By Edward Cox from Gollancz

The Relic Guild trilogy
The Relic Guild
The Cathedral of Known Things
The Watcher of Dead Time

The Song of the Sycamore

THE WOOD BEE QUEEN

Edward Cox

This edition first published in Great Britain in 2022 by Gollancz
First published in Great Britain in 2021 by Gollancz
an imprint of The Orion Publishing Group Ltd
Carmelite House, 50 Victoria Embankment
London EC4Y 0DZ

An Hachette UK Company

1 3 5 7 9 10 8 6 4 2

A CIP catalogue record for this book
is available from the British Library.

ISBN (Mass Market Paperback) 978 1 473 22687 6
ISBN (eBook) 978 1 473 22688 3

Typeset by Deltatype Ltd, Birkenhead, Merseyside

Printed in Great Britain by Clays Ltd, Elcograf S.p.A.

www.gollancz.co.uk

For Elsie
I never forgot ...

I

A Dream of Wolves and Dragons

They say that in the Realm, the sea is in the sky ...

Mai liked to wander the streets at night. In the small hours, when others were sleeping, she found solace in the quiet, peace in the dark. The air was fresher than it was during the day, salty from the sea, not choked by the fumes of automobiles. She had spent years travelling from place to place, enjoying the wind on her face, the open sky over her head, the honest earth beneath her back – but it was here in the town of Strange Ground by the Skea where her travels had finally ended, where she had at last come to feel at home even though her true home lay so very far away.

Ambling through a balmy night in the height of summer, Mai headed to her favourite nocturnal spot. She veered off from the soft sodium glow suffusing the main road, cutting down an alley to a residential area where the communal hum of electric fans came from wide-open bedroom windows. She smiled to herself, sadly.

The townsfolk had adopted Mai as something of a curiosity. The wise old woman of the streets, they called her; not quite a celebrity but certainly a mystery for gossips to discuss. She had many acquaintances among the earthlings, could claim to have at least one good friend, but none knew the truth of why Mai had adopted *them*. Strange Ground by the Skea was so close yet so far from her real home, but the town's lack of magic made it the perfect place to hide. Or had done, once.

Finally, Mai reached a horseshoe of small apartment buildings curving around a little private garden. Although the garden was fenced in by black iron railings and locked at night, the gate opened with a squeak at Mai's touch and welcomed her inside. Comforted by the smell of flowers and freshly watered soil, she sat on the solitary bench to contemplate a worry which had begun while she slept during the day.

Terrible visions had plagued Mai's dreams, nightmares of a dark Empress who commanded the foulest magic of the Underworld, who led a dragon horde into battle against a revolt of giant wolves. Once upon a time, the wolves had been loyal allies to the dragons, but now they were mortal enemies, and these two supernatural armies fought across the land without remorse or mercy. Innocent people died in their tens of thousands as the battle bathed their world in blood and fire. In the dream, Mai knew she had been given the power to stop the senseless destruction, but she didn't use it and awoke feeling disturbed by her decision, restless thoughts dominated by the home from which she had walked away.

The friends and family she left behind, the ones she had never said goodbye to – Mai missed them all dearly and it was only natural that they should cross her mind from time to time; but never had she questioned her decision to leave them, and never had they arrested her attention with as much force as they now did. Strange Ground by the Skea was full of bad omens on this night.

The sky was clear and bright with stars, yet the silvery glow of the moon rippled like a reflection in a pond. Beneath the taste of brine, a light breeze carried the scent of something wild, filled with desire and pursuit. A thin mist had begun forming on the ground like smoke sighed from the mouths of sleeping dragons. The atmosphere trembled as though warning of wolves on the hunt. There was magic in the air.

Startled by the sudden flapping of wings, Mai watched a gull swoop down to land on the bench's armrest. It cocked its head to one side and considered the elderly woman staring at it.

'Hello there, little thing,' Mai said. 'You gave me a fright.' She noticed the message tied to the gull's leg with some concern. 'You must have travelled a long way to deliver this.'

The gull offered no resistance as Mai untied the scrap of paper and read the message upon it. The words were few but stopped her heart. *We have failed. Come home.*

Mai's eyes welled, but a small sob was barely out of her mouth before she gasped. The wild smell of hunting wolves assaulted her nostrils with vigour – stronger, closer, announcing they had picked up their prey's scent.

Crushing the note in her fist, Mai jumped to her feet and held out a hand to the gull. 'No time for tears, little thing. It seems you were followed tonight.'

The gull hopped onto her arm and then up to her shoulder. Hurrying through the night, Mai took the shortest route to her dwelling. It wasn't much, a recess most would overlook, a nook between two buildings on the high street, but it kept Mai dry from rain and sheltered from snow, and it was lined with cardboard and blankets donated by kind townspeople. The mist had thickened by the time she arrived, and it carried a haunted chill.

'I'm afraid I have no food to offer you,' she said, placing the gull down on the floor. 'This will have to suffice.' She picked up a paper cup, removed the plastic lid and swirled the soured remnants of hot chocolate. 'My friend bought it for me.' Sadness grew inside her. 'He brings me hot chocolate every day. I wish

I could return his kindness better than I now have to.' Mai shivered and placed the cup before the gull. 'There, that should give you strength for the return trip. And return you must, little thing. This very night.'

While the gull dipped its head to the chocolate, Mai searched among her belongings at the rear of the nook until she found a pencil. *Forgive me*, she scribbled hastily on the back of the original note. *I am undone. You know what to do.*

The gull was still supping on cold hot chocolate when Mai tied the message to its leg. She lifted the bird, kissed its head, then stepped from the nook.

'Fly hard from this world, little thing,' she told it. 'Do not stop until you reach the Realm.' And she threw the gull into the air. With a burst of wings, it soared high and away.

Mai re-entered her nook and once again rummaged through her belongings. A decade ago, back when she lacked the strength to do what needed to be done, she had entered into a pact with a divine grace no longer worshipped on Earth. Such pacts were everlasting, never forgotten, and the ears of the divines could hear all places. Mai found the pact and carefully unwrapped the dusty old rag that kept it safe.

It came in the form of a spell contained in a glass vial, its every detail floating in clear liquid. Mai shook it and awakened the magic to a blue glow. Here was a promise. Here was a duty.

Out on the pavement, Mai crushed the vial beneath the heel of her boot. There was a hiss, a puff of steam, and then five streaks of ghostly blue sped away from her position. Three raced off into the town. Two shot up into the sky.

'For my granddaughters, for my friends and for the Realm,' Mai said as the spell disappeared among stars and watery moonlight like silent fireworks. 'Lady Juno, remember your servant's sacrifice and honour the promises you made ...'

4

A growl emanated from across the high street.

A wolf emerged from the mist, stalking between two parked cars into the orange glow of street lights. Mangy, black and silver, the beast was closely followed by a second. Mai stepped backwards into her nook. Only now did her nightmare make sense. How had she not seen this coming?

'Ten years ago, I would have given you a *good* fight,' she said, curling her lip. The wolves crept closer, growling, hackles raised. 'Tell my daughter that her mother's ghost will forever haunt her.'

And the hunters leapt at their prey.

2

Beneath the Skea

Princess Yandira of House Wood Bee had always boasted sharp eyes. The very sharpest, in fact – sharper than a hawk's. From her high rooms at the top of the north tower, she could see clearly the poppies growing wild at the edge of the castle gardens far below. Seated at her easel, she painted the flowers with a steady hand and intricate detail. While humming a happy tune, Yandira brought to life petals so red they practically bled onto the canvas.

Today was a good day.

In the corner of the room, beneath an ornate wardrobe, the Shade opened its eyes and whispered with the dry rustling of dead leaves, 'They are coming, my sister.'

'Yes, I'm well aware.'

With the thinnest of brushes and the blackest of paints, Yandira added veins to the petals of her poppies. She had heard the voices drifting up from the stairwell at the moment that four – no, *five* – people first entered the tower; like her eyes, her ears were as keen as any blade ever taken onto a battlefield. Two remained silent while three did their best to bicker quietly. Their footfalls scratched and echoed up the many spiralling steps to filter through the closed and locked door.

In a different life, Yandira fancied she would have made an

excellent gardener. She had a talent for recognising which soil was the richest and best for planting seeds. She understood how to encourage her flowers to take root and how to nurture them from sprout to bud. She could envision the grander picture and had the steely nerve to wait for her flowers to attain perfect colour and scent before plucking them from the ground. Patience and timing were just two of Yandira's very many specialities.

Her visitors believed they were bringing fresh news to the tower. But four large windows afforded a full compass view of Strange Ground beneath the Skea, of the city surrounding Castle Wood Bee and the lands beyond. Yandira had been watching and listening from her high perch for ten years, and very little escaped her attention.

Finally, after a lengthy climb, the visitors arrived at the door to her rooms.

'You are grieving, Highness,' said a crusty-voiced man, hushed but not hushed enough. 'I mean no disrespect, but are you thinking clearly?'

Unlikely, thought Yandira.

It was Hamdon Lark talking. The royal magician, elderly and full of creaky tradition, had been around longer than anyone in the castle could remember. Which was to say, *too* long.

'Highness, I share Hamdon's caution.' That was Ala Denev, the royal advisor. She was younger than Lark but still as stiff and fawning. 'Have you given yourself time to properly consider this?'

Doubtful.

'Please, Highness,' said Lark. 'At least let me come with you.'

'For your protection,' Denev pleaded. 'Her servant is missing and you more than any know the cruelty of which they are *both* capable.'

'My decision is made.' The third person spoke with no

7

gravitas whatsoever. She sounded as though she understood she was upset but that her temperament was entirely too airy to experience it. Which was a fair account of the truth. 'I would speak to her face, not through wood and spells. Wait here.'

As the protective wards and locking mechanisms on the door hummed and clunked, the Shade asked a dry, rustling question from beneath the wardrobe. 'Now, my sister?'

'Patience,' Yandira replied. 'Let's hear what she has to say first.'

And the Shade closed its eyes.

Yandira looked up as the door opened and two royal guards clanged their way into the room. Wearing full, pristinely polished armour and armed with long, silver pikes, they parted to allow Princess Morrad inside. Yandira caught a glimpse of Lark's and Denev's pained expressions before the princess closed the door and its spells and mechanisms locked. Morrad gazed around as though she was seeing through the veil of a dream. Her far-away eyes, dulled as though wreathed in grey mist, eventually settled on Yandira and she blinked, once, slowly.

'Sister.'

Yandira offered the slightest of nods. 'Sister.'

Morrad stepped in front of her guards and took a moment to admire the painting on the easel. 'You've always had such a good eye for detail.'

Although a few years older than Yandira, Princess Morrad had the unnerving quality of appearing neither old nor young. An unearthly creature in all ways, who some called a moon-calf, it was as though her skin was made from starlight and her clothes from spider silk and butterfly wings. Her hair tangled and wild, Morrad stared vacantly, offering nothing further by way of conversation. Yandira was pleased to see that her sister was as colourful and sweet-smelling a flower ever to have opened its petals. Ready for plucking.

8

Yandira returned to her painting. 'What do you want?'

'Oh.' The question jolted Morrad, as though reminding her that she was in the room. 'I bring grave news.' She took a deep breath. 'Queen Eldrid is dead.'

Yandira finished adding a touch of shadow to a petal before addressing the statement. 'Are you certain?'

'Murdered.' Tears like liquid moonlight welled in Morrad's eyes. 'Poisoned in her sleep. There are assassins in our House, Yandira.'

'Oh my, the queen is truly dead?' Yandira held a hand to her breast. 'How tragic.' She rolled her eyes and applied brush to canvas once more.

Morrad was aghast. 'Eldrid was your sister!'

'A shame she never treated me as such.'

'Shame?' Morrad cocked her head to one side. 'After all this time, you still fester so selfishly?'

'Eldrid was no more to me than my warden.'

'Where is your grief? Your remorse?'

'You honestly expect a show of compassion, Morrad? Ten years I have been locked in this tower. *Ten years!* And this is the first time either of my sisters has deigned to visit.' The first time *anyone* had visited, in fact; aside from the food hatch opening three times a day, the door had remained closed and locked throughout Yandira's incarceration. Or so her wardens believed. 'Your news grieves me not at all.'

'Have respect!' Morrad drew herself up regally, yet her voice remained sunshine light and no more admonishing than a mewling kitten's. 'After Mother left, Eldrid could have ordered your execution.'

'You think invoking Mother's memory will somehow soften my resolve?'

'It was an act of love that kept you alive.'

Love? Yes, there was truth to that, though others had warned it was a mistake. But that was yesterday, while today there was more to this news than even Morrad knew.

'Eldrid was poisoned by magical means,' Morrad said. 'My advisors warn me that you have not changed. I argued in your favour. I told them you could not achieve this foulness from your prison. Tell me I am right.'

Yandira did no such thing and placed the brush on the easel, wiping paint from her hands with a cloth. 'How is Princess Ghador taking the news of her mother's death?'

'She does not know.' Tears spilled onto Morrad's cheeks. 'Ghador is away from the city. We sent a gull with orders for her to come home, but she has not replied, and we fear ... we fear—'

'That silence from our beloved niece indicates the assassins got to her, too? Oh dear.' Yandira quashed a smirk. 'Though that contingency would make this a good day for you, Morrad. With Eldrid and her heir gone, the throne of Strange Ground is all but yours. The one rival left in your way is *me*. Or should that be the other way around?'

'Yandira ...' Morrad took a step closer. 'What have you done?'

Yandira's gaze rested on the two guards. Statue-still in their armoured shells, the visors of their helmets pointed and expressionless, their pikes sharp and menacing. They were waiting for the order that Morrad was hesitant to give. Behind them, beneath the wardrobe where no one was watching, the Shade opened its eyes like a piranha detecting blood in the water. At a discreet and silent order from Yandira, it slithered from its hiding place.

'If it's any consolation, Morrad, you would have made a truly awful queen.'

'Seize her.'

But the guards didn't move. The Shade had already sped across the floor to their boots. It split into two, slid up their armoured legs, over their back plates and disappeared inside their helmets before either of them could level their weapons.

Morrad watched, confused that her orders went ignored. The guards flinched as though shocked. Tendrils of shadowy smoke leaked from their visors.

Frantic knocking came at the door.

'Highness!' called Ala Denev.

'Is all well?' added Hamdon Lark.

Yandira pointed at the door and gave the guards her instructions. 'Arrest the royal advisor and magician. I believe they have startling confessions of high treason to make.' She clucked her tongue at Morrad, who looked more lost than ever. 'Such a wretched pair, don't you agree? Murdering our sister and niece like that.'

'*No!*' Morrad wailed at her guards. 'You will not permit her freedom.'

Yandira's laugh was bright and genuine. 'My freedom would only be yours to command if I had ever truly been imprisoned in the first place. The wait has been long, sister, but today *is* a good day.'

The door swung open as Yandira released the wards and locking mechanisms with a wave of her hand. Lark and Denev yelped in unison as the guards stamped towards them with sharp silver blades drawn. Its work done, the Shade fell from their helmets, its two parts merging in mid-air, spreading like a cloud as it drifted back into the room.

'Eldrid was wrong,' Morrad whispered. She didn't notice the Shade land in her wild hair and crawl into her ear. 'Letting you live was a mistake ... a mistake ...'

To the sound of Lark and Denev's panicked cries, Morrad

ceased functioning. Her misty eyes darkened to the colour of storm clouds. Her head bobbed, her shoulders sagged and she swayed on her feet.

Yandira rose from the chair and caught her, holding her upright.

'My dearest Morrad, we must summon the noble Houses to Castle Wood Bee.' She kissed her sister's forehead. 'It suits tradition that the Lords and Ladies of Strange Ground beneath the Skea should hear of your abdication from your own lips.'

3
By the Skea

The hot chocolate wasn't for Ebbie. A cappuccino would be his beverage of choice, sweet and frothy, dusted with cinnamon. The chocolate would belong to Ebbie's friend, but the friend in question was missing.

Everything else about the morning was as it should be. A normal summer's day had dawned over Strange Ground by the Skea and traffic trundled up and down the high street, ferrying townspeople to work. Shopkeepers swept away sand and the debris of night from their shopfronts, while gulls circled overhead against the perfect blue, crying as if to warn Ebbie that the temperature would rise and rise, forcing him to loosen his tie and roll up his shirtsleeves by midday at the latest. But the hot chocolate felt out of place in his hand because he had no one to give it to.

Sipping his cappuccino, Ebbie frowned. The narrow but deep nook between the launderette and Reg's Newsagents was where his friend usually dwelled. But today it was empty and that troubled him.

Every morning on his way to work, Ebbie stopped at Mrs Murdock's café and bought a takeout coffee for himself and a hot chocolate for Mai. Every morning she had a smile and a story waiting for him, and they would while away an hour

13

chatting and enjoying warm drinks in her nook. It was a daily, natural routine of his life, so why wasn't Mai at home today?

A nocturnal creature by habit, Mai preferred walking the streets at night, when the shadows were at their most secretive and quiet. 'The end of my day is the beginning of yours,' she always said. 'That's just how I am.' It might have been logical to assume that Mai had simply broken habit and gone for a morning stroll, but she was not the only absentee from her home.

Mai was a magpie, a collector, but every item she had gathered was missing. Her blankets and trinkets, the interesting things she hid at the back of her home – gone! The nook on the high street was entirely empty, swept clean, as though Mai had never lived there at all.

'Is something wrong?'

Ebbie wheeled around to see a woman standing outside the newsagents with a folded paper under her arm.

'Excuse me?'

'You look troubled.'

'Oh ...' Ebbie nodded at the nook. 'I was just wondering where my friend has got to.'

'Your friend?'

'Mai.' Ebbie lifted the hot chocolate as if it explained everything. 'She's usually at home in the mornings.'

'*Mai?*' the woman queried. Smartly dressed, hair iron-grey, she had the darkest eyes Ebbie had ever seen. 'Do you mean the wise woman of Strange Ground's streets?'

'That's her.'

'Then – oh my! I'm sorry to be the herald of bad news, but your friend passed away.'

Ebbie stared at her then snorted in disbelief. 'What are you talking about?'

'The man in the newsagents is spreading the *news* to all his customers.' There was very little expression on the woman's face. 'Reginald says he saw the authorities taking your friend's body away.'

The utter seriousness in her dark, dark eyes dispelled any chance of a mistake. Ebbie felt like he was deflating. 'What happened?'

'She was found during the early hours. I'm told the official cause of death is old age.'

'Mai was old, but ...' The hot chocolate felt suddenly heavy in Ebbie's grip. 'She was fine yesterday morning.'

'Perhaps she went peacefully in her sleep.' The woman gazed into the clear blue sky before offering a small smile. 'Perhaps the folk came to send her off.'

Ebbie shook his head. 'This can't be right.'

'I am sorry for your loss. Good luck to you, young man.'

The woman walked away and Ebbie stared into the nook.

Gulls cried overhead. Cars trundled by. The light breeze carried the taste of salt and the distant crash of waves. Ebbie placed the hot chocolate on the floor of Mai's home while everything else in Strange Ground by the Skea carried on as normal.

4
Keeper of Lifetimes

St. Meyers-Bannerman Library was a fading sort of building which hadn't seen a new carpet or lick of paint since the eighties. Computers were no more than theory and rumour belonging to the speculations of science fiction, and Wi-Fi was an undiscovered source of magic. Funding for the library was not high on anyone's list of priorities. Except Ebbie's.

He didn't really mind working with the lack of technology; there was something comforting about the double-thump of a stamp hitting an ink-pad and then banging onto a book's check-out card. Certainly, in this day and age, it was the long way to go about things, but somehow it felt like the *right* way, too; a truer, tactile respect for books and the stories they held instead of reducing them to information blinking from a screen. Not that there was much stamping to be done these days. Hardly anyone borrowed books from the St. Meyers-Bannerman Library any more.

Seated behind the main desk, Ebbie gave a weary sigh and looked up from the novel he was finding impossible to concentrate on. Cases and racks, once white but now a sickly yellow, divided the long, wide room into aisles, filled with books and no space to spare. A layer of dust coated each title and scented the air with the smell of forgetfulness. Over a month had gone by since Ebbie had last felt inspired to clean the library. The signs for various genres and topics dangled from the ceiling, hand-painted in a fancy font and paled to ghosts like the memory of readers wandering these aisles.

As for the ink-pad, it sat closed on the desk, the stamp lying atop it, dry and unused for days. On the other side of the desk was the library phone, an ancient thing now as sallow as the bookracks. The line had been cut weeks ago. All in all, Ebbie considered himself a witness to tragedy, and Mai would have agreed with him. If she were still here. The news of her death had failed to register with him. It didn't feel real. How could she not be alive?

Ebbie's breath caught and a sudden heat rose in his chest like heartburn. He rubbed the discomfort away and felt his mobile phone buzz in his pocket. A text from his mum, saying that she and his dad were looking forward to seeing him next week, adding: *I've made an appointment for you to see Father Tom.* Ebbie growled in annoyance. He didn't bother replying and went upstairs to make a cup of tea.

In the staffroom, Alice lay sprawled on a tatty, patched-up sofa, fast asleep. The window was open, the ceiling fan spinning, and a fug in the air carried the stale aroma of old beer. Ebbie watched Alice sleeping, a resigned smile playing on his face. In her cut-down black jeans, Doc Martens boots and un-ironed Metallica T-shirt, she appeared content, at peace with the world, and not for the first time Ebbie wished he was the pillow she was hugging.

'What are you doing?'

Startled, Ebbie realised Alice's bloodshot eyes were open and staring at him. Feeling like a guilty voyeur, he covered his tracks by waving a hand in the air and said, 'Bloody hell, Alice, what have you been smoking?'

She gave him a lazy grin. 'Just a little something to pass the time.'

'It's not even eleven yet.'

'What's your point?'

Ebbie didn't suppose he had one. 'Cup of tea?'

Alice nodded. She grabbed her glasses from an end table, then flinched and dropped them as a little *tick* of static shocked her. 'What is it with this bloody place today? Whatever I touch wants to electrocute me.'

'Really? I hadn't noticed.'

'Can't you feel it? It's like the air is supercharged.'

Now that she mentioned it, Ebbie could detect a heaviness to the air, prickling the back of his neck. 'Maybe there's a storm coming,' he said, filling the kettle and switching it to boil. He set out two mugs. 'Hey, did you hear about Mai?'

'Who?' Alice said, mid-yawn.

'Mai. The old lady who lives on the high street.'

Surrounded by smudged mascara, Alice's eyes searched her memory. 'Oh, I know who you mean. Always wandering around at night. What about her?'

'She died.'

Alice reached for her glasses again, received a second shock and gave up, crumpling on the sofa without them. 'Did you say she died? That's really sad. She spoke to me once. She seemed nice.'

'I still can't believe it,' Ebbie said, filling the mugs and squeezing the teabags. He added some milk and stirred in sugar. 'Old age, apparently. I was only talking to her yesterday and she sounded fine ...'

Ebbie froze mid-stir. Had she been fine? Mai had said something yesterday morning, something about the day feeling off – like an ill wind, she said, blowing in from the sea.

'Huh.' Ebbie turned to Alice. 'Maybe she knew it was coming. They say some people can tell when they're going to die—' He rolled his eyes. Alice had fallen back to sleep. He left her tea on the sideboard and took his own downstairs where he once again tried to pass the snail's pace of the day by reading a novel.

Roughly a year ago, Ebbie had been walking to work as usual, sipping a cappuccino while lost to his thoughts, when a voice had surprised him. It seemed to come from nowhere, and the kindness it carried stopped him in his tracks. 'Here,' it said again, this time from the nook between the newsagent's and the launderette. When Ebbie peeked into the nook, he saw a small, elderly woman sitting cross-legged on a pile of blankets, smiling at him.

'Sorry, are you talking to me?'

'Indeed I am,' she said. 'I was commenting on how nice it is to see someone looking so happy with life.' Her face was lined by age but her skin was clear and healthy. Dark hair, long and straight, sparsely touched by streaks of grey. Her eyes were a bright green that almost glowed. 'What's your name, child?'

'Uh ...' Being twenty-nine at the time, Ebbie found the title *child* a little odd, but in a satisfying way he didn't really understand. 'I'm Ebbie.'

'And your family's name?'

'Wren.'

Her smile widened. 'Well now, Ebbie Wren, what agrees with you today?'

Drawn to the warmth in her voice, Ebbie stepped closer and leaned against the edge of the nook's wall. The pleasant aroma of flowers met his nostrils. 'I've been made manager at work.'

'Truly?'

'It's my first day in the role.'

'Ah, no wonder you appear so pleased with yourself. Anxious, too, I should imagine.' Even though the day was hot, she wore a thick shawl over a heavy dress of dark material. 'Tell me your profession?'

'Librarian.'

'Well, of course you are.' Clearly delighted, her smile grew and beamed. 'Just look at the stories in your eyes, smell the dust from old pages on your hands. You could be nothing *but* a keeper of lifetimes.'

Ebbie chuckled. 'A what?'

'I know well the pride you're feeling. Once upon a time, I was something of a librarian, too. It is a noble pursuit.'

Ebbie had always thought so, though the people he had met who shared the opinion were far and few between. 'Which library?'

'Oh, it's far from here and a long time ago. I remember it fondly in my dreams now. Speaking of which ...' She rearranged the blankets she sat on, pulling one of them over her legs, preparing to bed down. 'I shan't keep you, Ebbie Wren, custodian of stories, but I should hope you might like to visit me again.'

'Uh ... sure.'

'Then it's settled. Good luck in your new position.'

It had been a brief but pleasant exchange, and the old woman had lingered in Ebbie's thoughts for the remainder of that day. He couldn't figure out why, but only later did it occur to him that he hadn't asked for her name. The very next morning, he had bought Mai a hot chocolate for the first time.

Ebbie had been happier back then. The library had five other employees under his management; they worked well as a team and he believed they were doing something important – *noble*, as Mai had said. A regular flow of townsfolk came to borrow books, or bring their children to activities during school holidays, or attend the author events Ebbie organised. Life had been moving in the right direction. But now, Alice was the only other employee, and she spent her days upstairs in the staffroom finding ways to relieve the boredom as the hours ticked down to five o'clock. Like Ebbie, she earned her wages doing nothing because there was nothing to be done any more.

Everything had changed two months ago when Mr St. Meyers-Bannerman had sold the library building to a property developer.

The heat of summer continued to rise and not one breath of breeze blew in through the open windows. A little after midday, irritated by the heat, and by the static shocks which now lay in wait on every surface and item, Ebbie loosened his tie and rolled his shirtsleeves to his elbows. Around one o'clock, the door opened and Mr and Mrs Walker entered the library. Ebbie stood to greet them like he'd never been happier to see other human beings.

With big smiles, the Walkers approached the desk, holding up the books they had borrowed for their grandchildren, proud to be returning them on time. Not that it mattered; it had been weeks since Ebbie last bothered chasing a late return.

'How are you today, dear?' said Mrs Walker.

'Plodding along, same as always.' Ebbie watched as she laid the books on the desk. His instinct was to reach for the ink-pad and stamp, but today he stopped himself. 'You can keep them, if you want.'

Mrs Walker's smile faltered. 'Keep them?'

Ebbie nodded. 'I'll rip out the cards and you can start a library for your grandkids. No one will know.'

Mrs Walker looked uncertainly at her husband, who said, 'Sounds a bit like stealing to me.'

'Not really,' Ebbie assured the couple, pushing the books towards them. 'They're in need of a good home now.'

But Mrs Walker wouldn't be convinced. 'I don't think it's right, dear. Besides, we don't have a lot of room on our shelves.'

Mr Walker concurred. 'Thanks all the same.'

'Well, if you're sure.' Disappointed, Ebbie dragged the books back across the desk.

Mrs Walker breathed in a lungful of the library's musty air. 'I'm going to miss this place.'

Her husband winked at Ebbie. 'Best of luck to you, sunshine.'

They turned and left, parting as they did so to reveal that Alice had been standing behind them. Her make-up was even more smudged and she looked as though she had smoked a second joint.

'I need food,' she mumbled, heading after the Walkers.

'Hey, before you go – what do they do with dead bodies?'

Alice screwed up her face. 'What?'

'I'm talking about Mai. Where would they have taken her?'

'I don't know, boss.' She shrugged. 'The hospital, the undertakers – try asking the police.'

'Yeah.' Ebbie rubbed at his chest as heartburn flared again. 'Yeah, I think I'll do that.'

Alice scratched the back of her head. 'Listen, Ebbie, I won't bother coming back after lunch, okay?'

She stumbled out of the library without waiting for a response.

Ebbie fished his phone from his pocket and saw his mother's message still on the screen. He stared at it a while before replying – *I'll see you next week. Please cancel Father Tom's appointment* – and then Googled the number for Strange Ground Police Station. Someone, somewhere, knew where Mai had gone.

5

The Other Side of the Skea

Backway Charlie had tried his best to deter her: 'All you'll do is bring a weight of trouble down on your head.' But his warning had been spoken with a defeated air because he knew she wouldn't listen to him. For she was Bek Rana, and Bek Rana was the best damn thief in Strange Ground beneath the Skea. What could go wrong?

Under the cover of night, Bek crept through a grove of oaks, stalking the shadows as silently and light of foot as any predator on the hunt. A dog barked in the distance, perhaps catching her scent; but it was a small, yappy sound, not the baritone of a wild beast straining at the leash to see off an interloper. Probably a ponced-up poodle having a final piss of the night under a servant's supervision.

'No one robs the nobles and gets away with it,' Charlie had said. 'They have uncanny ways of catching those who wrong them.'

Emerging from the trees, Bek came to an ivy-covered wall and scrambled to crouch atop it. Watery moonlight revealed a well-maintained garden beyond the wall: bushes and beds of flowers, ornaments and statues, a couple of fruit trees and a lush lawn that reached all the way to the back of a manor house, a house which appeared to be as still and dark as she had been promised.

The tip-off had come Bek's way early that morning. A letter had been left in her lodgings, written by someone who claimed to be a wealthy collector of rare items. It said that in the southern area, among the grandest residences in all the city, a priceless artefact was waiting to be stolen from the home of House Kingfisher. The Kingfishers and their staff were away and not due back any time soon. The collector wanted the artefact stolen tonight, and for Bek's services, a handsome price would be paid – more than enough to help her get out of Strange Ground for good.

Not a single candle-flame flickered from the many windows of the Kingfisher residence. The manor appeared as deserted as the letter had claimed it would be, and Bek felt a thrill. Not that she was entirely without caution. Backway Charlie's warnings might have fallen on deaf ears, but it wasn't as if the wily old fellow spoke without reason.

'You're too young to remember Fletcher,' he'd said. 'He thought he could get away with robbing nobles, too. What the guard dogs left of him was thrown in a dungeon, and that's where he spent his final hours.'

With this warning in mind, Bek issued three low whistles and waited. Nothing. She whistled again, but still no guard dogs were alerted to the sound, and that settled the matter: no one was home.

An empty scabbard hung from Bek's waist; she unbuckled its belt and laid it on the wall top before jumping down to land lightly on soft grass. Her dark clothes hid her well in the garden's shadows as she moved quickly and silently to the manor house.

After checking each of the ground-floor windows for signs of life, she turned her attention to getting inside. The letter had told her to forget conventional entrances; all the doors were locked and bolted from the inside and, like the windows, were protected from burglars with spells and wards. But the servants' entrance was a different matter: the owners hadn't been so cautious with that. At the side of the house, two flimsy panels of unfinished wood covered the entrance to a stairway that led down to the cellar, and they were secured by nothing more magical than a thin rusty chain with a small padlock.

Pulling her picks from her pocket, Bek made short work of the padlock. With a quiet but satisfactory click, the clasp popped up and she carefully slid the chain free. Lifting the double doors and leaving them open, she crept down the steps into the cellar.

In the dim moonlight, among barrels and crates and cobwebs, Bek was drawn to the dusty racks filled with wine bottles lining one wall. She knew enough about nobles' taste for expensive wine to be aware that selling any one of those bottles would bring her enough coin to survive a day or two in the city. In a different time, Bek might have fleeced this cellar for all it was worth and lived a few weeks without sleeping in flea-bitten beds and dining on the poorest cuts. But if the rumours coming out of Castle Wood Bee were true, then she needed to keep her eye on the real prize. Queen Eldrid was dead and so was her daughter. Dark times had returned to Strange Ground beneath the Skea, and Bek intended to be far from the city before it was swamped by madness.

Creeping up the stairs to the upper floor, wincing at the creak of each step, Bek found the door at the top unlocked and she slipped out into a narrow pantry and then into a kitchen where the stove was cold and pans hung from hooks. From there, she made her way down a long corridor, blinking in and out of moon-shafts spearing in through windows. Eventually, she came to the reception hall at the front of the house. Opposite the main door, a wide and grand staircase of marble swept up and split left and right to the next floor.

Bek was just thinking that it couldn't hurt to check one or two of the bedrooms for any well-filled jewellery boxes while she was here, when a glint of blue caught in a shaft of moonlight attracted her eye. It came from an open doorway to the left through which Bek discovered a small drawing room full of bookcases, a drinks cabinet and comfy-looking chairs with winged backs and soft leather upholstery. And she saw it, the thing that had caught her eye, the artefact she had been sent to steal: a sword, mounted on a wooden plaque hanging on the wall above the dark mouth of a fireplace.

Bek could spot fine craftsmanship from a mile away, and this sword had been hung in a place of pride, where visitors could hear the owner boast of its value and importance. The hilt was wrapped in dark, oiled leather; the guard curled like the ridiculous moustaches sported by some nobles. But the blade was like nothing Bek had seen before. Straight and true, a little shorter than her arm, harbouring not one nick or imperfection, it was made from polished stone that practically glowed in the moonlight with the deep blue of a clear autumn evening. This was a prized display piece, not a real weapon, but forged by a master nonetheless.

Bek gave the sword a closer inspection. The prickly aura of protective wards was absent, but writing sprawled along the flat of the blue stone blade. The light was too dim to make out what it said, but again, the engraving looked to have been done by a master hand. The sword was in perfect condition, obviously never intended to be wielded in battle, and it would fetch a grand price. The collector's letter had told the truth.

Pleased to discover that this unique prize wasn't fixed to the wooden plaque but rested freely on four small padded studs, Bek was just reaching for it when she heard a sound and froze. Voices. Muffled but close. Inside the house.

'Catshit!' Bek hissed.

There was a second door in the drawing room. It was shut, and the voices were approaching from the other side. Trapped between the decision to grab the sword and run or simply hide, Bek heard Backway Charlie's final warning rattling around her mind: 'Your trouble is you're nothing like as good as you think you are.' Her indecision was at last compelled into action when the doorknob squeaked and turned. Bek dived onto the varnished floorboards, crawled under a chaise longue and held her breath.

Heart thumping, she watched two pairs of feet enter the room, belonging to folk who were bickering.

'I don't like sneaking around in the dead of night, Genevieve,' one of them was saying. A nobleman, by his prim tones. 'You were supposed to leave with the rest of your House. What is going on?'

'Delaying my departure was imperative,' a noblewoman replied. 'No one but you knows I have returned to the city and I should like to keep it that way, so lower your tone and stop complaining about the dark.'

Bek knew that voice. Focused on staying as still as a dead thing while fighting a sudden urge to cough, she searched her memory and found a stern face framed by silvery hair staring back at her ... Genevieve Kingfisher, First Lady to House Kingfisher.

'Why have you not travelled to the city of Dalmyn?' the nobleman demanded. 'Remaining in Strange Ground puts everything in jeopardy.'

'Aelfric, will you please calm yourself.' *Aelfric ...?* Aelfric Dragonfly, First Lord to House Dragonfly? Had to be. These two were the highest-ranking nobles outside of House Wood Bee. 'I had indeed left with my family and staff, but then I received a courier gull carrying an urgent missive from our old friend.'

'You did?' Lord Dragonfly's voice was bright with hope. 'She is coming to help?'

'Alas, no.'

'Why?'

Lady Kingfisher didn't reply, and her reticence forced a noise of exasperation from Lord Dragonfly.

'Out with it, Genevieve!'

Lady Kingfisher spoke forlornly. 'Aelfric, listen to me. I will leave Strange Ground tonight, as planned, but the city of Dalmyn is no longer my first destination. Many things have changed, and ...' Her voice cracked. 'Our old friend is undone.'

'Undone?'

'Her message was the last she will ever send, and you know what this means.'

'Regrettably, I do.' Lord Dragonfly sat heavily in a chair beside the fireplace. 'Is there at least hope for Morrad?'

'Morrad is more lost to us than ever. At this moment, our friends are few.'

Bek knew what these nobles were talking about. Not only had the queen and her heir been murdered, but also Princess Morrad had released her sister Yandira from the tower prison. The folk of Strange Ground were talking of little else, and Yandira's freedom was the main reason why Bek wanted out of the city. She was cruelty personified.

Lady Kingfisher said, 'Yet we are not entirely without allies,' and began pacing the room. 'Yandira's strike was more calculated and effective than we could have anticipated. Tomorrow, she will have her sister gather the Houses. Before them, Morrad will relinquish her right to the crown, and Yandira will believe that no one can stop her from claiming the throne. But Yandira is unaware that while her assassins took the life of Queen Eldrid, they were not so successful with Eldrid's heir.'

'Ghador is alive?' Lord Dragonfly hissed out a relieved breath. 'Thank the Oldunfolk. I was beginning to believe that all rumours were true and she was as dead as her mother.'

Bek clenched her teeth. Yandira wanted the throne but the rightful heir still lived? Spiders crawled up her spine as it dawned on her what kind of conversation she was eavesdropping on.

'Where is Ghador now?' Lord Dragonfly asked.

Lady Kingfisher stopped pacing in front of the chaise longue, the tips of her fine boots mere inches from Bek's wide eyes. 'She evaded assassination, but where she fled to is ... secret.' She turned on her heel. 'Unless the rightful heir is returned to Strange Ground, Yandira will be our new queen, and she won't stop there.'

Backway Charlie's warnings were loud in Bek's mind now. This conversation was spiralling down into high treason, and she could be killed for just listening to it ... or she could get these two executed by repeating anything she heard to the wrong audience. Only the insane would try to piss on Yandira Wood Bee's affairs.

Wishing that deafness would strike her ears, Bek could do nothing but stay still and listen as Lord Dragonfly said, 'Do *you* know where Ghador is?'

'No, but blessedly Yandira is not yet aware she's still alive. For now, the heir has the chance to regroup and counter.'

'Then surely it is time to call for aid from the other cities.'

'They won't come, Aelfric, not while the situation remains so ... *local* to Strange Ground.'

'They must! Each Royal Family is a sworn Protector of the Realm. Yandira threatens them all.'

'And we will convince them of this how, exactly? You know as well as I that higher and lower graces are embroiled in Yandira's game. But if the Oldunfolk are willing, her threat will end before it spreads from this city.'

'Forgive me, Genevieve, but I do not share your confidence in the Oldunfolk's intervention, not this time. What don't I know?'

Lady Kingfisher began pacing again. 'Our friend bequeathed to me certain items along with a letter of instruction which I swore not to read unless the worst occurred. Events are now in motion, and I must step beyond the boundaries of the Realm in order for the true heir to be found. My apologies, Aelfric, but that is all I can tell you of my part. My secrecy is vital.'

Lord Dragonfly huffed, resigned. 'Then tell me of *my* part in these new plans.'

'Our one firm ally remains the Royal House of Dalmyn.'

'They are aware of the situation?'

'Yes.'

Dalmyn – ruled by Ghador's grandmother, whose First Heir was the princess's father. Bek clenched her teeth. This was all beginning to sound like war, even before Kingfisher said:

'Queen White Gold and Prince Maxis are sending Dalmyn's army to aid us. But that army is two days' ride from Strange Ground.' Lady Kingfisher sat in the chair opposite the noble lord. 'I'm sorry, Aelfric, but in the meantime I must leave you to face Yandira's spite and venom alone. I dearly wish it were otherwise—'

'I understand, Genevieve. What must I do?'

'Buy us some time. All of Strange Ground's Houses fear Yandira, yet while some would support her, others would oppose her with the right guaranty. Your talent for navigating the royal court is needed, Aelfric. Go among the Houses, stir them up and find which families will have the backbone to stand against Yandira when Dalmyn arrives.'

Bek really didn't want to hear any more.

Lord Dragonfly made a contemplative noise. 'I believe I already know where to begin. Lord and Lady Mandrake – their loyalty to Eldrid and Ghador has never been in question.'

'Yes, a fine start indeed. With more Houses like Mandrake behind us, Ghador might stand a chance of delivering the execution that Yandira deserved ten years ago.'

Oh no! No, no, no! Bek offered a prayer to Laverna, begging her to protect a faithful servant. *Stop them talking*, she pleaded. *Get me out of here!* And blessedly, the Oldunone of Thieves must have been looking out for her own on this night, because Lady Kingfisher said:

'Go now. And take great care. Yandira is always watching and we both know that dominating this queendom is but the first step in her ultimate ambition. But while Ghador lives, hope remains. Oldunfolk willing, I join with Dalmyn's army before long.'

They both rose from their chairs. A moment passed before Lord Dragonfly said, 'Then may Juno smile kindly upon you, dear friend,' and strode from the room.

With every fibre of her being, Bek willed Lady Kingfisher to follow him, but the noblewoman lingered for what felt like an age. Finally, thankfully, she muttered, 'May Juno smile kindly upon us all,' before walking out.

Bek waited until she heard the muffled thump of a door closing behind Kingfisher, and then found the patience to count to a hundred. Only then did she crawl out from under the chaise longue and stand. She came up facing the blue-stone sword on the wall. She had almost forgotten about it. A heartbeat of indecision came before she grabbed the weapon and fled the house, out of the cellar doors, across the long garden and up onto the wall, where she slid the sword into the scabbard she had left there. Jumping down into the grove of oaks, Bek buckled the sword belt around her waist and put as much distance between her and a treasonous conversation as she could.

6

Simple Pleasures

Ebbie was praying for the group of youngsters seated behind him to stop nattering about the most banal topics known to the human race. He was willing to pay good money if the man on the seat next to him would just eat a bloody breath mint.

Packed and sweltering, the bus made slow, chugging progress through the streets of Strange Ground by the Skea, and Ebbie regretted catching it instead of walking. The confining heat made him imagine that he and all the other sweating bodies were trapped in a deep dungeon beneath the ruins of a forgotten castle, crammed together without hope of ever again knowing the kiss of a cool breeze on their skin. Ebbie was feeling terribly sorry for himself.

Mai's body, he had discovered earlier, was now in the care of Mrs Cory's Funeral Home. It lay on the other side of town, a couple of miles from the sea, so Ebbie had caught the bus straight from work, but he wasn't sure what he planned to do once he reached his destination.

When the bus finally crawled out of town, Ebbie could stand its torturous confines no longer and got off a few stops early to walk the final mile or so. Relieved to feel the summer breeze, he wiped sweat from his brow and made his way along a country road, the name of which he had never known. With no pavements, he had to step up on the grassy embankment several times to let cars pass. Trees grew tall on either side, branches full of leaves reaching over to make the road a tunnel. Ebbie enjoyed the shade from the relentless sun beating down from a blue sky, and breathed in the wholesome smells of hot dust, flowers and manure.

As he batted away curious insects, he realised that he hadn't enjoyed anything as simple as taking a stroll in the good clean country air since Mr St. Meyers-Bannerman had announced the sale of the library.

'Hardships are a fact of life.' Mai's voice came unbidden from Ebbie's memory. He smiled to remember the sound of her. 'However,' she said, 'maintaining an appreciation for simple pleasures can help us overcome them—'

Ebbie stopped walking as voices in the real world disturbed his nostalgia.

Two men were talking unseen in the field beyond the trees to the left. Ebbie couldn't understand what they were saying, but they didn't sound happy.

'I said no!' one of them grumbled as they both barged their way out of the trees and stepped down onto the road several feet in front of Ebbie. 'We're already in enough trouble. What do you think will happen if we go back *completely* empty-handed?'

The other one growled like a dog.

'That's right, and worse besides,' said the first. 'It has to be here somewhere. We just need to find where she hid it ... hang on.'

The first man had noticed Ebbie, and so did his companion quickly after. Ebbie countered their hard stares with a small smile, which neither deigned to return. With thick, unruly hair and beards, they were dressed identically and might have been brothers. They wore long, heavy coats, buttoned up stiflingly

34

and as tatty as their muddy trousers and scuffed boots. The breeze carried their scent downwind, the scent of wet dog. They looked a little too wolfish for Ebbie's liking. And they were still staring.

'Evening,' Ebbie said with a nervous nod.

The man who had growled began sniffing the air, eyes narrowed in suspicion, teeth bared. The other one slapped his arm, said, 'Stop that,' and continued staring at Ebbie as they both crossed the road and disappeared through the trees on the other side.

Ebbie watched after them for a while. 'Interesting,' he murmured. With a shudder, he continued on his way until he reached the sign for Mrs Cory's Funeral Home and followed the short gravel drive beyond it.

In all his years of living in Strange Ground, Ebbie had never known this place was here. It was a small building, and inside he found the proprietor standing behind a desk in a neat but sparsely furnished reception room. A grey-haired woman with darker than dark eyes, Mrs Cory's face looked familiar.

'I recognise you, sir,' she said. 'You are the gentleman from this morning to whom I gave unfortunate news.' Ebbie nodded – yes, of course, she was the woman outside the newsagents. 'Unless I am very much mistaken, you are Strange Ground's resident librarian. Evidently, your sorrow has driven you to my doorstep.'

Ebbie looked at a glass coffee table set before the only sofa in the room. There were some spiritual well-being magazines on it and a pile of leaflets detailing the funeral services on offer. 'I'm not entirely sure why I came,' he said. 'It's just ...' He faltered at his ludicrous uncertainty. 'Mai was my friend.' His *only* friend, he realised.

'Perhaps you would like to see her? To pay your respects.'

'Is that allowed?'

Mrs Cory bowed her head in acquiescence. 'I must ask, have you ever seen a deceased body before, sir?' When Ebbie confessed that he hadn't, she added, 'Then I should prepare you. Your friend appears profoundly at peace, and some folk might find that disconcerting. This way, please.'

Much to Ebbie's relief, the room Mrs Cory led him to was more like an office than a mortuary. Warm with natural light, not cold and grey with rows of freezer drawers containing corpses like in crime books, there was a desk of varnished wood upon which paperwork had been neatly stacked, and thankfully no tools of Mrs Cory's trade were on display. Ebbie stood on the threshold, lacking the courage to step into the room. At the centre of the dark wood floor, Mai had been laid out on a padded gurney. She still wore her thick, dark dress, her hands clasped and resting on her stomach.

'I believe I already told you the official cause of death?' Mrs Cory said.

'Old age.' Ebbie's voice was quiet. He cleared his throat. 'You know, I offered to put her up in my spare room. I told her she could live with me, free of charge. But she said no. She preferred the freedom of the outdoors, she said, but I can't help wondering ...'

Mrs Cory patted his shoulder. 'Living on the streets is a harsh and uncertain existence, but is that always the reality? That *Mai* declined your kind offer has no bearing on her death. Do not feel guilty, sir. Age is an unavoidable truth of mortal life.'

Further words escaped Ebbie, along with the courage to step into the room, and the uncomfortable heat flared in his chest again.

'Do not think of this as an end but as the beginning it is,' said Mrs Cory. 'Compose yourself. I will give you a few moments to say your farewells.'

Quite gently, she encouraged Ebbie into the room and closed the door behind him. With a deep breath, Ebbie rubbed his chest and approached the gurney.

He stood at Mai's side. Her long hair had been brushed to a silky sheen and lay over her shoulders and down her chest. Mrs Cory had been right about her peaceful appearance. Her eyes were closed, her expression relaxed, serene, as though she meditated upon subjects far lighter than life and death. It was inconceivable that she was gone, that she would never take another night-time stroll. Ebbie reached out, paused, gathered himself, then laid his hand over Mai's. They were cold.

'Hello,' he said. 'I missed you this morning.'

Ebbie's earlier nostalgia returned and the sound of Mai's voice once again blossomed in his head:

'Reading a book, laughing with friends, finding the time to walk and ponder,' she was saying. 'These are simple, uncomplicated things that can remind us what we are living for.'

She had said that roughly two months ago, on a drizzling day at the end of spring, in her nook on the high street, while enjoying a hot chocolate in morning peace.

'I agree about the books,' Ebbie replied moodily. 'I couldn't be without them. People, not so much.'

Mai chuckled at that. 'The misanthropist judges! But what would a library be without its readers, Ebbie Wren?' She closed her eyes to savour the taste of chocolate, as she often did, like she was always tasting it for the first time. 'You're in rather a sour mood this morning. Could it be inspired by your unsuccessful attempts to win the heart of young Alice?'

There was some truth in that, he supposed, but on this occasion, he confessed to Mai that, no, Alice was not the main source of his sadness, for it had been the morning after Ebbie had received notice that the St. Meyers-Bannerman Library had been sold.

'We should always take responsibility for ourselves, no matter what hardship is thrown in our way,' Mai said, as saddened by the news as Ebbie. 'Some people don't have the luxury of choice and their world seems nothing *but* adversity. For example, I once knew a kind and sweet young girl who led a happy life until she lost *everything*.'

'Everything?' Ebbie managed a smile despite his mood; Mai addressed nearly all things in life with one story or another. 'I assume this girl's downfall was epic in some way?'

'Oh yes. She was orphaned. *Twice*. And after the second time, she lost her happiness for good, which changed her for the worse.'

Ebbie's smile widened. 'Let me guess, this all happened in a place far, far away from here?'

'Have my stories become so predictable?' Mai's wise old face screwed up while she considered. 'Let us say that this girl's story begins when what little family she had tragically died. Her misery was soothed, however, when a high-regarded family adopted her. She was taken to live in the castle of a grand city. She was cared for, loved and nurtured, and grew so close to the family's youngest daughter that she felt for the first time like she knew what it was to have a sister. But then tragedy struck again, and the girl was cast out onto the streets to live as a thief in a distant corner of the Realm, where they say the sea is in the sky.'

Of course she did. Mai's tales were usually about the Realm and the folk, and listening to them was the highlight of Ebbie's day.

'At first, she had no choice but to steal – scraps of food to stop her starving, rags and clothes to protect her from the weather.

And to sleep at night, she kept a sharp knife by her side and searched the streets for safe shelter, sometimes finding none and staying awake until the comfort of the dawning sun came. For she was now a denizen of the city's dangerous underbelly.

'Time passed and she adapted to her environment, clever and cunning – as unseen as a fox watching a chicken coop, if she needed to be. With these new-learned skills, her thievery outgrew a daily fight for survival, and she began coveting higher game than food and clothes. Tragedy fuelled her resentment and anger at the luxuries taken for granted by her fellow folk. Why should they enjoy what she had lost? And so she dedicated herself to stealing their joy and riches for her own selfish gain.'

Ebbie's smile faded. 'Yeah, that sounds familiar.'

'Ah, but the girl grew into *such* a bitter woman. If life would take everything from an innocent child – *twice* – then the thief would steal it all back, and she never changed her outlook. Even today, she roams the streets in a distant corner of the Realm, picking pockets and robbing houses, looking for her fortune while never taking responsibility for who *she* allowed herself to become. I hope that one day she will look in the mirror and remember the happy and kind girl she used to be—'

Mrs Cory cleared her throat and Ebbie wheeled around. He hadn't heard the door open.

'I wonder,' she said, 'are some deaths preordained? Was there a higher power steering your friend's life?'

'Excuse me?'

The funeral director came to stand on the opposite side of the gurney, her voice kindly but her ebon eyes full of intense curiosity. Ebbie couldn't decide if she was eccentric or creepy.

'Where was Mai from, what secrets did she keep?' Mrs Cory gave an exaggerated shrug. 'I have heard tales the townspeople whisper about her. Perhaps they are true. Perhaps her spirit travelled the Janus Bridge home to the Realm, and tonight she will celebrate among the folk before journeying on to Elysium. Is that a pleasing thought for you?'

'I ... I don't know.' Ebbie changed the subject but had to rub heat away from his chest before he could risk saying more. 'What will you do with Mai now?'

'I am afraid there will be no grand send-off from my end. It seems your friend was truly alone in *this* world – besides having you, of course. A cremation awaits her, I believe.'

'She'll have a proper service first? I'd like to attend.'

Mrs Cory paused, curious. 'Forgive me, sir, but I did not have you pegged as a man of faith and religion.'

'I'm not. I ... I just don't want her to be alone.'

'Yes. A friend, whatever his beliefs, should be there to ensure her legacy survives. I should imagine a local priest might recite prayers at her cremation. If given the opportunity.'

Ebbie looked at Mai's face, so peaceful, as if she might open her wise green eyes at any moment. He dearly wished he could afford to buy her a plot and a headstone engraved with a fitting epitaph. Would she have liked that?

'Can you let me know when her service will be?' Ebbie couldn't meet Mrs Cory's dark eyes. 'I'll leave my number.'

'No need, sir.' She patted Ebbie's hand and he snatched it away. Her skin was colder than Mai's. 'You are an easy man to find.'

'I'd better give you my mobile.' Ebbie shrugged hopelessly. 'The library closes tomorrow.'

'I know. Good luck, Ebbie Wren.'

7
Strange Ground

Bek Rana was pacing the room. She should have heard something by now. The collector's letter clearly stated that once the sword was in her possession, she should return straight to her lodgings where new instructions would be waiting. But there was nothing. Several hours had passed since returning from Kingfisher Manor, and now dawn was a small glow of promise through the cracked window. No one dallied when there was a piece as valuable as this involved. What if the collector had been arrested and was spilling Bek's name to the city guard at this very moment?

Backway Charlie had told her not to do it, but Charlie didn't appreciate the depth of Bek's situation. The trouble at Wood Bee Castle wasn't the only reason she wanted out of the city. She had a list of debts as long as her arm, owing money to the sort of people she really didn't want to be indebted to. Added to that, there were the already outstanding warrants for her arrest, plus the city guard were on the lookout for her. Bek didn't understand how her life had ended up like this, but it was getting harder and harder to move around the city, and this sword would buy her a new life in a new place.

Dalmyn, she had been thinking; it was the nearest city to

Strange Ground and the perfect place to begin again. But after hearing the treasonous conversation between Lady Kingfisher and Lord Dragonfly, she needed to think further afield, maybe Rooksmarch or Claddack. Wherever Bek decided to go, she needed to leave soon. She was burdened with knowledge her fellow citizens didn't have. War was coming.

True, Dalmyn was twice the size of Strange Ground with a much larger army, and if its Royal Family was indeed opposing Princess Yandira's claim to the throne, then its soldiers would likely save them all from the reign of the unhinged queen. But not before causing the kind of chaos that would trap Bek between a rock and a hard place. There was no limit to the dark magic Yandira Wood Bee would use to get what she wanted, especially if Lady Kingfisher was right about Princess Ghador still being alive.

But to escape, Bek needed her pay for stealing the sword. Where was the damn collector?

Whispers came from just outside the door. At least that was what it sounded like. When Bek pressed her ear to the rough wood, the sound stopped. She waited for it to come back, but it didn't. She had probably heard rats scurrying around in the walls. Or maybe the wind hissing through gaps in loose window frames. Her anxiety and paranoia were rising, and it was no wonder that every creak and whisper belonged to a henchman hunting payment on a debt; that every shadow on the dark street outside was cast by the city guard closing in.

Bek resumed pacing the tiny room – four paces up, four paces down. The confines were driving her insane. She needed to keep on the move, and she had been staying in one place for too long now – three nights in these lodgings, and this third night unpaid. The landlady would be asking for her silver coin as soon as the sun was up, but all Bek had to offer were the clothes she was wearing. Or the sword. And she wasn't about to give that away.

Why hadn't she heard anything?

Bek's ticket out of Strange Ground hung from her waist in a scabbard that was purposely old and battered, made of cheap and cracked brown leather, unworthy of a second glance. Bek reasoned that if the scabbard looked cheap and battered then the sword it held would be of a similarly poor quality, and no one would believe it was a sheath for a precious stolen heirloom. It was the perfect way to smuggle the sword from the Kingfisher Manor to this room without detection, so good that it would likely fool people on the street in broad daylight …

Bek stopped pacing.

She desperately needed to move on before someone caught up with her, but if the collector didn't show before sunrise, was that the worst thing that could happen? Instead of taking a cut for stealing the sword, what if Bek simply sold it herself and took a hundred percent of the profits? Finding a new buyer would take time, and safe houses were running low on the ground, but Bek could think of one remaining sanctuary where she might hole up and make fresh plans.

As for the collector … whoever it was had found their thief and left her in the lurch. If that was their game, then they deserved to lose the sword for good and never see Bek Rana again. It was time to move on.

From Mrs Cory's Funeral Home, Ebbie walked back into town and headed straight to the seafront. Down on the beach, he removed his shoes and socks and strolled with the feel of damp sand between his toes. The tide was out and twilight had closed in. The moon was already high, the sun an orangey blur on the horizon. A cool and salty breeze blew in from the west where, across the Skea Straight, the lights of the Penwith Peninsula twinkled like stars.

Strange Ground was an idyllic sort of getaway town. It sat on the east coast of the Isle of Watchers and turned over a fair amount of holiday trade with its ferry service to and from the mainland. Property there was expensive, especially around the St. Meyers-Bannerman Library, an area close to the train station. The direct line to Oldun City, the island's capital, made Strange Ground a desirable location for many commuters. But to Ebbie it was just home, the place where he had been born and raised.

Staring at the lights blinking across the sea, Ebbie wondered what would happen next for him. From childhood, books had been easier to relate to than the people in his life, and he had read as many as he could. When he wasn't reading about the Realm, he preferred to read works of fiction because, as Mai once said, 'These types of tales are more honest in their dishonesty, revealing the truths that *fact* likes to dilute,' which had been the source of many arguments between Ebbie and his parents.

The very existence of books, being surrounded by stories, was why Ebbie loved his job at the library so much. Their presence somehow defined him; caring for them gave him purpose – a fact which went completely over his parents' heads. They had never understood why he stayed in Strange Ground when they moved away. They saw the library's closure as an opportunity for their son to finally make something of his life, to find a new profession which was – at least in their eyes – worthwhile.

Tomorrow, Ebbie was losing *everything* because neither his parents nor Mr St. Meyers-Bannerman cared that the library wasn't just *a* library, it was *Ebbie's* library – the one place in the world where he felt confident, where he knew how to *be* someone.

Laughter and a gaggle of excited voices came from above. A group of people were making their way along the sea road in a wash of happy noise, like they knew how to enjoy the simple pleasures in life. Ebbie's jealousy rose when he spied Alice among them. She was laughing the loudest, undoubtedly half-cut. Did she care about what was happening tomorrow?

Alice carried a carefree attitude and nothing seemed to faze her. She was comfortable in herself and with others around her, whether she knew them or not. A fae creature, to Ebbie's mind, channelling personality traits which he found at once alien and painfully attractive. Not so long ago, he had summoned up the courage to ask Alice on a date. She had told him to meet her at a music pub on the seafront where her friend's band was playing. Ebbie had got as far as standing outside the pub, but the loud music and thick crowd of drinkers had frightened him away. The next day, he suggested a date at a quieter venue, but Alice said no; she didn't think they could be a good match, and dating the boss would be weird anyway – meaning she thought *he* was weird. Boring, too. And this was a recurring theme with Ebbie and *people*.

He never tried asking Alice out again, but his attraction to her remained. Which, to his shame, was probably why she was the only one he didn't make redundant as soon as the notice from Mr St. Meyers-Bannerman came in. He liked to think Alice stayed because of him but knew deep down that wasn't true. Her reasons remained a mystery. She certainly didn't love the library as Ebbie did, and he'd never once seen her reading a book. Maybe her carefree attitude was the mask she wore to hide from reality, like the shield of confidence Ebbie put up every day he stood behind the library desk. Was she scared of the world, daunted by the idea of making fundamental life changes by herself? Were Alice and Ebbie a better match than either of them realised? Maybe there was one day left to find out.

With her arms wrapped around someone else, Alice and her group moved on, and so did Ebbie.

Midsummer nights in Strange Ground never descended into full darkness. The horizon remained limned by the sleeping sun and the silvery moon shone like a floodlight. As Ebbie made his way along the beach, the ambience of town fell into the background. The smell of fish and chips lingered in the air, and with a mighty growl his stomach reminded him that he had skipped dinner.

Ebbie kept walking until his path was blocked by a high rocky bluff that reached out to sea when the tide was in. With the tide out, he could have walked around the rough and uneven wall, but he found himself staring into the dark mouth of a cave burrowed into its flank. There were lots of caves along the coast, but this one was famous in Strange Ground, and it reminded Ebbie of his absent friend.

Months ago, on a fresh spring morning, Mai had asked him, 'You are aware of the cave down on the beach, yes?'

'The old smugglers' cave?' Ebbie replied. 'Sure.'

'Do you know what its purpose was *before* the smugglers adopted it?'

'I know the legends.'

Mai raised an eyebrow. 'Are you certain?'

Strange Ground by the Skea was founded on an ancient settlement, and its myths and stories dated back so far that even historians gave up trying to trace their origins. Mai was referring to a legend which said that during a time long before smugglers moved in, the cave had been the location for a special sort of bridge – a Janus Bridge, to be specific, a magical con- duit which connected the Isle of Watchers with its invisible underside and twinned this town with its hidden half: the city of Strange Ground *beneath* the Skea. The Realm, where the folk lived.

'Where does everything you know about the Janus Bridge come from, Ebbie?' Mai had said on that fresh morning in spring. 'Experience or all those histories of the Realm you so love to study?'

'Given that I wasn't born hundreds and hundreds of years ago, books are all I have. And I think the histories are old enough to be mythologies now.'

'Do you, indeed? What about the stories I tell you?' Mai looked at Ebbie the way she did when she wanted him to challenge his own way of thinking. 'Would you discredit any truth in *them*?'

Ebbie chuckled and shook his head. 'So, what are you saying, Mai? We could go down to the cave and walk straight into the Realm right now, could we?'

'Ah, *that* is the question!' Mai's green eyes flashed brightly. 'Hypothetically, would you do it, Ebbie Wren? Would you cross the Janus Bridge and visit the folk of the *other* Strange Ground, where they say the sea is in the sky?'

'In a heartbeat!' The chance to visit the hidden parts of the world where the people worshipped the Oldunfolk, to experience the magic that infused *there* but not *here*; to reach the countless stories of mystery and wonder that he had been reading since childhood … yes, for a chance to see the Realm, Ebbie would dive head first into the cave and slide across the bridge on his belly like a penguin even if it were covered in broken glass. But reality was a little less adventurous.

'It's a nice dream,' he told Mai. 'I really want to believe the Realm is there.'

'What a curious thing to say.' Mai clucked her tongue. 'The

trouble with history books claiming to know the *truth* is that they fill in the gaps with wild speculation dressed as educated guesses posing as answers, because the authors wouldn't trust themselves or their readers with even a hint of ambiguity. Who knows, perhaps the same attitude prevails on the other side of the Skea. To the folk, are earthlings myth or history? Are Earth's stories taught in the Realm's schools?'

There were campfire tales told around the Isle of Watchers and across the world of Janus Bridges being discovered in more recent times, of people disappearing into the Realm, or of the folk appearing here. Many townspeople liked to joke that Mai herself had crossed a bridge to reach Strange Ground, that she wasn't an *earthling*. The truth was, if Janus Bridges ever existed then they stopped working, vanished, a couple of thousand years ago, and to this day academics, historians and mythologists debated over why. But all conclusions led to the same thing: campfire tales.

The Realm was embedded in global folklore, the pages of history, throughout the ages, and its legends were set in stone. But if it were in any way as readily accessible as the stories claimed it once was, then it would be nigh on impossible to keep that secret, not in a world of social media where a person couldn't sneeze in the street without causing a viral sensation. When Ebbie pointed that out, Mai had laughed with admonishment and ended the debate with a thought:

'Precisely because we are presented with a box and told not to open it, do not its contents become all the more intriguing? But what if the purpose of the box itself is to distract us from other questions? What if the designations of history and legend are founded on more than a *nice dream* as you believe?'

Could there be secret bridges dotted around the island, across the world, known to only a few both on Earth and in the Realm?

Ebbie loved the idea of it, but the cave he stared into, whatever its origins, was just a cave now. He knew that much, yet he wanted everyone to be wrong. Everyone except Mai. Because she hadn't just been Ebbie's only friend; she was the first *true* friend he had ever made, and the deepest part of him prayed that her spirit had found a Janus Bridge and tonight she rested with the people about whom she told so many wonderful tales.

'You're a good man, Ebbie Wren,' Mai said from his memories. 'A true hero, even if you cannot see it.'

The bothersome heat returned to Ebbie's chest. He tried to rub it away, but this time the sensation wouldn't settle and rose to his throat. Eyes stinging, he took a deep breath and looked out to the lights of the mainland.

'Goodbye, Mai,' he whispered to the sea.

And Ebbie cried.

Alone in the private council chamber annexed to the throne room of Castle Wood Bee, Princess Yandira celebrated her freedom while seated in a comfortable chair, enjoying the warmth of a crackling log fire. She had toasted her achievements with a glass of wine, but only a sip or two. It wouldn't do to dull her senses at this time. Wouldn't do at all.

For ten years Yandira had played along, pretending to be a hapless captive in the north tower while she had in fact spent the decade locating the main obstacle in her way. It had taken longer than she would have liked, but inevitably, inexorably, she had delivered herself to this moment where the Queendom of Strange Ground beneath the Skea was almost hers. But *almost* was not a word of which Yandira was particularly fond. *Almost* meant that while Queen Eldrid was now as dead as Yandira needed her to be, Eldrid's heir was not necessarily so.

A hiss of voices filled Yandira's ears. They came from the

wooden floor of the council chamber and the pool of oily fluid which she had earlier conjured upon it. The voices were the distant bestial roars of dragons, struggling to be heard from a great depth, an impossible depth into which the pool swirled away from the Realm to meet the ebb and flow of the river whose current ran to the Underworld. Lady Persephone was ever merciful and generous to the servants who prayed to Her domain, and the roars of Her dragons cleared the oily murk to show a crystal-sharp view of the lands outside the queendom's borders.

Yandira leaned forward for a closer inspection.

The vision in the pool swept along the miles and miles of the Queen's Highway which ran westwards from the city of Dalmyn all the way to Strange Ground's gates. It cut through forests and hills and fields, and Yandira saw farmers toiling, woodland creatures foraging for food and one or two bandit gangs lying in wait for unsuspecting travellers. But the vision, speeding in the direction of Strange Ground as it was, would not show her whom she hoped to see. Persephone's dragons told Yandira that her prey could not be located.

What did that mean?

Frustration boiling over, Yandira cursed softly and leaned away from the pool. Right now, down in the crypts, the cold, dead body of Queen Eldrid lay alone when she should have been lying beside her daughter. Official word around the castle was that Princess Ghador had fallen foul of the same treasonous plot which had killed her mother, and most had no reason to doubt it. The news was true; Yandira had arranged both murders personally, then made Morrad announce the deaths officially, placing blame upon Hamdon Lark and Ala Denev. However, Ghador's physical corpse remained elusive when it should have been returned to the castle by now. At this moment, Eldrid's heir was *presumed* dead but not *confirmed* dead. This did not sit well with Yandira. It was the *almost* in the next step of her ultimate ambition.

But still, alive or dead, the pool would show nothing of Princess Ghador. At the time of her mother's death, she had been travelling to Dalmyn to visit her father and paternal grandmother with a small army of her own, and on the highway between the two cities was the place Yandira had chosen for her assassins to stealthily slip into the royal convoy and take the princess's life. The convoy had not made it as far as Dalmyn, and it was yet to return to Strange Ground, and so it *had* to still be on the highway, somewhere.

Even while Yandira searched, the noble Houses were gathering in the throne room, summoned to address the tragedy of the royal assassinations. Or so they thought. Some of the Houses would support Yandira's right to the crown, most feared her too much to say otherwise, but a few were influential enough to oppose her. With confirmation of her niece's death, and while her sister Morrad posed no competition, Yandira's claim would be irrefutable. But until sure evidence of Ghador's demise bore witness, the more influential Houses would insist Eldrid's daughter remain the rightful heir. A technicality, maybe, but one that could raise the wrong kind of attention for Yandira. While there was even a hint of Ghador being alive, the Priests of Juno would not crown anyone else Queen of Strange Ground.

Forcing the priests to relinquish the crown was an option, but this would insult rusty traditions upon which the Realm was founded. In the long run, these traditions would mean little of consequence, but breaking them too soon could gain Yandira the kind of attention she was not yet powerful enough to repel. She needed her niece's corpse, and she needed it now, because the terms of the pact she had struck were quite clear: only when the crown was hers would Lady Persephone, Her Immortal Darkness of the Underworld, further Yandira's ambitions.

'Curse it,' she whispered. In the pool, the image of Strange Ground had come into sight, but still there was no sign of Ghador's convoy. The vision had travelled the entire length of the Queen's Highway, two days of riding in a few moments, but the dragons could not find what Yandira damn well knew had to be there.

Patience, she reminded herself.

She then realised the Shade had entered the chamber. It sat on the floor, expectant but motionless as a poisonous toad waiting for insects to fly by.

'What is it?' she said testily.

'The Houses are gathered, my sister,' the Shade rustled dryly. 'It is time to join Morrad in the throne room.'

Without Ghador's body, this was going to be trickier than she would have liked. But never let it be said that Yandira Wood Bee could not adapt.

With a sigh, she said, 'So be it,' then drew a small knife from the sleeve of her gown and pricked her fingertip. She gave blessings and thanks to Lady Persephone by squeezing a single drop of blood into the pool and begged that She might allow Her dragons to continue searching the Queen's Highway. The clear vision became black and oily, denying the request, and fury beat at Yandira's temples as she strode from the chamber to the throne room.

8

The Wood Bee Queen

Ebbie realised with stark clarity that he had to figure out life all over again. Did that mean a respectable job, good pay, a nice house, perhaps a wife and kids, faith – all the ingredients his parents claimed made a good life? Or should the future be the unknowable void of mystery he felt he was staring into?

Ebbie's home was a rented flat in the middle of town, an abode the brochure had politely described as *humble*, with a bedroom window overlooking a rowdy pub in a dingy side road, while the kitchen-sink window provided a grand view of the dirty brick wall belonging to an insurance company building. The flat was listed as a two-bedroom apartment, but the second bedroom wasn't much larger than a broom cupboard, so Ebbie had fitted it with shelves and used it as his personal library space. There were more shelves and cases laden with books in the main bedroom and the lounge-cum-kitchen, where a tatty sofa and comfy armchair lived, but no television or stereo. It wasn't much, but it was Ebbie's sanctuary, and if he didn't do something soon he'd be losing his home, too.

Sitting in the armchair with a cup of tea, the wrappings from his fish and chips dinner screwed up at his feet, Ebbie felt too dejected to think about the future. His current plan didn't extend beyond staying with the St. Meyers-Bannerman

Library until its final death, and then hopping on the ferry to the mainland to spend a frustrating week with his parents in Penzance. He wasn't looking forward to the trip; they would badger him with advice and demands, because Ebbie needed to stop avoiding some very serious decisions.

His savings would only stretch to cover another two months' rent on the flat – three if he didn't want to eat – yet he hit a mental block at the very thought of applying for another job. He had got as far as staring long and hard at the online form for a position at the university library in Oldun City, but didn't fill it in. Like a sulky child who wouldn't accept his favourite toy had been taken away, Ebbie refused to entertain the idea of working anywhere other than *his* library.

He sipped his tea.

On the coffee table in front of the armchair lay a single book. It was bound in a blank leather cover, appeared older than it actually was, and the thick pages inside were covered in words written by hand. Mai had donated this book to the library. She claimed that it came from her private collection, though Ebbie had never seen evidence of such a collection in her nook. Nevertheless, it was a precious thing with priceless emotional value and it deserved better than to be lost and forgotten.

Ebbie had started working at the St. Meyers-Bannerman Library as a means to pay for his college fees. His parents had refused to fork out because he was studying the Realm, studying the folk, their history and culture, their stories and religion, which to them was a redundant and blasphemous area of focus. Ebbie had defied his parents all the way to an A Level. After college, he continued working at the library, happier than he'd ever been, making his way up from a junior until eventually becoming manager – though, as it turned out, the manager of its demise.

Mr St. Meyers-Bannerman himself was something of a myth. Ebbie had never laid eyes on him, let alone spoken to him on the phone. He was the chair of the town council, which technically made him Mayor of Strange Ground, though this was more like an honorary position bought and paid for a long time ago.

Mr St. Meyers-Bannerman liked to pull the strings from the shadows, always to his own advantage. His influence came from inherited wealth accrued by the farming business that had been in his family for generations. The St. Meyers-Bannermans had owned most of the land to the south of Strange Ground for more than two hundred years, along with various properties in town, which included the library building. But he never wanted the library itself; the running of it had been a passion of his wife's.

They said Mrs St. Meyers-Bannerman fought a constant struggle to get any kind of funding from her husband. She had been a kind and sociable woman who often visited the library and had a friendly relationship with the previous manager and all the staff. Her belief was that books should be readily available to all. But sadly, a heart condition ended her life a few weeks into Ebbie's stint as manager. Everyone had hoped that her husband would continue patronage of the library in memory of his wife. And he did. For a while.

The man who Ebbie knew only as a myth obviously wasn't in possession of a long-lasting sentimental streak. Two months before, his secretary had sent Ebbie a memo stating that the library building had been sold to a property developer and redundancies would be paid at the legal minimum. A cold and officious declaration made by a cold and officious man.

Ebbie had tried contacting him, but phone calls and emails went unanswered. And when news spread of two luxury apartments soon to be on sale at the library's address, it was as though a curse had magically descended. Readers stopped coming to borrow books, townsfolk began referring to the library in the past tense, and redundancies whittled the staff down to just Ebbie and Alice, the only witnesses to the final days.

Mr St. Meyers-Bannerman had no idea of or interest in what kind of books his wife's library owned, whether or not rare or special editions graced the many racks and shelves. Which was why Ebbie had salvaged the leather-bound book on his coffee table. To his knowledge, no one had ever borrowed it, but he'd be damned if he'd let some property developer cart it away to burn on a bonfire with the all the other books. It was Mai's legacy.

Taking the book, Ebbie flicked through it, comforted by the crisp flapping of heavy pages. There was no author name accompanying the stories inside, which made Ebbie suspect that Mai had written it herself – though how she had afforded to bind the book so beautifully was a mystery. Each of the stories was a tale of the Realm and the folk, bearing titles that were familiar to Ebbie by now: 'The Close and Hidden Peril', 'The Trials of a Twice-Orphaned Thief', 'A Friendly Face in a Troubled Forest' and ... He blanched and flipped back a few pages ... 'The Wood Bee Queen'?

Ebbie frowned at the unrecognised title.

He had read Mai's book cover to cover at least twice but couldn't recall a story called 'The Wood Bee Queen'. He switched on his reading lamp and a big smile stretched across his face as he read the opening line, the same line which began all of these stories: *They say that in the Realm, the sea is in the sky* ... Ebbie read on and his smile grew and grew as he recognised not a word of this story.

Was this a hidden gem? A blessed ray of distraction on a day when he needed to forget the world and all it was throwing at him? Settling back in the armchair, Ebbie laid the book on his lap and dived from his life into the mysterious pool of a far-off land.

They say that in the Realm, the sea is in the sky ...

The Queen of Strange Ground beneath the Skea was proud to wear her crown. It would have been an understated circlet of entwining gold and silver if not for the two stones of majestic twilight blue set into it. One faced forwards and encouraged the Queen to consider the future; the other looked backwards and reminded her to learn from the past. Foresight and Hindsight, the stones were named; blessed, they said, by Merciful Lady Juno, the Oldunone of Queens. With these twilight stones, mortal monarchs had served their people well for centuries.

For most of her life, the Queen of Strange Ground dutifully fulfilled her role as Protector of the Realm and First Lady to House Wood Bee, and she had made her city a peaceful, happy queendom. But as the long years crept up on her, Foresight came to dominate her thoughts. What legacy could she leave behind which might inform her heir's Hindsight?

Venus, the Oldunone of Love, had favoured the Queen with the blessing of three daughters, three princesses of whom she was proud. Eldest Daughter was as shrewd and wise as her mother, though some might say lacking her mother's humour. Middlest Daughter was gentle and charmed with a mind for dreams and wonders and simple pleasures. Youngest Daughter preferred her own company and rarely aired her opinions: the Quiet One, her sisters called her; the Sulky Daughter, whispered the nobles in court. The princesses were who they were, brilliant, different, remote, and the Queen loved them as a mother would. That is to say, equally and without condition.

In the landscape of royal life, there were always subjects who sought to advance their position by currying favour or taking advantage of the misfortunes of others. The Queen was sure to make her children wise to this. Though Eldest Daughter's passions often drifted to hunting and swordplay, she made a sharp and attentive student while learning of the finer duties which came with the crown she would one day inherit. And the future queen shared what she learned with Middlest Daughter, her most loyal and loving sister, with whom she made a force to be reckoned with.

Middlest Daughter might have played well the role of an unfocused dreamer, but she was no fool. She bore no designs on the crown herself, harboured no jealousies towards her older sister's position as First Heir to House Wood Bee. Middlest Daughter knew how to charm the royal court and uncover the spiteful truths lurking behind honeyed words which might be of use to a monarch. She was a subtle but powerful ally to Eldest Daughter, and when combined their political prowess and cunning were not easily outsmarted.

And so the Queen slept well at night knowing that upon her final day in the Realm, the majestic stones of Foresight and Hindsight would sit on a wise and just head. But who could say what thoughts dominated the mind of Youngest Daughter? Perhaps she found contentment in her taciturn ways, or was it that she viewed the throne of Strange Ground with an eye of sadness, knowing that her turn to sit upon it would never come? Last in the line of ascension, overlooked and unconsidered by the folk and noble Houses alike, Youngest Daughter spent her days alone, brooding behind the books in her mother's library. No one conceived it possible that ill will might fester inside her like a cancerous growth.

All her life, Youngest Daughter had lived in the shade of her mother and sisters. If her position in the royal line was best described as *distant*, then it became all but invisible when Eldest Daughter gave the Queen the gift of a granddaughter. While the Royal Family and the folk of Strange Ground celebrated this glorious event, Youngest Daughter withdrew further from courtly life and descended into the dark mysteries of the past. If only the Queen's Foresight had noticed this.

Of all the leisures the Queen enjoyed outside duty and family, she took pleasure in her private library the most. It boasted some of the rarest books in all the Realm: histories by wise folk or those other people from that other place; tales of fancy and perilous adventure; old tomes with dry pages and fading knowledge written in dead languages – the Queen collected them all. She knew each and every one of her books, or so she thought. Until the day she discovered the forbidden text secreted among her collection.

From where it came was a mystery, for the Queen would certainly never procure such a book knowingly. It bore no title or name of author, though some now say it was written by a crazed royal magician from an ancient time in his own blood and bound in the skin of his unfortunate apprentice. The dark magic it radiated sickened the Queen so much she dared not touch its gruesome binding, let alone read the foul words inside. But read it she had to, eventually, when tragedy came calling on her House.

By this time, Granddaughter had grown into a fine young woman, the very model of her Grandmother, the nobles said with pride, and it was shortly after her thirteenth-birthday celebrations that her favourite aunt was struck down by the strangest ailment. Middlest Daughter fell into a deep and powerful sleep from which she could not be woken, no matter what was tried. The best and most learned physicians were called for, but they remained at a loss to explain the phenomenon. For two days they tended the princess with potions and remedies, while the Queen, Eldest Daughter and Granddaughter fretted by her bedside. Yet still she could not be roused.

On the third day, however, Middlest Daughter awoke, seemingly of her own accord, but confused and much changed from the woman the family knew. The dreamy wonders and simple pleasures of her thoughts were more real to Middlest Daughter than the natural world. She barely recognised her sister, her mother, her niece, or remembered her place within the Royal Family. Gone were the sharp eyes of that charming, cunning princess, replaced now with the faraway gaze of a lost mind, a mind that could not be found.

Dire science, the physicians proclaimed; dark magics, agreed the royal magician; and so the Queen's Hindsight steered her back to the mysterious and forbidden book in her library.

Though surely a damnable text and a danger to the eyes of any reader, the Queen scoured its pages, certain that it held answers. And answers she found. Knowledge from the foulest regions of the Underworld, secrets plucked from the nightmares of Cursed Persephone Herself, spells of terrible supernature which had no place in the world of mortals. The book contained them all, including black rites which explained perfectly Middlest Daughter's incongruous ailment.

The Serpent's Sigh, a vicious spell conjured from the spirits of dragons who long ago flew across the sea in the sky but now dwelled at Persephone's side in the Underworld. The Queen learned how the slightest touch from this magic would subvert even the most good-hearted person into a servant of darkness. The Serpent's Sigh could be used to steal the soul from a living body, not only rendering the victim a shell of their former self, but also gaining the caster a vile Shade, a murderous creature in the dark, a spy and assassin both. The Queen felt twice her age just reading the instructions. Damnable indeed! But who would bring such a *thing* into her library?

Even as the Queen's fury rose, her heart shattered, the pieces tumbling into despair. Those with permission to use the library with free rein were few, and there was only one who might benefit from casting the Serpent's Sigh upon Middlest Daughter, one who had been absent from her sister's sickbed.

Meanwhile, in her rooms in the high north tower of Castle Wood Bee, Youngest Daughter believed that physical absence from events ensured immunity from guilt. For years she had prayed to the Underworld in secret, plotting her ascension without raising a single eyebrow of suspicion, and now the first part of her long plan was done. With Middlest Daughter unfit to rule, she had stepped closer to the throne of Strange Ground. And now it was time to step closer still.

The Shade she had grown from her sister's soul was loyal and efficient, uncompromising and undetectable. On that very night, Youngest Daughter gave her servant the orders which would ensure her place as First Heir to House Wood Bee. In the dead of dark, the Shade stalked the castle shadows and struck murderously at Eldest Daughter then Granddaughter while they slept in their beds.

At last! Youngest Daughter thought in the safe comfort of her tower rooms. *I am my mother's most favoured child, the future Queen of Strange Ground beneath the Skea. Let any person, noble or not, deny my status at their peril!*

She prepared herself, Youngest Daughter, prepared her façade to exude emotions she did not – *could* not – feel any more. Emotions lost to her over a years-long slide into Cursed Persephone's domain. Devastation, heartbreak, horror over the death of her sister and niece — she was ready to receive the tragic news soon to be delivered to her tower.

But she did not realise that the Queen had discovered the catalyst for her wicked plan secreted amidst the books in her library. She did not know that wards and spells had been cast upon her royal rivals to protect them from the vicious Shade. She could not guess that a trap had been laid for her magical servant, and it had been captured by the royal magician the very moment it struck from the shadows. To Youngest Daughter's dismay, when the guards came to her rooms, they were not bearing tragic news but an order of arrest for the *attempted* murder of House Wood Bee's first and second heirs.

Powerless without her foul accomplice, prevented from summoning the Serpent's Sigh once more, Youngest Daughter confessed her crimes before the royal court, but not with re-morse or regret. With pride and malice, she cursed every House brought to bear witness, she damned the very ground upon which Castle Wood Bee had been built. *Suffering to every one of my mother's subjects*, she cried, *and may the lowest pits of the Underworld swallow them all.*

Many Houses called for execution. But the Queen, furious as she was, begged for mercy. Hindsight demanded penance, yet Foresight told her that in this matter a Queen's ruling could not be made separate from a mother's love. With the understanding of the nobles, she banished Youngest Daughter to the north tower where she would spend the rest of her days under lock and spell and close guard.

The folk rejoiced. The Quiet One, the Sulky Daughter, the Dangerous Princess was a threat no more. What they couldn't know, what Eldest Daughter and Granddaughter did not sus-pect, was how the Queen had laid the ultimate blame upon her-self. Try as she had to fashion a *good* legacy, she had been blind to the shroud of darkness falling on her queendom. The damage was done and too great to be healed. Youngest Daughter was lost to her spite and bile, and Middlest Daughter would never be the same again, for the Shade had corrupted her soul beyond redemption. The Queen had failed her people.

And so she prayed to the Queen of Queens, the Merciful Lady Juno, and she begged her Oldunone for a boon, a pact, a bargain for which she would pay with exile so that Eldest Daughter might rise to claim her birthright. And Lady Juno was listening. In Her divine wisdom, She acquiesced to Her mortal subject's request.

Under cover of night, when no one strode the castle halls, the Queen visited the three bedchambers where Eldest Daughter, Middlest Daughter and Granddaughter slept. Gently, she kissed their foreheads in love and farewell before placing the crown of Strange Ground beneath the Skea upon the seat of her throne, now knowing how Foresight and Hindsight could better serve her legacy. And then, the Queen travelled to no one knew where and was never seen again.

But it is said that the pact she made with the Oldunone of Queens allows her to watch over her city from a far and distant place, with a keen eye trained on Castle Wood Bee's north tower.

The throne room was a serious sort of hall, wide and long, all bare stone and high rafters, chilly even in summer. A lack of windows meant no sunshine lifted the spacious gloom to a cheerier shade. Torches burned night and day in sconces fixed to the rows of decorative pillars along the left and right walls. Though a gathering of noble lords and ladies covered the flag-stone floor to its halfway point, the light flickering of flames was the only sound to be heard.

Representatives from every House of Strange Ground beneath the Skea had been summoned by royal command to attend the throne room. Whether they had come out of fear or a sense of duty was beside the point; they had entered of their own volition, but the royal guards with their pikes standing between every pillar suggested their manner of leaving might be more complicated.

Shrouded in an eerie hush, noble faces were turned to the dais where Princess Morrad sat upon the throne – a worn and uncomfortable chair of preposterous size, forged from metal and wood to resemble a barren tree. Its armrests were more like branches, its base a knotted bowl; the back rose twisting and tall to form a parody of three oversized bees hovering in a line. With the huge banner of House Wood Bee hanging on the wall behind her, Morrad looked lost and useless on the throne, as indeed the nobles knew her to be; for on Morrad's left stood confirmation of an immediate and worrisome future.

To the gentle song of flickering flames and the silence of apprehension, Princess Yandira stared down any eyes that dared to meet hers. She knew these people of noble blood, and they knew her. So many of them had called for her death ten years ago, but they wouldn't be so keen to air their opinions now.

For the umpteenth time, Princess Morrad gave the impression that she would finally begin her address. She straightened on the throne, opened her mouth, and the nobles leaned forward as one, cocking their ears. But then, without breathing a word, Morrad closed her mouth and shrank into the throne, as though forgetting who she was and what she had to say. All in the gathering stirred with frustration, all except one who was not of noble blood: Ignius Rex, apprentice to the royal magician. His gaze was hungry, exhilarated by the current condition of his former master.

To the right of the throne, Hamdon Lark sat with Ala Denev in a cage hanging from the rafters on a chain as thick as a soldier's arm. The royal magician and royal advisor were a tangle of limbs on the cage's floor. Faces squeezed between iron bars, expressions lax, their beshadowed eyes stared out glumly. Beneath them, two royal guards stood statue-still in full armour, armed with pikes. Shadows leaked from their visors like tendrils of smoke.

A weak and ghoulish moan came from Lark's slack mouth. Denev answered it with one of her own. The nobles stepped back as though the floor were crumbling and a precipice drew near. This reaction pleased Yandira. *Let them see!* she thought. Not since the days of Lady Bellona, the last true Empress of the Realm, had prisoners been so publicly punished. Now there was a woman to be admired, and surely Bellona would have been proud of Yandira's ambition.

'Now, my sister?' The Shade spoke while clinging to its master's back like a spider. 'It is time?'

'Yes, why not?' Yandira whispered. 'The Houses have been kept in suspense long enough, I think—'

The tension Yandira had carefully orchestrated in the hall shattered in a moment when the throne room doors flew open and the nobles turned to see a late arrival hurry in. He was elderly, silver-haired and graceful on his feet.

'I beg pardon for my tardiness, Highness,' he said loudly. 'I was unavoidably delayed.'

Cold anger settled onto Yandira's face. Aelfric Dragonfly, First Lord to House Dragonfly, and one of the strongest voices in court. He took his place at the back of the gathering and adopted an expression of loyal attentiveness, but Yandira could detect that he carried one trick or another up his sleeve. These nobles needed bringing to heel.

The front row flinched as Morrad rose from the throne with

the speed of a puppet yanked to its feet by a puppeteer and said, 'My Lords and Ladies,' in a voice like cold floodwater seeping into the ears of her audience. 'Behold the traitors of the crown!'

She swept her arm towards the cage holding Lark and Denev captive. They moaned as Morrad continued, 'For years my sister, and my mother before her, trusted this magician and advisor with their very lives.' As she spoke, Yandira whispered along, conducting Morrad's words and movements. 'But who was it who failed to protect my family from the assassins these *betrayers* brought into my House?'

Morrad's finger shot out like an arrow of accusation. In the cage, Lark and Denev made a wretched pair. Together they stared miserably as though protesting their innocence, begging the nobles to save them from Yandira's trickery.

Yandira had Morrad bare her teeth at the nobles. 'Your lack of action mocks the very throne of this land. *Guilty!* Each of you! For now Queen Eldrid and her heir are dead.'

Some were surprised and confused to hear Morrad speaking so eloquently after all these years, while others were shocked by her accusation, turning their faces in shame. But one among them dared to speak out.

'Excuse my interruption, Highness.' It was Lord Dragonfly again. 'There is hope for Princess Ghador yet.'

Morrad's mouth opened and closed like a landed fish before Yandira regained composure and control of her voice. 'What nonsense do you bring, Lord Dragonfly? The tragic loss has been confirmed.'

'Perhaps too soon, Highness. I have this moment come from the city gates. Princess Ghador's royal convoy has returned to Strange Ground, but not carrying her body.' Yandira paled and bristled while a susurration of hushed voices rose among the nobles. 'It is true,' Lord Dragonfly told them. 'I know not the specifics, but it seems none witnessed the heir's demise. They say she is missing but not dead.'

And I'll wager you could not wait to have this happy news delivered to the Temple of Juno, Yandira thought darkly. How was it that she had not seen the convoy's return?

Lord Dragonfly addressed all in the throne room. 'Could it be we were wrong? Does Princess Ghador still live?'

Clever, thought Yandira, *but too little too late, Aelfric*, and she whispered instructions to the Shade. 'Discover if what this old fool says is true. Have the guards take every member of Ghador's convoy into custody, and then find Mr Lunk and Mr Venatus. They should have returned by now.'

'Yes, my sister.'

As the Shade melted away, Lord Dragonfly's news had raised the hushed voices to excited chatter and Yandira could not stand to hear their hopefulness.

'Enough!' Morrad's command silenced the room. 'Pray for this, if it comforts you, but we each of us feel in our hearts that we must weep for sweet Ghador alongside dearest Eldrid. And for their murderers, there can be no mercy.' She turned to face Hamdon Lark and Ala Denev. 'Execute them.'

The guards beneath the cage did not hesitate to obey. They stepped forward, wheeled around and thrust their pikes through the bars to slice the throats of the magician and advisor. The gathering struggled to contain gasps and retches of horror, unable to look. Ignius Rex could, however. The magician's apprentice enjoyed the execution of his former master, his gaze hungrier than ever. The grim spectacle proved too much for Lord Dragonfly, though. The old fool crept out of the throne room when he thought no one was watching. Let him go. Yandira would catch up with him soon enough.

Lark and Denev died without a sound. The guards resumed

their position beneath the cage, impassive as blood rained down and splashed over their helmets and armour. Stunned, sickened silence reigned until the bleeding slowed to *tinks* of the odd red drop striking silver metal.

'*I* am as guilty as *you*,' Morrad said softly. 'Only one among us saw the black web weaved by Hamdon Lark and Ala Denev. She tried to warn us, ten years ago. If only we had listened instead of laying our blame and judgement upon the head of poor, innocent Yandira.'

Among the horrified expressions, a few caught the lie and frowned. They remembered well that Yandira's conduct of a decade ago was far from innocent, but didn't the victor have a duty to rewrite history in their own image? The Quiet One, the Sulky Daughter, the Dangerous Princess had seized control of Strange Ground from under their very noses. And it was just the beginning.

Morrad was pointing at the gathering again. 'Like you, so quick was I to question the loyalty of my dear sister that I was blind to the truth. And how can a blind queen rule her people justly? She cannot.

'I stand before you as First Heir to my House and this queendom, but the folk of Strange Ground deserve better than *me*. There is neither the strength nor wisdom inside me to take up the crown of this city. I am unworthy to sit upon the Wood Bee Throne.' Yandira hid a smile as she formed her sister's next statement. 'Therefore, my abdication is imperative to the safety of Strange Ground. Let no one here object.'

The blood had stopped dripping from the cage. The nobles held their collective breath, none daring to speak.

Morrad stepped away from the throne and dropped to one knee before Yandira. 'Let the Priests of Juno hear that my beloved sister, Princess Yandira, is First Lady to her House.'

With an almost contented sigh, Yandira sat upon the throne and offered a thin smile to the noble bloods of Strange Ground. Each of them looked so ... *scared*. Except Ignius Rex, the new royal magician. His adoration shone brightly.

'Seal the doors,' Yandira ordered in a crisp, clear voice.

Three guards marched to the end of the throne room, closed the doors and stood with their backs to them. And then, as one, every guard present levelled their weapons at the gathering.

'Now then,' Yandira growled. 'I should very much like to address your loyalties to my throne.'

9

The Last Librarian

After a troubled night's sleep, Ebbie walked an alternate route to work – he couldn't face seeing Mai's nook on the high street, cleaned out and empty of her presence. The walk cleared his head, however, and he made a decision to do something he hadn't done for a long time: grab life by the balls. He summoned his courage, prepared himself to take one last plunge into the unknown: he was going to ask Alice for a date.

By the time he arrived at the library, he was ready to reveal his true feelings and prove to her how compatible they were. But, of course, Alice was late to work on the library's final day – just like every other day – so his declaration of love had to wait.

Ebbie was further disappointed when he reached the checkout desk and found a short, impersonal letter from Mr St. Meyers-Bannerman waiting for him: *To whomever locks up tonight, ensure you post your keys back through the letterbox.*

The gloom of desertion descended on Ebbie, and it felt like crashing to the ground when he collapsed into his chair behind the desk. He considered setting fire to the letter, or returning it to sender in box filled with dog poo. Instead, he stared at the library door, miserable and already too hot on this summer's morning. His phone buzzed. Another text from his mum, yet again reminding him that his dad would pick him up from the ferry next week and claiming that: *Father Tom is looking forward to seeing you.* He stuffed the phone back into his pocket without replying.

He couldn't bear facing the library's last day on his own. He willed just one more reader to show up and borrow a book for old time's sake. But in his heart of hearts, he knew it wouldn't happen. And with glum resignation, he realised Alice wasn't coming, either. Not for old time's sake, not even to say good-bye. Alice was gone from Ebbie's life for good. Like Mai.

Defeated and alone, Ebbie packed his stamp and ink-pad into the desk drawer and leaned back in the chair to catch up on the sleep he had missed last night.

A series of static shocks startled him awake a couple of hours later into the heat of midday. There was drool on Ebbie's cheek and sweat dampened his hair and shirt. He loosened his tie and rolled up his sleeves, then froze when a woman placed a glass of water on the desk before him.

'I'm sorry to disturb you,' she said. 'It seems as though you are in need of rest, but we have matters to discuss.'

The air around her was rippling. Ebbie rubbed sleep from his eyes and the effect stopped. The woman was smartly dressed. On the lapel of her jacket was a brooch made of cream and green onyx in the shape of a bird with a stocky body and long beak. A kingfisher, Ebbie thought. She encouraged him to drink. The water was cool on his throat and the glass a blessing on his forehead. Ebbie had never seen the woman before. Typical of his luck that a new reader should arrive on today of all days.

'If you're after a library card, I'm afraid you're too late,' he told her. 'We're closing down. But if there are any books you'd like to take . . . ?'

'A generous offer, I'm sure.' Her face was too stern to be sympathetic. 'But I've no interest in your books.'

Perhaps she was one of St. Meyers-Bannerman's cronies. Dressed in a brown skirt suit and ruffle-fronted shirt, her greying hair neatly tied up, he could easily imagine her striding around the offices of a successful business, the bane of any indolent worker. Had she been sent to turf him out?

'What do you want?'

'You are Ebbie Wren?'

'Yeah.'

'Good, good. I come to you at the behest of Her Royal Highness Lady Maitressa.'

'Who?'

'Maitressa, former First Lady to her House, Protector of the Realm and estranged Queen of Strange Ground beneath the Skea.' She smiled at Ebbie's sleep-fogged confusion. 'But I believe you were privileged enough to call her *Mai*.'

'Mai,' Ebbie said slowly. '*Mai*-tressa?'

'Her passing grieves us all,' the woman continued. 'She has named you the executor of her last will and testament.'

Ebbie wondered if he was still asleep and rubbed his eyes again. 'I'm sorry – what?'

'You have inherited the proud position of Lady Maitressa's executor. And she has left you a valuable heirloom to aid you in your duties.'

So saying, the woman placed what looked to be a homemade satchel on the desk. It was made from tattered cloth as dark as the dress Mai used to wear.

'An heirloom?' Ebbie looked up at the woman. 'I'm sorry, I don't want to be rude, but ... what are you talking about?'

'Further instructions will come to you as and when they are required. The queen said that I should remind you to look after this satchel with your very life.'

'The *queen* said?'

'Yes, she was quite insistent about it.'

Ebbie blinked at her. 'Sure ...' He lifted the satchel and scrunched it up. It was entirely empty, and a sudden anger rose inside him. 'Is this some kind of joke?' he demanded. 'Who the bloody hell are you ...?'

He trailed off. The woman now stood by the door, waving a farewell. She said, 'May the Oldunfolk smile upon you, Ebbie Wren,' and was gone.

With the satchel in hand, Ebbie rushed outside. Cars trundled up and down the road, a few pedestrians walked the pavement, but the woman was nowhere to be seen.

'What?'

His phone rang and startled him. He didn't answer for a long moment, but when he did, Mrs Cory from the funeral home was on the line.

'*Your friend's final send-off is at hand,*' she said in that stiff and weird way of hers. '*May I have your home address so you might receive a formal invitation?*'

'Uh-huh.' Ebbie gave his address distractedly and hung up.

He checked the street again, but no sign of the woman. Wondering what had just happened, he stepped inside and scrutinised the satchel in his hands. The raggedy cloth carried a peculiar scent, a curious mixture of flowers and woodsmoke and adventure. It smelled like Mai. *Maitressa* ...

His gaze drifted over the racks and shelves of dusty books, the faded paint on the walls, the worn carpet on the floor, and he saw the final death of the St. Meyers-Bannerman Library. His mind was racing but his heart had sunk into his stomach. Ebbie Wren was so very tired of caring.

While seated in a comfortable chair in her private council chamber, Yandira read a letter. It had arrived an hour or so ago by courier gull, and no matter how many times she read it, the details simply would not change for the better. Ghador's alleged survival was an unexpected obstacle, but not one that Yandira thought would be in her way for long. However, with the arrival of this letter, it had become clear that she had no choice but to step up her plans.

Dragons hissed from the dark pool on the chamber floor. The oily waters of the Underworld rippled and broke, allowing a figure to rise from its depths. Shrouded in black, the figure stepped into the chamber, waiting while the fluid drained away and slithered back into the pool, leaving not one stain upon the skin or robes of the man it revealed. His eyes glazed, his expression daunted, this was Ignius Rex, the new royal magician to House Wood Bee.

'Such knowledge,' he whispered. 'Such advancement.'

Yandira concurred with a nod, recalling how it had felt the first time she beheld the secrets of Persephone's domain. She almost experienced envy for how this magician was feeling.

'For all these years your promises spoke to my dreams,' Ignius said. 'Each night I prayed for your return, but never did I expect such wonders as reward.'

Ignius Rex had been apprenticed to Hamdon Lark near the end of Queen Maitressa's reign. A keen and talented pupil, but also sly and clever, for his sworn allegiance to the throne was never quite as loyal as he allowed his masters to suppose. His mind was curious for more than Lark was willing or able to teach, than the queen would allow him to learn, thus his desire for deeper arcane knowledge had to travel in secret the same dark road as Yandira.

The years had been kind to Ignius, though his temples were grey and lines of age were beginning to show on his face. Most importantly, his predilections had not been tempered over the last decade. This kind of fealty deserved a queen's favour, and such had been granted with his first taste of the Underworld.

'I was borne aloft by the spirits of dragons,' he said. 'They flew me to the gates of the Underworld, and through them I gazed upon the other side of the Skea.'

'You saw them, didn't you?' Yandira's voice was low with desire. 'You saw our allies.'

'I witnessed wingless dragons, Majesty, mightier than Persephone's pets, so powerful that one alone could destroy an entire city with its fire.'

'And the metal warbirds? Did you see how they hatch younglings in mid-flight to drop savage warriors directly into the midst of battle?'

Ignius nodded, awed by his memories. 'And sea beasts of monumental size, capable of sinking entire armadas.'

'With such an army at my command, could anyone stand against me, Ignius?'

The magician's eyes were drunk with knowledge and longed for the dark waters. 'I want to go back. I *need* to see more.'

'An understandable desire, commendable even, but caution and restraint! Many a soul has sought too much too soon from Lady Persephone, and none of them found their way back from Her domain. Your place is at my side for what is to come.'

Tearing his forlorn gaze away from the oily pool, Ignius nodded, albeit sadly. 'What would you have of me, Majesty?'

'Patience and cunning.' Yandira rose from the chair. 'The gates of the Underworld are opened but a crack. Lady Persephone permits a few of my agents to use it for travelling between worlds, but She has sworn to wrench Her gates wide open so my allies and their miracles of warcraft may join my cause. However, before Her Immortal Darkness will allow this, the crown of Strange Ground must first sit on my head, and to this end we have met an obstacle, Ignius. Juno's lackeys have joined the Oldunfolk's game.'

Yandira held aloft the letter she had been reading. 'The Queen of Dalmyn has sent me a missive. I am dismayed to discover that First Lady White Gold knows of things which she should not. Namely, that Eldrid is dead and Ghador is missing but alive. Regarding this matter, the queen is sending Ghador's father to Strange Ground with a delegation to aid us in –' Yandira peered at the letter and quoted '"– what must surely be a desperate and rigorous search for the *rightful* heir of House Wood Bee."

'She goes on to say, "I speak with authority as a Protector of the Realm when I say that all of Dalmyn stands with you. We have vowed not to sleep until the *rightful* heir is found, and pray that we will witness Princess Ghador's grand coronation, which must surely receive blessing from the Priests of Juno as *rightful* tradition dictates."'

'Rightful?' Ignius cocked his head to one side. 'Queen White Gold is threatening you.'

'Yes, it is clear enough, and to invoke her authority as a Protector is to say she suspects my ultimate ambition.' Yandira came to stand on the opposite side of the pool from the magician. 'Dalmyn's delegation will reach Strange Ground in less than two days. Whether Ghador is alive or dead, they are coming to stop *me*. I will not open my gates for White Gold's army, but *my* army is not yet large enough to repel them. They are forcing my hand, nonetheless, so war it must be, Ignius. Are you ready to do your duty?'

'For you, Majesty, anything.'

'Good.' Yandira fanned herself with the letter. 'I remember the time when you first came to the castle. You confessed to me your affiliation to a clandestine band of witches who worship the Underworld. You might recall that I advised you to remain in communion with them. It would please me greatly, Ignius, if you chose to follow my advice.'

'I did, Majesty.' The magician clenched and unclenched his fists as though testing newfound strength. 'The Coven of Bellona awaits your word.'

'Perfect.' Yandira closed her eyes, revelling in the sound of dragons hissing from the black pool like the applause of an audience. If they were pleased with her, then so was Lady Persephone. 'Cast your spells, Ignius. Command your kin to rise, tell them reward for their faith is at hand. Dalmyn's soldiers must not reach the city gates. Strange Ground's news must not spread across the Realm. Tell the coven that the Serpent's Sigh is theirs to cast.'

'It will be done, Majesty.'

'Sacrifice increases potency, Ignius, so feel free to endorse any ... *inspired methods* that were once prohibited to you.' Like a war hound let off the leash, the magician strode from the room, and Yandira whispered to herself, 'I will certainly be doing the same,' before making her way down to the crypts.

So it was that the St. Meyers-Bannerman library closed for ever and to no fanfare. Ebbie had hesitated only a moment before locking the door for the last time and posting the keys back through the letterbox.

Now, sitting in the lounge-cum-kitchen of his flat, he wasn't focusing on the loss of his library or Alice or the wreck of his life; it was the mysterious woman with all her talk of queens and Protectors of the Realm that dominated his thoughts.

She hadn't given her name, Ebbie didn't know how to contact her and she had shown him not one page of official paperwork let alone outlined the details of the will for which he had allegedly been named executor. This had to be some kind of wind-up, surely, but ... why?

'I didn't even sign anything,' Ebbie mumbled.

He was searching the satchel which Mai had supposedly left him, trying to discover a secret pocket or meaning. But the satchel remained a tatty, limp thing, very far from a valuable heirloom, while it undeniably smelled and looked as though it had belonged to Mai. She had been homeless, alone in the world. Why would she even need a will?

Throwing the satchel on the coffee table, Ebbie turned his back on it for the length of time it took to make a mug of tea, and that was when his already strange day took a truly surreal turn.

When he returned to the lounge side of the room, he almost dropped the mug in astonishment. The satchel was no longer empty. Quite clearly filled now with something bulky and square, Ebbie stared at it for a long time while his tea cooled in his hand. Eventually, with a supreme amount of caution, he took his seat, pulled up the satchel's flap, peeked inside and found a lantern.

'There's no way ...' Yet there it was. Ebbie stood the lantern on the coffee table. A simple item, unremarkable, which somehow made its impossible appearance all the more disturbing. A foot tall and around three inches wide, its front-facing panel was made of glass that reflected light with oily rainbow colours. But when Ebbie turned it around, he discovered the other three sides were plates of the same black metal which formed its frame and handle. He dared to look into the satchel again but found nothing else.

'There's just no bloody way ...'

Perplexed, Ebbie freed the catch on the lantern's glass panel. Little hinges squeaked when he opened it. Old wax had melted to a hard puddle around a little spike inside, but there was no candle. Instead, an envelope had been wedged into the lantern. Ebbie didn't want to touch it at first, but he did to discover nothing written upon its plain white surface. It had been sealed with red wax, though, stamped with a symbol that appeared to be a tree with a winged insect on its trunk – a wasp or a bee, perhaps? Ebbie thumbed the envelope; there was something hard and circular inside.

He looked around his flat helplessly, hoping to find someone who might explain to him what was going on, before snapping the seal and opening the envelope.

A ring tumbled onto the coffee table, a smooth band of cream-coloured stone shot through with green veins. At first, Ebbie thought it was onyx like the brooch worn by the woman who had delivered the satchel, but when he picked the ring up, he decided it wasn't any onyx that he knew. It was heavy for its size and too large for any of Ebbie's fingers or thumbs, but it didn't feel quite as solid as it looked. Not brittle, more like … ice that wasn't cold and didn't melt.

Ebbie lifted the ring and peered through its hole; light came through with a rippling effect, as though viewed from underwater. More bemused than ever, he placed the ring down and pulled a letter from the envelope. His heart skipped a beat when he saw it was from Mai.

My dearest friend, Ebbie Wren,

If you are reading this, then you have agreed to execute my last will and testament. There are not thanks enough that I could offer you, though I do not think you will be thanking me. There is little time for explanation, so I must be brief.

Along with this letter and ring, you have no doubt discovered my lantern and will note the candle is missing. It

*burned away many years ago and is not easily replaced. My
lantern requires a candle of specialist design, and those makers
who can work wax to the necessary specifications are rare and
not to be found in Strange Ground by the Skea. Nonetheless,
for you to be successful in your duties, you must be guided by
what is known in my world as a True Sight Candle. This,
however, is to be your second duty, for your first must be
escape!*

   *It is in desperation and with regret that I now place you
in mortal danger. Wolves are coming to your door and I am
powerless to stop them. This letter will hold more instructions
as and when they are required, so keep it safe. Keep the
lantern safe and guard my satchel as you would your own life.
Now put on the ring, Ebbie Wren. Put it on this instant and
prepare yourself.*

Ebbie dropped the letter to the table, scowling at it. Almost
unconsciously, he took the cream and green ring and slipped
it on. At first, it was far too loose to be anything approaching
a good fit, but then the stone squirmed and shrank, squeezing
around his wedding finger like a miniature python.

'Shit!'

Jumping to his feet, Ebbie shook his hand like he had been
burned. He tried to pull the ring off, but its grip was too tight
and wouldn't pass over his knuckle.

'Shit! Shit! Shit!'

Tugging and tugging, Ebbie spun around and fell over the
coffee table, landing on his back on the carpet. Air whooshed
from his mouth, and that was when he heard it. A noise coming
from somewhere, a rumbling in his ears, deep like the distant
roar of waves crashing on rocks.

He froze as a knock came at the door. Two hard thumps, a

pause, then a third. They sounded hollow and cold, like someone rapping their knuckles on a coffin lid. From the inside.

'Open up, please,' came a voice, muffled and gruff.

Ebbie remained silent and looked at Mai's letter lying on the floor beside him. *Wolves are coming to your door ...*

'Mr Wren?'

Ebbie stood up as quietly as he could. The crashing of the sea seemed to be coming from the ring. Somehow, it was rumbling from his finger, up his arm, shoulders and neck and into his head. But still the ring wouldn't budge.

'Quick as you like. We haven't got all day.'

Ebbie tiptoed to the door and peered through the spyhole. Two men stood out on the landing. They were tall and not particularly friendly looking, or clean, with unkempt hair and beards. They might have been brothers and carried a distinctly wolfish appearance. Ebbie recognised them as the men he had seen yesterday on his way to Mrs Cory's Funeral Home.

'I know you're in there,' said the one on the left, while the one on the right sniffed the door. 'I can hear you breathing.'

'What do you want?' Ebbie said, with panic in his voice. The waves crashed louder in his head each time he tugged at the ring.

'I believe you were left a particular item recently,' said the man. 'It doesn't rightly belong to you, Mr Wren, so we'd like to take it back.'

'Oh ...' Ebbie looked at the lantern and the satchel on his coffee table. 'Sorry, I don't know what you're talking about.'

'Let's not mess around. Mrs Cory told us you were friends with Maitressa. She was very accommodating, before we set fire to her home and left her inside. Looks like your friend wasn't the only one to get a cremation.'

The other man smiled, revealing pointed teeth.

'I'm calling the police,' said Ebbie.

'As you like.' The man shrugged. 'But they won't get here before we smash this door off its hinges. We just want what's ours, simple as that.'

Ebbie whimpered. The sound of the sea was making it hard to think. 'All right. Give me a minute.'

'No. I'll give you to the count of five. One …' Ebbie rushed over to the coffee table. 'Two …' He thrust the lantern into the satchel – 'Three …' – followed by the letter. 'Four …' Maybe he could shout for help from the pub over the road and – 'Time's up, Mr Wren.'

Clutching the satchel to his chest, Ebbie yelped when the first blow hit the door, followed by another, and another. The wood complained and cracked, the frame shuddered. Ebbie's insides turned to water but not just because he honestly believed he was about to be murdered. The sound had risen to deafening levels and the light dimmed as though a tidal wave were casting its shadow. The whole flat began shaking and the ring clung to Ebbie's finger tighter than ever.

Another blow to the door and splinters flew. The flat was shaking so much, the mug of cold tea juddered across the coffee table and upended onto the floor.

'I can smell your magic, you sneaky bastard,' the wolfish man shouted. 'Stay where you are!'

A fist smashed through the door. Thick, dirty fingers with cracked nails pulled and tore at the wood.

'Help!' Ebbie screamed and sank to his knees, covering his ears, his very bones rattling, as darkness crashed in to carry him away on a roaring sea.

10

Strange and Stranger Still

Afternoon and the city had relaxed into the lull that always followed the lunchtime rush. A few shopkeepers took the opportunity to wash their windows and signs and sweep their doorsteps, while citizens wandered the streets and perused wares. Smoke from taverns and smithy forges laced the air, along with the aroma of horse manure. In Jester's Tavern, where a few candles shed light onto empty tables and chairs, where the fireplace had burned down to glowing ashes, Backway Charlie, the landlord of this establishment, was preparing for the suppertime stampede while playing host to a single customer bringing shady business.

'It wasn't easy, let me tell you.' Bek paused to take a dramatic swallow of ale before thumping the tankard down on the bar top. 'Guards and dogs patrolling the grounds, wards protecting every door and window, servants wandering the halls – none of them a test for my skills.'

'Utter catshit,' said Backway Charlie. Behind the bar, he looked up from the sword in his hands and raised an eyebrow. 'You got lucky, didn't you?'

Bek hid a grin behind another swallow of ale.

Charlie frowned. 'Who did you steal this thing from?'

'Probably better if you don't know.'

'So you actually went and did it. You robbed a noble.'

Bek shrugged.

Charlie hissed out an exasperated breath and turned the sword over to study the design of the hilt. His expression remained unconvinced. 'Did you really steal this by yourself?'

Bek rolled her eyes. 'Just tell me what you think.'

'It's a well-made piece.' The landlord tested the sword's weight, swishing the blue blade through the air in a figure of eight. 'Nice balance, but ... obviously too brittle for fighting.'

'That blade's sharper than a butcher's cleaver.'

'Still made of stone. Likely shatter first time it met metal. And see here?' Charlie pointed to an oval frame just above the curling quillions where a rain-guard might have been. He flipped the sword over to show a matching oval on the opposite side. 'I reckon jewels were set into this thing at one time, and it doesn't surprise me they're missing. They were probably what gave the sword any real value to begin with.'

'You don't know that for sure.'

'Maybe not, but ...' Charlie peered down the blade's length to check its straightness. 'Honestly, Bek, how much can it be worth if it was so easy to steal?'

'Look at the craftsmanship, Charlie. That's not some tossy old display trinket you're holding. That sword's worth a mint and you know it.'

But Charlie wasn't listening. He was scrutinising the flat of the blue stone blade. 'There's writing on here. What does it say?'

Bek could have made something up about the smooth, flowing script on the blade; Backway Charlie had never learned to read. But he was no fool and could smell a lie from a hundred yards away, so she went with the truth.

'I've no idea,' she admitted. 'I don't even recognise the language. At first, I wondered if someone had engraved a ward—'

'Bollocks!' Charlie threw the sword onto the bar top like it had bitten him.

'Careful!'

'What are you trying to do to me, Bek?' He wiped his hands on his apron. 'Wards can be traced. They can lead the wrong kind of people to *my* doorstep!'

'Oh, pipe down, Charlie. I said I *wondered* if it was a ward. But it's not, trust me. I don't know what the writing means, and the owner doesn't know the sword is missing. They're not even in the city.'

'You sure about that?'

Mostly, thought Bek. She hadn't dared tell Charlie about the treasonous conversation she'd overheard between Lady Kingfisher and Lord Dragonfly. In truth, she was trying to forget all about it.

Charlie glared at her. 'Get it out of my sight.'

Bek took the sword and slid it into the old and battered scabbard at her waist.

'You have an awful sense of timing,' Charlie said. 'Doesn't matter how fine a piece you've got your hands on, no one in their right mind will buy it, especially now.' He shrugged at Bek's scowl. 'What did you expect?'

'A decent offer, at least.'

'I tried to warn you. Don't thieve from the nobles. Leave their stuff well alone. And with what's going on up at the castle, it's like I said – your timing couldn't be worse.'

Fresh news from the Royal Family had been filtering down to the streets of Strange Ground all day. Lady Kingfisher's predictions had been spot on: Princess Morrad had abdicated her position in favour of her younger sister. Princess Yandira was now First Lady to House Wood Bee and heir to the throne.

Charlie leaned across the bar and lowered his voice. 'No one with a smidgeon of wit would risk pissing off the nobles while there're queen-killers on the loose. You keep a low profile, because Yandira Wood Bee is free, and you remember what it was like last time. Even a hint of suspicious activity will likely get your bloody head lopped off. And you more than most need to stay out of that madwoman's way, you hear?'

That was true, but Charlie didn't know the half of it. Rumour was that Hamdon Lark and Ala Denev were behind the assassins who killed Queen Eldrid, but those old fools weren't capable of something so foul. It was Yandira's doing, just as Lady Kingfisher said, but who would dare speak out against House Wood Bee's new First Lady? Anyone standing in her way was in danger. She had killed her own sister to get to the throne, for Oldunfolk's sake! But ... not necessarily her niece. Could Princess Ghador still be alive?

Bek didn't want to think about it.

'I'll never understand you,' Charlie said. 'Why get involved in something this dangerous at this time?'

'It's like my grandma used to say, Charlie. Sometimes you have to dream big.'

'Your grandma was an honest fisherwoman who never stole from anyone in her life. She had morals.'

'And look how her *morals* struggled to keep a roof over our heads, every single day of her life.'

'She did right by you, Bek Rana. Oldunfolk rest her soul, if she could see you now.'

'Let's leave my grandma out of this.' Bek swallowed her anger. She *really* needed to get away from this city. 'Come on, Charlie,' she pleaded. 'You must know someone who'd be interested in the sword?'

'Whether I do or I don't, I want no part in it.' Charlie brushed his hands together, cleaning away his involvement. 'Even in the best of times, goods stolen from the nobles will always – *always* – come back to bite you on the arse. Count me out.'

Bek stared at him slack-jawed for a moment. 'So that's it? The infamous Backway Charlie has finally lost his nerve?'

He gave her a sobering look. 'Backway Charlie isn't as stupid as the thief he's talking to.'

Growling in disappointment, Bek turned on her heel, crossed the tavern floor and stepped up to the window. Outside on the street, citizens milled. In the distance, the dark shape of Castle Wood Bee rose above the rooftops. Bek dreaded to wonder what kind of plans Yandira was making up there, especially if she knew Princess Ghador was alive. What was it Lady Kingfisher had said? Something about the rightful heir hiding where no one could see—

'Anyway, I thought you already had a buyer?' Charlie said. He had moved from the bar and was shovelling ashes from the fireplace into a pail. 'All lined up and ready to go, you said.'

'I did,' Bek replied miserably. 'It fell through.'

'Oh, this gets better and better.' Charlie shook his head. 'Who was it?'

'No one you need to worry about.'

'Catshit.' Charlie looked up from the fireplace. '*Who*, Bek?'

'I don't know, all right?' Her shoulders slumped. 'I got a tip-off from someone calling themselves a *collector*. Whoever it was bailed on me once I'd stolen the sword.'

Charlie groaned. 'You want my advice, you'll return that thing to the house you took it from before the owner comes back.'

'Not a chance.'

'Then you're on your own.' Charlie resumed shovelling ashes. 'I don't want to see that sword in my tavern again, you hear?'

'All right, fine, but ...' Bek licked her lips nervously. 'Can you lend me some money?'

The landlord barked a laugh.

'I'm serious, Charlie. I'm skint, not a coin to my name. I'll sell the sword in another city. Just give me enough for wagon fare.'

'Nope.'

'Then let me stay here with you while I find a new buyer.'

'Listening's never been your strong point, has it?' Charlie began laying fresh kindling in the fireplace. 'Put the sword back where it belongs, Bek, then go and pick some pockets for your wagon fare. Getting out of this city is the smartest thing you can do now.'

'I don't need reminding!'

Bek swung back to face the window just in time to see a man fall to the ground right in front of the tavern. But not falling as though he had tripped, she thought; more like thumping to the street as if dropped from a height. He appeared to be gripped by a powerful swirl of wind that whipped his hair and twisted him onto his back before petering out.

Bek scoured the street; no one else had noticed the man's fall. He got to his feet, swaying unsteadily as he looked around in alarm. Was he drunk? Addled? No. He was panicked and wide-eyed, but if Bek's instincts were as sharp as she liked to think they were, then this man carried the fresh-faced look of the countryside. He was new and naïve to the ways of a city, typified by the fat coin-purse openly hanging from his belt.

'Nice,' she whispered.

Charlie stepped up beside her, intrigued himself. The man outside looked like a lamb caught in the hungry gaze of wolves. Charlie clucked his tongue at the sight of him. 'I think that fool might pay your wagon fare.'

Bek was already heading for the door. 'See you around, Charlie.'

'Laverna's luck,' he called. 'Happy travels.'

Ebbie was checking his skull for signs of damage when the wagon trundled towards him. The driver called out a rude warning and Ebbie skipped back on the cobbles. The donkey gave him a bored glance and dropped a healthy amount of dung as it clopped by, while the driver, a grizzled sort of man, muttered something about folk using the eyes in their heads. The wagon, creaking under a full load of burlap sacks, was quickly gone and Ebbie once again gazed upon a street he didn't recognise filled with people looking like extras from a period drama.

He must have hit his head, he decided, and hit it *really* hard. What else could explain what he was seeing? There were parts of Strange Ground by the Skea that were centuries old, but no streets or buildings preserved to this degree of authenticity. The design and architecture had been plucked straight out of history; thick wooden beams like exoskeletons held up shops and businesses, some of them so crooked they were practically falling over. Windows were criss-crossed with lead. Chimneys rose from a landscape of thatch and slate, pluming smoke into the air from just about every rooftop. And there was a castle!

In the near distance, above the roofs and beyond the smoke, it sat on a hill. Not some ancient ruin or preserved landmark refitted as a museum, but a place where someone lived, complete with flags flying and tiny figures patrolling the ramparts. A big proper castle, and Strange Ground by the Skea definitely didn't have one of those.

A boisterous shout erupted on the street. A roar of laughter answered it.

The people around Ebbie were massing into a thick crowd, their chatter rising like grasshoppers singing in a field of crops on a balmy night as they strolled along, going in and out of shops; and the way they were dressed ... Ebbie might have been staring at a scene from the village of Bree.

A shop bell jingled.

Ebbie slapped a hand against the satchel hanging from his shoulder and felt the lantern inside. There was something re-assuring about its bulky presence. He thought of his flat, Mai's letter, the wolves at his door ... the ring! He looked at his hand. There it was, cream and green and still wrapped tight around his wedding finger. At least the roar of angry waves had stopped in his head.

His memory of leaving his flat was a panicked blur. He remembered being cold. A watery sensation that wasn't wet. Tumbling breathlessly through darkness like a tidal wave had swept him away until he crashed down onto this street like he had fallen from the sky. Only ... only the sky wasn't just a sky in this bizarre place.

Where wispy clouds should have been drifting lazily across a vista of vibrant summer blue, waves rolled serenely on a vast expanse of clear water. The smudged orb of a golden sun blazed above it, its wavering rays filtering down through spume and frothy crests to shine warmly on Ebbie's upturned face. The sky was the sea.

A whimper escaped his lips.

Heart racing, a sense of vertigo dizzying him, Ebbie looked away from the impossible sky, and his eyes came to rest on a woman standing outside a tavern. Her posture appeared frozen, as though he had caught her sneaking up on him.

'Hello there,' she said, relaxing. 'You look lost.'

Ebbie nodded. She was dressed similarly to the people around her, albeit a little more frayed around the edges, and she frowned, concerned by the obvious distress on Ebbie's face.

'Are you all right?'

'No, not really.' Ebbie wished his hands would stop shaking. 'I don't know where I am.'

'Strange Ground.'

'Strange Ground?'

'Beneath the Skea.' The woman gave him an easy smile. 'You've not been to a city before, have you?'

Ebbie rubbed his forehead. 'Can you help me?'

The woman sucked air over her teeth. 'I usually charge for my help.'

'Okay, I suppose that's fair ...' Ebbie groaned. In his mind's eye, he could see the dish on his kitchen counter where he kept his keys and phone and wallet. 'Shit, I left my money at home.'

'Is that right?' The woman chuckled and rested her hand on the hilt of the sword sheathed at her waist. 'Word of advice, if you're going to lie, be smarter about it.'

She pointed at Ebbie's midriff. Hanging from his belt was a pouch bulging with ... clinking coins, he discovered when he jiggled it. Ebbie didn't know where the pouch had come from, or the belt itself, or the trousers the belt was holding up. He was wearing a thick green jacket that he damn well knew he didn't own, along with a matching waistcoat and a dark grey shirt. His black woollen trousers were tucked into buckled leather boots that reached halfway up his shins.

'What the hell ... ?' Ebbie turned this way and that, examining his mysterious new clothes in a flap. He was dressed like the people on the street. '*How?*'

'Whoa, calm down,' the woman said. 'What's wrong?'

'What's wrong?' Ebbie's voice had risen a couple of octaves. He opened and closed his mouth, not knowing where to begin. What had Mai's letter said? First, escape; then ... something he had to find. His hand felt the lantern in the satchel again. 'I need a candle,' he said, as though it was his only salvation.

'What's that now?'

'I don't know. Please help me.'

'For a candle?' The woman shrugged. 'Go to the candle-maker.' She aimed a finger across the street. 'Just over there, between the butcher's and the baker's.'

Ebbie wheeled around, trying to glimpse what she was pointing at through the gaps in the throng of people. But he couldn't see a sign for a candle-maker or a ... Butcher's? A Baker's?

'Wait a minute ...' Ebbie turned back, but the woman was gone. And so was his money pouch. 'Oh, bloody hell.'

Once again gripped by panic, Ebbie scoured the street for the thief. But she had already disappeared into the crowd along with his money. He screwed up his fists and pressed them against his temples. 'What money?' he hissed. 'I didn't bring any! I don't own these clothes!'

This was it. This was the moment he broke down and his mind imploded. He crouched right there on the street and made himself into as small a ball as he could.

'You're under arrest!'

Thinking the loud, angry shout was aimed at him, Ebbie snapped upright to attention. But the commotion came from further along the street, where people were parting to make way for three soldiers, each wearing leather armour and carrying swords. The crowd formed a circle around them. Ebbie stood on tiptoes to peer over heads, ducked to spy through gaps and finally caught sight of the thief. She was surrounded by the soldiers, poised, ready to fight.

'On your knees!' one of the soldiers demanded. 'Put your hands behind your head!'

But the woman grabbed the hilt of her sword instead, and Ebbie held his breath as she prepared to draw. She looked like a warrior from a story of old. If only her willingness to use the sword was as strong as her bluff.

Two of the soldiers darted forward before the blade cleared an inch of sheath, while the third manoeuvred behind the thief and pounced to smack a sap across the back of her head. She went down like a lead weight and the fight was over before it could start.

While one of the soldiers began dispersing the crowd, the other two placed the woman in cuffs before dragging her limp body away down the street. Ebbie waved at them and was about to shout for his money when a voice stopped him.

'I wouldn't do that, if I were you.' Behind Ebbie, a man was leaning on a broom outside the tavern. 'Best not to get involved.' Tall, portly and balding, he watched the soldiers hauling the thief off with a sad expression. 'Damn shame, though.'

'Shame?' said Ebbie. 'She stole my money.'

The man sighed. 'Listen, if you're going to keep your purse on display in this part of the city, then you're asking for trouble.'

'Am I?'

'Not from around here, are you?'

Ebbie couldn't quite catch his breath. He placed a hand on his chest, as though he could grab his heart and stop it thudding, and pointed upwards. 'They say that in the Realm, the sea is in the sky.'

The man furrowed his brow. 'Are you having a funny turn?'

'Yes.' It sounded more like a grunt from Ebbie's mouth. 'What's happening to me?'

'Don't worry, you're not the first to be fleeced by this city.' He smiled with understanding. 'Why don't you come inside, have a drink, get your head straight.' He jabbed a thumb at the tavern behind him. The peeling paint on the sign depicted three multicoloured juggling balls above one fading word: Jester's.

'What do you say? I'm about to open a barrel of honey beer. Best time to taste it is when it's fresh.'

Ebbie stammered over his reply. Alcohol sounded like a very good idea, but, 'I-I lost my money.'

The landlord waved the comment away. 'Least I can do is shout you a pint. Come on.'

In the sallow light of torches, Yandira crossed the damp stone floor of the crypts. Her footfalls barely making a sound that might echo around the cavernous space, she felt at peace amidst the high archways, the stonework walls and pillars, the large niches rising floor to ceiling in which past monarchs had been interred – some in sarcophagi, others old enough to be linen-wrapped mummified husks. Deep in the foundations of Castle Wood Bee, she found the dingy, smoky atmosphere a perfect place for reflection.

She stopped to look at a small tomb. Age-old and more than a little crumbling now, the engraving of House Wood Bee's crest was difficult to discern through the cobwebs and dust covering its door. For generations the rulers of Strange Ground had been laid to rest in the crypts, but some commanded more exalted positions than others. Like this tomb, for example, with its door sealed by high, unbreakable magic and unopened for centuries. It was the resting place of Lady Minerva, the first and most cherished Wood Bee Queen according to the history books; she who had ended the days of the Imperium and given the Realm new founding traditions. Not an ancestor Yandira aspired to emulate.

Moving on, Yandira soon arrived where the last Queen of Strange Ground awaited her place among the dead. The Chapel of Elysium was a small, open chamber where Juno's likeness had been intricately rendered upon the wall. The Queen of

Queens' cold eyes stared into the chamber's centre, where candles burned around a stone table upon which lay the body of Yandira's oldest sister.

'Dear Eldrid,' she said, approaching the table. 'Groomed to rule from the day you were born, always mother's favourite.' She stared down at her sister's pale and lifeless face. 'You look so much like her.'

The line of her nose, the height of her cheekbones, the way her brow was slightly furrowed as though contemplating one conundrum or another, Eldrid could be none other than the daughter of Lady Maitressa Wood Bee. Even her gown of emerald green, embroidered with gold thread, mimicked their mother's style. In death, a faint line indented her forehead, a ghost from when she had worn the crown of Strange Ground. But the crown itself, with its legendary stones of Foresight and Hindsight, remained in the custody of the Priests of Juno, kept securely in their temple as tradition dictated. And there it would stay until the priests decreed there was a new and rightful queen to coronate.

Yandira's anger flared.

'You were never a true queen,' she told her sister. 'Like mother, you were Juno's pretender, a proxy, and I will outmatch your achievements tenfold, a *hundredfold*! In Persephone's name, my Empire will cover the Realm.'

Yandira took a breath to calm her spite and wondered: had Eldrid awoken when her assassin struck, or had she passed in her sleep never knowing death had visited her?

'Our sister Morrad believes I should have been executed long ago. I think you and mother would agree with her now. Surely I haunted your mind, dear Eldrid? Did you not fear that my ambitions remained alive, that I would return for you one day, for you and your daughter?'

No, was the short answer. Eldrid had always been so assured, so confident, arrogant, ignorant ...

Yandira sensed a presence. The Shade emerged from gloomy torchlight beyond the Chapel of Elysium. It slithered across the floor and crawled up Yandira's back to perch on her shoulder like a vulture expecting fresh battlefield carrion.

'They have come, my sister.'

Yandira smelled her servants before they entered, the stink of meaty breath and damp pelts. They loitered at the edge of the chamber, hesitant, unwilling to come forward, and Yandira bristled to feel their eyes on her back.

'Fools!' she snapped. 'Present yourselves.'

Two wolves padded across the floor to the opposite side of the stone table, as though Eldrid's corpse offered a defensive barrier. Their yellow eyes would not meet Yandira's icy gaze. With the light of candles flickering upon the silver in their black pelts, the wolves changed shape, growing, stretching, rising tall into the bedraggled and sheepish forms of Mr Lunk and Mr Venatus.

'Well?'

Neither of them spoke. Yandira dug deep to remember her tolerance. After all, there was only so much initiative one could expect from men less smart than the wolves inhabiting their souls.

'It is vexing enough that Princess Ghador's convoy somehow managed to return to Strange Ground without my detection,' Yandira said. 'Why isn't the princess lying dead beside her mother?'

'Umm ...' Mr Venatus glanced at Mr Lunk, who, as ever, remained unhelpfully silent. 'We're not sure, Majesty.'

'Explain.'

Mr Venatus looked at his scruffy boots. 'She wasn't where

you said she'd be. The royal convoy didn't get as far as Dalmyn. When we caught up with them, they'd already turned around and were heading back to Strange Ground.' Mr Lunk growled a confirmation of events. 'Princess Ghador wasn't on board, Majesty. She'd disappeared.'

'This much I've already been told. I want an explanation, Mr Venatus. How is it that a convoy comprised almost entirely of soldiers somehow manages to lose their charge and avoid my detection? What did you discover?'

'Nothing, Majesty. When we realised the princess was gone, we didn't see the point in hanging around.'

On Yandira's shoulder, the Shade picked up on its master's mood and rustled with the smallest of whispers. 'We will kill them, my sister?'

Lunk and Venatus stiffened in fear.

'Not yet,' Yandira told the Shade. 'Though I wish these imbeciles were half as efficient as you.'

'Yes, my sister.'

'Did you hear me?' Yandira said to her wolfish servants. 'My Shade had no trouble killing Queen Eldrid when I told it to.'

'Forgive us, Majesty,' Mr Venatus pleaded. 'We reckoned the smartest thing to do was go back and finish the other job. We had some problems, see?'

'Problems?' Yandira's heart froze. The *other job*, their visit to the Earthly side, to Strange Ground by the Skea. 'Mr Lunk and Mr Venatus, for your own sakes, my mother had better be dead.'

'No doubt about it, *definitely* dead, Majesty. And we didn't leave a single mark on her, just as you ordered.' He bit his bottom lip. 'Told us to give you a message before she went, though.'

'And?'

'She said her ghost would always haunt you, Majesty.'

How like Lady Maitressa it was to try and have the last word. Ten years of searching it had taken to finally discover where she had hidden herself. Even the lands outside the Realm were not beyond Yandira's reach, not with Lady Persephone on her side. Killing her mother had been a vital act, because while Maitressa lived, observing and listening, she could have ruined everything.

I do so hope your ghost is watching me, you old crow, Yandira thought. *Witness how your beloved queendom is now mine!*

But still, a bad feeling crawled up inside her. 'What problems did you encounter?'

Mr Venatus shared another nervous look with Mr Lunk. 'We took care of your mother then came home to deal with your niece. But your niece was missing so we went back to Earth because ... I'm sorry, Majesty, we searched everywhere for the heirloom you wanted, but all we found was this.'

From a deep pocket in his coat, Mr Venatus pulled out a leather-bound book and placed it on the edge of the stone table, between two candles. Yandira immediately knew it to be one of her mother's books, a collection of stories she'd been writing before she fled Strange Ground. Its presence was vexing.

'This is not the sword I asked you to procure,' Yandira said.

'Your mother – I mean, Queen Maitressa ... the-the *former* queen—'

'Spit it out!'

Mr Venatus took a breath. 'We think she gave her possessions to an earthling before we got to her. We found out who it was and tracked him down. His name is Ebbie Wren. B-But he escaped.'

Yandira clenched her teeth. 'Mr Venatus, you'll understand if my patience wanes dangerously at this point, yes? That sword belongs to me, and you allowed some mundane earthling to escape with it?'

Mr Lunk growled and huffed unintelligibly, to which his cohort agreed with vehement nodding. 'It's true. He was more than mundane. He summoned a bridge.'

'A Janus Bridge?'

'That's right, Majesty. We followed him back to the Realm, but he'd already got away from us.'

A Janus Bridge was divine magic and not what Yandira was expecting, or wanting, to hear. 'Tell me more of this Ebbie Wren. He is a warrior? A magician, perhaps?'

'No, Majesty. As far as we know he's a librarian.'

Yandira scoffed. 'How precious. And you say he has come to the Realm?'

'Without a doubt. We picked up his scent around Strange Ground, but ... but then—'

'But then what, Mr Venatus?'

'Begging your pardon, Majesty, but then you summoned us here.'

Yandira scowled at Eldrid's corpse and the book lying next to her. *Haunt me, indeed.* 'You are certain this Ebbie Wren has my sword?'

'Well, didn't see him holding it with my own eyes, but who else could have it?' Mr Venatus cleared his throat. 'Do you want us to search for him, Majesty?'

'Of course I bloody well do!' Yandira shouted with all the fury she stored in her heart. 'If my mother has embroiled an earthling lackey into this game, then he knows more than a little something about Princess Ghador. Find him and bring him to me. *Alive and with my sword!*'

Lunk and Venatus scurried from the chapel quick-smart, disappearing into the smoky murk of the crypts along with the echoes of their master's shout.

The Shade said, 'What now, my sister?'

'A good question.' Simmering, Yandira picked up her mother's book. 'The soldiers and servants of Princess Ghador's convoy have been detained?'

'In the castle dungeons, my sister. We will go to them?'

'Soon.' Yandira opened the book. 'First, I want Lady Kingfisher and Lord Dragonfly taken into custody. It's high time they and I had a long chat about their old friend.'

As the Shade slithered away, Yandira flicked through the book, recognising her mother's handwriting, and then held the dangling pages over the flame of a candle. Once the paper had caught and burned brightly, she let the ashes snow down onto her sister's face.

II

The Ultimate Ambition

Juno damn you, thought Lord Dragonfly. Yandira Wood Bee had struck faster than a snake and her venom was flowing through the veins of the noble Houses with impeccable lethality.

'Would you like some tea?' Lord Mandrake asked, and not for the first time. On two other occasions he had enquired, and although Dragonfly had said yes to both, no refreshments had arrived. This time, he said nothing.

Lady Mandrake looked about the room, struggling to focus on her husband. 'Did you mention tea?' she said. 'That would be lovely.' But again, no servant was summoned and the pair settled into torpid vacuity as though largely unaware they were sitting in the presence of a visitor.

Honed by decades of courtly protocol, Lord Aelfric Dragonfly had an unerring gift for sensing when he was in danger. No candles or fire had been lit in the drawing room of Mandrake Manor, and thick curtains were drawn against the afternoon sun. Sitting in gloomy twilight, postures stiff and straight, the First Lady and Lord of this House were acting most out of character. Their voices carried a ghoulish emptiness, but it was their eyes which signified the real danger in the room.

'You are both adjusting well, I trust?' Dragonfly said carefully. 'Given the grisly events we all witnessed.'

Lady Mandrake's face screwed up spitefully. 'Ala Denev and Hamdon Lark got what they deserved.'

'And curse the rest of us for not seeing the treason in their hearts,' said her husband.

'Quite, quite.' Dragonfly expressed a perfect measure of remorse while his hosts stared at him.

Even in the dim light, it was clear to see that the Mandrakes' eyes were dulled as though shrouded in a film of smoke. This effect was heartbreakingly familiar to Dragonfly; he had first witnessed it ten years ago in the eyes of Princess Morrad, after her soul had been dragged from her body to create a vile Shade. And now he was seeing it again, stronger than before, and not just in this room. The royal guards were marching around Castle Wood Bee with shadowy tendrils leaking from the visors of their helmets; the general staff loitered, still as scarecrows, while their smoky gazes observed anyone who wandered the castle grounds. Yandira had conjured the Serpent's Sigh and it was spreading like a plague. Her spies were everywhere, watching and listening.

Damn it all! Dragonfly thought. He had come to the Mandrakes to make allies, not to see them at the mercy of a deranged usurper. It was time to leave and rethink his plans.

Before he could make his excuses, Lady Mandrake said, 'What do you believe, Aelfric?' She looked surprised that she had spoken and touched her lips.

With a frown, Dragonfly said, 'Apologies, my Lady, but to what do you refer?'

'Is there any chance for Princess Ghador?'

Senses alerted, Dragonfly kept his expression thoughtful. Surely a question to test his allegiance, and no doubt the Mandrakes would be reporting his answer to Yandira, if she wasn't already listening through the ears of her subjugates.

With care, he said, 'I fear Ghador's return is no more than hope and prayer in these tragic times.'

'A blessed thing, then, that Princess Morrad stepped aside so her strong and canny sister could lead us through our troubles.'

'There can be no mistake,' Dragonfly said smoothly. 'Yandira Wood Bee will indeed make a strong queen.'

'Strong enough to be the Queen of all Queens, I should say.' Lord Mandrake's smile bore more resemblance to a skeletal grimace. 'Surely if any among us has the courage and wisdom to reinstate the Imperium then it is Blessed Yandira.'

A provocative statement designed to goad Dragonfly. He choked down a venomous retort and covered his anger with a soft and kind chuckle. 'A score of centuries have passed since an Empress last ruled over the Realm's Royal Families, but perhaps you are right. Perhaps it is time for change.'

Feeling the chill of his seventy winters biting down to his bones, Dragonfly rose from his seat. 'My Lady, my Lord, thank you for your hospitality, but I really must be going.'

They stared at him, saying nothing.

'Then until we next meet.' Dragonfly nodded farewell, then walked from the drawing room and down the hall to the main doors. The few servants he passed watched him closely with smoke-filmed eyes but didn't prohibit his departure. Seeing himself out, Dragonfly gave a silent plea to the Oldunfolk as he strode for his manor.

Mandrake was the first name on his list of potential allies, but how many more Houses were already infected with the Serpent's Sigh? Most of them, was no doubt the answer, high and low, and each in between. Yandira Wood Bee was already steps ahead of anyone with the power and influence to stand in her way. Right now, the soldiers who formed the ill-fated royal convoy to Dalmyn were imprisoned – Princess Ghador's closest and most loyal guards, every last one of them locked away in the castle dungeons – which left the princess herself with only one sure ally in Strange Ground beneath the Skea: House Dragonfly. But there was naught else its First Lord could achieve while he remained in the city. The Serpent's Sigh would infect them all in the end.

Outmanoeuvred and undone, he arrived at his manor and headed straight for his study, ignoring the fearful glances from his staff. They all recognised what evil had returned to plague Strange Ground. In his study, Dragonfly found a slim strip of paper, hastily scribbled a message on it and then took it out to the gull coop in the gardens. On the way, he found Wilden, his head servant, waiting for him by the back door with a worried expression.

'My Lord?' he said. 'You look troubled.'

'Indeed, Wilden.' Dragonfly rubbed his forehead and exhaled heavily. 'We must prepare the House for departure. Gather the staff, tell them to leave everything behind. We head for Dalmyn. Tonight.'

The old servant looked shocked. 'My Lord?'

'Just do it, Wilden. There's no time for debate.'

Leaving his servant, Dragonfly strode across the lawn of his expansive and cherished gardens. The very idea of abandoning his home, this city and its people sickened him, but he had to trust that Genevieve had reached Dalmyn by now, that an army was assembled and on its way, because if Yandira had already converted the other Houses to her cause, then the corruption of her magic would spread among the general populace next. That craven would put swords in the hands of children to defend her position.

The gull handler was an uncommunicative woman called Gray who preferred the company of her charges to her fellow folk. Surrounded by gulls dipping their beaks to water bowls or pecking at feed cages, she bowed her head when Dragonfly swept into the coop and thrust the slim piece of paper into her hand.

'Your strongest and fastest bird,' he ordered. Gently, he lifted Gray's chin so her eyes left the paper in her hand and met her Lord's. 'That message must reach First Lady Kingfisher with all haste. Understood?'

Gray nodded. Satisfied, Dragonfly headed back to the manor to help with preparations for departure. But as he neared the door, Wilden rushed out to meet him in something of a flap.

'My Lord,' he said breathlessly. 'You have been summoned—'

Before he could explain further, two royal guards emerged from the manor, barging the old servant out of the way as they marched towards Dragonfly. To his dismay, their pikes were levelled, and thin lines of smoke coiled from the visors of their helmets.

'You will come with us,' ordered one. His barbed voice echoed as though his armoured shell enclosed him in a huge cavern. 'Her Imperial Majesty Yandira Wood Bee commands your presence.'

The lad was old enough to have a patchy fuzz of beard-growth but young enough to be strong-hearted and pure-blooded. An apprentice horse-groom, the shadow of Her Imperial Majesty was upon him, wreathing his eyes in a smoky film and voiding his face of expression – the same state which now afflicted most who lived within the castle walls. While the lad was undoubtedly all misery and torment on the inside, outside he had been subservient and compliant when ordered from the royal stables to this private chamber where Ignius Rex had once studied magic under the tutelage of Hamdon Lark.

Surrounded by books and ingredients and apparatus for magical experimentation, the lad was sitting upon the cold floor. He clutched his knees to his chest and swayed gently from side to side under candlelight. His vacant eyes stared at the spell Ignius was drawing in chalk upon the flagstones before him.

This was an exhilarating moment for the magician. What he drew on the floor looked more like artwork, a configuration of swirls from a divine language not often used in a world where the sun shone through the Skea. That fool Hamdon Lark would never have dared teach his pupil the dark tongue of the Underworld, but now the ancient, forbidden words in this spell marked the point of no return, a declaration of intent from Her Imperial Majesty. Yandira was bringing havoc to the Realm and Ignius felt proud to be her messenger.

'Blessed be the Underworld and all the worlds it touches ...'

His lips twisting into an excited smile, candlelight shining upon eager eyes, the magician's deft hand chalked symbols and words with fluent speed. The stable-lad watched on.

There had been times when Ignius doubted this moment would ever arrive. For years he had dutifully attended to his studies, feigning loyalty to Lark and Queen Eldrid with perfection, cursing the youngest Wood Bee daughter's name while secretly longing for her return. Of course, Yandira had never truly been a prisoner, for she was Lady Persephone's most favoured, and the spells and wards Lark had cast on the north tower had been no match for the Underworld's Immortal Darkness.

Yandira had always been free, but having learned from past mistakes, she knew she must play a waiting game. Like a spider at the centre of the web she had woven over Strange Ground, Yandira remained in her tower, acting the prisoner, while she searched for her mother. During that time, Ignius had to dig deep for ten long years of patience, but doubt and sufferance were far behind him now. Rivals had been removed, Ghador would soon follow them and once the crown sat on Yandira's head they would both wield the havoc of Persephone's promise.

Finishing his spell, the magician laid aside the chalk and picked up a ceremonial dagger, a small weapon with a curved blade, no more threatening than a letter opener in appearance. The stable-lad issued a low groan but didn't move as the blade came towards him. Neither did he recoil or gasp when Ignius opened the veins in his arms. Without a hint of panic on his face, he watched his lifeblood raining from his fingertips onto the spell. A pool of red quickly spread to cover the chalk and stained the edge of Ignius's robe. The dragons of the Underworld caught the offering's scent and the blood began to steam.

Ignius's handiwork shone through its thickness with fiery lines and swirls. He marvelled as the Underworld accepted the sacrifice with a greed like no other, a fierce, insatiable thirst which drank and drank from the stable-lad's life force until all that remained of him was a dried, withered husk that crumbled to ashes in a puddle of steaming blood.

The roar of dragons filled the magician's head. He fell back, writhing, as a surge of fire threatened to burst his heart. Divine force blinded his eyes but thrust his vision from the chamber, far beyond the confines of the castle, and for an instant Ignius Rex was one with the very earth of the Realm. In less time than it took a butterfly to beat its wings, he pulsed a message across the land. In the darkest shadows of the forests and the deepest burrows of the hills, the wild things stirred and listened to the voice speaking from their souls.

The time is now, the voice told them. *Rise in the name of Her Imperial Majesty Yandira Wood Bee, breathe the Serpent's Sigh into our enemy's midst, let it devour all magic and living things.*

Though the voice spoke no more, the Coven of Bellona had heard. All along the Queen's Highway, from Strange Ground to Dalmyn, witches emerged from their hiding places.

And as Ignius Rex passed out, he whispered in divine reverie, 'Blessed is the Underworld and all the worlds it touches ...'

Funny, thought Lord Dragonfly, even with braziers burning warmly between every stone pillar, the throne room of Castle Wood Bee remained a cold hall. It had always felt this way, now and back in happier times, cold as spring nights and a sombre place in which to find oneself alone. Only, standing at the bottom of the steps leading up to the dais where the empty throne was positioned, Dragonfly was surprised to realise that he wasn't alone at all.

Hardly noticeable in the shadows, Princess Morrad was sitting beside the throne on a chair small enough for a child's classroom. Hunched, silent and still as a woodland animal hiding in its burrow, she stared vacantly up at the rafters, hands in her lap fretting at fingernails. Her mouth hung open like a hatch someone had forgotten to close, and Dragonfly feared she was about to drool.

He looked over his shoulder. The guards who had accosted him remained outside the throne room doors, so he cleared his throat and leaned forward. 'Apologies, Highness. My old eyes struggled to see you there. Are you well?'

Startled by the question, Morrad cast her gaze about the room as though just as surprised to learn of another presence close by. Unable to focus on the speaker, she said, 'Are you a ghost?'

'No, Princess. It is me, Aelfric Dragonfly.'

'Oh ...' This confused her somewhat. 'Then *I* must be the ghost. Please leave me be.'

Lord Dragonfly lowered his gaze. She sounded so fragile and lost. *Ah, what has become of this House?*

He had known the Wood Bee sisters since the days of their births, watched them all grow into womanhood. Morrad became charming, quick and clever, while Eldrid was brave and steadfast, and they had made an imposing team, respected by the court and the folk alike. But any good they ever achieved was counterbalanced by the conduct of their youngest sister.

Sulky, petulant, antagonising – perhaps it had been Yandira's destiny to become such a dangerous creature from her earliest age. The rumours that spread around Strange Ground about her, the things nobles whispered behind her back – if only they had been taken seriously at the time. Because now, with Maitressa gone these last ten years, Eldrid dead and Morrad more lost to herself than ever, the end of a great House was drawing near. And Dragonfly knew that his summons to this throne room spelled the end of his House, too.

'Escape, Highness,' he told Morrad with sudden heat. 'While you still can, flee this queendom.'

Morrad straightened, her eyes gained focus and she saw Dragonfly for the first time. 'Despair, my Lord, warn the Realm that my sister has dire plans—'

Whatever moment of clarity Morrad had achieved shattered when the door behind the dais swung open. She crumpled into the chair and her gaze returned to the rafters as Yandira swept into the hall.

'My dear Aelfric,' she said, positioning herself on the throne without acknowledging Morrad in any way. 'It has simply been too long.'

Not nearly long enough, thought Dragonfly. At the bottom of the steps, he bowed and adopted an amiable expression, while his heart rabbited in his breast. Yandira looked down on him from the throne, neither smiling nor scowling, as unreadable as ever. Wherever she went, her vile Shade was sure to be close behind.

'Of late,' Yandira said, 'I have felt my mother's hand on my shoulder. You must miss her terribly, Aelfric. Childhood friends, were you not? Scamps together and the bane of your teachers?'

'A long time ago now, Highness.' Dragonfly managed a smile. 'Happy memories, nevertheless.'

'But you were a triumvirate of scamps, yes? Lady Kingfisher was also one of Mother's childhood cohorts.'

'She was.'

'I should like to have seen dear Genevieve after my sister's abdication, but I gather that House Kingfisher has left Strange Ground?'

Lord Dragonfly didn't reply, for Yandira didn't need him to, and he still retained a degree of pride even in the face of such hopelessness. 'Perhaps we might do away with any preamble, Lady Yandira, and arrive at the reason for my summons?'

Darkness descending onto her manner, Yandira flapped a folded letter in the air. 'Ghador's paternal grandmother has aimed veiled threats at my House. Oh, she speaks prettily of tradition, of hopes and *rightful* things, but what I hold here is an intent to invade, and no mistake. Dalmyn is coming with an army, Aelfric, for Queen White Gold believes her granddaughter should be sitting on my throne. And I find it telling that this event coincides with Lady Kingfisher's departure.'

Dragonfly, bolstered by his relief to hear that Genevieve had made it to Dalmyn and they were on their way, dropped all pretence of his courtly charade. 'What did you expect, Yandira? You killed Eldrid. You wrung the life out of poor Morrad.

Who else should preserve your mother's legacy but her oldest friends?'

'You are clever, Aelfric, I'll give you that.' Yandira settled back into the throne. 'I believed I controlled all from my tower, but it escaped my notice that you and Lady Kingfisher remained in communication with my mother during her exile. And now, with Dalmyn on the way, I find myself *fixed* to Strange Ground for the time being. The expansion of my domain is hindered. Clever, but not enough to stop me.'

'I know what's in your heart,' Dragonfly said hotly. 'You think of Strange Ground as a necessary beginning for an ultimate ambition, but there is very good reason why your ancestor ensured that a single Empress has not ruled the Realm for generations.'

'My ancestor was a fool.'

'Light will follow dark, Yandira. The Good Lady Juno will not allow you to become Empress of this world or any other, no matter what Cursed Persephone has promised you. And it is for the love your mother commanded that the Protectors will stand in your way. Stop this. *Please.*'

Yandira sat forward, eyes blazing. 'I found her, you know, your precious Maitressa. I had her killed, too.'

It stung to hear it said with such hateful pride, and Dragonfly suspected this would be the moment when Yandira summoned her guards to put an end to his life. But she didn't. Instead he heard the dry rustle of leaves blown in hot wind and knew the Shade to be close. On the little chair beside the throne, Morrad's cheeks were wet with tears, and Dragonfly's face flushed with anger.

'But you did not kill Ghador,' he growled.

'And how well I know it.' A sudden, icy calm descended on Yandira as the Shade appeared on her shoulder. 'I wonder, what else have you *scamps* been cooking up against me?' The Shade scurried down her body and legs to the floor like a scorpion, then descended the steps towards Dragonfly. 'I am particularly interested to hear of a plot involving an earthling named Ebbie Wren.'

12

Unlikely Friends

For at least an hour, Ebbie sat frozen, clutching the satchel to his chest while tucked away at a corner table in Jester's Tavern. The only customer, he stared into a flickering candle-flame with his back turned to the window, a part of him believing that if he couldn't see the world outside then it couldn't see him. The tavern was surprisingly gloomy given the sun was so ... what? High in the sea? Underneath it? Over it? He tried not to imagine the vast expanse of water hanging above his head. What if it fell down?

Earlier, the landlord had placed a tankard of golden-brown beer on the table, telling Ebbie, 'Strange Ground's not such a bad place once you get used to it.' His words did nothing to calm Ebbie, and so far he had sipped not one drop from the tankard.

Mai had once asked him what he would do if presented with an opportunity to enter the Realm. *I'd take it*, he had believed, as if he had never been more certain of anything in his life. Now, it was different. This couldn't be Strange Ground beneath the Skea, *couldn't* be, yet here he was, stuck in the Realm. He looked at the immovable ring on his finger. Even if he knew how to get back home, would the wolfish men be lying in wait? And then it dawned on him ...

Whoever those men were, they had found out where Ebbie lived because they had gone to the funeral home. They said they had burned it down. Had they killed Mrs Cory to get to him?

Ebbie grabbed the tankard and gulped from it. Sweet and warm and earthy, like nothing he had tasted before – honey beer, the landlord called it. He drained half the tankard, trying to find reason in the wholesome flavour, trying to convince himself that Mrs Cory was still alive.

'All right?' someone grunted. A gaunt man had entered the tavern. Unshaven, bleary-eyed and looking a little drunk, he said, 'Do you need me this afternoon?'

'Of course I bloody need you!' said the landlord while he lit the fire. 'Who else is going to cook for supper time? Go and get the oven ready, you miserable sop.'

With a curse on his lips, the gaunt man walked behind the bar and disappeared out back, presumably to the kitchen.

Two young women followed him into the tavern. One of them greeted the landlord in a bright and breezy manner before she, too, disappeared out back. The other stopped to eye Ebbie suspiciously. The landlord spoke to her in a quiet voice, evidently explaining who he believed Ebbie to be. Her suspicion turned to amusement and she failed to hide a snort of laughter behind her hand as she went behind the bar and began straightening bottles and tankards on the shelves.

Ebbie drank more honey beer. These people mistook him for one of the folk like themselves, a clueless bumpkin blown in from the countryside and turned over by the city – which wasn't far from the truth.

While humming a pleasant tune, the first woman returned with a bucket of water in one hand, a cloth in the other, and proceeded to wipe down the tabletops. She sang while she worked, and it sounded comfortingly normal. This was just another day for the folk. Jester's Tavern had a worn and battered look – spit and sawdust like any number of pubs back home. Obsessed with the Realm since childhood, Ebbie had imagined thousands of times what it might look like. But never did he imagine it could appear so ... *mundane*.

Was Mrs Cory dead?

Gulping down the remainder of the beer, Ebbie delved into Mai's satchel and pulled out her letter. In it he hoped to find something he had missed which might explain what the hell was happening to him. But when he read the letter, he was astonished to find the words had changed, the originals replaced by an entirely new message:

> *My dearest Ebbie Wren,*
>
> *You have arrived safely in Strange Ground beneath the Skea, and for that I am more relieved than I can express. You have also been robbed of the coin I provided, so let this be a lesson to you. My Strange Ground is not your Strange Ground. Remember it. You will find a second purse inside the satchel.*

Ebbie checked, and there it was: another pouch nestled against the lantern. Its appearance, along with the words that had changed as if by magic, should have surprised him, but he was no longer sure that he was capable of ever experiencing surprise again. Discreetly, he opened the pouch, saw a flash of copper and silver and gold, then cinched it shut quickly.

> *You have been informed of who I used to be, and there is no time to waste on disbelief and confoundedness. My granddaughter is missing, Ebbie. Her name is Ghador. She is lost and faces great peril. In death, I can help her by asking*

*you to find her. It is my last wish, my final plea, that you
see my granddaughter returned to where she belongs. In this
matter, there are few others I can now trust.*

Vaguely aware of people arriving at the tavern to order food and
drinks, Ebbie was mesmerised by the words on the page, the
perfect handwriting of his old friend Mai – *Queen* Mai. She had
a granddaughter, children? He had never known that about her,
always assuming she was alone, never asking about her past;
and yet it was comforting, calming, to have her speak to him
about them, to hear her voice in his mind saying how much she
trusted him. This was really happening.

*I wish I could tell you where to begin your search. Your way
must be guided by the light of the True Sight Candle. This
light is as rare as the people who can manufacture the candle
itself. But I trust you to find it, Ebbie Wren, as I pray you can
trust me.*

    *You cannot do this alone, so remember that wealth talks.
As it is in your world, so it is in mine, a universal language.
You will need help to navigate my city and its lands. There are
individuals roaming the underbelly of Strange Ground who
possess the necessary skills and temperaments to aid you, and
you have already encountered one such individual who now
owes you a debt, yes? Gaining her loyalty will be difficult,
therefore I bequeath to you the sigil of my House.*

Yet another item had magically appeared inside the satchel.
The sigil in question was a glass stone the colour of honey, big
enough to cover Ebbie's palm and smooth like a pebble on the
beach. On one side, engraved in white, a flying insect clung to
the trunk of a tree – the same picture used on the stamp to seal

the letter's envelope. But the sigil wasn't the only new item to have appeared.

Putting the stone away, Ebbie found a sheet of paper which proved to be a contract of employment when unfolded. It was simply written, promising the signee great wealth in return for their services, and there was a watermark in the top-right corner. It was hard to make out in the dingy light, but the mark appeared to depict the same image from the sigil. Ebbie started and shoved the contract back into the satchel, certain he had just seen the bee on the tree trunk move.

He grabbed the tankard, remembered it was empty and put it down.

Your thief goes by the name Bek Rana. She will not be quick to give her loyalty, but use my sigil wisely, discreetly, and it will grant you privileges that might just gain her trust. Gather your courage and do not rest on your laurels, Ebbie, for Bek Rana will steer you to the light of the True Sight Candle and the salvation of my granddaughter Ghador. My hopes and Juno's blessings go with you.

More soon,

Mai

Ebbie stowed the letter in the satchel and again tried to drink from an empty tankard. The details of the letter, the things Mai knew ... was she watching him from beyond the grave?

Ebbie looked around for the landlord and was startled to discover his burly form already looming over him.

'Fancy another?' he said, pointing at the tankard.

'Ah, no, thank you.'

'What about some food?'

Ebbie shook his head. 'The woman who stole my money – is her name Bek Rana?'

'Why do you ask?'

'I'd like to talk to her.'

'Be a bit difficult, what with her locked in a jail cell and all.' The landlord scratched the stubble on his chin. 'Listen, if you're after your money, I wouldn't bother. The city guard don't get much by way of pay. They'll already have divvied up whatever coin Bek was carrying.'

'So you know her?' The landlord nodded. 'Where was she taken?'

'City Guard Jailhouse, most likely.' The landlord ensured there was no one in earshot, then dropped his voice. 'Bek Rana lacks some smarts, but she has a good heart, so I'd ask you kindly not to add to her woes.'

'What? No, you misunderstand. I don't want to get her in trouble, I ...' Ebbie rubbed his temples. 'When will they release her?'

The landlord sucked air over his teeth. 'Not sure they will this time.'

Ebbie stared at the satchel in his hands, felt the ever-increasing items inside. *Gather your courage* ... He looped the strap over his head and rose from the table. 'How do I get to the jailhouse from here?'

The landlord gave him an appraising look. 'Step outside, turn right, then straight on till you see it on the left. Big building, can't miss it.'

'Thank you.'

'What are you up to?'

'I *think* I'm going to set her free.'

It was while Yandira began the long, spiralling descent into the castle dungeons that she realised how tired she felt. Fatigue was crawling through her leg muscles, forcing her to take the stairs slowly and with care. She could feel it probing at her mind, too – a cloud attempting to obscure her thoughts. This wasn't the kind of weakness that was easily remedied by a few hours of sleep; Yandira recognised it as a form of admonishment: her enemies had hindered her progress and Lady Persephone was not pleased.

Lord Aelfric Dragonfly was one such enemy. Maddeningly, he had revealed little during his interrogation that Yandira hadn't already guessed: he and his oldest friends had vowed to keep a watchful eye on the youngest sister and counter any move she made to further her ambitions. However, Maitressa and Kingfisher had denied Dragonfly the finer details of their plan, telling him little of the parts they played, nothing useful regarding Ghador and this earthling Ebbie Wren. And any questions about the sword which had been hidden away among the Wood Bee heirlooms for generations, Dragonfly had answered with silence. Perhaps unsurprisingly, he didn't even know it truly existed.

Yandira muttered to herself angrily as she reached the bottom step, for down here in the gloom yet another problem had presented itself.

The dungeons were as large as the throne room and the illumination of many torches staved off complete darkness. Despite her fatigue, Yandira kept her back straight and walked regally past the rows of cage-like cells filled to bursting with around fifty folk. Most of them were soldiers, plus a smattering of diplomats and servants, but none of them dared speak as the First Lady of House Wood Bee headed to where a captain of the Royal Guard stood between two jailers. Yandira stopped and studied the captive.

Stripped of armour and weapons, the captain gazed into the First Lady's unblinking stare with as much confusion as fear.

His name was Gavith. The jailers – a man and a woman, their clothes covered by stained and filthy leather aprons – carried evidence of the Serpent's Sigh on their faces and in their eyes, subservient to the core. But this soldier remained unaffected by the Underworld's magic.

'So,' said Yandira. 'Princess Ghador's convoy was under your command, correct?'

'Yes, Highness.' The captain's gaze flittered to the torture rack which had been left on display for all to see. As of yet, no prisoner had been strapped to it. 'But ...' The captain licked his lips nervously.

'But *what*?'

'I cannot tell you what happened, Highness, for I do not know.'

'I find that difficult to accept, Captain.'

The rest of the prisoners watched in tense silence. Each of them had believed they were valued members of the Royal House when they set out for Dalmyn with Ghador under their protection. They had returned home to discover otherwise. But a strange charm had been cast upon these folk, a powerful charm that not only made them impervious to Yandira's spells, but also invisible to her magical sight. Inexplicably, they retained free will before the might of the Serpent's Sigh.

'You have failed my House, Captain,' said Yandira. 'Your queen is bitterly disappointed.'

In the dungeon's humid and oily atmosphere, rife with the smell of sour bodies and torch smoke, a look of indignation came over Gavith's face, rising above his fear. As the convoy's commander, he knew that blame for losing his charge lay on his shoulders alone. Yet he hadn't returned to Strange Ground to face Queen Eldrid's wrath, but to discover his queen dead and Yandira free and sitting on the Wood Bee Throne, even if she was missing a crown.

'You have an opinion?' Yandira purred. 'The current state of my queendom does not meet with your approval, perhaps?'

The captain looked away. Yes, he had an opinion, all right; had there been a sword in his hand, he would happily have plunged it into the First Lady's chest. With a mental command, Yandira made the two jailers stand a little closer to him.

'Where is Princess Ghador?'

'Please, Highness, the princess is missing.' Gavith gestured at the folk in the cells. 'Not one of us knows what happened to her.'

'A somewhat ridiculous statement, and here's why.' If her legs hadn't been aching so much, Yandira would have started pacing. 'I know for a fact that Princess Morrad sent a courier gull to you bearing news of Queen Eldrid's death. Convenient, I think, that my niece should then *disappear* without one of her *oh so* very loyal subjects knowing what became of her. You took it upon yourself to send her on to Dalmyn, didn't you, Captain?'

Gavith shook his head, perplexed. 'I don't understand, Highness. We received no gull. We knew nothing of our queen's death until returning to the city.'

Yandira gave him a dangerous smile. 'Let us pretend your ludicrous statement is true. Am I to then believe that upon discovering the princess's absence, the first instinct of her protector – a soldier with years of training, specifically chosen for this duty because of his deep loyalty – was to abandon his charge on the Queen's Highway and return home?'

'No, I-I ...' The captain took a moment to think through his story's logic and found it to be as absurd as Yandira did. 'I can't explain why I did it, Highness. Returning to Strange Ground just felt like the right decision, like ... what I was supposed to do, I-I—'

'Enough.' Yandira's patience had grown as tired as her legs. 'Seize him.'

The jailers grabbed Gavith's arms and made to drag him to the torture rack, but he struggled and shouted, 'Please, Highness, by the oath I swore to your House, I am telling the truth. There was a disturbance—'

'Stop!'

The jailers obeyed, though they didn't release their grip.

Yandira stepped forward. 'What disturbance?'

Breathing hard, the captain spoke hurriedly, keeping one eye on the rack. 'Less than a day out from Dalmyn, we made camp on the Queen's Highway, and ... and it all happened so fast. The guards saw nothing unusual, but then there was an unnatural light—'

'What kind of light?'

'It came suddenly, flaring from nowhere, and encompassed the camp with a blue glare. It hurt no one and its only effect was to dazzle our eyes. But when it receded, Princess Ghador was gone. The light came and went, like ... like ...'

'Like magic?' Yandira finished.

Gavith nodded, thus exposing the reason why he and his charges could hide from the Serpent's Sigh. An unnatural light of glaring blue: it sounded familiar to Yandira, even if this fool could not hazard a guess at its origins. The Oldunfolk did so like to complicate matters. As did Lady Maitressa Wood Bee.

'I swear to your House,' Gavith pleaded. 'We received no message from Princess Morrad. I cannot understand why I failed to order a search after the blue light faded, but I do not know what became of Princess Ghador, Highness.'

Could it be that he was telling the truth?

Yandira curled her lip into a snarl. 'The correct form of

address is *Imperial Majesty*. And your Empress has heard quite enough, Captain.'

Fatigue continued to beset Yandira and she folded her arms to hide the fact her hands were shaking. She let her eyes drift over the folk in the cells. Squashed together with no room to sit, many of their fearful faces looked out from between metal bars. This magical blue light which had infected their camp might have saved them from subservience, but it could not protect them from physical harm. Someone here knew more about Ghador than they were saying.

'Take him,' Yandira ordered.

'No!' Gavith struggled but could not shake the jailers' vice-like grip as they dragged him to the rack and forcibly strapped him in.

'My mercy can be bought with information,' Yandira told the prisoners. 'Perhaps witnessing the punishment for defiance will loosen your tongues.'

Captain Gavith's first scream echoed around the dungeon as Yandira made her way out. Reaching the spiralling stairs, she stopped to catch her breath. This fatigue would only get worse. She needed to get her hands on that earthling and squeeze him for every drop of information. Ebbie Wren knew where Ghador was hiding.

The games of the Oldunfolk were founded upon a golden rule: no Oldunone was permitted to reveal their true self to a mortal.

It was less harmful to corporeal existence if Oldunfolk remained in the shadows while manipulating their chosen champions. The game then became a challenge of moves and countermoves, unpredictable to a degree given mortal-kind's penchant for considered actions followed by visceral reactions. It was delicious to watch them manoeuvring against each other while confused as to whether they acted of their own free will or if divine edict steered their every decision.

However, when manipulating from the shadows, an Oldunone had to remain vigilant and wary. The temptation to break the golden rule was constant, and there were penalties for doing so. Direct and heavy-handed gameplay set in motion dangerous precedents which a divine opponent could take advantage of. Patience and subtlety were key to outmanoeuvring one's adversary, but by thrusting Ebbie Wren into the chaos of the Realm, Lady Juno, Queen of Mortal Queens, had revealed a hand which She would have rather kept hidden. And now, trickery and lies would further reveal the plans She did not wish *Her* adversary to know.

Moves and countermoves.

Emerging from the steaming breath of dragons, Mrs Cory conjured a door: a simple thing with no other design than to connect two spaces. Through this door, She stepped onto the well-worn carpet belonging to the second floor of a lodging house on Earth. She closed the door behind Her and hung a brass No. 7 on it. Never before had this floor boasted a seventh apartment, but She made space for it now, stretching the hallway to a length that accommodated a new abode perfectly and snugly beside No. 6.

Concerning No. 6, its own door had been smashed and ripped until only a rough L-shape of wood clung to one hinge. This would not do at all. Not only did it sully the hallway's bland but neat aesthetic, it also mocked the door's sole purpose in life: to cast the illusion that while it stood, proud and closed, it would protect inhabitants from all the bad things in their world.

With but a thought and a gesture, Mrs Cory gathered every piece of broken wood, down to the last chip and splinter, and put them back into their proper place. Once the door to No. 6

matched the same lacklustre brown of the other doors on the second floor, She turned her attentions to Her own aesthetic.

Disguises, like actions and reactions, required engineering to specific situations. But how to act, what to wear, for this one? The funeral director would be too impenetrable, too aloof to be trusted to any helpful degree. This disguise needed to be kindly, unthreatening; it needed to represent something *good*. A replacement, of sorts, for a lost ally and loved one. Calm affection amidst tragic chaos. And Mrs Cory knew just the thing.

She aged her features and fashioned a skirt suit of thick woollen plaid to fit a shrunken body and withering limbs. Her shoes were ugly but very comfortable. She covered Her iron-grey curls with a floral headscarf, then stooped Her shoulders, adopting the gait of an elderly mortal. She cleared Her throat and tested Her voice. 'Hello, dear.' No, too commanding. She tried adding significant frailty. 'Hello, dear.' Perfect.

And then She waited outside the door to No. 6.

Why would Yandira Wood Bee bother to consider this humble abode on Earth? Now that Ebbie Wren had flown to the Realm, with Mr Lunk and Mr Venatus hot on his heels, surely this place had played its part in the game and was now an empty nest? *No one* would bother checking on it, not even the earthling's parents. And Ebbie Wren certainly did not have any friends who might come calling – well, there had been one, perhaps, but she was dead anyway.

This was Lady Juno's reasoning; She had gambled on no one watching this apartment because She believed Herself smarter than Her opponent, who would undoubtedly consider this location nothing more than the site of an old move and unworthy of further investigation. But Juno was not as smart as She thought. The only mystery in Her gameplay was why She had allowed Ebbie Wren to be one of Her champions. If

Mrs Cory did not know better, She would say Juno had made a mistake.

But clearer insight into mysteries and secret strategies would come when apartment No. 6 was occupied again in ... 'Three, two, one.'

A noise came from the other side of the door, like the *whoosh* of a gale over an angry sea. Next, the muffled thump of a body hitting carpeted floor. Then, a strangled cry from a panicked throat. A brief respite, during which the new arrival was surely clambering to her feet to gaze at her environment in stunned silence. Finally, a string of curses, each one spat with venom and fear, invoking the names of many Oldunfolk; a tirade which ended with a sharp gasp when Mrs Cory chose that moment to knock at the door.

She didn't expect an answer at the first attempt, nor did She at the second. Her third knock resulted in the creak of a floorboard as No. 6's new occupier wondered if the door separated her from friend or foe.

Aware She was being viewed through the spyhole, Mrs Cory wrung Her hands and expressed sympathetic concern. 'Are you all right in there? Sounds like you arrived with a bump.'

No response. While the door remained closed, nothing bad in this world could get inside. The thrill of mischief was almost too much to bear. After all, why should the mortals have all the fun in this game?

Kindly and frail, She said, 'I knew you were coming,' then lowered Her volume to imply secrets and conspiracy. 'Your grandmother asked me to watch out for you.'

The lie was swallowed and the door opened a crack. Green and suspicious eyes peered out.

'Hello, dear. I'm Mrs Cory from number seven, just next door.'

'You ... You knew my grandmother?'

'Yes, dear. Me and Maitressa go back a ways.'

Which was actually the truth, in a manner of speaking. The crack in the door opened wider and revealed a tired woman in her middling mortal twenties.

Mrs Cory feigned surprised upon seeing her face by forming Her mouth into a large 'O' and exclaiming, 'Oh my ... there's no mistaking whose granddaughter you are, is there?'

Like a sleepwalker terrified to wake worlds away from the place in which she fell asleep, Princess Ghador Wood Bee tried and failed to find words, then burst into tears.

The cell stank of old vomit and urine.

Sitting on the edge of a narrow and rickety bunk, Bek was trying not to think about how many lice infested its stained, straw-stuffed mattress. She wished she wore something on her feet to prevent them from sticking to the tacky flagstones, but along with her jacket and money, the guards had taken away her boots for reasons that made sense to them alone. More importantly, they had taken the sword, too.

Very little light shone in through the tiny barred window high on the wall, and in the dimness Bek shuddered to hear once again the muffled voice of the inmate in the next cell, making sounds like he was doing things to himself he ought not to be. She rubbed the back of her head; the guard's sap had given her a lump and an ache but hadn't broken the skin.

One big job. That was all she had needed. A job paying enough for a new life in a new city. Like her grandma used to say, 'Catching fish every day will keep food on your table, but hooking a chest full of gold from the belly of a shipwreck will change your fortunes for ever.' Well, Bek honestly thought she had hooked her treasure chest this time. She had come so close. It was enough to make her weep.

In other cells, other prisoners were airing their opinions of the guards or singing drunkenly like they didn't realise they were no longer in a tavern. All in all, this was the worst day of Bek's life. She hadn't been told for what crime she was being held; it might've been for any one of seven outstanding warrants, by her count. But deep down Bek knew it was the sword that had landed her in trouble. Had to be. Why hadn't she listened to Charlie?

Putting her face in her hands, Bek rocked back and forth on the bunk, blocking out the noise of the jail, searching for a scenario in which this ended well for her. She tried focusing on memories of a happier time, years before the streets, setting out across gentle waves at dawn in a small boat to catch fish with her grandma. But all that did was remind her of what she had lost, then and now, and her misery deepened. If she could only get her hands on the mysterious collector who had set this job in motion, then she'd have a throat worth strangling.

Hushed voices came from just outside the cell door.

A key scraped in the lock and clunked it open. The door swung inwards revealing a grubby guard on the threshold. She looked perturbed and was practically cowering, wringing her hands.

'That's her,' she said, pointing at Bek.

The guard stood to one side, allowing a man to step into the cell. A satchel hung from his shoulder. Bek's jacket was draped over his arm. In one hand, he held her boots; in the other ... the sword — *her* sword, still in its battered scabbard. Bek didn't know whether to shy from it or stare at it with longing. She did both.

The guard cleared her throat. 'Is there anything else I can do for you?' she simpered. 'Anything at all, my Lord?'

The man said, 'Ah, no. I'd like to speak with her alone.' There was a nervousness to his tone, a lack of confidence. 'Thank you for your help.'

'Pleasure's all mine, my Lord. Grady's the name, if you've a mind to mention it.' She gave an oily chuckle. 'Promotions aren't easy to come by, if you follow me.'

The man hesitated. 'Okay. Grady – I'll remember.'

'Much obliged, my Lord.' Stooped in a rough approximation of a bow, the guard scurried away, adding, 'I'll be at the duty desk, if there's anything else.'

When she had gone, the man pulled the cell door to and exhaled in relief. Bek's hungry gaze left the sword in his hand to settle on his face. He smiled crookedly at her, embarrassed, and Bek's shoulders sagged.

'Great,' she huffed.

The last time she had seen this man, he had been wittering on about a candle while she stole his purse. Not the naïve farmer she had supposed, but a lord, apparently. Just her luck that she would rob a second noble. She could practically hear Charlie laughing at her.

'Hello again,' he said.

Bek gave him a sour look. 'If you want your money back, talk to your new friend at the duty desk.'

The man failed to hold his smile in place. 'I'm not here about the money. I know who you are – Bek Rana, right?'

Bek said nothing.

'My name's Ebbie Wren. I need help and I've been told that I can trust you.'

'Oh, you were told that, were you?' Bek scoffed a laugh. 'I don't recognise your House's name, *Lord* Wren. Where are you from?'

He pressed a finger to his lips. 'I'm not a lord,' he whispered. 'I'm a librarian.'

Bek frowned. 'Who sent you? Was it the Kingfishers?'

'Who?' He waved the question away. 'I've been dumped in a situation I don't really understand.' To Bek's surprise, he passed her the jacket and boots. 'I'm lost and need a guide.' When he gave her the sword, Bek was tempted to kiss it before calmly placing it on the mattress beside her and covering it with the jacket. 'I'd like to hire you.'

Bek blanched and almost laughed. 'You what?'

From his satchel, he produced a folded piece of paper. Bek took it but didn't read the contents, keeping her dumbfounded expression on this Ebbie Wren who sounded prouder to call himself a librarian than a lord.

'It's a contract of employment,' he said, encouraging her to look at it. 'I need someone with your skills, someone who knows their way around.'

'Uh-huh.'

Dubious, but liking the direction of this conversation, Bek unfolded the paper. It was hard to read in the dingy light, but there was no mistaking the genuine contract of employment in her hands. It promised great riches for services rendered, but all Bek really wanted was her sword and freedom back.

'So, you can get me out of here, can you?'

'I've already arranged your release.'

'You sure about that?'

Ebbie Wren flapped a hand at the contract. 'Just sign at the bottom and we'll walk right out through the front door.'

Bek kept her face neutral but smiled inside. Perhaps she had hooked her treasure chest after all.

'We shouldn't hang around,' Ebbie said. 'I haven't got a pen, I'm afraid, but the contract says you don't need a signature—'

'A thumbprint in dirt or blood will suffice,' said Bek. 'I do know how these things work.' She leaned forward and rubbed her thumb on a grimy flagstone, then smudged a print on the bottom of the page. 'Here,' she said, passing the contract back. 'I suppose I'm all yours.'

Ebbie Wren, lord or librarian, practically deflated with relief as he folded it and slipped it into his satchel.

'I've got a lot to explaining to do,' he said. 'Can you take us somewhere safe to talk?'

Bek pulled on her boots and smirked. 'I know just the place.'

13

The Back Way Out

Ebbie was scared and exhausted and wanted to go home, but he felt relieved to no longer be alone in this sphere of madness. Though he was far from convinced that Bek Rana was anything like the loyal accomplice that Mai's letter suggested she would be.

'Let me get this straight,' Bek said as they made their way along the street. 'You walked into the jailhouse posing as a lord, ordered the guards to drop all charges and set me free, and they did?'

'It wasn't quite like that, and I'm not posing as anything,' Ebbie said. He still couldn't quite believe he'd summoned the courage to enter the jailhouse in the first place. 'The guard *assumed* I was a lord, so I went along with it.'

'So you're really, honestly just a librarian?'

'Yes.'

Bek laughed. 'I've heard some things in my time, but this tops them all.' She laughed some more, enjoying the situation entirely too much for Ebbie's liking. He felt exposed.

'Look, I sprang you, didn't I? Can we please get off the street?'

With a mocking bow, Bek led Ebbie deeper into the hubbub of Strange Ground beneath the Skea, through an area of the city known as Golder's Fairway, according to her. Ebbie had managed to summon the armour of confidence he wore at the library, but it was a brittle coping mechanism behind which his earlier panic bubbled, and it could shatter at any moment. He didn't dare look up; he couldn't face the sea rolling so serenely across the sky.

The folk on the street didn't pay any attention to their passage, but Ebbie, though dressed like them as he was, looking like them as he did, still felt he stuck out like a sore thumb. There were people aplenty, but Bek cut through their comings and goings as smoothly as a slippery eel navigating the current of a stream. Following in her wake, struggling to keep up, Ebbie apologised a hundred times to those he bumped into. Gulls cried overhead, and he wondered, absurdly, if they were flying upside down in the impossible sky.

'Keep up,' Bek called cheerily. 'Not far now.'

Ebbie bumped into yet another person and gritted his teeth.

Bek strode ahead like she owned the place. Her confidence was encouraging, as was her obvious familiarity with the city, and Ebbie would have felt comforted if not for Bek's rushed and distracted manner. As soon as she stepped unimpeded from the jailhouse, she had become breezy, dismissive, like she couldn't be touched, like she had more important things to do and wouldn't be hanging around for long. And it was odd, Ebbie decided, that she carried her sword in her arms, wrapped in her jacket, clutched to her chest like a closely guarded secret.

By the time Bek led Ebbie to their destination, he was holding his satchel protectively, too. He trusted Mai but feared she had suggested a guide who was planning to rob him a second time.

'Here you go.' Bek jabbed a thumb at the tavern where, only a short time earlier, Ebbie had been drinking honey beer. 'Jester's, also known as Backway Charlie's. No safer place to talk.'

Jester's was much busier than it had been earlier, jam-packed with customers, sitting and standing, filling the tavern with chattering voices. The smell of beer and cooking food hung in the air along with clouds of pipe smoke. The landlord – Backway Charlie, apparently – caught sight of Bek from behind the bar and made a beeline for her, dodging and weaving between his customers with a stunned smile on his face.

'I don't believe it,' he said. 'Thought they'd put you away for good this time.'

'They haven't yet made a cell that can hold me, Charlie.' Bek chuckled and tilted her head towards Ebbie. 'Actually, I've got my new friend to thank for my freedom.'

'Oh ...' Charlie noticed Ebbie for the first time and he nodded in both appreciation and recognition. 'Hello again. Man of your word, I see.'

Bek looked from one to the other. 'You two already met?'

'After a fashion,' said Ebbie.

'I was clearing up your mess like always.' Charlie opened his arms wide. 'Come here, you.' He pulled Bek into a big hug.

'Careful,' she said.

Charlie's happy demeanour changed, and he pushed Bek away until he was holding her at arm's length by the shoulders. He scowled at the jacket-wrapped bundle in her arms which had prevented her returning the hug.

'That better not be what I think it is, Bek.'

'Don't get angry, Charlie.'

'I told you—'

'I know what you told me, but not now.'

'*Yes*, now. Come with me.'

The landlord stalked back to the bar like an angry bear and Bek gave Ebbie a forced smile. 'Why don't you find a table while I get us some drinks?'

'What's going on?'

'It's nothing. Old business between friends. Go on, I'll join you soon enough.'

Bek headed to the bar where the scowling Charlie waited for her, and Ebbie pushed his way through the throng of customers. He found an empty corner table and settled onto a chair, holding the satchel in his lap, trying to make himself as small and unnoticeable as possible. Anxious for Bek to join him, he peered through a gap in the crowd, caught sight of the landlord jabbing a finger at her angrily, but then his view was obscured by bodies. When he next saw her, she was thankfully heading his way carrying two tankards of honey beer.

'Sorry about that,' she said, taking her seat and drinking a long draught from her tankard. She wiped foam from her lip and gazed expectantly at Ebbie. 'What's the job, boss?'

She said it like she didn't care, dismissive again, but only then did Ebbie realise he had no idea where to begin. The first crack appeared in his brittle self-control. He wanted to go home.

'Well?' said Bek. 'Tell me why a librarian pretending to be a lord was so keen to spring me from jail.'

'I wasn't pretending ...' Ebbie gave up. He shook his head and took a drink. 'A friend of mine died.' He pushed his tankard to one side. 'And she named me the executor of her will.'

Bek's ears pricked up at the mention of a will, but she looked disappointed when all Ebbie produced from the satchel was nothing more valuable than a lantern, which he placed on the table.

'Look inside,' he said. 'See anything missing?'

Bek opened the glass front and grinned. 'Ebbie, I'm grateful for my freedom, and I'm sorry your friend is dead, but you didn't go to all this trouble because your lantern is missing a bloody candle, surely?'

'Bek, I don't want to be in this situation, but I am, so ... I've recently been told about something called a *True Sight Candle?*'

'Ah, right – that makes more sense.'

'You know what it is?'

Bek lifted her tankard to her lips. 'I've certainly heard of them.'

'Good. I need you to find me one.'

Foam sprayed as Bek scoffed into her beer. 'Are you mad?'

'What?'

'Do you have any idea what you're asking for?' Ebbie shook his head and Bek pursed her lips. 'True Sight Candles are very rare, very expensive and *very* illegal.'

'Why?'

'Because their light shows the way to folk who often don't want to be found. So, the big question here is, who are *you* trying to find?'

'Mai's granddaughter.'

'Mai?'

'My friend who died. Her granddaughter's missing and she wants me to track her down.'

Bek gulped from her tankard and gave Ebbie an appraising look. 'Are you going to kill her?'

'No! Why would you ask that?'

'I'm not judging.' Bek raised her hands. 'I've heard stories of assassins using True Sight Candles to hunt down their victims, so I need to know.'

'I'm not an assassin.' Ebbie was appalled. 'Mai wants her granddaughter returned home safely. She's in trouble. I think. I can't understand why Mai chose me to do this. I'm a librarian! Anyway, I need a True Sight Candle to find her granddaughter. Can you help?'

'Tricky. True Sight Candles are outlawed in this city, so you won't have much luck around here. You might have to buy us passage out of Strange Ground to find one.' Bek's eyes lingered on the satchel. 'Can you afford that?'

Ebbie wrapped his arms around what was his. 'Maybe.'

'This granddaughter, she in for an inheritance? Executor of a will, you said, so what's the handout? Money? An estate?'

'I'm not sure. Might be both.' Ebbie gave an apologetic smile. 'Seems that Mai was something of a dark horse.'

'I'll say she was if she left you enough coin for a True Sight Candle.' Bek looked around and lowered her voice. 'Listen, who am I *really* working for? Did this Mai come from noble blood?'

'It's complicated.'

'Then you'll have to explain it, Ebbie. I'm not a fan of the nobles, and they don't much like me.'

In thought, Ebbie drummed his fingers on the table, then delved into the satchel. 'This might help explain things.' He pulled out Mai's honey-coloured sigil stone and placed it beside the lantern. 'That guard mistook me for a lord as soon as she saw that symbol. She practically jumped out of her skin and couldn't do enough for me. I think it's because … What's wrong?'

Bek had paled. She was staring at the white tree and insect engraved into the stone like it was a vision of her death.

'Put it away,' she snapped. 'The lantern, too. Put them both away. Now!'

Ebbie quickly swept the lantern and stone back into the satchel. Bek leaned across the table and beckoned Ebbie to do the same until their faces were inches apart.

'Very quietly,' she whispered, 'tell me who your friend is.'

'That's just it,' Ebbie replied. 'Apparently, she's not who I thought she was. After she died – I mean, this sounds crazy, I know, but someone brought me this satchel, told me it was a valuable heirloom. It was empty but then things started appearing in it. And then there's this letter, too, you see, and it changes, it … it—'

'*Who* is Mai, Ebbie?'

'She used to be a queen. Queen Maitressa.'

With a hissing sound, Bek pushed herself away from the table, face furious. 'Is this a joke? Did someone put you up to it …?' She trailed off and her eyes widened with fear. She seemed to collapse into herself, shrivelling on the chair, and the strangest sound rattled hoarsely from her mouth, '*Lunkenvenatus.*'

Ebbie wondered if he had given her a stroke. 'What?'

'Just walked in. Mr Lunk and Mr Venatus.'

Ebbie turned around and his heart froze. Two men in long coats stood by the tavern door. Dishevelled and hairy, they scanned the crowd like wolves searching for sheep.

A flashback to his apartment made Ebbie duck down. 'Shit,' he told Bek. 'They're after me.'

Bek took a second to acknowledge these words before grabbing her sword and coat then slid off the chair to the floor. Her hand came up and pulled Ebbie down after her.

'Follow me,' she growled.

On hands and knees, they crawled through the legs of patrons to the end of the bar where Charlie was washing tankards in a basin of water.

He frowned when he saw them. 'You all right down there?'

Bek shook her head. 'Backway, Charlie.'

The landlord stiffened. 'How bad is it?'

'Bad as it gets. By the door.'

Charlie's face clouded darkly when he caught sight of the wolfish men called Lunk and Venatus. 'Oldunfolk, no,' he hissed through clenched teeth. 'I told you there'd be trouble, Bek.'

'They're here for *him*, not me. Please, Charlie, before they see us.'

'I'll keep them busy,' he said with a curt nod. 'You know what to do.'

Bek and Ebbie crawled behind the bar and out into the back of the tavern, where they scurried through the kitchen and down the stairs to the cellar. Surrounded by barrels and cobwebs, Bek headed to the far side where candlelight didn't quite reach. She grabbed a sconce on the wall beside a wine rack and pulled it like she was playing a one-armed bandit. The rack clicked and swung open, jingling bottles, and a small hidden room was revealed. Once inside, Bek pulled the rack-door closed. Firelight flickered up through a large hole in the floor, and Bek pointed at the ladder descending into it.

'Go!'

Ebbie half-climbed, half-fell down into a chamber where a few torches burned in sconces. A low wind moaned from ahead, but the light couldn't penetrate the gloom.

'See that box on the wall?' Bek said as she jumped from the ladder. 'Put two gold coins in it.'

Ebbie fished around in his satchel until locating the money purse. He saw the box on the wall. It was made from wood, about the size of a birdhouse, the little door on the front secured by a padlock. Ebbie dropped two gold coins through the slit in the top. They clinked as they hit other coins.

'What's going on?' he asked, breathless, fearful.

'What's going on, he says.' Bek swore as she pulled on her jacket and buckled the sword belt around her waist. 'You've got some cheek asking me that.'

On the wall behind the ladder, a line of rucksacks hung from hooks. Bek grabbed one, shrugged it onto her back and then rushed to a barrel filled with unlit torches.

'Bek, who are those men?'

'Shut up!'

Having selected a torch, she held its end to the flame of another on the wall. It spat then flared to life with a *whump*.

'Laverna curse you, Ebbie Wren,' she said as she headed into the gloom and moaning wind. 'I'd have stayed in jail if I'd known Lunk and Venatus were after you.'

Gulls were clever little creatures. As sly as thieves but as stouthearted as warriors, not governed by divine lore, dismissive of whether or not the pathways they travelled were forbidden. Worlds were in their feathers, their skin, their blood and meat and bones. They saw everything beneath the Skea. And by it. If gulls could tell their tales, they would speak of a history older than folk and earthlings, because they belonged to all places, the messengers who would brave tempests to deliver their missives.

So why wouldn't they fly today?

Lady Genevieve Kingfisher huffed at the four gulls housed in the cage on the back of her wagon. Two had vital messages tied to their legs. Yet, even though the cage door remained open, they wouldn't budge, perched with heads tucked to their breasts, not touching feed or water.

She and the soldiers of Dalmyn were taking respite on the Queen's Highway. It had been a relentless journey so far, and the bounces and jostles of the wagon were harsh on Kingfisher's aging back and bones. As anxious as she was to reach Strange Ground, she felt glad for the chance to stretch her legs, but the weather had taken a sudden ill turn, and the gulls weren't the only ones affected by what had become a sorry sort of day.

Around eight hundred soldiers were camped on the Queen's Highway and those closest to Kingfisher looked miserable, their horses skittish. All was ominously quiet around their fires as smoke rose thick and acrid from dampened wood. A chill breeze blighted the air. The ground and grass glistened with dew. The few trees on the roadside were hazed by mist, a mist that was thickening to fog on the highway. Up above, the Skea was grey and restless. It felt as if they were camping during a midwinter's morning rather than a summer's evening. There was something wrong with the land. The gulls knew it, the soldiers knew it and so did Kingfisher.

'Come now,' she cooed softly into the cage. 'Why won't you fly?'

Thank the Oldunfolk that Queen White Gold had already received word from Ghador's convoy and ordered half her troops to march on Strange Ground. Kingfisher had joined them on the road straight after her return from Earth, and she had arrived to find a courier gull waiting for her, sent by Lord Dragonfly.

His message was concise and clear: *Situation uncontainable. Alert all Protectors. Look for me on the road.*

Lady Kingfisher's anxiety had quickened in her breast upon reading it, imagining the kind of foulness Yandira was serving to the folk of Strange Ground. She must have grown powerful indeed if she was forcing dear Aelfric to abandon the city, more so than even Maitressa had foreseen. So, in desperation, the First Lady of House Kingfisher had written two messages.

The first was intended for Dragonfly, assuring him that she and an army were on the Queen's Highway and heading for Strange Ground. The second was for Queen White Gold, who awaited word and further instructions back in Dalmyn, and it told her that Yandira's curse now threatened more than just Strange Ground. But neither message could be delivered.

'Damn you,' Kingfisher told the gulls. 'Fly!' But still they wouldn't leave the cage's sanctuary.

'Perhaps they fear the weather, my Lady.'

Kingfisher turned to see Prince Maxis approaching, leading his horse by the reins.

'Feels like the season's changing right before our eyes,' he said. Ghador's father cut a tall and broad figure in his armour, and he was the sort of man who, as Dalmyn's First Heir, believed deeply in his own importance. 'Seej Agda worries that some force of supernature is afoot. I've told her she worries too much.'

Seej Agda, a High Priest of Juno. There had not been time so far for Kingfisher to get properly acquainted with her, but she trusted the priest was as loyal to the Royal Family she served as she was to her Oldunone. From what little Kingfisher knew of her, if Seej Agda had cause to worry then there was definitely something to worry about, despite the prince's dismissive attitude.

'How long till we reach Strange Ground, Highness?'

'A day, perhaps, if the fog doesn't worsen.' Maxis let his horse wander a little way to feed on grass before looking up at the Skea, where waves swelled and fell, churning the greyness with frothy crests. 'Though I'm not entirely sure what to expect at our destination.' He wiped moisture from his beard and fixed an expectant gaze on Kingfisher. 'My mother was a little secretive with me regarding this mission. She said you would counsel me on the road.'

'Indeed, Highness,' Kingfisher said. 'Queen White Gold is well aware that our *mission*, as you put it, will be difficult to predict. The strange weather and Seej Agda's misgivings might evidence this.'

Maxis rolled his eyes. 'The priest sees signs and omens wherever she looks, but from you I was hoping to hear the level-headed counsel my mother promised. And please, don't try to tell me I'm leading eight hundred soldiers because your city has lost its princess.'

A princess who just happens to be your daughter, Kingfisher thought bitterly while offering a polite smile.

Upon learning of Eldrid's death and Ghador's disappearance, Maxis had insisted he lead Dalmyn's troops to Strange Ground, but out of a prince's pride and honour rather than a father's concern. Maitressa had once told Kingfisher that Ghador was the result of a drunken tryst during one of the traditional banquets which followed the frequent hunting competitions that Maxis and Eldrid enjoyed organising. They were well suited, in their way. Like Eldrid, Maxis was impulsive and hot-headed, susceptible to acting before thinking. Thank the Oldunfolk that Ghador had learned her grandmother's temperance. She and her mother often hadn't seen eye-to-eye. She and her father barely knew each other.

'Well?' Maxis was still looking at her. 'When did Strange Ground become so impotent in dealing with its own troubles? Why does Yandira Wood Bee's threat warrant Dalmyn's intervention?'

Kingfisher turned to face the immobile gulls in their cage, the message from Dragonfly burning a hole in her mind. 'Highness, rest assured the search for your daughter continues along its own path. You and your brave soldiers are here to help me secure Ghador's queendom before Yandira leads us to war.'

'*War?*' Maxis chuckled as though he spoke to an old fool. 'Between Dalmyn and Strange Ground? What nonsense is this, Genevieve?'

'Strange Ground, Dalmyn, every city in the Realm – make no mistake, Highness, we are all under threat. I know it to be true, and so does your mother.' Kingfisher turned from the gulls and gave the prince a sobering look. 'Yandira has made a terrible pact and the foul sorceries at her command cannot be underestimated. I will counsel you further, but first we must—'

She was interrupted by a horse approaching at a gallop along the road. Soldiers watched with interest as the rider, wearing dark blue robes, reined up beside the wagon and pulled down a hood to reveal the shaven head and deep brown eyes of Seej Agda.

'Highness,' she said, face as deathly serious as her tone. The horse snorted, its flanks heaving for breath. 'You must order your soldiers to break camp.'

'Calm yourself, priest,' Maxis growled. 'We have not long stopped to rest, and you will remember to whom you are talking—'

'I was right!' Seej was flustered and spoke as though to a petulant child. 'Dark magic is abroad that I cannot yet explain. We are not safe in this place. You *must* signal departure.'

The High Priests of Juno did not make demands of royalty without good reason. Though Kingfisher was encouraged to see she might have an ally against the prince's pomp and bluster, the priest's words and manner stirred her anxiety. Maxis evidently felt the same as he relaxed his pride and said, 'Very well, Mother Seej,' albeit reluctantly.

Seej reined the horse around and looked back at Kingfisher. 'We will talk more on the road, my Lady.' And she departed as abruptly as she had arrived, riding through the soldiers, barking out the order to break camp for her prince.

Maxis watched after her with a scowl. 'Dark magic,' he grumbled. 'You mentioned Yandira's sorceries, Lady Kingfisher?'

'Indeed. Might you spare me a rider, Highness?' She glanced at the gulls in their cage. 'The situation worsens by the moment and it is imperative we send word to your mother.'

Beneath Backway Charlie's was a network of tunnels which offered a number of alternate routes out of the city for those in need of a hasty and secret escape. The warrens, Bek called them, saying she knew the tunnels like the back of her hand,

and Ebbie believed it as she jogged purposefully ahead, turning left and right, leading the way under torchlight.

'Who are Lunk and Venatus?' Ebbie said, struggling to keep up.

'Bad people.' Bek sounded angry with him.

'I-I think they killed someone to get to me.'

'Sounds like the sort of thing they'd do.' Bek swore. 'Haven't seen them around for years and I thought they were dead. It helped me sleep better at night.'

'Why are they after me?'

'If you haven't worked that out by now then you're in deeper shit than you realise.'

'Bek, tell me.'

'Later,' she snapped. 'If our luck is holding then Lunk and Venatus didn't see you and Charlie threw them off your scent. Now, come on!'

The torch flame growled above Bek's head as she cut a quick right at an intersection. Firelight danced over hard dirt walls and thick support beams. Reminiscent of mineshafts, the tunnels must have been years in the digging. Bek took more twists and turns than Ebbie could count, but he asked no more questions, following in silence for quite some time before a fresh breeze blew in from ahead. The path rose to an opening covered in shrubbery. Beyond that, they walked into thick woodland.

Evening was heading into night. An animal crashed through the undergrowth, startled away by the sudden glare of Bek's torch. Trees were tall and looming all around. Ebbie bent, placing his hands on his knees while catching his breath.

'They would have caught up with us by now if they were following.' Breathing hard as well, Bek looked exhausted, like she had been too long without sleep, too tired to remain angry. 'Good old Charlie. We should be safe for a while.'

Ebbie peered up through a canvas of leaves. In a darkening sky, rippling water filtered the glow of the setting sun. 'Where are we?'

'Watcher's Forest, west side of Strange Ground.'

'I'm scared, Bek.'

She nodded, agreeing, and adjusted the straps on the rucksack. 'We can't stay this close to the city for long, but we need to talk so let's find a good spot to catch our breath.'

They crept through the trees and soon reached a clearing next to a narrow stream. A fire pit had already been dug, lined with blackened stones. Ebbie helped to collect firewood before sitting on a fallen log, clutching the satchel, nausea churning his stomach. Lost and frightened, he watched as Bek lit the pile of wood with the torch. The flames rose quickly. She pulled a small black iron kettle from the rucksack in agitated fashion; she whispered a curse as she filled it from the stream and then set it to boil.

Delving into the rucksack again, this time producing two tin cups, Bek crouched beside the flames and broke the ominous silence. 'Queen Maitressa disappeared, Ebbie, must be ... ten years ago now, so how did you get your hands on her House sigil?'

'She gave it to me.'

'Right. Because you were friends.' From a wax paper packet, Bek tipped crushed leaves into the cups. 'You'll understand if I'm struggling to believe you.'

Something in her voice set Ebbie on edge, something dangerous. 'It's true,' he said. 'I didn't know she was a queen. She came to live in my town, Bek. She was homeless, had nothing and no one. She lived on the streets.'

'What town?' By this time the kettle was boiling. 'Where do you come from?'

'Strange Ground.' Ebbie swallowed. '*By* the Skea.'

'Catshit.' With a sour chuckle, Bek pointed up at the sky. 'You really expect me to believe you crossed the Skea?'

'I'm not lying.'

Bek poured steaming water into the cups then carried them over to Ebbie and stood in front of him, limned by firelight. 'Nobody has found a Janus Bridge for centuries.'

'Well ... Mai gave me this.' Ebbie showed her the cream and green ring that wouldn't come off his wedding finger. 'I don't know how this thing works, but somehow it brought me here.'

Bek stared at the ring while shadows danced between the trees and a night bird hooted in the distance. 'Drink this,' she said, passing him a cup.

Ebbie wrapped his hands around it and took a sip. To his surprise, it was tea. He took a second sip, and a third, and the heat settled the anxiety churning his stomach, though the tea itself carried an odd aftertaste.

Bek drank her own. 'Let me get your story straight. Queen Maitressa crossed the Skea to the other side of Strange Ground where she lived as a simple vagabond called Mai, and that's where she died?'

'Yes, of old age.'

'Old age, uh-huh.' Bek's expression was unreadable but her voice was low with warning. 'She makes preparations for an earthling to be the executor of her will, and after she dies he's sent to the Realm to find her granddaughter – am I getting this right?'

'Spot on.'

'Do you have any idea who her granddaughter is?'

'Mai said her name is Ghador, but ...' Ebbie paused mid-sip and started. 'Is she some kind of princess?'

'Oh, she's certainly that all right. Ghador is heir to the

Queendom of Strange Ground beneath the Skea. Now, I don't know what that means to you, but Mr Lunk and Mr Venatus are working for the most dangerous person in the city. She wants the queendom for herself. Her name is Yandira, and *she* is Maitressa's daughter.'

Ebbie frowned and drank more tea.

'Don't you get it?' Bek's expression was pained. 'If Lunk and Venatus are after you, then Yandira knows you're here and what you're doing. She's already killed Queen Eldrid – her own *sister* – and by the sounds of it she got to her mother, too.'

'What?'

'I'm sorry to tell you, but I very much doubt your friend died of old age.'

'You think Mai was murdered?'

'I think you should be more frightened than you've ever been.' Bek swigged from her cup and then chucked the dregs on the ground. 'Time to go. Finish your drink.'

Ebbie stared at her as she walked back to the fire. He drained his cup, spat out a few errant tea leaves and shook his head. 'This is mad.'

'You're telling me,' Bek muttered. The fire hissed and died as she emptied the kettle onto it and shoved it back into the rucksack. 'I only pray that Lunk and Venatus don't know I'm with you, otherwise there's no safe place for me.'

Her statement carried an inflection, almost apologetic like a farewell. And strangely, her voice had lowered in tone, slow and deep, while her face rippled like the glow of the moon.

'Wait,' said Ebbie, rubbing his eyes. 'What ... what do you ... mean?'

He struggled to get his words past a sudden fog in his thoughts. What had Bek just said? He smacked his lips. The odd aftertaste of the tea had become so bitter it was drying the inside of his mouth, sticking his tongue to his teeth.

'I-I don't feel ... right,' he said thickly.

The dark forest was moving, tilting sideways. Colours blurred and swirled in the gloom. Ebbie dropped the tin cup and grabbed the log to stop himself falling off.

'I won't be dragged into this,' Bek said from somewhere distant. 'I'm sorry, but you're on your own.'

Ebbie slid from the log, unconscious before he hit the leafy ground. But the ground didn't stop him falling ...

14

The Last Empress

They say that in the Realm, the sea is in the sky ...

Down and down Ebbie Wren tumbled, through the pages of books flapping like gusting wind, alive with words coloured by every shade of emotion. And then he was falling no more but standing in a forest that he somehow knew he had once read about in a story.

A dense and dark setting, full of secrets and dangers, the name of the forest escaped him, but he recalled that it had an old heart and was so vast it took a band of questors three months to cross from one side to the other. He remembered how many of those characters had died in the story, and terror gripped him as he realised he was now one of them, lost and alone in the old heart of a forbidden place where he wasn't welcome.

Wolves were calling. Their howls rose in a wild hunt for the earthling who had dared to trespass on their territory. *I had no choice*, Ebbie wanted to tell them. *I was abandoned here!* But the wolves cared nothing for that and their howling grew louder, drew nearer. Hiding would not fool them, fleeing would only work if Ebbie knew where he was heading ... *There!* Like a blessed ray of hope, blue light shone liquidly through the trees from a short distance away. It beckoned with the warmth of safety, and Ebbie ran for its sanctuary.

But the forest was no friend to him. Branches scratched at his face, roots tripped him, walls of undergrowth rose to block his path. Whichever way he turned, Ebbie could not reach the source of the blue light, and he began to hear maniacal laughter in the voices of the hungry beasts closing in on him. The sound of their speeding feet could be heard now, crashing through the trees. With a yell of desperation, Ebbie launched himself at the undergrowth, caring nothing for the thorns that tore at him, the vines that strangled him as he begged the forest to relent.

And mercifully, it did.

The undergrowth opened a gap, a sliver of salvation, and Ebbie seized the chance, slipping through to the other side where he arrived at a trail, a clear path running straight between the trees, all the way to the sanctuary of liquid blue. He pumped his legs with all the strength remaining to him, praying for death to the wolves who would not be deterred from the chase. But halfway down the trail, a tree twisted its trunk like it was scything wheat and spun one of its branches into Ebbie's midriff. Air whooshed from his mouth as he was propelled backwards and landed hard on his back.

Gasping for breath, Ebbie struggled onto his hands and knees, dismayed to see the wild hunt in sight. A pack of wolves was creeping down the trail towards him. Teeth bared, hungry eyes glowing, their growls seemed to be discussing what terrible things they might do to their prey.

'No,' Ebbie groaned. He had not the strength left to push himself to his feet let alone run. He closed his eyes, accepting his fate, and that was when he felt a tug on his leg.

Before he could react, Ebbie was face down on the leafy ground being dragged backwards. He managed to glimpse a tentacle of blue light coiled around his ankle before his attention was shocked away by many voices unified in a single, mighty howl. Seeing their prey escaping, the wolves bounded forwards. Ebbie screamed and his fingers clawed little trenches in the forest floor.

His scream died as warm blue flowed over his body, his straggling arms and fingers, and formed a wall between him and the grisly predators. Fluid as water, wispy as clouds, the wall sparked when the wolves nosed at it and they skipped back yelping.

With a surge of strength, Ebbie jumped to his feet, heart pounding in his chest. Beyond the blue, the beasts prowled and paced the trail, but they dared not approach the shimmering wall again and soon departed, no doubt to search for another path to their prey. They wouldn't find one. The wispy, watery wall flowed all around, between tree trunks, overhead through a leafy canopy, to cocoon a clearing at the end of the trail, a clearing in which a single person waited for Ebbie Wren.

'Mai!'

She was smiling at him, albeit sadly, sitting in the clearing like she used to in her nook on the high street: legs crossed, back straight, hands clasped in her lap. She wore her dark dress, her hair long and straight, her eyes as green and bright as a cat's.

'I wouldn't blame you at all if you're feeling angry with me,' she said.

Ebbie's mouth hung open.

'Come and sit,' Mai urged. 'The wolves can't reach us here.'

Ebbie took a few tentative steps towards her. 'But you're dead.'

'Yes, murdered on the orders of my daughter.' On the ground before Mai was a china teapot and two matching bowls. 'Come, let's talk like we used to.'

Ebbie sat on the leafy ground, facing her. 'Am I dreaming?'

'You must be. This can't possibly be real. Can it?'

Mai stirred the contents of the teapot. The sweet aroma of

hot chocolate reached Ebbie's nostrils. Comforting, familiar, it induced rich memories of a more comprehensible time. No, this couldn't be real, yet he felt as though nothing had ever been more so.

'Tell me,' Mai said. 'How are you getting along with Miss Rana?'

'Bek!' Ebbie had almost forgotten about her, but he remembered now with a touch of despair. 'She's gone. I think she drugged me. She left me on my own ...'

He trailed off as Mai actually had the audacity to laugh at his situation.

'I did warn you that she wouldn't be easily convinced. You must forgive Bek her nature. She's the product of a harsh life, as are many in Strange Ground's underbelly.' Mai narrowed her eyes when she noticed the anger flushing Ebbie's cheeks. 'Perhaps you'd prefer not to talk about her?'

'This isn't funny,' he said. 'You sent me to the Realm.'

'Magnificent, isn't it?' Her eyes sparkled as though she had bestowed a great gift. 'I only wish I could have shown you my home personally.'

'People are dying, Mai. There was a woman. She was looking after your body.' Ebbie paused as tears filled his eyes. 'Lunk and Venatus murdered her so they could find me—'

'Stop!' Mai said, all signs of enjoyment banished. 'I know Mr Lunk and Mr Venatus all too well, Ebbie Wren, and I can see where your darker thoughts are leading you. But listen to me, now.' She lifted the teapot and filled the bowls with hot chocolate. 'It is not your fault that my daughter and her henchmen are murderous cravens. I burdened you with this quest without asking for your consent, and I would do so again. If innocent blood has been spilled along the way then it is on *my* hands, not yours.'

Her words did little to make Ebbie feel better. Mai offered him one of the bowls. He accepted it but didn't drink, keeping his eyes on his friend's familiar face.

'Let me ask you a question,' she said. 'If I had told you that my granddaughter was the rightful heir to Strange Ground beneath the Skea, that I was sending you into danger to save a queendom and prevent Ghador from becoming another of Yandira's victims, would you have said *yes* or *no* to this quest?'

Ebbie's silence pleased Mai and she gestured at the bowl in his hands. 'Drink, before it gets cold.'

He sipped hot chocolate. Its warming flavour dampened his anger, his fear, and he accepted that this dream of blue light was a fragile moment of respite where he was safe from wolves and assassins, though it made the reality to which he had to return eventually all the more difficult to anticipate.

'You chose the wrong person, Mai. How can I help your granddaughter? I'm a librarian.'

Even as the words left his mouth, Ebbie heard how ludicrous, pointless, they sounded and spoke again before Mai could reply.

'You're not real,' he told her. 'These people, these events – you only know about them because this is my dream. You're repeating what Bek already told me.'

'Oh, Ebbie.' Mai looked saddened, almost ashamed. 'You've experienced too much too quickly, but you must accept a daunting truth. Yandira has been made promises by a vile power, and should she add my granddaughter to her list of victims, then she will have free rein to wreak her terrible ambition upon the Realm.'

'I can't do this, Mai.'

'Whether you would choose it or not, Ebbie Wren, you have been given a role in a pact I made with my Oldunone years ago.'

'You're not making sense. None of this makes sense.' Ebbie stared into his now-empty bowl. 'I just want to go home.'

'*Home* is the hardest place to leave and the easiest to miss, especially when you are feeling lost and alone.' Mai closed her eyes to savour the taste of hot chocolate. 'Therefore, I have a story, if you'd like a distraction from your homesickness.'

'A story? *Now?*'

'Why not? It's the perfect time, for its telling will help you understand what you are embroiled in.'

A wistful smile came to Ebbie's face. Maybe it was simply because he was hearing Mai's voice again that the offer felt like a moment of perfect magic in a bad situation. This was just a dream. 'Yeah. Tell me a story, Mai. Like old times.'

'*Old times* is a rather apt phrase,' Mai said as she offered the teapot and refilled Ebbie's bowl. 'For my tale is of a time *so* old that any mortal who witnessed its events crumbled into the dust of history long ago.'

Ebbie cupped the bowl in his hands and his eyelids suddenly felt heavy. He wondered if it was possible to fall asleep inside a dream.

Mai said, 'It was an era when the Queendoms and Kingdoms of the Realm were ruled by an Empress who oversaw all the lands beneath the Skea from her grand throne in Imperium City. She was wise and just, and the folk gave her unquestioning love and fealty. But tragically her rule heralded a war which ended the reign of the Imperium for good.'

Maybe *all* of this was a dream and Ebbie would wake up back at home to discover nothing bad had happened. Would Mai be alive, waiting in her nook? Would the library still be open?

'Hold on.' He perked up. 'The folk don't have an Empress any more?'

'Indeed not.'

'I never read about that, and I've read just about everything that's been written about the Realm. You've always had an Empress—'

'Who is telling this story, Ebbie? Me or your history books which have gleaned no fresh information for century upon century? Try listening and maybe you'll learn something astounding.'

'Sorry,' Ebbie said, smiling again. 'Carry on.'

Mai cleared her throat. 'While the Empress of my story was wise and kind, her daughter was intolerant, cruel as a winter storm. And in this, I must confess to sharing a degree of empathy with her mother.

'Even back then, the Priests of Juno were keepers of the strong traditions which decided who sat upon a throne. But unlike the queendoms of today, the Imperium of the Realm did not follow a line of succession, there was no heir of which to speak. The priests themselves judged which candidate from the Royal Houses best suited the position, based on worthiness alone, and they could not be curried for favour. The Empress's daughter was not high on their list, and this did not sit well with her.

'Bellona was her name. And as she watched her mother grow old and frail over the years, she came to realise with despairing clarity that her time in Imperium City was coming to an end, yet she was not prepared to relinquish the privileges to which she had grown accustomed. Therefore, in a fit of envy and desperation, Bellona murdered her mother and seized the Imperial Throne.'

Mai placed her bowl down beside the teapot, the hot chocolate unfinished, her face becoming a mask of stone. 'You see, Bellona needed a sacrifice for the darkest of domains. The blood of an Empress, the blood of her blood – a forbidden offering but the grand price to pay in the pact she had made with Cursed Persephone.'

'I know that name,' Ebbie said. 'Oldunone of the Underworld.'

'And a black-hearted trickster.'

'Yeah, I've read the stories about Her.' More than that, at college Ebbie had written an essay about Persephone's influence on the folk's culture and beliefs, which was to say a *bad* influence.

Mai continued, 'Cursed Persephone ordered Bellona to bathe the land in the Underworld's glory. In return, Persephone would reward Her disciple with divine magic and dangerous allies, all the power Bellona would need to secure the Imperial Throne by force.

'But Bellona didn't truly understand for what she was asking. You know as well as I that the Oldunfolk are fickle creatures, Ebbie, easily amused by mortals, and it indeed amused Persephone to reward this Imperial sacrifice. Bellona received all that she craved, but with it came a terrible transformation. Iron-hard scales covered her skin; her tongue became forked, her fingernails like claws. Leathery wings burst from her back and a bestial fire raged in her gut. Persephone had kissed Bellona's soul with the spirit of a dragon. Powerful, merciless, bestial, Bellona secured her empire by waging war across the Realm.

'The queendoms and kingdoms were enraged and banded together to end this sickening madness, but their united efforts to stand against Bellona were in vain. Not only had their enemy called down the wild things from the hills – wolves and monsters to fight in her name – she also commanded the Serpent's Sigh, the foul breath and essence of Persephone's dragon horde. This dire magic was sent onto the first battlefields as a choking fog. Armies stood and fell against it, in spirit as well as body. It altered their perceptions, subverted their nature, subjugated their allegiance in favour of the Underworld. Bellona's army grew stronger, but it was not enough. The Serpent's Sigh produced mindless drones. True dominance could only come if allegiance was given with free will, even if Bellona had to break the Realm to get it.

'And that was when the earthlings came.

'You see, Earth had empires of its own, and Persephone knew the most powerful of them had long desired to include the Realm among its *many* territories. Fortunately for the folk, Lady Janus had never allowed their armies to use Her Bridges to enact their desires of invasion. Unfortunately, Persephone was amused enough to honour Her promise of allies by opening the gates of the Underworld. Legions of earthling soldiers She brought to Bellona's side, tens of thousands of battle-hardened warriors, eager to invade. City after city fell to a force of monstrous size. In hopelessness and desperation, House after House offered Bellona fealty if she would only spare them. In less than a year of war, the new Empire covered more than half the Realm, and all seemed lost.'

Mai looked up at the ceiling of blue light, a fierce pride filling her eyes. 'Yet Lady Juno was watching, from Her High Throne in Elysium. She saw the game Cursed Persephone was playing and decided to enter a champion of Her own. She chose a hero from among the folk, one with the strength to stand against Bellona's madness: Queen Minerva Wood Bee, the first of her House to wear the crown of Strange Ground beneath the Skea. Her faith remained unwavering when all others had lost theirs.

'Juno came to Minerva. She took the crown of Strange Ground and removed its majestic stones, Foresight and Hindsight. She blessed them with divine protections and then set them into a weapon forged by Her own hand. This weapon Juno bequeathed to Minerva. A blade which never dulled, inscribed with magic written in the divine language of Oldunspeak, and its purpose was to destroy darkness wherever it poisoned mortal light.

'Meanwhile, Bellona had grown troubled. As her Empire spread, her power waned, even with the daily blood sacrifices she made to her Oldunone. Her terrible appearance no longer inspired fear in her earthling soldiers, and they began to act as though she would be subservient to them in the end rather than the other way around. Yes, Bellona was gravely troubled when the last free Houses massed on the fields of Imperium City for the final stand against her.

'It was on those fields that Queen Minerva appeared, wielding Juno's blade like a beacon of hope. With the divine magic imbued into Foresight and Hindsight, she blessed her army with a shield against evil and led the charge into the final battle. Minerva cleaved darkness left and right. Monsters and wolves fled from her onslaught, the Serpent's Sigh recoiled from her path. And while the folk engaged the earthling army, Minerva at last came face to face with the Evil Pretender, the False Empress, Bane of the Realm.

'Bellona dug deep into her reserves of magic, casting the wildest spells she had learned, but she could not best her foe's defences. Minerva, fuelled by the strength of divine blessings, did not tire or relent, and soon Bellona crippled her own wings, broke her own claws and exhausted her own power. In despair, she prayed to Cursed Persephone, begging for more.'

Mai leaned forwards with a smirk. 'The Oldunfolk are ever fickle creatures, Ebbie. Perhaps Persephone had simply grown bored with this game, perhaps She could not best the might of Juno, but no amount of blood sacrifice could encourage an answer to Her disciple's plea. In Bellona's greatest moment of need, the Underworld abandoned her. Weakness set deep and the dragon's fire cooled in her gut. She could not prevent

Minerva from sinking the divine blade through her scaly skin and into her heart.'

Mai clapped her hands sharply and Ebbie flinched, spilling chocolate over his hands. Mai's green gaze was intense, her voice full of mystery.

'Some say that while Bellona's body remained as a boneless sack on the battlefield, her soul drained away as venomous black oil that seeped down into the foulest regions of the Underworld to fill Persephone's mead cup. With Bellona's tyranny ended and the earthling army vanquished, the Houses rejoiced, and the Priests of Juno decreed Minerva Wood Bee saviour of all and the Realm's new Empress.

'But Minerva did not want this.

'They had been through too much, the land had suffered too greatly, and Minerva would not allow this to happen again. With Foresight, her first and last act as Empress was to abolish the Empire for good, because Hindsight taught them that no single person should ever hold the corrupting power to dominate the Realm. And to this end, Minerva bestowed upon every queen and king the title of Protector. Together, in harmony, let them all be the keepers of peace and just traditions.'

Mai bowed her head. 'As for the earthlings, whose greed and lust for domination had grown to match Bellona's own ... well, not one of them made it home, and their actions convinced Lady Janus to hide Her divine bridges, thus the two worlds were forever separated.' She waited as Ebbie took a moment to absorb that last part. 'Didn't I say you'd learn something astounding?'

Ebbie snorted an uncertain laugh. 'This isn't true.'

'Of course not,' Mai said, 'you're only dreaming,' while her smile suggested otherwise.

'The Janus Bridges vanished because of this war, an event which has no documented record whatsoever, anywhere?'

'You can only say that's true on Earth.'

'Okay, right.'

'Ask around, if you don't believe me.'

'It's a good story, Mai.'

'Think as you will, but you *are* living this tale's aftermath.' Mai looked around the clearing bathed in blue light and a weight seemed to descend on her shoulders. 'I tried so very hard to stop Yandira finding me. I thought I could watch her prison from a distance, inhibit her actions without anyone else in the Realm suffering, and in this I failed in my duties as a Protector. Dream or not, Bellona's ambition is a source of inspiration to my daughter, Ebbie, and she has made a pact of her own. The Realm needs its Minerva more than ever.'

'Your granddaughter?'

'I've asked you to find Ghador because she cannot stop this madness alone. Yandira has reached the point of no return. Should she claim the crown of Strange Ground, her ambitions will spread like fire in a bone-dry forest, and Ghador is the only one who can bring the cooling rains. Such is the nature of this game.

'I see in you what you refuse to see yourself, Ebbie.' Mai got to her feet and stretched her back. Blue light cast shadows on her face as she stared down at him. 'So I ask – will you help my granddaughter or search for a way home?'

Ebbie looked at the ring on his finger, cream and green and irremovable, and he knew that she already had her answer. 'I'm lost, Mai. Bek left me stranded in the middle of a forest. I don't know how to get a True Sight Candle on my own.'

'Don't give up on Miss Rana just yet.' Amused again, Mai turned her back and approached the wall of watery blue wisps. 'She is a slippery eel, though not quite as hard to catch as she believes.' She laid her hands upon the light and immediately it began to dim. 'The quest stretches before you both, and it will be a hard road. I will watch over you as best I can, but for now I would advise finding a magician's help.'

The light was darkening at an alarming rate and Ebbie jumped to his feet. 'No, don't leave me—'

Mai disappeared as the magical wall blinked out completely and steeped Ebbie in utter blackness. 'Mai,' he called, but the only answer he received was a shock of cold water splashing his face ...

Old friend – that was the term Lady Kingfisher and Lord Dragonfly had used when referring to a mysterious absentee during their secret meeting at Kingfisher Manor. *Of course* they had been talking about Maitressa Wood Bee – Bek just hadn't needed to acknowledge it until now. She had been thrust into a living nightmare and she wouldn't stick around to see how it ended. But once again, fate had other plans for her.

The first time she tried to escape, she cursed a bad sense of direction as she somehow led herself through the darkening forest in a circle to arrive back at the small clearing. The second time, she couldn't quite believe she'd done the same thing again. On the third she grew angry with herself, but on the fourth and fifth she began to panic with the realisation that something was terribly amiss.

It didn't seem to matter in which direction Bek headed, however much of a straight line she damn well knew she was walking in, she always returned to where Ebbie was sleeping off the opiates she had slipped into his tea. After an hour of trying to get away from this supposed earthling, she finally gave up and spat her repertoire of curses into the night that now shrouded Watcher's Forest.

The fire pit was filled with damp ashes. Bright moonlight

shone down into the clearing. Ebbie sat where Bek had propped him up against the fallen tree. His face twitched while he huffed and whispered in the grip of dreams. His arms were wrapped around his precious satchel, and that bloody thing was yet another source of frustration. It was enchanted. Bek had tried to steal the coin-purse it held, but as soon as she opened the satchel, its contents disappeared. She had searched inside, but there was no mistaking its emptiness, so she had to slip away penniless. But now, the satchel was bulky again with returned items as though the enchantment was mocking her.

Bek felt no guilt over trying to abandon Ebbie Wren. She thought she might play along until he paid their wagon fare to another city before ditching him, and she hadn't given any serious thought to finding a True Sight Candle. But now Ebbie had proved himself to be a wagonload of trouble, and the less Bek knew about his plans the better. So she had decided to leave Strange Ground on foot, right away, no looking back. There was some distance to cover between here and the nearest towns and cities, not to mention some pretty dangerous roads full of bandits and wild things, but better to risk them than hang around for Lunk and Venatus to catch up with her; better to take her chances over open ground than fall foul of Yandira Wood Bee.

Someone, somewhere, would buy the sword, but evidently, Bek was stuck in Watcher's Forest, and there was a reason for that.

She considered punching Ebbie awake, but then filled a tin cup from the stream and stood over him. 'Wake up,' she growled and threw the water in his face.

Ebbie coughed and spluttered, rubbing his eyes. Bek skipped back when he looked straight at her and shouted, 'Bloody hell! I'm in the Realm!'

With an angry noise, Bek jabbed a finger at him. 'You've got a lot to answer for, you bastard.'

'What?' Bleary-eyed, Ebbie wiped water from his face and took in the dark trees around them. 'Wait a minute,' he said, his sluggish thoughts evidently catching up with the situation. 'Did you drug me?'

'Shut up.' Bek held out a hand. 'Show me our contract.'

'Why?'

'Just do it, Ebbie.'

With a frown, he opened the satchel and pulled the contract out. Bek snatched it from him and unfolded it angrily. She held it up to the moonlight, scrutinised every word of the page before turning her attention to the top right corner. Her grip on the paper tightened and her shoulders sagged.

'There's a royal watermark on this contract.' It was an accusation.

'Yes, I know.' Ebbie was rubbing the back of his head, looking groggy. 'If you stare at it long enough, it starts moving.'

'That's because it's a spell.'

Ebbie froze. 'Really?'

'Yes, *really*! It enforces the signee's obligation.' Bek threw the contract back at him. 'All night I've been trying to get away from you, and now I know why I can't.'

Ebbie looked offended, upset. 'We had an agreement. Why did you renege on it?'

'Why do you think?' Bek seethed. 'It doesn't matter anyway, because I can't leave you until I fulfil my obligation to that contract ... or if my *employer* dies. And I'll be honest with you, Ebbie, I'm seriously thinking about running you through with my sword.'

Ebbie recoiled then narrowed his eyes shrewdly. 'No you're not.'

'Well, it's no less than you deserve. The spell in that water-mark is a trap, a magical bind, and *you* tricked me into putting my thumbprint on it.'

'Bek, I didn't know.' Ebbie was looking the contract over. 'Didn't you check what you were signing first?'

'I was locked in a jail cell!' Bek shouted. 'I would've signed anything to get out. I didn't expect to end up bound to you.'

Ebbie folded the contract and slipped it back into his satchel before standing up and stamping his feet against the night's chill. He grinned as though remembering something. 'Some eels are easier to catch than they believe, eh?'

'What's that supposed to mean?'

'I forgive you, Bek.'

Taken aback, she watched open-mouthed as Ebbie looped the satchel strap over his head and walked to a tree to relieve himself.

'You want to run that by me again?'

'I forgive you.' Ebbie looked at her over his shoulder. 'I forgive you for stealing my money. I forgive you for lying when you said you'd help. For welching on our contract and trying to ditch me when you know I'm lost and clueless, I forgive you, Bek – though I actually don't mind that you spiked my tea. I feel quite fresh and clear-headed now.'

'Oh well, then, I'm very happy for you.' Bek's tone was shot through with simmering anger, which she wasn't of a mind to take off the boil, especially when Ebbie dared to chuckle.

He finished watering the tree and gazed around at the forest, breathing in the heady, earthy air, smiling at his surroundings as though he was ... *happy*?

'I also want to thank you,' he said, 'for saving my life and leading me to a safe place. Thank you for coming back, even if you had no choice.'

Bek clenched her teeth, preparing to spit a curse at this earthling, but Ebbie stopped her with a raised hand as he came to stand on the opposite side of the fire pit.

'Most of all, I want to apologise. If I'd known what the contract was, I would've warned you but still begged you to sign it. I'm sorry, but I'm glad we're stuck together. I can't do this on my own.'

On hearing this, Bek reasoned there should have been steam coming out of her ears. 'I wouldn't be so quick to feel *glad*, if I were you.'

'Bek, I was born confused and awkward, and I've never had any friends, apart from Mai. Being a librarian was all I knew, all I wanted. She was the only person in my world or yours who made me feel important. But she was taken from me and so was my library. I lost everything that made me believe I was worthwhile, and now I'm here.'

Sympathy? This idiot thought he deserved her sympathy? 'Do you have any idea how much trouble your *friend* has landed us in?'

Ebbie pursed his lips. 'I know this much – Mai was a queen to you, but to me she was a dear, sweet person, kind and honest, and her dying wish was for me to find her granddaughter. And I'm going to find her, Bek, because it's the right thing to do. So, I'll make you a promise. Once I have the True Sight Candle, I'll rip up the contract and you can be shot of me for good. Just help me get that far. What do you say?'

Bek stared long and hard at the hand Ebbie offered over the fire pit. 'I could still run you through,' she said.

Ebbie grinned. 'Yeah, but you won't.'

'Fine.' Bek grabbed his hand and gave it one stiff pump. 'Let's find your stupid candle before Lunk and Venatus see me with you.'

On the blood-smeared floor of Jester's Tavern, amidst the wreckage of smashed glass, broken chairs and upturned tables, a sliver of magic flickered into being and crawled among five corpses. It searched for the body with the fewest broken bones and found one: a man whose name and life were of little consequence, whose neck had been shredded to the arteries and one arm dislocated from its socket. The corpse stirred, rose awkwardly to its feet, and Yandira Wood Bee gazed through the eyes of a dead man to look upon the red-spattered visions of Mr Lunk and Mr Venatus.

'I told you to hunt for the earthling,' she said, her voice deep and coarse from an unfamiliar mouth, 'and yet I find you festering in this rat pit instead. Why?'

'Ebbie Wren was here, Majesty,' Mr Venatus said quickly.

'*Was* here?'

'Oh yes.'

Surrounded by carnage they had undoubtedly caused, the wolfish pair shared a look, clearly proud of some imagined achievement. Yandira's weakness was growing and using this possession spell was only worsening her fatigue.

Between her servants, a portly man with wide, fearful eyes had been tied to a chair, a rag stuffed into his mouth. His face was beaten, bloody and swollen, and splinters of wood had been pushed beneath his fingernails.

'My revulsion is at a premium,' the corpse growled, and the pride slid from her servants' faces like melting wax. 'I do not enjoy wasting power to inhabit a sack of meat whose last act in life was to soil himself, evidently. So explain what happened in this place, and do so quickly.'

'Charlie here started a fight, Majesty.' The man in the chair winced as Mr Venatus smacked a hairy hand down on his shoulder. 'Whipped the whole place up into a frenzy. He did it on purpose. To distract *us* while Ebbie Wren slipped out.'

And it was a clever distraction technique. As wolves, Lunk and Venatus were impressively stealthy assassins; but as folk they did so enjoy answering the call of a good fight. This collaboration of souls made them brutally efficient and, at times, maddeningly distracted, as evidenced by the wreckage and corpses left in the wake of what must have been a very rowdy bar brawl.

'Mr Venatus, I'm assuming there's a reason why you have delayed your hunt for the earthling?'

'Information,' he said, gesturing the bodies on the floor. 'We questioned some of the locals. They didn't know anything, but Charlie here knew plenty.'

Mr Lunk nodded with an unintelligible growl and Mr Venatus continued, 'You won't believe this, Majesty, but Ebbie Wren's not alone.' He looked excited. 'He's running with Bek Rana.'

'Bek Rana?' The man tied to the chair whimpered as the walking corpse took a few shuffling steps towards him. 'I *do* find that difficult to believe, Mr Venatus. Are you quite certain?'

'There's nothing Charlie knows that he wouldn't tell us, Majesty. She's definitely with Wren.'

Bek Rana. Not a name Yandira ever expected to hear again. She would have thought – or maybe *hoped* – that Rana would be dead by now. How very curious that she should resurface at this precise moment.

'That's not all, Majesty.' Mr Venatus's grin split his beard with a line of discoloured and pointed teeth. 'Looks like we know where your sword is, too.'

From surprise and tiredness, the corpse staggered, setting its dislocated arm swinging. 'Explain yourself.'

'By the sound of things, your mother didn't take the sword to Earth like you thought. It was here in Strange Ground all the time. Charlie says that Rana stole it from a noble's manor. He doesn't know which House, but he says the sword had a blade of blue stone.'

'You are sure? There was writing upon it?'

'In a language no one could understand.'

The corpse shuffled closer to Charlie, crunching broken glass underfoot. 'Did he happen mention what Rana intends to do with the sword?'

'Sell it, by all accounts, Majesty. I don't think she knows what she's got her hands on.'

Unlikely, not while she was in cahoots with Maitressa's earthling lackey. No, Rana's involvement was far more than simple coincidence, and this gave Yandira an insight into her mother's plans.

'Get after them,' she ordered Lunk and Venatus. 'They know where Ghador is hiding.'

'Do you still want Wren kept alive, Majesty?'

'No. Find my niece then kill them all. And bring me my sword.'

Lunk and Venatus barely remembered to bow in their eagerness to rejoin the hunt. They headed for the tavern's main door but Yandira stopped them by having the corpse clear its throat. 'What are you doing, gentleman?'

After sharing a confused look with his companion, Mr Venatus said, 'Pardon me, Majesty, but didn't you say—'

'Did you spend so long away from Strange Ground that you forgot all detail of the city's underbelly?' The dead man's left foot was dragging, smearing a pool of blood as he came to loom over the man in the chair. 'Perchance you can recall that Jester's Tavern is also known as Backway Charlie's?'

Another confused look was shared, during which Mr Lunk shrugged and Mr Venatus screwed up his face. 'Majesty?'

'There's a secret way out in the cellar, you cretins!' Yandira bellowed. 'Your prey escaped through the warrens.'

Venatus slapped Lunk's arm and the wolfish pair ran behind the bar and disappeared into the back of the tavern. The sound of their heavy feet could be heard thudding down wooden stairs.

Yandira turned her attention to Charlie. It physically pained her now to keep possession of this body. Persephone's displeasure was growing inside her. Perhaps consulting her old books of forbidden lore would reveal a way to hold off the weakness until she appeased her Oldunone.

Charlie moaned. He expressed terror as the corpse reached out with bent fingers to pull the rag from his mouth.

'Mercy,' he gasped. 'For the love of the Oldunfolk, mercy!'

'There is little mercy to be found in the spirits of dragons.' Charlie's struggles were in vain as Yandira grabbed what remained of his hair and yanked his head back. 'I bestow to you the Serpent's Sigh, to share with your customers, for them to share with their families, their friends.'

Yandira planted the corpse's lips on Charlie's, muffling his scream of fear and revulsion with a deathly kiss. She pulled away, but a dark line of smoky drool remained between them. When it dropped from the corpse's bottom lip, it slithered into Charlie's mouth. He coughed, gagged, before his panic eased while his eyes darkened and his face fell lax.

'The Empress calls her people to arms,' said Yandira. 'We must prepare for war.'

The corpse collapsed onto Charlie as Yandira relinquished control and returned to the weakness haunting her own body.

*

Ebbie Wren's Earthly dwelling was rife with the aroma of baking fish. Mrs Cory waited by the oven as a timer counted down to announcing the seafood pie She had prepared for the little princess was baked and ready to devour.

On the kitchen counter, a mobile phone gave a deep buzz. She investigated the alert and supressed a smirk. Mr Wren had a message from his mother.

'I was travelling to see my father when it happened,' Ghador said. A slight tremor affected her voice despite years of royal training teaching her to hold her nerve in any situation. 'I fell asleep in my carriage, but when I woke up, I was lying on the floor of this place.'

There was more to it than that, of course. Just as Yandira Wood Bee had made her pact, so had Lady Maitressa. Juno Herself had whisked the little princess out of harm's way by thrusting her onto the Janus Bridge before Mr Lunk and Mr Venatus could get their hairy hands on her. This move was made fairly in the game, to counter Her decision to allow Yandira's cronies access to Earth via the Underworld.

'I-I don't even know how long I was asleep,' Ghador said. 'Or what became of my convoy.'

The entourage of soldiers and servants were, of course, locked up in Castle Wood Bee's dungeon, having first gained the protection of Juno's Blessing from *somewhere*.

'You must be horribly confused, dear,' Mrs Cory said while Her thumbs tapped away on the mobile phone's screen. 'I can only imagine the shock of waking up so far from where you fell asleep. Horrible.'

Ghador nodded in a distant way, while Mrs Cory pressed *send* and Mrs Wren received a reply from her 'son'.

The little princess did not bat an eyelid at the strange device as the elderly woman placed it down on the counter; she was too wrapped up in her shock and grief and anger to consider much else outside her predicament.

Ghador sat on a patched-up armchair on the lounge side of the room wearing Ebbie Wren's bathrobe. Her eyes were puffy from a restless night's sleep and her hair was still wet from the shower she had taken. She was not at all awed by the concepts of hot and cold running water, central heating, electricity, kitchen appliances and all the other devices earthlings took for granted but might seem like high magic to the folk. Strictly speaking, her awareness had been nudged in the right direction, just a touch, enough to focus her on important matters instead of wasting time marvelling at Earth's technological wonders. Ghador and the Realm could worry about *those* later.

Right now, Mrs Cory wanted to understand the tactics behind sending the little princess here instead of a more obvious location, like the queendom ruled by her paternal grandmother. And who had been casting divine blessings upon the folk? Certain not Lady Juno Herself, for casting high magic without the filter of proxies or relics would break the golden rule and set a very dangerous precedent of which Juno's adversary would take full advantage.

Ghador said, 'I saw blue light as I slept ...' She paused in a way that could only mean a significant omission was being placed within her story. 'I dreamed of my grandmother. She came to me with news of terrible things. I ... I know it was a dream, but somehow it was really her, in spirit, and the things she told me were true.'

'I believe you, dear,' She said with the intensity of one who empathised. 'You're not the only one Maitressa visited from the grave.'

Ghador expressed surprise that this frail and harmless-looking old lady called Mrs Cory had been the recipient of at least one of these ghostly visits.

'I told you,' She added with a smile, 'me and your grandmother go back a ways. Her spirit didn't say much, but she told me what your aunt did.'

'Yandira ...' Ghador's expression darkened like a storm cloud. 'For years I've lived with what that monster did to poor Morrad, but now she has murdered my grandmother. *And* my mother.'

'It's a terrible thing she's done, and I'm sorry for your loss. But at least you're still alive. You're safe now.'

'*Safe?* How can you think I'm safe when Yandira is free to cause chaos and spill innocent blood? You have no idea what she's capable of now she has made a pact with her foul Oldunone.'

Foul was a little judgemental, especially with regard to divine nature in general, and could not stand to pass unadmonished. 'There aren't many earthlings left who believe in the Oldunfolk, dear, or remember their names. But the way *I* remember them, one's as bad as another, and I don't believe your wicked aunt is alone in getting Their help, is she?'

But Ghador had stopped listening and was grinding her teeth. 'I'll have revenge on Yandira. I swear by Juno's Light that I'll make her pay for her crimes with her life. Or I'll die trying.'

It was all Mrs Cory could do not to roll her eyes. The mobile phone buzzed again. Mrs Wren had sent a delighted reply to her son's surprising and alleged news. These mortals were simply too much fun.

'Damn it!' Ghador said, smacking the arm of the chair. 'It's maddening to be trapped here with no way home while Yandira tears everything I love apart. Strange Ground needs me. The *Realm* needs me.'

'I don't really understand what you're supposed to do next,' Mrs Cory said while tapping out another message to Mrs Wren. 'But you're not trapped on Earth for good, are you?'

'No,' Ghador replied cagily. 'For the time being, I must *wait*.'

'For what, dear?'

Ghador locked eyes with Her. She said nothing, but her hand slipped into the bathrobe's pocket, unconsciously, protectively.

Ah! Mrs Cory thought. *What do we have here?*

Ghador's fist bulged in the pocket, gripped tightly around a secret she was keeping hidden. Her expression was uncertain, as though she wanted to show what she had, unburden herself of the secret, but wondered if she could truly trust this elderly woman before her.

It was tempting to make Ghador free her hand and reveal what she was hiding, but that would be akin to walking into a trap. Subtly manipulating a mortal's decisions created a level playing field; outright forcing them into doing One's bidding tipped the balance too far and led to wild escalation. There was good reason for the golden rule. Ghador would have to take her own sweet time deciding how much she trusted Mrs Cory, and her game face was already beginning to slip.

The oven timer *pinged* and She opened the door to release a heady cloud of baked mash and seafood steam. Ghador gazed hungrily at the pie, her mouth watering, but failed to notice that Mrs Cory didn't wear protective mitts to take the roasting-hot dish out of the oven and set it aside to cool for a moment.

Ghador said, 'I'm waiting for a man – an earthling, a librarian.'

'Oh,' She replied. 'You must be talking about Ebbie Wren.'

'My grandmother said they were friends, that he is trust-worthy. What do you know about him?'

'Not much, to be honest. He's lived next door to Me for years, but I hardly saw him about the place. Quiet man, good-natured, keeps himself to himself, bit of an academic, but ...' And then, to Her own surprise, She told the truth. 'Why your grandmother has trusted your fate to the hands of a librarian is beyond Me. Sure, Ebbie Wren has spent his life learning about your side of the Skea, but if you're waiting for a hero to turn up, he might just disappoint you. I can't even begin to guess what trouble he's in right now.'

That was also the truth. She had not checked in on the Realm for a while, and for all She knew, Mr Lunk and Mr Venatus might have captured Maitressa's champion and discovered what quest he had been given. Which was to say, everything Mrs Cory did not yet know Herself. Ebbie Wren was more the sort that Yandira Wood Bee would swallow whole for a light snack, so why send him to the Realm and bring Ghador *here*? The reasoning behind this divine strategy was elusive and tantalising.

'When my grandmother left Strange Ground,' Ghador said, 'my mother tried to find her.' She was relaxing in the armchair with an air of deep contemplation. Her hand remained in her pocket. What was she keeping there? 'The truth is, I already knew grandmother couldn't be found, would never return, and perhaps I was the only one she told. I was sworn to secrecy, could tell my mother nothing of *her* mother's sacrifice. For ten years I've kept my secrets, lived with them, praying they would never have to be revealed. But obviously my prayers went unanswered.'

Because prayers, like games, only met with success if they weren't boring.

Mrs Cory took a plate from a cupboard and a serving spoon from a drawer, then began dishing up a healthy portion of seafood pie for the little princess.

'Yandira found Queen Maitressa and ... here I am, waiting for a librarian.' Ghador drew a breath, marshalling her resolve.

'Grandmother had her reasons for choosing Ebbie Wren, and I'll trust in that. It's his choice of companion who troubles me.'

'*Companion?*' Mrs Cory almost dropped the plate She was carrying to Ghador. The thrill of unknown things tingled through Her. 'I don't know anything about a companion, dear.' Another truth – as far as She knew, Ebbie Wren was alone in the Realm.

'I was surprised when my grandmother told me who it was.' She gave Ghador the plate along with a fork. 'Who?'

'An old friend of mine.' Ghador chuckled sadly as she flattened mashed potato with the fork. 'We were close, once, but our friendship didn't end well, and I can't imagine she'll be too eager to help me now.'

'I wouldn't be so quick to say so, dear. Whether folk or earthling, hard times often bring the best out of people.'

'Well, hard times brought out the *worst* in Bek Rana.'

Bek Rana? Oh, how perfect! She really had not seen this move coming.

Ghador offered a wan smile. 'My grandmother was a wise woman, Mrs Cory. I don't need some damned hero to come and save me. I'm waiting for a thief and a librarian to bring me a nasty surprise for *dearest Aunt Yandira.*'

The little princess stabbed her food like it was a foe and shovelled a forkful into her mouth. But her free hand – well, that remained in the robe's pocket, closed around a secret.

How interesting, Mrs Cory thought. It was high time She checked up on the Realm. Yandira should have fulfilled her promises by now. Though it was amusing to watch the would-be Empress's slow realisation that her plans were nothing like flawless. She was not responding swiftly enough to her Oldunone's last admonishment, but was that entirely her own fault?

'So,' She said, plating up seafood pie for Herself. 'Tell me more about this friend of yours. What's the *nasty surprise* you've all got planned for your aunt?'

On the kitchen counter, Ebbie Wren's phone buzzed.

15

A Familiar Tale

Throughout the night and well into the morning, Ebbie followed Bek through Watcher's Forest. They walked fast and ate dried beef and hard oatcakes – provisions from the rucksack purchased at Backway Charlie's. Ebbie had never been in a forest as large as this before. The trees appeared to be endless and the scenery added to a state of well-being that had been welling inside him since waking from his dream of Mai.

The ambience of these woodlands, the shade of a verdant canopy rustling in the breeze, the scent of the earth, the texture of bark, the song of birds – they somehow dispelled his anxiety and the aches in his legs. Even while listening to Bek's dark tale of Mai's youngest and most dangerous daughter, Ebbie felt at peace beneath watery sunlight filtering through the sea in the sky.

'Yandira spent the best part of ten years locked up in her tower,' Bek told him as she pushed ahead. 'This isn't her first foray into high treason, Ebbie, and I remember the last time she tried to take the throne ...'

They were terrible days, Bek said. Yandira's servants – murderers like Lunk and Venatus – prowled the underbelly of Strange Ground, stirring up ideas of rebellion, making sure that those who showed too much loyalty to the crown *disappeared*.

Bek told Ebbie how Yandira had stolen the soul of her other sister Morrad to create a Shade, a creature of sinister magic; how she wanted to use the Shade to kill Eldrid and Ghador, her rival heirs. But Yandira didn't succeed, not back then, and it was only by the love of her mother that she was spared execution and imprisoned instead. In the aftermath, Eldrid became queen because Mai abdicated out of remorse and went into exile.

It was all beginning to sound familiar to Ebbie, but he couldn't pinpoint why until Bek said, 'And now Yandira is getting what she's always wanted. She's already First Lady to House Wood Bee.'

'Wood Bee?' Ebbie stopped walking. 'I know that name.'

'Everyone knows it.' Bek turned to face him, hand resting on the hilt of her sword. 'It's the name of the Royal Family.'

'No, it's more than that.' Ebbie felt a chill. 'The crown of Strange Ground has two stones, one called Foresight and the other Hindsight.'

'You needn't make it sound like some big secret. If the priests give Yandira that crown, she'll be queen by rightful tradition and no one could deny her.'

'You don't understand, Bek. I first heard the name *Wood Bee* back in *my* Strange Ground. The story you just told me – I already know it because it's one of Mai's stories ...' Ebbie stared into the middle distance. 'Yandira had a secret book in Mai's library, didn't she?'

'A book?'

'Some kind of forbidden text. Dark magic. Mai discovered it and that's how she knew what Yandira was doing.'

Bek frowned, looked uncertain, then shrugged. 'I don't re-member anything about a book.' She stuck her thumbs under the straps of the rucksack and turned away as though Ebbie's epiphany was of no consequence. 'Let's keep walking.'

As the journey continued, the warmth of the day rose and Ebbie removed his jacket, wondering what else Mai had told him that he hadn't realised was true. Had she spoken more about her past and family than he ever knew?

After a while, Bek dropped back beside Ebbie and said, 'Maitressa might have sent you here to find her granddaughter, but you're not the only one looking out for her.'

And she explained about a city called Dalmyn and how its Royal Family were well aware of House Wood Bee's troubles.

'Dalmyn's sending an army to stop Yandira – at least, that's what I've heard. It makes sense, though, given Ghador's other grandmother is Dalmyn's queen and her father is the First Heir.' Bek became cagey and gave Ebbie the side-eye. 'But you must know all about that already.'

'Must I?'

'I reckon your job is to make sure Ghador meets up with Dalmyn. Am I right?'

'This is the first I'm hearing of any army.'

'But you're going to keep her safe, help her take back the Wood Bee Throne, surely?'

'I suppose, but ...' How could he do that? Ebbie thought about his dream of Mai. She had said many things pertaining to this situation, as though she had been more than just a dream, but that was ludicrous. He shook his head. 'Mai asked me to find her granddaughter and help her get home. That's all I've been told to do.'

Bek clearly didn't believe him but didn't push the matter and strode ahead, saying, 'Fine. The less you tell me the better, anyhow.'

Ebbie's sense of well-being drained away as he trudged through the trees after her. He felt for comfort from the weight of the lantern in the satchel, concerned now by what he did or didn't know. This was far more complicated than a simple case of finding a missing person. Mai's granddaughter was heir to a bloody queendom! There were murderers after him. He didn't really understand all this talk of Royal Families and armies, but Bek made it sound like war was brewing and Ebbie was standing in the middle of it.

His mind trundled through the story Mai had told him in the old forest bathed in blue light. What if the dream was like the letter, a way for her to communicate from beyond the grave? *Minerva Wood Bee* – Mai's ancestor? He thought about *all* the stories she had told him of the Realm. What if each and every one was true? Perhaps she had told them as a means to ease her grief over what she had lost, or perhaps she had been preparing Ebbie for this moment and what he had to do once he found Ghador.

Tired and fretful now, with dull aches gnawing at his legs, Ebbie struggled to keep up with Bek's quick pace. Around midday, they stopped to rest awhile beside a brook. Bek built a small fire and brewed some tea. She assured Ebbie that she had nothing left to spike it with this time. For a while, they drank in tired silence to the lazy voice of Watcher's Forest, sitting in dappled sunlight.

Ebbie opened the satchel and pulled out Mai's letter. If there was ever a time for new instructions, then surely it was now. Frustratingly, not only did he discover that no new words graced the pages, but also that there were no words at all. The paper was entirely blank, and Ebbie swore.

'What's that?' Bek asked.

'A letter Mai left me.' Ebbie folded the pages. 'I don't know how, but it keeps changing, giving me different instructions. It's like Mai's ghost is watching over me or something.'

Bek harrumphed. 'Probably enchanted like your satchel. Magic is a weird and dangerous thing, Ebbie.'

'You should be grateful. Last time I read this letter, Mai told me to get you out of jail.'

Bek sat up straighter beside the fire. 'Lady Maitressa Wood Bee mentioned *me*?'

'By name.'

Bek held out a hand for the letter. 'Let me see.'

'No point, it's blank now.'

'But she definitely told you my name, you didn't get it from Charlie?' She became wary when Ebbie nodded. 'What did she say about me?'

'That you were a friend in a fix, even though you tried to screw me over. She sounded fond of you, actually, like you were the only person who could help me.'

'Why?' Bek appeared trapped midway between looking disturbed and confused that a dead queen should know her name. 'I mean ... why would she think that? She doesn't know me.'

'I've asked myself the same question, more than once.' Ebbie gave a small smile as he slipped the letter back into the satchel. 'Mai had a gift for just ... *knowing* people, and I trust her judgement. But there was this other woman, Bek. Before I came here, she gave me this satchel and everything in it. She said they were from Mai. I never found out who she was, but she must've been from this side of the Skea. You said there were other people looking out for Ghador?'

'I did.' Bek sounded relieved to move on from what Mai did or didn't know about her. 'What did this woman look like?'

'Stern.' Ebbie sipped his tea. 'Businesslike, well-to-do. She wore a brooch, cream and green like my ring. It was shaped into some kind of bird, maybe a kingfisher.'

'Huh.' Bek stared at Ebbie for a moment, then shook herself. 'Could've been anyone,' she said, poking the fire with a stick.

'Well, anyway ...' Ebbie gulped the last mouthful of tea. 'Tell me about this other sister, the middle daughter – Morrad, is it?'

'What about her?'

'Whose side is she on?'

'No one's. Morrad's about as decisive as a cow's moo, and she's been that way for years.' Bek sighed. 'Wasn't always like that, though. Before Yandira ruined her, Morrad was quick, clever – nothing got past her and Eldrid. Or so they say.' She tapped her temple. 'That Yandira was able to outsmart them and their mother should give you a clear warning of who you're up against.'

'But she didn't outsmart Ghador,' Ebbie said with uncertain brightness. 'She hasn't stopped us.'

Bek grumbled something about the day being young as she extinguished the fire and stowed the kettle. 'There must be one or two Houses left in Strange Ground who'll to stand up to Yandira, but they're of no help to you right now.' She turned her back so Ebbie could put his cup in the rucksack. 'Which is why we're headed in the opposite direction from the city.'

Ebbie cinched the rucksack shut. 'Where *are* we going?'

'A place called Singer's Hope. If anyone can point you to-wards a True Sight Candle, it'll be someone from there.'

An hour or more of walking later, Watcher's Forest finally ended and they came to the edge of a road that ran alongside the treeline. The early afternoon had cooled somewhat and throughout the Skea, grey clouds were pestering the sun. Ebbie looked up and down the road; it was formed from grassy dirt, sliced by thin wagonwheel tracks and flanked by trees and wild bushes. It suddenly occurred to him how many adventures he had read that began on roads just like this one.

'I'm actually here,' he said. 'I'm in the Realm.'

Bek smiled at his moment of awe. 'This must all seem pretty astounding to you.' She pointed to the right. 'Follow the road that way and you'll skirt around Strange Ground to join the Queen's Highway which runs straight to Dalmyn.' She leaned in to Ebbie. '*Not* where we want to go.' She pointed left. 'There are some villages and farming settlements in that direction, but beyond them the way becomes unused and overgrown, abandoned for centuries and for very good reason. If you travel far enough, you'll come to the old Imperial Road and eventually reach Imperium City. No one wants to go there. Ever.'

'Imperium City?'

'Or what's left of it. Now there's a long and terrible tale from both our histories ... What's wrong?'

Ebbie was staring intently at Bek. 'Imperium City? Where the Empress of the Realm lives?'

'*Used* to live. Nothing but ruins now.'

'You don't have an Empress anymore?'

'Of course not.'

'Right. Because ... because the Protectors took over after what happened between Minerva and Bellona?'

Bek looked impressed. 'That story's as old as the hills, Ebbie. They must teach an awful lot about the Realm on your side of the Skea.'

'Uh-huh.'

'We don't talk about you lot much. We have stories and legends, but given what Bellona and her army did to the Realm, the word *earthling* is often used as a curse. You'd do well to remember that.'

'It's not just a story, then?' An icy sensation gnawed at Ebbie's gut. 'Minerva ended the Imperium?'

'She made all the kings and queens Protectors of the Realm,

and the Oldunfolk forbid travel between our worlds. Or so they say, eh?'

She sounded like she was combing through common folklore, but she clearly didn't realise that *earthlings* had no idea why the Janus Bridges vanished; and Ebbie didn't want to admit that despite having a college education in the subject of the Realm, it was a dream which had apparently drawn him to the answer to a question that had stumped Earth's academics and historians for two thousand years. This was mad.

He cleared his throat and tried to keep his voice light with innocent curiosity. 'They say Bellona made a pact with the Underworld. Is that part true?'

'Maybe. Stories get warped over that amount of time.' Bek shrugged. 'But the aftermath of the war can still be felt in Imperium City.' She shuddered. 'I've heard the ruins are full of ghosts and monsters and all kinds of bad magic. Wouldn't know personally. Never been stupid enough to go there.'

Ebbie's fingertips were tingling while his memory raced through the dream, searching for something Mai had said. His mind screeched to a halt when he found it: *Bellona's ambition is a source of inspiration to my daughter ... The Realm needs its Minerva more than ever.* What did that mean? Something important. *She has made a pact of her own ...*

'Anyway,' Bek said, aiming her finger directly ahead, 'Singer's Hope is in that direction.'

On the other side of the road there was a scattering of trees but no visible path. The terrain became rocky beyond the foliage – almost coastal-looking, with pale, chalky stone more suited to cliff faces. The rocks rose high in the near distance but their detail was blurred by a shroud of mist.

'For what it's worth, this is nothing personal,' Bek said, encouraging Ebbie to cross the road with her, eager to reach their destination. 'Whatever your friend thinks she knows about me, I don't intend to hang around. Once you have a True Sight Candle, our contract is done and I'll be off.'

At the top of the stairs coiling around the outside of Castle Wood Bee's south tower there was a balcony. And on this balcony, high above the castle grounds, a royal guard hacked away at the door to the tower's topmost chambers. With tireless routine he would lift … *strike!* lift … *strike!* while clearly under the influence of the Underworld's sorceries. The guard should have reduced the door to kindling by now, yet each impact produced an erroneous *chinking* sound like a pick chipping at ice rather than the deep *thud* of an axe biting into wood. Every *chink* stabbed at Princess Yandira's impatience; and somewhere deep inside himself, Lord Aelfric Dragonfly was pleased by her frustration.

'A pox on all doors,' Yandira said.

Whether she was talking to the guard or her audience was unclear. Yandira's face was ashen, her posture hunched and she looked frail, fatigued, weak. Was it too much to hope that her power was waning?

The afternoon breeze was stiff atop the tower, bringing with it the smell of forge smoke and the sound of hammers on anvils. The wind forced tears from Dragonfly's eyes, but he could not blink them away or alter his line of sight. He felt as though his eyes had become the windows of his prison cell, and his view was only ever what Yandira allowed him to see. Next to Dragonfly, Princess Morrad stood as docile as he, and together they watched Yandira who in turn watched the guard working with his axe.

The Serpent's Sigh felt like drowning in icy blood which froze you an instant before filling your lungs with death.

'You are a disappointment to me, Aelfric,' said Yandira without looking at him. 'But it makes sense that my mother and Lady Kingfisher would keep secrets from you. Strike it harder!' she ordered the royal guard, whose efforts only succeeded in producing louder *chinks*.

The door led to the private library of the former Queen of Strange Ground. Mysterious enchantments had sealed it shut after Maitressa went into exile; no one knew why, but the library had remained inaccessible for the last ten years. Although Yandira's magic was terrible and seemingly unstoppable, her attempts to break the spells on this door, and the other door inside the tower, had failed. Whether or not this was another sign that she was exhausting herself and her abilities, Dragonfly could only hope, but it hadn't stopped her resorting to more mundane methods to gain access.

Chink, went the axe, and Yandira's hands balled into fists.

'I have my own books secreted among this library's collection. I hoped to gather them, but evidently my mother wanted me never to see them again. The stench of divine Oldunspeak is upon this door, the filthy touch of Juno's Blessing. I am of a mind to pile all of my mother's tomes in the courtyard, douse them in oil and watch them burn. Should I ever get this bloody door open, of course.'

Yandira turned to Dragonfly and her sister; her face looked old and grey. 'My mistake ten years ago was not making mother my first victim. I didn't kill her because it felt so important to become her First and only Heir. For tradition's sake, irrefutable right to the crown in the eyes of all. In hindsight, my ambitions called for less subtlety and more direct action. I am older and wiser now, and Persephone has taught me the virtue of foresight.'

With a shuddery exhalation, Yandira winced as she moved

to the balcony wall, as though each step was made painfully on arthritic legs. Out of breath, she placed her hands on the wall to steady herself, while the guard continued hacking in vain at the library door.

'The Protectors of the Realm is a tired tradition, buried beneath centuries of complacency.' Yandira gazed down onto the castle grounds. 'Queens and kings across the land, dry and covered in dust, dogged by formalities, all tripping over each other's self-importance – entitled cretins, the lot of them. The Realm is ready for an Empress again, but *tradition* would deny my *ambition*.'

She looked up at the Skea, now partially obscured by a fog. 'My sword,' she sighed. 'Some believe it no longer resides in the Realm. Others that it was sealed in Minerva's tomb, safe behind Juno's high magic – much like this pox-ridden library. But I knew it was in my mother's possession, a secret passed down from her mother, who received it from her mother, and so on and so forth. I was certain Maitressa had taken that sword to wherever she exiled herself, but I was wrong ...'

Yandira looked at Dragonfly. 'Aelfric, do you remember Bek Rana? I'm sure you do.'

If Dragonfly could have expressed surprise, he would have. Bek Rana was a name he had not heard mentioned in the last decade.

Yandira said, 'I was surprised to learn that she is not only embroiled with an earthling, but also in possession of the sword. It is a Wood Bee heirloom, which makes it mine by rights.'

This wasn't the first time Yandira had spoken about the sword; she had questioned Dragonfly about it during his torturous interrogation, but only to discover that Maitressa had never told him about such a legendary heirloom among her possessions. And who was this earthling Ebbie Wren?

'However,' Yandira continued brightly, 'beyond my surprise and outrage at this news, I believe it has given me deeper insight into Maitressa's role in the Oldunfolk's game. Bek Rana is helping Ebbie Wren to deliver the sword to Princess Ghador. They must know where she is hiding, thus I regain the upper hand. Now come here, both of you.'

It was disconcerting to move under someone else's control, like being strapped to an untamed horse that wandered to its own whims. Morrad and Dragonfly came to stand on either side of Yandira.

'Over there is another door refusing to open for me.' She pointed to the inner bailey where a large dodecagonal building was surrounded by vibrant gardens. 'The Temple of Juno. I had planned to receive my coronation the *rightful* way, as tradition dictates. It seemed the simplest, quickest method of upholding unbreakable promises I have made to my Oldunone. But you might say my mother and my niece have hobbled my horse somewhat. Juno's priests wait for the rightful heir and won't willingly crown anyone else queen. *Willingly* being the operative word.'

Angrily, Yandira smacked her hand down on the balcony wall. 'If Lady Bellona taught us anything, it is how petty a single queendom is in the grand scheme of the Realm, but I will not make the same mistakes as her. I shall reduce Juno's Temples to rubble before the end. In their place, Houses of Persephone will rise.' She turned her grey face to Dragonfly. 'It must break your heart to know your old friends were so ready to sacrifice you. A decoy, Aelfric, a means to buy my enemies time – that is all you were to them. But hark, can you hear the ringing of the forges?'

Indeed, the distant clang of hammers on anvils, the hiss of hot metal dipped into water, continued to accompany the strikes of the guard's axe. And now that Dragonfly thought on it, he had been hearing this sound since morning and it had replaced the general ambience of the city's hubbub.

'That sound is the beginning of my Empire,' Yandira said, once again looking down onto the Temple of Juno. 'The Serpent's Sigh is spreading through the city, ensuring the smiths of Strange Ground will forge swords and arrowheads, day and night, never stopping until every citizen, young and old, stands with weapon in hand to fight in my honour. I would have given them the choice to follow me, Aelfric, but you – you *and* your friends – forced my hand to this.'

Every citizen ... nearly ten thousand innocent folk. Dragonfly wished he could grab Yandira and topple her over the balcony to the certain death of the flagstones far below. If only the royal guard could break his conditioning and sink his axe into her head.

Footsteps reached the top of the stairs. Like puppets, Dragonfly and Morrad turned with Yandira to witness the arrival of Ignius Rex, Yandira's lackey and the foul magician who had encouraged this dire situation every step of the way.

'It is done, Majesty,' he said with a bow, clearly excited. 'The Coven of Bellona is your shield on the Queen's Highway.'

'Excellent,' said Yandira, then she pouted at Dragonfly. 'Oh my, I pray you didn't place too much hope in Dalmyn's army—'

She staggered, as though the last of her strength was draining away. Ignius Rex was quickly at her side, holding her arm.

'Majesty?' he said worriedly.

'I can wait no longer, Ignius.' Yandira's voice was low and hoarse. 'Walk me to the temple. The time has come to snap the Realm's precious traditions in two.'

As she held the magician's arm and let him lead her to the tower's outer stairs, she called, 'You two, stay here. I want you to witness my coronation.'

While the guard's axe *chinked* off the library door, Dragonfly and Morrad endured the cold wind, unable to look away from the Temple of Juno.

The path to Singer's Hope was narrow and weaved through a landscape of pale rocks. Each boulder the size of a house, they were clustered together so closely – balancing at precarious angles, resting upon one another to fashion rough archways and overhangs – that it looked as though an entire mountain had fallen apart on this ground. Cold mist pervaded the area, wet enough to dampen clothes now the Skea was drizzling rain into it – or maybe that should've been *spraying* rain. Although the mist hid the Skea from view, the distant sound of unsettled seas could still be heard.

Ebbie was lost to thoughts as troubled as the sky, mulling over and over his dream of Mai. But when he licked rainwater from his lips, it suddenly occurred to him that it didn't taste as it should.

'Huh,' he said. 'It's not salty.'

Bek stopped walking and turned to face him, her appearance damp and miserable. 'What?'

'The rain.' Ebbie tasted his lips again. 'It's not salty.'

For a moment, Bek looked at him as if he were daft, then she said, 'Hang on, are you saying the rain is salty on your side of the Skea? How does anything grow?'

'No, I'm not saying that.'

'Then what's your point, Ebbie?'

'Where I'm from, the sky is just a sky, and the rain isn't sea-water. So how comes *your* rain isn't salty?'

'I don't know. It just isn't, all right?' With an irritated air, Bek adjusted the rucksack on her back, turned and trudged on.

'Hey,' Ebbie said, hurrying to catch up with her. 'I've been thinking about something Mai told me.'

'Writing you letters again, is she?'

'What? Oh ...' Ebbie rocked his head from side to side but said nothing, deciding it was better to let her believe he was talking about the letter rather than try to explain the dream he'd had.

'Did she mention me this time?' Bek said.

'No. It's about her daughter.'

'Then I don't want to know.'

'Mai said Yandira's made a pact.'

'Keep it to yourself, Ebbie.'

'But what if it's with the Underworld? What if she wants to be Empress like Bellona?'

Bek huffed. 'Can't happen. That's what the Protectors are for.'

'Then where are they?'

'Exactly.' Bek stopped and glared at him in annoyance. 'I don't know what it's like on your side of the Skea, but the Realm is a *big* place. We have our fair share of troubles and wars, but the kings and queens don't all band together over every storm in a teacup at the arse end of nowhere. That's why *Dalmyn* is taking care of Yandira. In the grand scheme of things, it's a small problem.'

'But is it? Nobody knew Bellona had made a pact with Persephone until—'

'*Don't* say Her name!'

'What?'

'She can hear you whenever you say Her name.' Bek made a curious gesture with her hand, which Ebbie guessed was a ward against evil. 'Call Her the Great Trickster, or say *cursed* before you mention Her, all right?'

Ebbie would have laughed if not for the serious look on Bek's face. 'Okay. Nobody knew Bellona had made a pact with *Cursed* Persephone—'

'Give it a rest!' Bek snapped. She pinched the bridge of her nose and reined herself in. 'Yes, like Bellona, Yandira uses dark magic, but so does every witch and bad magician. It doesn't mean she's in cahoots with the bloody Oldunfolk. Trust me, she would've succeeded last time if the Great Trickster was involved.'

'But *She* is called the Great Trickster for a reason, Bek. Mai clearly said Yandira has made a pact, and pacts are two-way agreements.'

'So?'

'So what if there's something Yandira has to do before Persephone – sorry, *Cursed* Persephone – will help her? Like killing off her rivals and claiming the crown of Strange Ground … What?'

Bek's nostrils had flared angrily. 'I don't care what *Mai* said. I don't care about Yandira's *pact*. We might have given Lunk and Venatus the slip, but they won't abandon the hunt. We need to stay ahead of them, so stop talking and start walking.'

After less than half an hour of miserable silence, they came to a clearing in the looming rocks. Up ahead, fires glowed in the mist as a line of hazy figures came in from a different direction from Bek and Ebbie, pushing carts or riding creaking donkey-drawn wagons. This small procession headed towards a huge shadow which rose up to the Skea beyond the fires like a dark wall.

Bek drew Ebbie to a halt and explained that these people were delivery workers returning from selling goods in Strange Ground or its outlying settlements. They were arriving from the main road to and from Singer's Hope.

'We're sneaking in the back way,' she added. 'The folk here tend to be suspicious of travellers coming from this direction, so let's wait a bit and join the end of the line. And, Ebbie –'

Bek gave him a stern look '– under no circumstances tell *anyone* you're an earthling.'

They fell into step behind an empty wagon pulled by a single donkey and driven by a hunched figure hidden beneath a travelling cloak and a wide-brimmed hat.

'A lot of trading companies operate out of Singer's Hope,' Bek said quietly. 'It's Strange Ground's main harbour.'

Ebbie looked up at the Skea, though he couldn't see it through the mist. 'Harbour?'

'And there's a toll to pay, so you'll need two silver coins. Let me do the talking, all right?'

Ebbie fetched the coins from the money pouch as they followed the procession towards the great shadow looming behind bright flames burning in braziers. The shadow turned out not to be a wall, but a tower made from rock and metal, rising wide and high into the mist. Several young folk took possession of empty carts and wagons, leading donkeys over to an open-faced stable. The delivery workers then formed a queue before a checkpoint staffed by four guards armed with swords or bows, along with a grizzled woman sitting behind a table, who Bek explained was the harbourmaster's deputy.

'But the sea is in the sky,' Ebbie whispered. 'How can this place be a harbour?'

'You'll see.' A wistful smile played on Bek's lips. 'I was born and raised in Singer's Hope. Me and my grandma had a little fishing business. We did all right for ourselves.'

One by one, the workers handed over payments from their deliveries to the harbourmaster's deputy, who, once she had updated a ledger, allowed them to enter the tower through tall double doors. In front of Bek and Ebbie, a man and woman struck up a conversation.

'I stopped off at Mag's farm this afternoon,' said the woman.

'She reckons there's something foul in the weather. Since yesterday morning, she said, her cows been giving sour milk, and now she reckons her gulls won't fly.'

'I don't know what to make of it all,' said the man. 'I was in the city this trip. All sorts going on there.'

'Aye, Mag told me about Queen Eldrid.' Ebbie and Bek shared a surreptitious look. 'Maitressa's youngest is out of prison, is that right?'

'Looks to be the way of it. They say she'll soon be queen.'

'Oldunfolk preserve us. I'll be needing a drink tonight.' The woman *tsked* and stamped her feet against the chill. 'If you ask me, the season's getting ready to change too early.'

She handed over small money bags to the harbourmaster's deputy, and then it was Bek and Ebbie's turn at the table. Bek placed the silver coins down, saying, 'Two visitors from the city.'

The deputy looked from the coins to Bek's face. 'State your business.' Her voice was as stern as her gaze.

'None,' Bek said with a casual shrug. 'Except the pocketful of gold we're itching to spend.'

The deputy's eyes flickered to the sword hanging from Bek's belt before she scooped up the coins, dipped her pen in the inkwell and scribbled something in the ledger. 'Cause any trouble and we'll throw you in the Skea.'

Ebbie was wondering how one might go about throwing someone up into the sky when Bek led him by the sleeve into the tower, where they joined the delivery workers. It wasn't crowded, and the large floor-space was formed from a latticework of thick metal bars. To Ebbie's surprise, the tower's interior was hollow, rising to a patch of daylight high above.

'If you don't know the drill,' said a guard as he closed and bolted one half of the double doors, 'keep your arms by your sides and stay away from the walls.'

When the second door closed, the tower became as dim as a cloudy night. With a clunk of gears, the rattle of chains and the turning of wheels, the floor began to rise.

Butterflies fluttering in his stomach, Ebbie gripped Bek's arm. 'It's a lift,' he whispered. Bek chuckled and looked up at the patch of daylight they were headed towards.

The ascent didn't last long and Ebbie was the only one perturbed by it. When the platform stopped, he was swept up in a wave of disembarking folk who quickly dispersed in all directions to leave him staring dumbfounded at Singer's Hope.

Buildings tall or squat, high or long, crooked or standing proud – all of them sat above the water on great stilts. Folk hurried along walkways and over bridges, punting down canals in leaky-looking gondolas. Singer's Hope was like a version of Venice from history, and the harbour town enthralled Ebbie so much, his mouth agape, his eyes filled with wonder, that he didn't realise he was walking backwards into danger. If Bek hadn't shouted his name, jumped forwards and grabbed his arm, he would have tipped over the edge of the dockside.

'Be careful,' Bek snapped.

A few dockhands were watching, some of them laughing at Ebbie's close call. He supposed he must still look like a country bumpkin to them, but his attention was now arrested by how many ships were moored at Singer's Hope. Big, old-fashioned ships of dark wood with masts and sails and figureheads, accompanied by smaller fishing boats and skiffs of varying shapes and design. Folk crossed gangplanks, loading and offloading cargo, while ropes and pulley systems lifted large crates and pallets. The dockside swept away left and right as far as Ebbie could see, and all these vessels, their moorings thick and tight and creaking, bobbed on a gentle sea that stretched far and green to a few islands and a hazy horizon.

'How ... ?'

Ebbie turned around to look at the tower. Its rock and metal top was domed, protruding from the worn but chunky wooden beams that made the dockside. Beneath, the tower must have sunk into the sea, but that didn't make sense. Ebbie looked up. A blanket of grey cloud continued to drizzle but there were no rolling waves or any hint of a watery covering.

His face split into a grin of childlike awe. 'The sea is where it should be,' he told Bek. 'It's not in the sky.'

'Will you pipe down?' Bek hissed.

'But it's impossible.' Ebbie pointed at the sea, the sky, the tower. 'There's nothing like this on my side of the Skea.'

Bek silenced him by stepping in close. 'Do you know what you sound like? An earthling seeing the Realm for the first time. Stop enjoying yourself so much and start blending in.'

Shoving Ebbie ahead of her, Bek steered him off the dockside, away from the sea and into the Venice-like town of Singer's Hope.

16

Secrets

Dalmyn's army made painfully slow progress along the Queen's Highway. They should have been nearing Strange Ground by now, but they remained at least half a day's ride out, perhaps more, if the weather had its say. Throughout the night and morning, thick fog had forced a trundling pace, and by early afternoon visibility became so low the company was ordered to stop and make full camp. Much to Lady Kingfisher's chagrin.

If not for the fires illuminating the shapes of tents, wagons, horses and soldiers, Kingfisher fancied she wouldn't see her hand in front of her face. But that was no excuse to delay the mission. Before she had the chance to seek out Prince Maxis and air her dissatisfaction, a soldier came bearing a summons from him. Cold, miserable, eager to be travelling again, she followed the soldier to where the prince had decided there was time enough to erect his command tent. Inside, her mood was not improved.

Maxis sat at a small table, staving off the chill by sipping hot wine from a cup beside glowing coals in a brazier, looking for all the world as though he was enjoying himself and as unhurried as you like. High Priest Seej Agda sat next to him, appearing far less comfortable; she, at least, had the manners to look apologetic. Kingfisher's hackles rose when Maxis invited her to join them.

'Highness, it is a mistake to delay,' she said. 'The company must continue to Strange Ground.'

'My Lady,' Maxis said with a soft, patronising chuckle. 'I sympathise with your frustration, but I will not order my soldiers to march another step before they are rested and I better understand what we are heading towards.'

'Your queen—'

'Is not here, and *I* am in command. Now, before we go rushing into whatever supernature has befallen your city, Mother Seej is of the opinion that there are one or two details we *all* need to understand.'

'My Lady,' Seej said before Kingfisher might utter something she'd regret. 'We have much to discuss.' The priest filled a third cup with steaming wine from a pitcher and pushed it across the table towards an empty chair. 'Please, take a moment's respite. Tell us how Strange Ground came to be facing this horror.'

Something in the priest's eyes cut through Kingfisher's impatience, something pleading, filled with unspoken meaning. Relenting, Kingfisher picked up the cup and took a grateful sip of warm wine, but did not sit down, instead pacing before the table.

'Highness, if you require confirmation of exactly what kind of maleficent your daughter's aunt is, then let me tell you ...'

Maxis listened with a heavy frown as Kingfisher told him of Eldrid's murder and Ghador's disappearance, and the cruel way Yandira had freed herself from the tower prison. He was suitably astonished to learn how Yandira had found her exiled mother living on Earth and then had her killed – though she left out details of her own trip to the other side of the Skea, and how Maitressa had entrusted his daughter's fate to an earthling named Ebbie Wren. By the time Kingfisher had finished, the prince understood just how deeply Yandira Wood Bee was diving into darkness to achieve her ambitions – though Seej Agda did not act surprised at all.

'It should not have been this way,' Kingfisher concluded, almost apologetically. 'But so it is, and now time is of the essence. Highness, your mother has already informed Yandira that we know what her game is.'

After a moment's contemplation, Maxis looked at the High Priest. 'Could Yandira reach us here from Strange Ground?'

'Yes, perhaps.' Seej's face was as troubled as it was thoughtful. 'Bargaining with the Underworld has no doubt gained her many allies in these parts. Witches. They, too, pray to Cursed Persephone.'

'The Coven of Bellona,' said Kingfisher, nodding. 'Queen Eldrid had trouble with them several years ago, but I thought the coven was stamped out.'

'*Scattered*, never eradicated,' Seej corrected. 'These witches keep themselves as elusive as forest creatures, impossible to root out, but rarely do they band together. In Yandira, they have a worthy leader behind whom they can rise as a single force.'

'So we have witches to thank for this fog?' With a shiver, Maxis placed his empty cup on the table and warmed his hands before the coals. 'I have heard the coven's ways are indeed foul. We should have brought magicians with us.'

'Highness, I'm not convinced they could make a difference,' Seej said with warning. 'If this fog comes from the Underworld, then we are witnessing the beginning of the Serpent's Sigh. Yandira and her witches are commanding the spirits of dragons, which means Cursed Persephone is truly on their side.'

'Ah, well,' Maxis said offhandedly. 'A sharp sword will stop a witch as surely as magic.'

'Hear what I am saying, my Prince. The Serpent's Sigh is truly dark, fuelled by sacrifice to the lowest form of divinity. It is corrupting, powerful enough to turn your sword against your own daughter's claim to the throne.'

'And we have all read Lord Dragonfly's missive,' Kingfisher added before Maxis could bluster. 'Time is running out.' Desperate impatience nipped at her along with the wintery cold, and she implored both prince and priest. 'Strange Ground is at the mercy of a madwoman who would steal our crown to achieve the cruellest ambition. We must keep Yandira contained and buy Ghador time to claim her rightful place. We must get the citizens out to safety while Yandira festers in her castle.'

'The folk of Strange Ground may already be lost.' Seej sat forward, dull light shining off her shaved head. 'The Serpent's Sigh's mastery over mortals will only grow stronger the closer they get to its summoner – Yandira Wood Bee. We cannot save your people, help Ghador, if we go blindly charging at the gates of your city.'

'Then what are you proposing?' Kingfisher snapped. 'Should we stay here and allow the witches to surround us, pick us off one by one?'

'No, my Lady, you misunderstand me—'

Whatever the priest intended to say next was cut short by Maxis. 'The answer is clear,' he said. 'We return to Dalmyn.' It was a command.

Seej shook her head. 'Highness—'

'My mind is set, Mother Seej. We ride home come morning.'

'No!' The thunder in Kingfisher's voice startled the prince. 'To turn your back now is to condemn the folk of Strange Ground.'

'And would you so gladly sacrifice my every soldier attempting to save them?' The prince clenched his teeth and aimed a finger at Kingfisher. 'We ride for Dalmyn and gather reinforcements.

With greater numbers, we stand a better chance against these sorceries.'

'Reinforcements alone won't help us,' Seej said.

'And they are already on their way,' Kingfisher stated. 'The message I sent to your mother called for her to summon the Protectors of the Realm.'

'Then we will meet them on the road and make our plans.'

Kingfisher softened her voice with a pleading edge. 'Highness, I beg you, let them follow in our wake as we continue to Strange Ground. Ghador has—'

'I've heard enough, Genevieve.'

'You must listen to me.'

'Oh, but I am.' Maxis fixed her with a stern eye. 'You say Yandira has perverse ambitions, but to achieve them she must first deliver the crown of Strange Ground to Cursed Persephone? Then *I* say Yandira has won the day. After all she has done, do you honestly believe she would allow Juno's traditions to stand in her way? She would slay every priest in her queendom to get that crown. Surely, it is hers already.'

That put Kingfisher on the back foot. She hadn't considered it before, always believing Maitressa's promise: *As long as Ghador lives, the throne can never be Yandira's.* But now she saw the awful, daunting truth in the prince's words. Yandira Wood Bee had shattered the Realm's traditions ten years ago. What chance did they stand against the Underworld's power? Retreat to Dalmyn might be their only option.

'You will now listen to me, both of you.' Seej Agda spoke with a low tone that carried the full, commanding gravity of a High Priest. 'Yes,' she said to Maxis, '*if* Yandira claims the crown, she will win the day, but there will be no returning to Dalmyn for us.' She switched her gaze to Kingfisher, her face alive with secret things. 'Achieving her goal will not be so easy for Yandira. And between us, Lady Kingfisher, we should tell my prince *why*.'

'Quiet!' Maxis raised a hand curtly, this time with a soldier's command for silence, not a prince exercising his privilege. He cocked his ear. Shouts were coming from the camp.

'Highness!' The tent flap flew open and a soldier rushed in. 'Prince Maxis, a rider is approaching.'

Maxis was up and heading out of the tent in a heartbeat. Kingfisher and Seej followed him. In a few moments, they had pushed their way to the front of a crowd of soldiers who were watching uncertainly as a horse walked slowly into misty campfire light. The horse stopped, but the man riding it didn't dismount, only stared at the company, his face deathly pale.

'It is Nellin,' Maxis whispered to Kingfisher. 'The rider I sent with your message to my mother.'

'Something is wrong with him,' Seej said.

Which was clearly the truth when Nellin spoke. 'Hear me.' A cold voice, radiating ill will. 'I bring tidings from Strange Ground.'

'Strange Ground?' said Kingfisher.

Nellin's horse was of no common variety. The beast wasn't just steaming, it was as smoky as the fog but black as if created from shadows.

'The coven must have got to him,' said Maxis.

Seej issued a warning. 'Highness, keep your soldiers clear,' and she stepped forward. Maxis motioned for the company to move back as the priest addressed the rider. 'What tidings do you bring?'

'Change has come.' With the slow, stiff movements of a clockwork toy, Nellin faced Seej. 'Dalmyn and all its Houses are commanded to pledge allegiance to the new Empress of the Realm, Her Imperial Majesty Yandira Wood Bee.'

Worried, confused murmurs arose among the soldiers, quickly ordered to silence by their commander.

'Prince Maxis,' Nellin continued. 'Lady Genevieve Kingfisher is found guilty of high treason. You are ordered to execute her where she stands.'

Kingfisher took a fearful step back. Maxis laid a reassuring hand on her arm, his eyes scouring the thick wall of fog beyond the firelight, searching for whatever threat might have accompanied this rider. 'Bear arms!' he ordered. The sound of swords being drawn rang through the camp. 'Watch your surroundings!'

Seej was taking slow, cautious steps towards Nellin. She clutched something in her right hand, something that leaked a faint blue glow between her fingers. Nellin remained statue-still on the shadowy horse's back, watching. Kingfisher stayed close to Maxis, who drew his sword.

A sour breeze blew through the camp. As Seej moved closer, Nellin opened his mouth and issued a moan, low like a tormented spirit calling from the Underworld. Seej raised her hand above her head. The blue glow intensified, shining through her skin and blood, and she cried, 'With the Blessing of Juno, I stand in your way!'

Nellin's moan rose to a wail. He and his mount began shedding tendrils of black shadows into the misty air, fat as tentacles. They stretched forward, reaching for the priest. Seej stood her ground, her glowing hand lofted like a beacon. As the darkness neared, the blue light flared blindingly.

With a drone, it blazed in waves across the camp. Soldiers cried out in panic as it passed through them. Kingfisher held up her hands, expecting impact and pain, but all she felt was a strange sense of cleansing. The light chased away the mist and spiralled around the unnatural horse, tearing a scream from its rider's mouth. The horse and its darkness dissipated as though fleeing with a hiss like water on fire, throwing Nellin to the ground. His neck snapped audibly as he landed on his head.

The light receded, flowing back into Seej's hand to shine no more. The priest stumbled, failed to right herself, then collapsed.

Grandma Rana once told Bek, 'If you're in trouble and need a place to hide out, the Old Flagship is where you go. No one asks questions there.' Which was why Bek had led Ebbie directly to a dive of a tavern that clung to its stilts like an old drunk desperately trying not to fall into the Skea.

With Ebbie's coin they paid for a night's lodging in a small and musty room, dingy with its one cracked, grime-covered window. They took up with them a supper of stewed eels and potatoes, and sat on the hard mattresses of their bunks, eating from their laps. The room was so cramped their knees almost touched across the narrow space between them.

No, no one asked questions in the Old Flagship, but if they did, Bek would tell them that Ebbie was grinding on her last nerve. Ever since she had tried to ditch him, he had been gripped by childlike awe – never more so than when he was led across Singer's Hope's bridges and walkways to the shadier parts of town – and even now he gazed happily around this shitty little room while chewing his food, looking like he'd never been more amazed to be anywhere in his life. The sooner Bek could find that True Sight Candle, the sooner she could get rid of him.

Ebbie swallowed what he was chewing. 'You used to live in Singer's Hope?'

'As a child.'

'With your grandma, you said. Did she raise you?'

'Yep. Till the day she died.'

Ebbie expressed sympathy that Bek didn't care for and said, 'How old were you when she passed away?'

'Not old enough.'

'Oh. What about your parents? Where are they?'

Bek shrugged.

'You don't know?'

'Nope. I've never even met them and never wanted to. Grandma was enough.'

'Who took care of you when she died?'

Bek didn't like these questions. 'I took care of myself. End of story.'

Sympathy returned to Ebbie's face. His gaze drifted up into the distance and he made a confession. 'I wish I could be more like you. Sometimes, I don't want to know my parents, either. I'm supposed to be visiting them next week.' He grinned, adding sarcastically, 'Be a shame if I couldn't make it.'

Narrowing her eyes, Bek used a piece of bread to mop up parsley sauce and stuffed it in her mouth. 'You'd rather be stuck here in this mess than visit your parents?'

'No, not really.' A sad smile came to Ebbie's lips. 'But we don't see eye to eye. We argue. A *lot*. About everything and nothing.' He placed his empty plate on the little bedside table and licked sauce from his fingers. 'My parents moved away from Strange Ground when I was eighteen. They were upset when I didn't go with them, but I was glad to see the back of them both. I needed some distance between us.'

'Are they that bad?'

'No, they're not bad people, just ... single-minded.' Ebbie picked up his satchel from the floor and held it in his arms as he scooted up on the bunk to sit with his back against the wall. 'My mum and dad are deeply religious, and they're ashamed that I'm not. They think there's something wrong with me, and they're always trying to *fix* my faith, while never bothering to understand that it's *my* choice to believe whatever I want, you know?'

Bek nodded, not really caring. 'I've met a few people like that.'

'My mum's the worst. She's embarrassed of me.' Ebbie huffed and his expression darkened. 'Every single time I visit, she arranges for me to see her priest. She's convinced that Father Tom is the only one in the world who can ... *drive out my evil spirits*. It's like I'm their pagan enemy. Of course, I never make the meetings with Tom, and that's what usually kicks off the arguments. My parents think I'm some kind of renegade.'

The idea that *anyone* might mistake this earthling for having a rebellious nature amused Bek, but she couldn't fathom why Ebbie thought she was a good type of person to share his feelings with.

'Everyone has faith of some kind,' Bek said, finishing her meal and putting the plate on the bed beside her. 'The sailors and fisherfolk, they pray to Neptune. For magicians, it's Hecate. Travellers whisper to Janus, while witches ... well, we all know who they worship. Me, I pray to Laverna, and it's never done me any harm.' *Until now*, she added mentally. 'But if I had to guess, I'd say your parents fit Juno's bill. Am I right?'

'Juno?' Ebbie sounded surprised by her words.

'I used to believe in Her myself,' Bek said. 'The Queen of Queens, the loftiest, most pious Oldunone who sits above them all. I quickly learned that the biggest isn't necessarily the best, and your parents sound a lot like Juno's priests ... What?'

Ebbie was shaking his head. 'Um, you wouldn't know, but ... after the Janus Bridges vanished, religion became quite complicated on my side of the Skea. Earthlings don't pray to the Oldunfolk. Not really. Not any more.'

A world without Oldunfolk? Bek tried to comprehend that. She was on the cusp of asking Ebbie who his parents worshipped, then, but swallowed the question instead. It didn't matter; he'd be gone soon.

'I have to go out,' she said, getting to her feet, offloading a satisfied belch, then buckling on her sword belt. 'On my own.'

'On your own?' Ebbie looked like a startled deer and sat bolt upright. 'Why?'

'Because there're parts of this town you're not ready for.'

'You're leaving me here? Alone?'

'And I'll need some money, too.'

Ebbie gripped the satchel, sinking into himself, face full of suspicion. 'What's going on?'

Bek rolled her eyes. 'Look, you've seen what happens when I try to run away, Ebbie. The spell on our contract reads the signee's intent, and I *intend* to honour our agreement.' Because she had no choice and it was the only way to get shot of him. 'You have to trust me now. To get a True Sight Candle, I need to grease a dirty palm or two, and it's safer if I do that by myself. I won't be long and I don't need much. A few coppers and silvers should be enough.'

Ebbie mulled it over for a moment, clearly not liking it, but deciding Bek was telling the truth. Slowly, he opened the satchel and dipped a hand inside. 'So, what do I do in the meantime?'

'Stay in the room.' Bek took the handful of coins Ebbie offered and stuffed them into her pocket. 'Keep the door closed and don't go out. *For any reason.* All right?'

Ebbie nodded, eyes wide with worry as Bek opened the door and made to leave. 'Try and get some sleep,' she said from the threshold. 'I'll be a couple of hours at most.'

*

208

Yandira sat on the Wood Bee Throne, the crown of Strange Ground nestled in her lap. Brazier flames flickered and licked at the brooding silence permeating the air, the throne room's usual lonely cold gloomier than ever. For what felt like hours, she had sat staring at the crown in her lap. Dragonfly couldn't begin to imagine what dark thoughts possessed her current mood, but he experienced a seed of pleasure as he witnessed her condition.

On Yandira's shoulder, the Shade spoke in its dry, crackling voice. 'There is another way, sister.'

Yandira's gaze moved from the crown to Dragonfly and Morrad standing side by side at the base of the steps leading up to the throne. 'Not yet.' Her voice was barely a whisper. 'We will await word from Ignius before it comes to that.'

At some point, Yandira was bound to erupt in fury. Dragonfly wondered if she would kill him or Morrad first to sate the frustration that had come from this latest foiling of her ambition.

The sacking of the temple had made a terrible spectacle. Dragonfly wished he could have turned away, but he and Morrad, enthralled and transfixed and sickened, could do nothing but watch from the south tower balcony. Surely, if the divine wards of Oldunspeak preserved Maitressa's old library, then it would bless the Temple of Juno and the dutiful servants inside. But no; the Oldunfolk's reasoning was not for mortal minds to comprehend. When Yandira arrived, it was as a savage tempest that smashed down the temple doors. And Ignius Rex had been her wildfire.

The screams and wails of the dying had been the stuff of nightmare. Priests had fled the temple's sanctuary ... at least, they had tried to. Some were already ablaze and only made it a few steps before falling to the ground. No matter how much they rolled and thrashed, they could not douse the magical fire which burned their priestly robes and cooked their flesh.

Others had been blinded, bleeding holes where their eyes once were, and they ran sightless into the temple gardens where they keeled over from supernatural death with ghoulish cries.

Smoke had poured from the ruined doors, slate-grey and thick like viscous fluid which flowed in all directions, covering the ground, rising to the height of folk, the height of rooftops, creeping up the south tower's length. The Serpent's Sigh moved with a curious intelligence, knowing, seeking, as it slithered away into the city. The spirits of dragons had desecrated Juno's Temple, Her priests, the divine traditions which had held the Underworld at bay since the foul days of Lady Bellona. With this act, Yandira Wood Bee had announced her ambition to the Realm. Now the crown was hers, Cursed Persephone would help spread fire and poison across the land by sending a dire army of monstrous size and power, led by Her disciple.

But it hadn't happened.

Yandira had emerged from the temple weaker than ever, leaning heavily on Ignius Rex, walking on frail legs. Oh, she had claimed the crown of Strange Ground as her Oldunone demanded, but it was ... *incomplete*.

Now, Yandira struggled for breath as she brooded over the spoils of her vicious act. The crown itself was of simple design, a circlet of twisting silver and gold metal. What had always made it remarkable were the two majestic stones of twilight blue set into its front and back. The legend of Foresight and Hindsight was well known, for it was said they had been blessed by divinity during ancient times. But the stones now set into the crown carried no legends or higher grace ... because they were imitations.

The throne room doors opened and Ignius Rex marched in. His face was angry and his jaw muscles rippled as he ground his teeth.

'Sorry news, Majesty,' he said, bounding up the dais steps to kneel before the throne. 'Ghador's entourage has been searched, all possessions examined ... not one of them carried the missing stones.'

Yandira wasn't moved by the news. 'Go,' she told her Shade. 'Ensure the entrances to this city are barred and guarded. I want weapons in the hands of every citizen able to walk.' The Shade slithered like a snake down to the floor and disappeared to carry out its orders. 'Curse you,' Yandira told the crown. Even the act of speaking was painful to her.

Somehow, Foresight and Hindsight had been replaced with impressive replicas, while the originals were ... where? It didn't matter; the further away from this queendom the better, as far as Dragonfly was concerned. Without the true stones, Yandira could not fulfil her promise to her Oldunone. Cursed Persephone would not accept *fakes* in return for Her dark favour. Surely Yandira was undone. Dragonfly prayed she would wither and die before his eyes.

She said, 'I have suspicions, Ignius. Walk me to my council chamber.'

With no choice in the matter, Dragonfly and Morrad followed Yandira as she held on to the magician's arm and headed slowly to her private chambers where the black pool to the Underworld bubbled on the floor. Ignius helped his master sit in an armchair beside a dying fire then stepped back as she whispered serpentine words of magic. The pool cleared with a hiss to show woodlands where two wolves prowled between trees, sniffing the misty air.

'Present yourselves,' Yandira ordered.

Both wolves stopped in their tracks and changed into the craven Mr Lunk and Mr Venatus. They looked around, searching for the source of the voice.

'Where are you?' Yandira demanded.

'Watcher's Forest,' Mr Venatus replied to the air.

'What news of your prey?'

'They're travelling west, Majesty. The scent is faint, hard to track, but we reckon we can guess where they're heading. Rana's going home.'

'You think she's taking Wren to Singer's Hope?' A wry smile curled one side of Yandira's mouth. 'Of course she is.' She coughed and specks of blood appeared on her lips. 'Listen to me carefully. When you have Ghador in your clutches, search her corpse for two stones of twilight blue. They will be small, slim and oval, and you will take every measure to ensure they do not touch my sword when you bring them to me. Do you understand?'

'Utterly and completely, Majesty,' said Venatus. 'We should reach Singer's Hope around midnight.'

As he and Mr Lunk reverted to their wolf forms and bounded off through the trees, the pool blackened and Yandira sagged in the armchair, exhausted.

Ignius was quickly at her side. 'I have made preparations for you, Majesty. The threat of interrogation is loosening tongues. A soldier has come forward. He claims to have information about Princess Ghador.'

'Then quickly, Ignius.' Yandira placed the crown with its fake stones on her head, then gripped the magician's arm with a withered claw. 'Lead me to the dungeons.'

Grandma Rana had known every inch of Singer's Hope. The nooks and crannies, every establishment, every ship – along with their captains and secrets. To accompany her advice about the Old Flagship, she had once told Bek of the dingiest, dirtiest tavern in town, where decent folk were few and calculating eyes watched from the shadows. She said, 'If you're ever looking for the type of information you ought not to know, the Rudderless Swine is the place for you.' She had meant it as a warning, of course, adding that if a person ever needed either tavern then that person had met some trouble in life. Which was why Bek sat alone at the bar of the Rudderless Swine, while Ebbie was safely stowed away at the Old Flagship.

Grandma had been a good soul, the best of folk. Bek raised her tankard of ale in a silent salute to the memory of a woman who had tried her hardest to bring her granddaughter up right.

'Shit!' someone said from a table behind Bek. A gang of salty dockhands were playing cards. Evidently one of their number was getting fleeced.

Bek smiled sadly.

Dockworkers and sailors began to crowd the tavern now the working day was done, and Bek let the wash of voices flow over her. Here in this sordid place, if she sat and listened long enough, someone would tell her what she needed to know; and it was better she did this without Ebbie's fresh-faced naïvety alerting every pickpocket in the vicinity.

Bek nursed her ale and listened.

She hadn't been back to Singer's Hope since her grandma died – twelve years ago now, when Bek was a child of eleven. Before arriving at the Rudderless Swine, Bek had been curious to see if the place had changed, so she walked the long way to the tavern. Singer's Hope remained mostly as she remembered, along with the smell of brine and fresh fish, the noise of the docks and the bustle of town – she had been filled with a bitter-sweet sense of *home*. Bek had walked to a row of fishing shacks at the far end of the dockside, run-down, abandoned-looking buildings with dirty windows and peeling black paint.

The shacks were dark inside and locked for the night. Bek

kept walking until she stood before the shack where she had spent her childhood, which had once belonged to Grandma Rana. Nostalgia, heartache, anger swirled inside her to see it. Twelve years since she had died. Had it really been so long?

Although the shacks were small and cramped, Bek and her grandma had lived in theirs, eating and sleeping, talking and laughing, rising at dawn each day to cast off in their little fishing boat to earn their money from the Skea. They never had much, but always enough to get by. Such a simple and happy life. On the waves, listening to her grandma's wisdom while waiting for the net to fill with fish – that was the best education she had ever received, where she felt the most love, wanted for nothing. Grandma filled every absence in Bek's life.

She hadn't lied to Ebbie. She really didn't know her parents, wouldn't recognise them if she ever laid eyes on them. Bek's mother was named Lores. She was a sailor, which was the polite way of saying *smuggler* around these parts. Grandma would never have a word said against her, but Bek knew how disappointed she was in her daughter's choices in life. As for Bek's father, Grandma always said that he was just a night's fun at whatever harbour in the Realm Lores happened to be docked at. As far as Bek knew, the last time her mother had come to Singer's Hope was to give her new-born daughter to *her* mother before sailing away again. She left Bek behind and never returned. Maybe she was dead now, too.

But Grandma had stepped up, like always, and she did the right thing by her granddaughter every step of the way. 'One day, what little I have will be yours,' Bek remembered her saying. 'I won't be around for ever, sweetheart, but I'll make sure you're ready to face it all without me.'

It hadn't happened that way. The morning when Grandma hadn't risen to make breakfast, when she lay in her cot, cold and grey, and couldn't be woken, Bek hadn't felt ready at all. With Grandma's death, the harbourmaster at the time decided that eleven was too young to run a fishing business, however small. He rented the shack to someone else – no doubt someone who had greased his palm. And then, within a few hours of Grandma's sea burial, Bek had been shipped off to an orphanage in Strange Ground where she learned that life could be painfully sharp. And unintelligible.

'Don't waste time blaming others for your misfortunes,' Grandma used to say. 'Pick yourself up and try again.' She had been determined not to let her granddaughter become like her daughter. She would be so disappointed with how Bek had turned out.

A nearby conversation grabbed her attention.

'I'm telling you straight, old Cyrus reckons he's seen it with his own drunken eyes,' a woman was saying. 'The Oldunfolk, he says, They've cast winter on the Queen's Highway.'

The woman she was talking to laughed. 'Funny how Cyrus sees divinity when he's been at the gin. Mind you, it's that fog on the Skea what's bothering me.'

'Aye,' said the other, suddenly grim. 'It ain't natural.'

'They're saying it came from Oddridge Island.'

Funny – Bek had been thinking about Oddridge Island on the walk to Singer's Hope. When it came to True Sight Candles, Bek had never actually seen one, but she had heard all kinds of stories about them. Now, Oddridge Island was close to town, less than fifteen minutes' sail away, and a magician lived there who might well have a True Sight Candle to sell. But magicians were tricky to deal with, and this one had a dangerous reputation, so Bek had already decided that Oddridge Island was her last resort. Plenty of other places to try first.

One of the women muttered something about Neptune

saving her from darkness, and the other said, 'Have you heard what the sailors have been saying about the island—'

Whatever she said next was drowned by roars of laughter bursting from the table behind Bek.

The person getting fleeced at cards was a young sailor, as green around the ears as Ebbie Wren by the looks of him. Bek had seen dockhands working this kind of con before. The sailor was probably on shore leave for the first time since signing up to whichever ship he served on, pockets filled with coin itching to be gambled away. An easy target.

'I know what you're doing,' the sailor said, slamming his hand on the table. 'You can't cheat me like this.'

'Careful, boy,' said one of the dockhands, 'else we'll have the shirt off your back, too.'

The others laughed, as did many of the tavern's patrons who were watching.

The sailor, raging, jumped to his feet and shouted for his money back, which made him an even funnier spectacle. But then he said the thing Bek was waiting to hear.

'I'll tell my skipper about you. I serve on the *Admiral's Teeth*, you know.'

With a fresh round of laughter, the dockhands waved him away and the sailor conceded defeat, slumping against the bar and ordering an ale. The landlord brought him a tankard and waited while he searched his pockets for what money remained in them. When it became clear that he had nothing left, Bek slid alongside him and placed a copper coin on the bar. The landlord took the coin and wandered off to serve someone else.

The sailor gave Bek a suspicious look.

'Your skipper should've warned you about this place,' she said. 'Still, once bitten, twice shy, eh?'

The sailor slurped his ale then scowled over his shoulder at the dockhands. 'I'll get my money back.'

'No, you won't. And I'm not in the habit of buying drinks for every sad story I meet, so …' Bek held up two silver coins. 'I'll repay some of your losses if you deliver a message for me.'

The sailor's eyes lingered on the coins, his young face suspicious again. 'A message for who?'

'You're serving on the *Admiral's Teeth*, did I hear that right?' Bek waited for the sailor to nod. 'Is she in dock?'

'Aye, for the next day or two.'

'I take it Konn is still her captain?' When the sailor gave a second nod, Bek slid the silver coins across the bar top. 'Then my message is for him. Tell Konn that Bek Rana is in town and needs his help.' The sailor reached for the money, but Bek didn't take her hand off it. 'He can find me at the Old Flagship.'

Bek made the sailor repeat the message before letting him take the coins. 'I want it delivered now. I'll know if you don't.' She tapped her sword to underline the threat. 'Be sure to tell Konn it's urgent.'

First draining the tankard, the sailor left the Rudderless Swine with a final scowl for the dockhands. Bek waited a few moments then followed him out.

The sun was a bloody glow shining through grey clouds, half-sunk into the horizon, shedding a last streak of red on the glimmering Skea. A few dockhands were still unloading cargo from ships, and a lamplighter was making his way along the dockside adding the warm yellow glow of oil flames to the chilly rain. With a shiver, Bek pulled her collar up and made her way to the Old Flagship.

When she arrived, Ebbie was fast asleep in their rented room. A candle burned on the small table between the two bunks.

Ebbie snored while sitting upright with his back against the wall. His satchel lay open on his lap.

Bek stopped herself waking him. Instead, she stared into the satchel, her fingers suddenly itching with a pickpocket's curiosity. She leaned forwards, peeked inside and saw the lantern and coin-purse. She dipped her hand in, and the items didn't disappear because Bek wasn't interested in stealing them this time. With slow movements and a delicate touch, she located the enchanted letter which Ebbie claimed had been left to him by Queen Maitressa Wood Bee.

Ebbie snorted in his sleep as she pulled it free but didn't wake. Bek stepped back from him and unfolded the letter, expecting it to be as blank as Ebbie said it was. She nearly threw it away when she saw words on the page and read who they were addressed to: *Hello, Bek ...*

Heart thumping, Bek's brain told her to slip the letter back into the satchel and forget all about it, but her eyes refused to stop reading:

Are you still angry with me? I suppose it is too much to hope for your forgiveness after all these years, but the Bek Rana I knew was never given to hate, nor was she a believer in coincidence. Though I wonder if she is losing that unwavering curiosity with which she once viewed everything.

Aren't you intrigued by Ebbie Wren, where he is from, what he has seen? Are you so determined to save your own skin that you don't wonder what his world is like? If you believe your paths have crossed by accident, that you are an unfortunate victim of his circumstance, then you are denying the morals and instincts honed in you by your grandmother. Ebbie Wren has a brave heart, but he cannot complete

*his quest alone, and you know better than most what my
daughter will do should he fail.*

*There is no coincidence here, and you, Bek Rana, were
never a coward. Be angry with me if you wish, but do not
use it to excuse what you are planning. Instead, ask the truest
part of you if your loyalties have become so self-serving that
you would allow old friends to fall in the dust in your wake.
The decision, the responsibility, is yours alone. Do not deny
that. I may not be your flesh and blood, but I am your adopted
family, and I taught you better than this. I give you one last
chance to confess the true nature of our relationship, or I will
tell Ebbie Wren myself.*

With disappointment,
Lady Maitressa.

Bek's eyes refused to look away from the signature until Ebbie
mumbled in his sleep and made her flinch. Mouth agape, she
slipped the letter back into the satchel. In something of a daze,
she unbuckled her sword belt and sat on the free bunk, staring
into space.

Bek's teeth clenched. Was she angry? Damn straight she
was, and perturbed. Whatever magic had brought that letter to
Bek, Lady Maitressa Wood Bee of all people had no right to
question her loyalty and sense of responsibility. She had some
nerve accusing *anyone* of denial. Her words were the words of a
hypocrite, and they couldn't prey on Bek's conscience.

With a grim expression, she pulled the sword from its scabbard. In the candlelight, the writing sweeping along the blue
blade was easy to discern, though in an indecipherable, alien
language. Old friends had already let Bek Rana fall in the dust
long ago. Her mind wouldn't be swayed from her plans, for
her plans were just. This unique sword would buy her the life

she deserved, far from bad memories and hypocrites, where she would recover the happiness she had lost when her grandma died and Queen Maitressa abandoned her—

'Hey, you're back.' Ebbie's voice startled Bek. Awake now in his sitting position, he blinked bleary eyes at her. 'What kind of weapon is that?'

'What kind of weapon?' The question chafed against Bek's mood. 'It's a bloody sword, Ebbie.'

'Well, I can see that.' He noticed the satchel still sitting on his lap, open. Bek tensed, fearing he would check the enchanted letter and see what was written on it, but he didn't. Closing the flap, he placed the satchel on the floor and sat on the edge of the bunk. 'I mean ... it has a blue blade. Doesn't that make it special?'

'No.'

'What about the writing?' He was eager, excited again. 'Is it a spell?'

'*No.*'

'Then what does it say?'

Rankled, Bek lifted the blade and pretended to read. 'It says, *Happy Birthday, Bek, love Grandma.* All right?'

'Oh.' Ebbie's shoulders sagged. 'It's just a sword, then?'

'I'm very sorry if that disappoints you.' Bek slid the blade into the scabbard and put it aside. 'Listen, I might've found a way to get you a True Sight Candle.'

'Really?'

'The *Admiral's Teeth* is in dock. Her captain is an old family friend and if anyone in Singer's Hope can help you, it'll be him. But it won't come cheap.'

'Okay.' Ebbie rubbed his face. 'Let's go down to the docks.'

'Doesn't work that way. Konn has survived in the smuggling game for more years than even he can remember. You don't approach his ship without invitation. I've sent him a message. With luck, we'll hear back before long.'

'So, we wait, then?'

'Yes, we wait. And get some sleep.'

Ebbie was glad for the chance to rest some more, judging by his enormous yawn. With a little noise of contentment, he lay down on the bed and put his hands behind his head, saying, 'Sweet dreams.'

Bek rolled her eyes and blew out the candle.

Listening to rain tapping on the window, Bek lay there staring up at the ceiling. She'd been a long time without sleep, but her mind was too busy to shut down just yet. The letter was pricking at her. She probably should've told Ebbie about it, explained what it meant, but was there any point? He'd be gone for good soon. Even so, Maitressa's words tugged at Bek's soul.

'What's it like?' she asked in the growing dark.

'Hmm?' Ebbie said drowsily.

'Your side of the Skea. What's it like?'

'Different,' he said in a whisper. 'Very different.'

Bek didn't ask any more and lay there staring at the ceiling until the gentle rhythm of Ebbie's breathing lulled her to sleep.

After less than an hour, a gang of sailors kicked open the door, pulled sacks over Bek and Ebbie's heads and dragged them from the room.

17

Old Friends

'Bek,' Ebbie whimpered.

'Keep your mouth shut,' she snapped.

Though Ebbie found a small measure of comfort in Bek's proximity, he was struggling with panic. Hands tied, eyes blinded by an itchy sack over his head which stank of fish, he was led roughly through the rain drizzling down on Singer's Hope. There was a lot of shoving and sharp prods and grunted threats from the sailors who had so rudely stolen them from the Old Flagship, but they gave no explanation for why this was happening.

No one stopped or questioned the group, and it was a short march to the dockside. After crossing what Ebbie presumed to be a gangplank – a rather flimsy one by the precarious way it bowed and bounced underfoot – he was led down steps to a warmer place, drier.

He froze when he felt the sharp tip of a knife held against his stomach. Someone began searching his pockets, airing disappointment to find them empty of coin. They tugged at the ring on Ebbie's finger, but of course it wouldn't come off. He panicked for a moment that the sailor might try to cut it free, but evidently the ring was judged to be worthless and left alone.

Ebbie wondered where his satchel was as a woman began asking questions in a tone that said she wasn't in the mood to tolerate lies. He let Bek do the answering. By the tightness in her voice, she was being held at knifepoint, too.

Though Bek admitted she was in the market for a True Sight Candle, she lied when she said it was for tracking down the man who had knocked up Ebbie's sister and then left her in the lurch. By the time the woman had finished asking her questions, she revealed the captives had been brought to the hold of a ship called the *Admiral's Teeth*, abducted on the orders of its skipper: Captain Konn.

Ebbie didn't know how many were with the woman, but it sounded like a lot as their feet thumped up wooden stairs and a door slammed behind them. The stillness was disturbed by the ship's creaking as it bobbed on the Skea, the movement not helping to settle the anxiety roiling Ebbie's stomach.

'You can take off the sack,' said Bek.

Ebbie whipped it from his head and took a deep breath of air that smelled worse than the sack did. The hold was dingy, filled with crates and barrels. Water dripped. Wide stairs led up to a big hatchway, closed and probably locked.

Bek sat on a barrel, staring up into a shaft of weak moonlight shining through a gap in the decking. Her hands rested in her lap. Like Ebbie's, her wrists were bound with rope.

'I thought you said Konn was a family friend?' Ebbie whispered, scared and angry.

'That might've been a stretch.'

'Well, obviously.'

'The truth is, my grandma got on better with him than I ever did.' Bek sucked on her bottom lip thoughtfully. 'Now I think about it, I do owe Konn some money. He cheated me at cards a couple of years ago, back in Strange Ground. I refused to pay up and ducked out. But it wasn't enough to warrant this kind of treatment.'

'Are you sure?' Ebbie tried and failed to pull his hands free of the rope. 'Pissing off a smuggler doesn't sound like a clever thing to do.'

'I'd advise against calling Konn a smuggler to his face. Be careful around these folk, Ebbie. You don't know them, and they don't know you—'

The shaft of light blinked as someone moved through it. The sound of footsteps and muffled voices approached the hatch at the top of the stairs.

'I'll do the talking,' Bek whispered. 'But if you *are* pressed to speak, remember they're not *smugglers* – they're *sailors*, all right?' The hatch opened and lantern light shone into the hold. 'And how ever much you might want to, *don't* tell them the truth.'

Three folk descended the stairs. The first was a shaven-headed woman covered in tattoos and carrying a long knife. The lantern-bearer followed her, a scrawny youngster who looked like he had many weapons concealed about his person. Lastly, another man, aged and weather-worn, tall and broad, his beard bushy and hair streaked with grey. While his companions hung back, this man came forward and studied first Ebbie and then Bek with eyes as blue as ice. Dressed in a red, billowing shirt and dark trousers, he appeared unarmed, though his hands looked big enough to strangle a neck each.

'As I live and breathe,' he said, grinning to reveal a few gold teeth. 'The one and only Bek Rana.'

To Ebbie's surprise – and dismay – Bek answered with hostility. 'What in Laverna's name are you doing, Konn? I ask for your help and you treat me like *this*?'

The captain shrugged meaty shoulders. 'That's what happens when you run out on a debt.'

'You can't be serious? This is because of ten miserable gold pieces?'

'Aye, it's the principle. And it's twenty gold now. See, I doubled your debt on account of you being a sneaky, cheating bastard.' Konn hissed out a disappointed breath. 'Grandma Rana would be shamed by your conduct. Now there was a woman I could trust.'

Behind the captain, the tattooed woman nodded in agreement. Bek's cheeks flushed angrily.

'Don't you dare talk about my grandma.'

Ebbie held his breath, but Konn was amused rather than offended by the threat in Bek's voice, doing no more than folding his thick arms across his wide chest in reaction.

'When I heard Bek Rana was back in town, looking for me, I knew she wasn't here to square her tab. She's always up to something, I thought. So ...' Konn looked at Ebbie. 'Who are you?'

Ebbie opened his mouth, but Bek jumped in. 'He's no one, from the country.'

Konn laughed. 'Well then, *No One from the Country*, I'm told someone put your sister in the family way then did a runner. Now you want a True Sight Candle to find him. Is that right?'

Again, Bek answered. 'Yes.'

'True Sight Candle.' Konn sucked air over his teeth. 'A rare and expensive piece of merchandise for the likes of countryfolk.'

'Don't worry, he can pay you,' Bek said, with more confidence than Ebbie possessed.

'How?' said Konn 'You don't have a single copper between you. Or will you sell what you *do* own? I'm sure you'll get a fine price for a rucksack, a crappy old sword and an empty satchel.'

The sailors laughed at their captain's sarcasm, but Ebbie felt the bite of anxiety at the mention of his satchel. It was empty? Did that mean the crew of the *Admiral's Teeth* had already helped themselves to what it held, or something else?

'Your story's utter catshit, of course,' Konn said. 'There's always more to Bek Rana than she reveals.'

Bek did her best not to look shifty. 'Listen, Konn, I need your help and you'll get paid well for it.'

'Oh, I doubt that. But ...' Digging his fingers into his beard, Konn studied his captives with icy blue appraisal. 'I *could* get your friend a True Sight Candle. Tonight, as it happens. I could also square away your debt. If you're up for a bit of business?'

He left it hanging and Bek's face became an unreadable mask. Konn's gold teeth flashed in the lantern light as he headed for the stairs.

'Cut her bonds,' he ordered his sailors. 'Bring her to my cabin. Leave *No One* down here.'

Ebbie didn't want to be left alone, but a warning look from Bek told him to keep quiet as the tattooed woman grabbed the sack from the floor and pulled it back over his head.

Down in the hot and shadowy dungeons, Lord Dragonfly was feeling sick in his heart. The Serpent's Sigh was slowly draining the life from his soul. He wondered if Princess Morrad retained enough of herself to be able to feel the same as, side by side, they witnessed the grim events taking place beneath Castle Wood Bee.

Captain Gavith, the commander of Ghador's convoy, was dead. His corpse remained strapped to a torture rack, on open display for the rest of Ghador's soldiers to see from their cells. Gavith's eyes had been burned out, a few of his fingers cut off and multiple lacerations ensured he was slicked with his own blood before death. On either side of the rack, two jailors sat on the floor, still and drooling. Their hands and aprons were bloody and glistening.

The rest of the entourage, packed together like animals in

cages, bruised and dishevelled, had once been happy and loyal to the throne; now these poor folk were gripped by silent fear and hatred as Yandira confronted her latest victim.

'I've been told of a confession you have made.' Yandira's voice was ragged, barbed like a spider creeping over its web towards its catch. 'Before returning to Strange Ground, you received an important message. Is that right?'

'Yes, Majesty.' The young soldier was named Barrek. In charge of the convoy's courier gulls, he had come forward too late to save his commanding officer's life, but now believed he could spare his fellows a similar fate. 'A gull was sent from Castle Wood Bee. It carried news of Queen Eldrid's assassination and Princess Morrad's order for her niece to be returned home swiftly.'

'Yet you did not share this news and order with Captain Gavith.'

The apple of Barrek's throat bobbed and he shook his head, too afraid to speak further.

Dressed in a grimy doublet and hose, he stood in the circle of a spell written in chalk on the flagstones. A royal guard stood between him and Yandira. Motionless in full armour, the guard had levelled a wicked pike at the prisoner's gut. Behind Barrek, Ignius Rex observed in deathly stillness, standing close but not so close as to be inside the chalk spell. Yandira had positioned herself and the royal guard in such a way as to allow Barrek a clear view of Gavith's corpse. She wore the crown of Strange Ground, albeit with the fake stones of Hindsight and Foresight.

Dragonfly hoped it wasn't a trick of the dungeon's flickering torchlight, but Yandira appeared to be withering before his eyes. She was grey, her skin dry and flaky, her every breath taken with great effort as she stared expectantly at the young man from behind her armoured guard.

'Then what *did* you do with the information, Barrek?'

With eyes fixed fearfully on the silver blade mere inches from his stomach, Barrek's voice trembled as he said, 'I wrote to Dalmyn. I informed Queen White Gold that Strange Ground had fallen to ... to ...'

'To me?'

He confirmed with a whispered, 'Yes.'

Yandira frowned at Ignius. 'This explains Dalmyn's swift response, but not how this fool or anyone in Ghador's entourage knew I was responsible for Eldrid's death. When Morrad sent her message to the convoy, requesting Ghador's return to Strange Ground, I was still locked in my tower. Curious, don't you agree?'

'Perhaps, Majesty.' The magician looked more concerned about his master's increasing frailties. 'But then we know clandestine forces have been working against you from the beginning. This *boy* has more to tell.'

'It was the blue light!' Barrek cried but averted his gaze when Yandira whipped her spidery attention back onto him.

'Ah, yes, our mysterious magic.'

From what Dragonfly had gathered from Yandira's dark mutterings and her conversations with Ignius Rex, the charm which had been cast upon the prisoners was a divine one: Juno's Blessing, a shield against dark magic like the Serpent's Sigh. It encouraged a beat of hope in his ailing heart, hope for this queendom, hope for Ghador.

'Majesty,' Barrek said, quickly, breathlessly, 'Princess Morrad's gull arrived mere moments before the blue light swept through the convoy. And I saw from where the light came. Princess Ghador's carriage.'

Yandira sized him up. 'You only confirm what I have already reasoned.'

'When the light faded, the princess was gone, and I ... I cannot explain it, but somehow I knew the truth behind the queen's assassination. Sending a gull to Dalmyn was the greatest imperative of my life.'

'Divinity compelled you,' Yandira said mournfully. 'And Captain Gavith.'

More hope beat in Dragonfly's heart. Legend said Foresight and Hindsight had been blessed by Juno Herself. Surely Ghador had used the real stones to release her Oldunone's Blessing upon the entourage before making her escape with them, taking them far, far away from Yandira. But ... how had Ghador stolen them from the crown when her mother wore it on a daily basis?

'Ignius, our enemy has gained an advantage, and I am disturbed.' She steadied her wobbling stance by placing a hand on the royal guard's armoured back. 'I *must* have those stones.'

'And have them you shall, Majesty, along with your sword.' Ignius was fretting now, clearly pained by his master's appearance. 'It is time to gather your strength for what is to come.'

Yandira's hooded gaze scoured the prisoners in the cells. The soldiers, stripped of armour and weapons, glared back with open hostility. Gavith's first officer stood right at the front. Lieutenant Davil was a tall woman with unreadable blue eyes. Did she see what Dragonfly saw? Without the promises of her Oldunone, Yandira was shrinking, wasting away, her courtly gown loose and ill-fitting over what now looked to be a skeletal frame.

Barrek shied from Yandira's hard and dark eyes, which, to Dragonfly's astonishment, turned pale and rheumy as if milk had been dripping into them. She then asked a question that surprised the young soldier.

'Are you angry with me?'

'Majesty?' Uncertain, Barrek searched for help or courage from the faces in the cells. Lieutenant Davil's grim expression stared back at him.

Yandira said, 'Do you fear that Captain Gavith's fate now awaits you?'

'Yes,' Barrek admitted.

'You and your fellows must be horrified by who now sits on the Wood Bee Throne.'

Not knowing what to say, Barrek worried at the cuff of his sleeve while looking to his commanding officer.

'You don't seem particularly brave to me, Barrek. *Unassuming* and *expendable* are the words I'd use. How could anyone possibly perceive you as a threat?' Yandira rapped her knuckles on the guard's back. He lifted the pike and stepped aside to leave clear space between his master and her prisoner. Yandira swayed on unsteady legs. 'Your fellow soldiers spied an opportunity when you volunteered to come forward, didn't they? You were given *very* specific orders, weren't you?'

'Do it now!' Davil roared.

His face creasing in rage, Barrek cried, 'Traitor!' and pulled a stabbing dagger from his sleeve. He leapt forward, punching the blade into Yandira's stomach.

Morrad groaned, desperate shouts came from the cells and a thrill of triumph coursed through Dragonfly's subjugated body. But the moment of jubilation was short-lived. Yandira hadn't even flinched. The guard didn't act, and Ignius Rex only raised an eyebrow. Barrek's dagger had rebounded and he staggered back into the chalk circle, gawping at the red stain blossoming on his doublet from a wound he'd made in his own stomach.

From the cells came more desperate and encouraging shouts. But Barrek didn't launch a second attack. He stared fearfully as darkness appeared on Yandira like a breastplate.

'Juno's Blessing will spare you from the Underworld's magic,' she said, almost kindly, 'but not from an assassin's blade.'

The darkness had formed a diamond-like shape on Yandira's chest, setting hard and shiny like an arrowhead of obsidian. The Shade, Dragonfly realised with despair.

Barrek cried out and stabbed for Yandira's throat with the dagger. The Shade was far quicker and much more deadly, springing forward to open a deep gash on the side of Barrek's neck.

Blood sprayed, spattering Dragonfly and Morrad, while the Pretender to House Wood Bee watched impassively.

The dagger slipped from slick fingers and Barrek sank to his knees, clutching his neck, failing to stem the gushes of lifeblood pumping from his wound, soaking his clothes, pooling on the spell beneath him. The fetid, slimy presence of dark magic filled the dungeons. Gasps and retches came from the prisoners. Crushing misery descended on Dragonfly as the Underworld opened its filthy maw.

The spell's lines and swirls shone through steaming blood with fiery detail. Serpentine voices, an untold number, hissed spitefully from unknown depths as black tentacles rose and searched for a sacrifice.

Panic and terror contorted Barrek's young face as the tentacles probed at him with their tips like poisonous snakes tasting with their tongues. He managed a final scream when they struck, coiling, squeezing, and pulled him down into his own blood, down through the spell, and dragged his body into the bowels of Cursed Persephone's domain. As a final act, the tentacles claimed the royal guard, too. His pike clanged to the dungeon floor as silver armour flashed and followed Barrek into darkness.

Breathing hard, Ignius Rex appeared excited, relieved. But

then he jumped clear, yelping, as something happened that he was clearly not expecting.

The Underworld belched a gout of red fire that wreathed his master in flame. Sour heat washed over Dragonfly. Head thrust back, Yandira bellowed at the dungeon ceiling, but not in torture. It was a bellow of victory as her body absorbed the fire until the Underworld closed its mouth, leaving nothing behind except a patch of scorched blood on the flagstones, the spell burned away.

The prisoners were all sobs and cries of despair by this time. When they saw Yandira's transformation, they tried to back away in their already cramped cells, including the immovable Lieutenant Davil. Ignius Rex's face expressed shock.

Empowered by something more than strength from blood sacrifice, Yandira stood straight, unharmed by the Underworld's fire, her clothes burned away, replaced by shadows that roiled like smoke. The skin of her face and hands had toughened as though changed to iron-hard scales, and her blackened eyes glared from a demonic face.

'I will care for you,' she told the cowering prisoners, her voice stronger than ever. 'I will feed and water you.' She clenched and unclenched long fingers now tipped with claws, and her voice rose to a shout of wild fury. 'Blessed by Juno, your blood tastes all the sweeter to the Underworld! With your sacrifices, Lady Persephone will nourish my Empire!'

'Majesty,' said Ignius. He cowered when she snarled at him like a beast. 'I beg you hear my wisdom, Majesty.' The magician turned fearful eyes to Princess Morrad. 'The time has come. It must be now.'

The *Admiral's Teeth* wasn't a particularly big ship, but the right size for navigating the narrow inlets and hidden coves used for smuggling. Up on deck, a couple of sailors in cloaks stood by a hanging lantern, watching the dockside. Above, moonlight split dark clouds with silver cracks in the sky. The tattooed woman and the young sailor who had delivered Bek's message to the captain remained outside after ushering Bek into Konn's cabin, which was more like a storeroom. Amidst barrels and piles of folded cloth, stacks of books and rolled maps were a simple bed and a desk, behind which Konn sat, looking over a map.

The captain was a touch greyer than the last time Bek had seen him, but still every inch the strong shark she remembered. He didn't look up from the map at first, and Bek's heart skipped a beat when she noticed the items on his desk.

The rucksack was there, as was Ebbie's satchel. Flat and empty again, the enchantment had obviously prevented Konn from discovering its contents, otherwise this would have been a very different kind of situation. But next to the satchel was Bek's sword, her precious treasure, and it was unsheathed, lying alongside its battered scabbard, blue blade bare to the world.

'Been some troubling rumours coming out of the city lately,' Konn said, looking up from the map. 'Don't suppose you can tell me anything about that, can you?'

Bek considered her answer carefully. 'I could, but the less you know about it the better.'

'Is that right?'

'Just … steer clear of Strange Ground for a while. Trust me on that.'

'*Trust you* – that's a good one.' Konn pointed at the rucksack. 'This right here is an emergency pack from Backway Charlie's, which tells me you had to leave in a hurry.' The chair creaked as the captain leaned forwards. 'You and your friend are on the run. Tell me I'm wrong.'

Bek swallowed. 'Listen, Konn—'

'No, *you* listen. Grandma Rana always dealt fair, so out of respect for her memory, I'll give you the chance to be straight with me.' Konn laid aside the map and picked up Bek's sword. 'Clever, keeping this thing in an old scabbard. My crew didn't give it a second glance, but you and me know it's got some worth. Looks like it used to have gemstones – I suppose you sold those already, did you?'

'No. It came without them.'

Konn ran a thumb over the stone blade's keen edge then inhaled sharply when he nicked himself. Bek could have sworn she saw a spark of blue when it happened but didn't say anything as Konn dropped the sword on the desk, sucked the blood from his thumb and said, 'There's writing on it. Never seen the like before.'

'Nor have I,' Bek confessed. The opportunist in her suddenly reared its ugly head with an idea. 'I'm selling it, if you're interested. Make me an offer and I'll knock off the gold I already owe you. Plus a bit more. In memory of my grandma.'

'Shameless as ever, eh?' Konn leaned back in his chair, clearly amused. 'If I wanted this sword, I'd take it without your permission, but I don't. See, when such a fine display piece winds up in the hands of someone so untrustworthy, my instincts are more inclined to give it a wide berth. Didn't anyone ever warn you that thieving from nobles brings nothing but bad luck?'

'What?'

'Who else could afford this kind of craftsmanship? Come on, Bek, I told you to be straight with me.'

Her shoulders deflating, Bek conceded defeat. 'You're right. Charlie warned me not to steal it, but I wouldn't listen.'

'And now you want to scam your troubles onto me?' Konn chuckled. 'There's good reason why even smugglers won't deal with this kind of merchandise. What have you got yourself into, Bek Rana?'

Where did she begin? 'Look, the rumours you've been hearing about Strange Ground are true and worse.' She rubbed her forehead. 'I need to get as far away from the city as possible, and you damn well know why. But ever since I stole the sword, trouble's been following me around like a bloody curse.'

'Trouble like your friend down in the hold?' The captain narrowed his eyes. 'Does he know half the truth about you?'

'Let's not get into that, Konn.'

'Who is he really?'

'A pain in my arse who won't go away. I would tell you more, but—'

'The less I know about it all, the better – aye, I heard you the first time, but my gut's inclined to believe you now.'

'The quickest way to get rid of him is with a True Sight Candle.' Bek looked at the captain hopefully. 'You said you can fix him up with one?'

'I did at that.' With care, Konn slid the sword back into the scabbard, then picked up the map he had been studying, issuing a huff. 'Been having troubles of my own, lately. Strange weather's messing with smuggling routes, sailors are talking about *things* hiding in the fog, and now a merchant I trade with has disappeared with a *lot* of my gold.'

'Disappeared?'

'Well, not exactly. I know where she is, so let's say she's become *aloof*. Nobody's heard from her for a couple of days now, and she's withholding merchandise from a fair few traders who have already paid for their wares. Traders like *me*.' Konn's expression soured. 'I've got a line of unhappy customers who'll be demanding their money back if I don't deliver their orders soon. Reputation's everything in this game, Bek.'

True as that was, Bek didn't like where this tale was heading. 'You want me to go and collect your merchandise. Konn, I'm begging you, I don't have time for this.'

'Well, given one of the items I ordered just happens to be a True Sight Candle, I reckon you'll make time.'

In her head, Bek was asking Laverna what she had done wrong. Why was the Oldunone of Thieves allowing so many folk to piss on her plans?

Konn said, 'Get me my merchandise and I'll let you keep the candle. I'll square away your debt, too, then you and your friend can be on your merry way. How does that sound?'

It sounded like the only resolution Bek was going to get. There was always a catch when the smugglers of Singer's Hope were involved, and Konn was the sneakiest shark in the Skea.

'This merchant,' she said. 'If you already know where she is, why haven't you gone after her yourself?'

'It's tricky, Bek.' He winced, almost embarrassed. 'Me and her, we've done a lot of trade over the years, but we don't much like each other. For whatever reason, she's obviously got a new beef with me, so there's more chance of claiming what's mine if I use a neutral face in a parlay.'

'Parlay or burglary?'

'Whichever best suits.'

Bek mulled that over. 'Who is she, Konn? *Where* is she?'

In reply, the captain handed over the map. Bek held it up, seeing it was of a small land mass just off Singer's Hope. She recognised the shape before reading its name.

'You've got to be joking.' Bek lowered the map. 'You want me to go to Oddridge Island?'

'I'll take that as a *yes*. Of course, I could always keep you here for that noble you robbed. Bet there's a nice price on your head.'

Konn's gold-toothed grin wasn't kind. 'Now, go and fetch my merchandise, you sneaky bastard. And while you're about it, get this sword off my ship.'

18

Truth, Lies and Letters

The *Admiral's Teeth* slipped away from Singer's Hope, stealthy and secretive as it cut across the Skea. The ship's mission involved a brief sojourn over calm waters, and in less than fifteen minutes – barely enough time for the sails to catch the wind – it had dropped anchor just off a small beach belonging to its mysterious destination: Oddridge Island.

Oddridge ... The crew on deck acted wary of the name. Ebbie decided not to ask why, surrounded as he was by unfriendly sailors or smugglers or whatever they called themselves. He really wasn't cut out for this kind of company.

Dampened by cold drizzle, with shafts of moonlight peeking through the clouds, Bek was uttering a never-ending line of curses as she helped Ebbie down a rope ladder into a rowing boat. Ebbie didn't know why she was so angry, but he was glad Bek's angst was aimed at the captain and not him for a change.

'We'll wait for you here,' Konn said, grinning over the side of his ship, flanked by several sailors who were as amused as him by Bek's bad mood. 'And I suppose I should wish you Neptune's luck. Or would you prefer Laverna's?'

He laughed at Bek's choice retort, and then at Ebbie as the boat rocked and his lack of sea legs caused to him fall hard into a sitting position. Ebbie clutched his limp and empty satchel to his chest, worrying over its missing contents. Bek used an oar to push off from the ship's hull. Her sword and the backpack were sitting in the boat between them. Swearing with every heave, Bek rowed towards the beach with Konn's voice drifting after them: 'If you're not back with the sun, I'll assume the worst and set sail without you.'

Ebbie didn't know what that meant; he had yet to discover why they had come to the island or what had occurred during Bek's private meeting with Konn, but he once again decided it was better to keep his mouth shut so Bek could vent her anger on the oars.

Halfway to the island, he realised with some astonishment that the satchel was full again. He looked inside; the lantern, the sigil stone, the letter, the money pouch and the contract had all rematerialized. Bek noticed this, too, but instead of expressing surprise she growled something best left unsaid. Ebbie pulled out Mai's letter, shielding it against the drizzle. His heartbeat quickened to see she had written to him again.

My dearest Ebbie Wren,
  As you sail on troubled waters, heading into the unknown, it is time you learned a few truths about your travelling companion. Bek Rana is angry, bitter, and this has made her stubborn and self-serving. Therefore, it falls to me to inform you of her omissions ...

Ebbie looked at Bek. She glowered at the paper in his hands as she heaved on the oars. Ebbie resumed reading, all the way to the end of the letter. And then he read it again, and again, because he couldn't quite believe what Mai was telling him. He stared at the words until the hull scraped against sandy shallows.

'Help me,' Bek grunted.

Ebbie splashed into chilly, knee-deep water and helped to drag the boat up onto the island's stony beach. Once it was safely stowed behind some rocks, they stood side by side, looking inland to where the beach ended and trees began.

Bek said, 'Konn will give us a True Sight Candle. But only if we do him a favour first ...'

And she explained how the captain was having trouble with Oddridge, the magician who lived on the island. He had paid a lot of gold for specialist merchandise which she was withholding. Konn had given Bek, and by extension Ebbie, no choice but to collect what he was owed. If they failed, there'd be no True Sight Candle and they'd be stuck in the mud till someone like Lunk and Venatus caught up with them.

But Ebbie was only half-listening. 'Mai wrote to me again.' He took the letter out of the satchel. 'I think you might want to read what she said.'

'I don't need to.' Bek's eyes were hard, staring into the dark trees. 'I know what Maitressa told you.'

Ebbie stowed the letter, frowning. 'Then it's true? You knew each other?'

'A long time ago.'

'Why didn't you tell me?'

'Because it makes no difference.'

No difference? 'Bek, you're Mai's adopted granddaughter.'

'Drop it.' Bek's voice was as stony as her eyes. 'You need a True Sight Candle, and to get one ... well, Lunk and Venatus might be the least of our problems now.' She buckled her sword belt then hefted her rucksack. 'Magicians are dangerous folk, Ebbie, so focus on that. Forget about anything that bloody letter told you.'

Ebbie watched as she set off for the trees. How could he forget about it? She had been close to Mai for all that time and she had hidden it from him. And that wasn't the only secret Bek Rana was keeping.

Sparing a final glance for the lantern lights blinking from the *Admiral's Teeth* bobbing on the Skea, Ebbie hurried after her.

A path of large, worn stones snaked through the wood. Bek said it should lead them straight to Oddridge's house, if all the stories she'd heard were true. 'And there are a *lot* of stories about this island, few of them good. I've been taught to fear Oddridge since I was a child. She doesn't like uninvited guests.'

'So what do we do?'

'Don't know. Never tried visiting her house before—'

Ebbie nearly walked into the back of Bek as she stopped abruptly. She was scanning the wood, scowling at fog now creeping in from all directions, grey like smoke drifting through the trees.

'But then again, maybe Oddridge already knows we're here.'

Ebbie stepped closer to Bek. The fog acted unnaturally. Glowing with moonlight spearing through the clouds, it rose up to form a wall on either side of them and cover the path several paces ahead and behind. But it didn't close in on them.

'Is it magic?' Ebbie asked fearfully.

'Maybe.' Bek's fingers curled around her sword's hilt. 'Stay behind me.'

They walked on at a cautious pace, and the fog continued to act unnaturally, never letting them get too close, always receding to stay nine or ten paces distant as though steering their passage. It was growing thicker, too, rolling sluggishly like viscous fluid and concealing the trees beyond those flanking the path with their dark and twisted shapes.

A twig snapped. Ebbie flinched. Things were moving unseen in the fog. Had to be wildlife scurrying about, he convinced himself, simple as that. He was walking so close to Bek that he practically shadowed her footsteps. This time, he did bump into her when she stopped.

'We're being watched,' she whispered, slipping three inches of blue stone from the scabbard. 'Someone's out there.'

Ebbie gasped, tapping Bek's shoulder urgently and pointing to the right. Two figures had appeared, no more than black silhouettes behind the misty treeline. Rustling came from the left and a third figure appeared, but none of them stepped onto the path.

'We come as friends,' Bek declared. 'To parlay with Oddridge.'

No reply and the figures remained where they were. Statue-still, the three of them seemed content to keep their distance and stare at the island's interlopers.

'Hello?' Again, no reply, and Bek drew the sword a few inches more.

'Who are they?' Ebbie asked.

'Might be trolls.'

'What?'

'Way too small for ogres, but I didn't think this island had any trolls—'

Bek broke off as a ghostly light shone through the fog. A pale illumination, glowing from somewhere ahead. A voice cried, 'Begone!' A woman, full of authority. 'You've tormented me enough.' The light brightened and Bek yanked the sword fully free. The dark figures scattered like startled rabbits, disappearing into the grey.

'Parley!' Bek called. 'We're here on behalf of the *Admiral's Teeth*.'

There was a pause. 'Konn sent you?' Ebbie heard surprise in the woman's voice. 'That old smuggler can only think of merchandise at a time like this?'

'Are you Oddridge?'

Another pause. 'Come forward and keep your hands where I can see them.'

Bek sheathed the sword and put her hands in the air, then motioned for Ebbie to do the same before approaching the source of the light. The trees and the fog cleared when they reached the end of the path. Woodsmoke laced the air and the ghostly light blazed like an interrogation lamp. Ebbie shielded his eyes, but still couldn't see much of the woman who held the light aloft. Her face was hidden in the hood of a russet robe.

'Who are you?' the woman – Oddridge, apparently – said, her voice an enigmatic growl. 'Tell me your names.'

Ebbie was about to reply when Bek gave him a swift elbow to the ribs. 'We're no one,' she said. 'Travellers, down on their luck and in a bind.'

'I should think you are if you wound up here,' Oddridge said. 'But tell me, how is it that your wits are not poisoned?'

'I ...' Bek faltered with words. 'Look, if it's all the same to you, we'd like to collect Konn's merchandise and be on our way.'

The magician considered them. 'Follow me.'

The pale glare dimmed to a gentle glow, revealing its source as a glass ball in Oddridge's hand. With the light now low, a house could be seen behind her, a sizable building the shape and design of an Earthly church, Ebbie thought. Oddridge headed towards it. Her uninvited guests followed.

The entrance to the house was a sturdy and old-looking wooden door. It didn't creak or groan when Oddridge opened it to reveal a darkness that her light couldn't penetrate. She beckoned her visitors inside before stepping forward and disappearing into the gloom.

Ebbie took a step back from the darkness which had evidently swallowed their host. Rolling her eyes, Bek grabbed his hand and pulled him in after her. Crossing the threshold felt like stepping through a veil of thick air. Ebbie's ears popped and then his eyes were filled with the warm glow of orange flames burning low in an open woodstove.

Still hidden within the hood, Oddridge faced them in the kitchen of her house. Pans and dried herbs hung from the ceiling; on a table a dead chicken waited to be plucked and gutted. As tall as Ebbie and slender in her robe, hands tucked into her sleeves, Oddridge looked every bit as mysterious as Ebbie always imagined a magician would be.

'How did you get past the fog?' she said with a low voice befitting her mysterious appearance. 'What protection did you bring?'

When Bek said nothing, Ebbie decided the question must be for him, so he answered. With a shrug.

Oddridge clucked her tongue. 'Some might say that deceiving a magician is a foolish thing to try.'

'We didn't bring anything,' Bek said, taking two steps closer to the magician. She shook off her rucksack and placed it on the floor, showing none of her earlier apprehension. 'We rowed ashore from the *Admiral's Teeth* and walked through the fog, simple as that. All we want is Konn's merchandise.'

'No, there is magic upon you. *Both* of you.' The opening of Oddridge's hood turned from Bek to Ebbie. 'That ring on your finger. Where did you get it?'

Ebbie looked at the cream and green band, weighing the pros and cons of keeping information from a magician, but then Bek said, 'Don't tell her anything.' Her gaze travelled around the kitchen, eyes narrowed, calculating, as she took another couple of steps towards their host. 'What's going on here? Where's Oddridge?'

Ebbie found it a strange question, given the person in question was standing right there in front of them, but his confusion turned to panicked surprise when Bek drew her sword, quick as a flash, and pointed it at their host.

The magician's hood tilted to one side, studying the weapon. 'You dare to threaten *me*?'

'Give it a rest,' Bek growled.

Ebbie gulped. 'What are you doing?'

'I saw Oddridge once. When I was a child, she bought fish from my grandma. She was five feet tall, if that, and so bent she needed a staff to walk.' Bek tapped the magician's chest with the sword tip. 'So, who are you?'

'All right, calm down.' The magician's voice had lost its menacing and mysterious tones. 'Let's not get nasty.'

Encouraged by the sword at her chest, she raised her hands submissively and Bek pulled down her hood. The face belonged to a woman around thirty, much too young to fit a legend's profile. Her black hair rested about her shoulders in a tangle of matted locks. Her eyes were sheepish, but her smile was warm.

'Hello there,' she said. 'The name's Karin, Oddridge's apprentice. Well, I was until she died.'

Bek gave Ebbie a perplexed glance before saying, 'Oddridge is *dead*?'

'Couple of years now. Passed in her sleep, poor love.'

'That can't be true. I would've heard.'

'Oh, well, I never told anyone, see? I'd show you where I buried her, but ...' She looked at Ebbie and puffed her cheeks. 'I've been having a shite time of late.'

The pans in the kitchen began rattling together and Bek screwed her face up. 'What—?'

A rumble came up through the floor tiles, light at first but gaining momentum until bursting into a wail, disembodied and ghoulish, and tongues of red flame licked out from the stove. The wail rose and fell, shaking the whole house. Ebbie covered his ears as pans danced and clanged on their hooks and two plates jumped from a cupboard to smash on the floor.

And then, as though stolen by a vacuum, the wail fell silent and all was quiet in the kitchen besides the low crackling of burning wood.

'What the hell was that?' Ebbie said.

'One of Oddridge's wards,' Karin replied. 'It's reminding me there are bad things outside the house.'

To Ebbie's surprise, the magician had used the moment's distraction to slip away from the sword at her chest, which Bek still held out straight. The sphere of pale light was in her hand again, and she was shining it upon the flat of the stone blade, studying the writing engraved into it.

'I knew it!' She grinned at Bek. 'Brilliant. I've been waiting for you two.'

The Queen's Highway was saturated with forbidden magic, magic greater than any witch or magician could conjure without divine intervention. The night was cold, unseen enemies hid in the fog, but there would be no stopping until Strange Ground beneath the Skea for the eight hundred soldiers of Dalmyn.

Prince Maxis had abandoned his plan to return home. The message Kingfisher had written to his mother had been found on Nellin's corpse, undelivered, its wax seal unbroken. There were no reinforcements coming, no way to alert the Protectors of the Realm, and Kingfisher had to fight through Maxis's princely pride to hook the reason of a father. His daughter needed him, she pleaded. The Coven of Bellona was poisoning the land with the Serpent's Sigh and the fog would only grow, spreading from Ghador's home to his home, to the next city, the next town and settlement, unless Yandira was stopped, here and now. Time was running out but the heroes of Dalmyn could secure his daughter's throne.

Of course, it helped that he and his soldiers were now protected from dark sorceries.

'The Priests of Juno have a saying,' Kingfisher said. She and Seej Agda sat facing each other in the back of a wagon. '*When darkness comes, lightness must follow, but never to shine upon a clear and easy road.*'

The High Priest was shaken by her recent ordeal. Upon regaining consciousness, she had taken a while to gather her wits. Even now, she didn't look too sure of herself. Seej shivered, pulled her thick travelling cloak tightly around her, then drank deeply from a waterskin.

'In this situation, I'd pray for all the help in the Realm,' Maxis grumbled as he drove the wagon. Straight and tense in his armour, he had set a careful pace for the company, and they expected to reach Strange Ground before dawn. Maxis swung his head from side to side, scanning the fog for enemies. 'But for now, Mother Seej, I'd settle for an explanation.'

'As would I,' said Kingfisher.

The priest didn't seem to know where to begin. The source of the mysterious magic she had cast was still wrapped in her tight fist. Even while unconscious, she hadn't relaxed her grip. All around, the enchantment's effects could be seen. It cleared the cold fog from the road ahead and kept it at bay so the soldiers on horseback travelled within a protected circle, flanking the wagon train. Kingfisher could not feel it affecting her person, but when the magic first flowed through her, it had felt comforting and familiar. It had reminded her of the old days, back when Maitressa was queen.

Kingfisher took Seej's closed hand in hers and spoke kindly.

'Juno's priests are not known for their spell-casting, yet *this* priest is able to cast spells I don't believe were meant for mortals.'

'I-I didn't cast anything. It wasn't my doing.'

'Then you have a story to tell, Mother Seej.'

Managing a weak smile, the High Priest said, 'The Oldunfolk have a story for us all, my Lady.' She opened her hand to reveal an oval stone of twilight blue nestled in her palm. 'And a part to play in their game.'

It took Kingfisher a moment to realise she had been looking at this stone all her life. She chewed on words, but could only think to say, 'When Cursed Persephone's darkness comes—'

'Juno's lightness must follow.'

'Will you two talk sense?' Maxis snapped, looking back at them with a heavy scowl. 'What is that thing?'

'Something old, something divine,' Seej answered, keeping her gaze on Kingfisher. 'I think you know its name, my Lady.'

Kingfisher recoiled. The stone sparkled in flame-light from the torch burning in the sconce beside Maxis. She saw words hiding in the little glares, alien words, unintelligible to mortal eyes, and she knew they came from a higher grace. As majestic as the stone was, had ever seemed, Kingfisher had always assumed its legend was hogwash. Had the Wood Bee Queens truly worn divinity upon their heads?

'Foresight,' said Seej. 'It carries the light that shields against dark.'

'Juno's Blessing,' whispered Kingfisher.

'Foresight?' Maxis blustered. He flicked the reins then asked the question which was already on Kingfisher's lips: 'Mother Seej, how in damnation's name have you come to possess a jewel from the crown of Strange Ground?'

'Highness, I have been its guardian since I ascended to High

248

Priest,' Seej explained, 'and learned that this divine stone was given to your mother ten years ago.'

Maxis considered that and liked what he was hearing as little as Kingfisher. 'What nonsense is this? I would have known.'

Seej stopped Kingfisher airing her agreement with a raised hand. 'Some secrets queens share with their High Priests, but not with their princes, *or* their closest friends. Before she went into hiding, Maitressa Wood Bee entrusted Foresight to Queen White Gold's custody.'

'Impossible!' Maxis said. 'You seem to forget that I have been in Eldrid's company countless times since Maitressa's exile, and her crown was *never* without its stones.'

'And I can say the same,' Kingfisher added.

The priest shrugged and simply stated, 'Maitressa swapped the originals for imitations.'

Kingfisher was momentarily taken aback. 'Imitations?'

'Fakes. And she did so while informing only a select few, which did not include her heir.'

Oh, Maitressa, Kingfisher thought, *I never questioned you, my dear one, but what is going on here?* 'No, no. Eldrid must have known, if this is true.'

Seej shook her bald head. 'The replicas play their parts well, mysterious and magical to the eye, but make no mistake – Maitressa Wood Bee swapped them both and delivered the real Foresight to Dalmyn after Yandira's first attempt to steal the throne. To keep at least one of the stones beyond her easy reach.'

Kingfisher saw the logic, but still ... '*Both* stones are replicas, you say? What happened to Hindsight?'

'I'm not sure. Maitressa told my queen that Hindsight would be their granddaughter's to find. Perhaps Ghador has it already.'

Her mouth suddenly dry, Kingfisher took the waterskin and

drank. So much tragedy could have been avoided if Yandira had been executed ten years ago. 'Am I to understand that Ghador might have been keeping Hindsight hidden since she was a child?'

'At this stage, only she could answer that. Ghador learned much from a wise grandmother. The rightful heir is a credit to your city.'

'And the pride of her father!' Maxis declared. 'Who cares how this came to be? With Foresight and Hindsight, Juno's Blessing will be our shield and the weapon which strikes down Cursed Persephone's damned disciples. My daughter *will* have that stone, and then she and I will be the vice that crushes Yandira Wood Bee.'

The prince's fighting spirit always remained within easy summons – he and Eldrid had been such a good match on that front – but this time Seej Agda threw cold water over his heat.

'If only it were that simple, my Prince.' Concern furrowed the priest's brow. 'Foresight acts upon a will of its own. A divine will. And I can only imagine it is the same with Hindsight. I do not control this stone's actions but follow its edicts. It ... it speaks to me.'

'That thing has a *voice*?' Maxis said.

'A whisper, a ... *feeling*. Foresight steers me, giving information in the strangest language, and it says that Juno's Blessing is a shield, and shield alone. However ... it has whispered the existence of a divine weapon to me.' The priest's eyes bored intently into Kingfisher's. 'Perhaps it is time to tell your side of this story, my Lady.'

A shout from ahead disturbed them. The Serpent's Sigh parted and a soldier on horseback rode through the convoy.

'It's Lina, my scout,' Maxis said. 'What news?' he called.

'My Prince!' The scout reined her horse into a trot beside the wagon. 'There's no end to this damn fog, and there's a problem a mile or so down the road.'

'Witches?'

'No, Highness. We need to break out the axes.'

The warrens were older than the city which sat atop them. No one knew who had made them, or for what purpose, but they had been there, far below the ground, when the first settlers had built their homes in the long-forgotten past. Well before there was a castle with a monarch sitting on a throne – a time, in fact, before the ancient dragons themselves had died out – the warrens had snaked and criss-crossed through the earth; and they had remained unchanged as, over the epochs, that first settlement grew into the city of Strange Ground beneath the Skea.

At least, that was what Backway Charlie had learned from his mother. He remembered her teaching him. As the landlady of the infamous Jester's Tavern, her job was to prepare her son in the ways of the business he would one day inherit – both its legitimate and shadier sides. The warrens were paramount, she said; they'd keep gold in his pockets for life, if he was shrewd enough to ask no questions.

So, every day, Charlie had spent his time studying maps of this ancient network and wandering the tunnels by torchlight. He learned the twists and turns, which paths were blocked, which ones led to forbidden areas. The warrens had any number of exits both inside Strange Ground and out in the surrounding countryside. Charlie learned them all, and for a while he served as a guide for folk who didn't like questions but needed to get out of the city quickly and undetected. As long as they paid, they got good service.

In more academic circles, Backway Charlie might be

considered an *authority* on the warrens, but it was becoming a struggle just to remember his own name, let alone his mother and his education.

In a distant sort of way, he was wandering the tunnels like he had in his youth, following some instinct belonging to maps imprinted onto a buried part of his brain. He had no memory of fog ever filling the warrens before, but there was fog none-theless, somehow clouding his vision while allowing him to see through it at the same time. In his hand, he held a cudgel. Made of hardwood with a thicker battering end, he knew he used to keep this weapon behind his bar, as a deterrent for troublemakers. But now, it was for stopping anyone trying to sneak into – or out of – the city. And in that duty, Charlie wasn't alone.

A man came from the opposite direction, carrying a butcher's knife. Charlie might have known him, but they didn't acknow-ledge each other when they crossed paths. There were many folk traipsing through the warrens, dragging their feet like sleepwalkers in the dark grey fog of dreams, eyes filmed with smoke, patrolling for interlopers without consideration for their actions. That was how the Serpent's Sigh worked; it made them understand they were doing Yandira Wood Bee's bidding, and somehow that was a good thing.

It had started with a kiss from a corpse. A seed of something bad had been sown in Charlie. It had grown in his mind, spread through his body, taking control until he was able to infect his customers with the slightest touch. They carried their own bad seeds to their friends and families, and within hours a plague was spreading. Then the breath of dragons had come and filled the city with fog, above and below.

Charlie arrived at a narrow tunnel somewhere around the centre of the warrens. He recalled that it led to a forbidden zone, a dangerous area even criminals steered clear of, unless they wanted more trouble than they were already in: the grounds of Castle Wood Bee itself. This tunnel was blocked by heavy gates warded with dangerous magic positioned well before an interloper might reach the royal home. Beyond the gates, it led to the castle dungeons. Once, this tunnel had been used for smuggling prisoners in and out of Strange Ground, but as far as Charlie could recall, no one had used it for that purpose in centuries. Someone was using it now, however ...

A glow illuminated the fog in the narrow tunnel, preceding the sound of footsteps. Surely an insurgent, out to depose Her Imperial Majesty. Charlie raised the cudgel, ready to beat to death whoever appeared.

But the person who emerged from the fog wasn't alive. A youngster, twenty years at the most. A deep gash on the side of his neck had drenched his doublet in blood; his skin had the pallor of the dead. He walked on bandy legs, arms swinging and body bouncing as though his spine was made from jelly. His eyes were the source of the glow: blue illumination shining from sockets like lantern lights. He didn't *emerge* from the fog; the fog parted before him as though frightened into retreat. He looked at Charlie with a cleansing gleam, cool and pure, that felt like needles on his skin.

And then, the dead man spoke.

My adversary believes She is subtle and clever and I will not see the mischief She causes. The voice *radiated* from the youngster instead of coming from his mouth. It felt ... older than time. *She underestimates Me and is blind to how one freed soul among thousands possessed will spring the trap into which She is walking.*

Charlie dropped the cudgel, doubling over as his stomach cramped. He collapsed to his hands and knees, retching and gagging until he brought up a vile spew of darkness. The puddle writhed and squealed like a lobster in the pot. Charlie scrambled away from it, watching with fearful eyes as it boiled down to nothing. And it was then he realised his old self was flooding back. It was painful, like someone repairing his mind at a forge. On an anvil. With hammers and fire. But Backway Charlie was himself again.

Cool blue light blinded him, and the voice ... *that* voice, so old and alien, spoke once more: *Moves and countermoves – this is how the game is played. And you, Master of the Warrens, will hold for Me a reserve strategy.*

'I never told anyone that Oddridge passed away,' Karin was saying while rooting through a big pile of scrolls. 'See, most folk take me more seriously when they think I'm doing Oddridge's bidding. Not that I kept quiet about her death out of greed, you understand. A magician needs to earn a living.'

Despite Karin's earlier attempts at deception and intimidation, Ebbie had to confess he had taken to her. Since her charade had been uncovered, she had revealed a kind and welcoming manner. She carried a general oddness and had an endearing, unfiltered way of speaking.

'The truth is, I thought I'd abandon the island if Oddridge went away. But when she died, leaving this place somehow felt wrong, like I was supposed to stay. I understand why, now.'

Bek clearly didn't share Ebbie's feelings about Karin; suspicious and irritated, her calculating eyes were more interested in the collection of small chests stacked up against the far wall. Around twenty-five of them, each allegedly filled with smugglers' merchandise. Ebbie wasn't sure what to think of his travelling companion at present. There was a *big* conversation waiting to happen between them.

Karin had led her guests from the kitchen to this room – a

study or workshop, Ebbie couldn't decide which. Two head-sized globes hung from the ceiling, shedding pale light onto a desk and bookcases and a number of scrolls, which, before the magician began rummaging through them, had been stacked into a neat pyramid. A wooden table, heavy and worn like an old-fashioned butcher's block, served as the room's centrepiece, and on it was the kind of apparatus usually found in a chemistry room at school.

With genuine affection, Karin had spoken about her time with Oddridge. She had come to the island seven or eight years ago – she couldn't be certain – to study the magical arts with the most powerful magician in the Realm. Although wise beyond measure, Oddridge was not quite as mysterious and dangerous as she had allowed her legend to become. With a wicked sense of mischief and a deep love of nature, Oddridge encouraged her fearful reputation because she simply preferred to be left alone. But she tolerated her apprentice and had been a caring mentor for Karin. Apparently, all three people in the room had lost the most important person in their life.

'I miss Oddridge every day,' Karin said. 'My happiest memories died with her.'

Bek spared a glance for the magician and huffed. She sat on a stool beside the table, drumming her fingers impatiently upon the worn and scratched top, wearing an empty scabbard while her sword lay unsheathed beside a bell jar.

'Look, I'm sorry for your loss,' she said, 'but we just need Konn's merchandise, then we'll be out of your hair.'

'You can't fool me,' Karin replied, unrolling then discarding yet another scroll. 'You two are more than lackeys for Captain Konn, and I know what you're really after.'

Bek gave Ebbie a look, warning him to say nothing. But Ebbie was sick and tired of keeping his mouth shut. Standing close to the magician in case he could aid her search for ... whatever she was looking for, he said, 'You say you've been waiting for us?' much to Bek's dismay. 'You knew we were coming?'

'Actually, I was *told* you were coming,' Karin said. 'A couple of mornings ago, the strangest thing happens. I wake up to find a ghost sitting on my bed. Bold as you like, the ghost of an old woman, smiling at me. "Greetings, Karin," she says, all posh like a noble. Thought I must be dreaming at first, but I *really* wasn't.'

Bek muttered darkly under her breath. 'Karin, please – Konn's chest?'

'Shut up, Bek.' Ebbie shot her a look. 'I want to hear this.'

'Ah!' Karin unfurled a scroll and her eyes darted from side to side as she read. Then she *tsked*, grumbled, 'Nope, that's not it, either,' and let the scroll snap back into a tube before throwing it over her shoulder.

Ebbie caught the scroll and placed it with the others so far discarded. 'A ghost told you we were coming to your island?'

'Juno's Champions, she called you.' Karin had dived back into the pile. 'Said the Queen of Queens and Cursed Persephone were once again pitting Their wits against each other, while you two were playing out Their game in mortal lands. Took me a while to realise who I was talking to, to be honest. I knew this ghost, see? At least, I'd heard of her proper title. But you, Ebbie ... *you* call her Mai.'

Bek groaned and Ebbie's breath caught. 'You saw Mai's ghost?'

'Lady Maitressa Wood Bee, in the flesh ... spirit ... you know what I mean.'

'I do,' said Ebbie. 'Her ghost talks to me, too.'

'And I doubt we're the only ones she's visited. Maitressa warned me, Ebbie. She said that when the Oldunfolk play, any move made by light would be countered by dark, and vice versa, so on and so forth, while we mortals are left to navigate the game blindly. I didn't know what to make of it all until that bloody witch arrived.'

'Witch?'

'Oh, have I not told you about him?' Karin looked back at Ebbie, a scroll in each hand. 'Well, if Juno's move was to send Maitressa's ghost, then the witch was the Great Trickster's counter, see? He came from the Coven of Bellona – a dirty, vile bunch of arse-faces. By the time I realised he'd sneaked onto the island, he'd already spread the Serpent's Sigh.'

'Serpent's Sigh?' Ebbie's thoughts sifted through his dream of Mai. 'That's something to do with dragons, isn't it?'

'The spirits of dragons, the breath of the Underworld – call it what you like, it's *very* bad magic.'

Was that why the fog outside acted so unnaturally, because it came from the Underworld? Ebbie shuddered to think he had walked through it.

'I've tried warning Singer's Hope about it,' Karin said, 'but my gulls won't fly and any spell I cast can't leave the island. The captains don't realise what's going on here, so they keep sending sailors to collect the merchandise I owe them, even though those sailors don't make it home again.' She gave up on the scrolls and began studying the titles of weighty books crammed into a big case. 'That poxy fog is trapping anyone who walks into it. Besides you two, of course.'

'Look, this is all very interesting,' Bek said, rubbing her forehead. She pointed at the chests and did her best to smile. 'But I'm begging you to tell me which one of these belongs to Konn – Wait!' She sat straighter on the stool. 'This has been going on for days? The folk we saw in the wood, they're sailors?'

'They won't stop coming and the fog keeps claiming them,'

Karin said. 'The Serpent's Sigh takes them over, bends their minds, turns them into servants for darkness, and if I stray too far from the house, it'll do the same to me.'

'Then ... then Konn must have known sailors were disappearing.' Bek jumped to her feet, fists clenched like she was ready to fight. 'That's why he wouldn't come himself. He knew something was wrong on the island, so sent me instead. He didn't even warn me ...' She swore viciously.

'But *we* got to the house unscathed,' Ebbie said, 'because Bek's sword protected us?'

'Yes, but let me confirm something first,' Karin said. 'Here, take this.'

She passed Ebbie a heavy, leather-bound book, then selected a second from the case which she carried over to the desk. The chair creaked as she sat down, as did the book's spine when she opened it on the desk with a thump. Bek had lied about where the sword came from; Mai's letter had told Ebbie that. She said it was special, an ancient Wood Bee heirloom – and yet another of the secrets Bek was keeping.

'Why are we wasting time?' Bek said through gritted teeth. 'If the sword got the two of us onto the island, then surely it can get the *three* of us off? There's a ship anchored nearby, but it'll leave without us if we're not there by dawn, so if you tell us which chest is—'

'If I were you, I wouldn't trust the *Admiral's Teeth* to hang around,' Karin said, flipping dusty pages. 'I know you need a True Sight Candle, but if Konn let you think there's one in his chest, then think again. He never ordered that particular item, and I wouldn't know how to make one if he had. I'm not sure Oddridge could've done it, either. Do you even understand what a True Sight Candle is?'

Bek wasn't listening. A blustery storm was gathering on her face, but the magician jumped in before she could blow.

'Forget about Captain Konn and his ship. Your business is with me now. Maitressa's ghost told me who you're looking for. She told me all about what happened in Strange Ground. Queen Eldrid is dead. Yandira has seized control, and if she delivers her niece's crown to her Oldunone, she'll have the forces of the Underworld at her command.' Karin looked at Bek. 'I also know that *you* are running from your past, while *you* –' she looked at Ebbie '– aren't from around these parts.'

The magician smirked as Ebbie found a multitude of ways to say precisely nothing and all expression dropped from Bek's face.

'That ring on your finger,' Karin continued, 'it's made from Hecate's Onyx – not as rare as the sword, but rare enough. It was used a *long* time ago by High Priests for the purpose of storing magic the Oldunfolk wanted hidden from mortals. Divine magic, like the Janus Bridge.' Karin closed the book and pushed it one side, grinning as she took the one Ebbie was holding. 'I've never met an earthling before. How do you do?'

'I don't care *who* you think you've seen,' Bek said, her voice tight. 'I don't care *what* you think you know. You're wrong about us and we're leaving with Konn's merchandise.'

'Oh no you're not.' Karin stabbed a page in the second book with her finger. 'And here's why.'

Ebbie followed the magician to the centre table, peering over her shoulder as she laid the book down, open at the page she'd chosen. Script in a language Ebbie couldn't read surrounded a few pictures. The artwork was rough, ancient-looking, the colours faded, but it crudely depicted dragons lying dead beneath a representation of a sword with a blue blade.

'I must be dreaming,' Karin said. 'Look at the writing on the blade.' Her face lit up with wonder. 'Maitressa said it would be, but I didn't believe her, I *couldn't*, I ... This sword carries Juno's Blessing. It once belonged to Minerva Wood Bee. You've got the blade that slew Bellona.'

A moment of silent reverie passed.

'What catshit is this?' Bek snapped. 'Minerva's sword is a myth. It doesn't exist.'

'It bloody well does,' Karin said, sliding the book towards her. 'Read for yourself. It's all here.'

Bek shoved it away. 'I don't need to read it.'

'Hold on.' The magician peered closer at the sword on the table. 'The stones are missing.' She checked with the book's illustration. 'I'm not wrong. It's supposed to have two gems.' She tapped the page. 'Foresight and Hindsight.'

'I know those names,' Ebbie said. 'The stones from the crown of Strange Ground.'

'Maitressa told me they were stolen from the crown to use with this sword. One's supposed to go here –' Karin pointed at an empty oval frame just above the guard '– and one matching it on the opposite side, both blessed by Juno Herself. Where are they?'

'I don't know!' Bek shouted.

'Well, that's a problem, see? Those stones are what gives the blade power enough to slay dragons – or, in this case, Yandira Wood Bee and whatever darkness the Underworld's put in her.'

'I don't care.' Agitated, Bek grabbed the sword and drove it into the scabbard. 'I stole this thing fair and square.'

Ebbie felt a rush of anger. 'I thought your grandma gave it to you.'

'I lied, all right? I stole it, and now I'm going to sell it.'

'*Sell it?*' Karin laughed at the very idea.

'No,' Ebbie said. 'The sword doesn't belong to you, Bek.'

They glared at each other. A hostile silence bloomed, disturbed when the house's defensive ward activated once more with its tortured wail. As it had in the kitchen, it rose to a deafening pitch before dipping again, shaking the glass apparatus on the table. Once it had faded to nothing, Karin's eyes narrowed thoughtfully and she closed the book.

'Why don't you two have a quick chat,' she said, heading for the door. 'I need to check on something.'

As soon as the magician left the room, Bek moved to the chests piled against the wall and began searching through them. But each chest was locked, and every lid she tried to lift wouldn't budge. She swore, pulled a set of lock picks from her pocket, then noticed Ebbie still glaring at her.

'What?'

'I have to believe you didn't know what you were stealing, because otherwise ...' Ebbie shook his head in dismay.

'Think what you want. The sword belongs to me.'

'How can you believe that now? You heard what Karin said.'

'Will you wise up, Ebbie!' Bek threw her hands in the air. 'Karin has spent too much time on this island alone and she's clearly a donkey shy of a full farmyard. You can bet your life she's making it up about Konn, too. One of these chests belongs to him. Right here, in this room, is your True Sight Candle and *my* freedom.'

She was acting far too desperately in her quest for self-preservation to be making any kind of rational argument. At that moment, Ebbie trusted his host way more than his travelling companion.

'I should've guessed you knew Mai the moment she told me to spring you from jail,' he said. 'But it's not just her, is it? You know Yandira *and* Ghador, too. You know the whole Wood Bee family, and they know you. Personally.'

'And I've been trying to forget the lot of them for the last *ten years!*' Bek shouted.

'You should have told me they adopted you.'

Bek hissed out an angry breath. 'It's not important, Ebbie.'

'Not important? You lived with Mai, she cared for you.'

'*Cared* for me?' Bek made fists, and Ebbie thought for a second that she might hit him. 'Oh, you need setting straight, *earthling*. When my grandma died, they shipped me off to an orphanage, and your precious *Mai* came looking to buy a friend for Ghador. She chose *me* like I was a pet dog for a spoiled princess.'

'That's not true. You and Ghador were great friends, as close as sisters, Mai said.'

'*Hah!* She kicked me out of the castle as soon as her grandmother disappeared. What does that tell you?'

'No, there must be more to it than that. All the time we've been together, you haven't said a word about this. Why not?'

Bek gave a sour chuckle. 'Because it's none of your business.'

The look on her face told Ebbie she wouldn't discuss it further, but he wasn't to be deterred. 'The sword belongs to Ghador. Mai wants us to take it to her. This is how she beats Yandira. Bek, we've been in this together from the very beginning – can't you see that?'

'There is no *we*, Ebbie!' Bek was raging again. 'You can stay here and become the best of friends with Karin, for all I care, but as soon as the True Sight Candle is yours, I'm leaving, and you'll never see me again.'

Ebbie bristled at the cruelty in her voice. 'You know what … if you can only think about yourself, then here –' he took the money pouch from the satchel and threw it at Bek's feet '– payment for your services.' Next he took out their contract, ripped it in two, then four, then eight, and sent the pieces fluttering into the air. 'Consider your obligation fulfilled. Go on – *leave*! But that sword stays with me.'

Bek watched the pieces of paper drift to the floor like snow, looking offended. Then the house began wailing again and Ebbie covered his ears. Karin returned, shouting something about *moves* and *countermoves* and how she wished she could be left alone.

'Here's what I reckon,' she said like she was angry with her guests. 'The Serpent's Sigh was supposed to stop you reaching me. But you countered with the sword, which got you through. So now, the next move is for the opposition to play. And the opposition has just played it.'

'What?' said Ebbie.

'You were followed to the island. You need to come with me. Right now.'

Bek picked up her rucksack and rushed after Ebbie as he followed the magician into the kitchen. They arrived just as three hard thumps rattled the front door. A moment of silence, then two more thumps. Absurdly, Ebbie thought he recognised the knocking style – like someone banging on a coffin lid from the inside ...

'Can't be a dark magician,' Karin whispered. 'Wouldn't have made it to the house if it was. But don't worry. Oddridge cast wards and defences on all the doors and windows years ago, and no one's getting past those—'

'Rana!' The voice, muffled by the door, was almost a bark. 'I can smell you in there. You and that rotten earthling.'

'Oh no,' said Ebbie.

'Lunk and Venatus,' said Bek.

'Ah,' said Karin. By her tone, the magician knew well the reputation of her guests' pursuers. 'Now *they* might be able to get in.'

'Yandira's not forgotten you, Rana,' Mr Venatus bellowed. 'She wants us to cut your head off with Minerva's sword.' And this time the thumping on the door sounded more like a dedicated assault to smash it down.

'Give me a hand,' Karin said.

Ebbie helped her shove the kitchen table aside. There in the floor, two wooden flaps had been set like cellar doors. Karin pulled them up, revealing a flight of stairs leading down into gloom. She took a glass ball from her robe's pocket, shook it until it gleamed with pale light.

'Time to go,' she said, descending the stairs.

'Wait,' Bek hissed after her. 'What about the True Sight Candle?'

Karin's voice drifted back. 'You've already got one, you tit.'

19

Hindsight

Yandira could barely sit still in her council chambers. She buzzed with raw energy, as if time passed at twice its normal speed and she couldn't keep up with it. A heat like no other burned in her gut, yet it could not warm the chills that shivered her skin. Thoughts were too many, too fleeting, too fast, and Yandira felt like screaming. Or roaring.

A fiery pain caused her to grip the chair's armrest. Her heart thudded with two beats now; one her own, the other belonging to the beast growing inside her.

Ignius noticed his master's discomfort with some concern. 'Not long now, Majesty,' he promised. He was on his hands and knees, drawing spells upon the floor around Morrad, who stood with a vacuous expression before the oily pool of the Underworld.

Tucked into the corner of the room, Lord Dragonfly stared at Yandira with eyes as watery and docile as a mooncalf's. But inside he was all seething hatred – no doubt about that. Yandira wondered why she bothered keeping him around. Killing the old fool would provide a grand distraction, if only for a moment, and the Oldunfolk knew she needed one. This was not supposed to have happened.

'Faster, Ignius,' Yandira hissed. 'Tame this beast before it consumes me.'

'I beg your patience a moment longer, Majesty.' Ignius didn't look up as his deft hand chalked words of magic. 'I *cannot* get this wrong.'

Her Immortal Darkness Lady Persephone was displeased. The purpose of Yandira's transformation was to inspire haste in fulfilling the promises she had made to her Oldunone. It told her that time was running out. Yandira's skin was segmenting into hard scales. Her jaw ached as teeth became more pointed by the moment, her tongue slowly thinning and splitting to a serpent's fork. Fingernails were darkening like talons, and her eyes saw with such clarity she had discovered new colours that were painful to behold. And her clothes ... her clothes were liquid shadows, painted thickly onto her body and set as tough as leather armour. She would lose herself to the transformation unless the beast was fed.

'*When*, Ignius?'

'Soon, Majesty.'

Yandira stifled a groan as a deep ache flared in her back. Wings, she realised, threatening to sprout from her shoulder blades. Lord Dragonfly continued to stare at her. Did he hope to see his Empress ripped to shreds? Did he understand what her Oldunone had done?

Long ago, dragons flew across the Skea, the bane of the folk. Persephone's Pets, they called them, for their pestilence was always conducted in Her name. Time passed and the dragons died out one by one, but their spirits flew to the Underworld where Persephone wrapped them in immortal darkness, rewarded their devotion by making them Her personal guard. And by Her side the dragons remained for evermore. However ...

When Yandira had sacrificed the young soldier Barrek to the Underworld, Persephone had not only deigned to rejuvenate Her disciple's strength but also to infuse her soul with the spirit of a dragon. It was no high honour; Yandira had not the power to control the beast, the fire in her stomach, the fury pounding at her temples. If she didn't appease her Oldunone soon, the dragon would break her every bone, burn her alive from the inside out, and she would suffer the same fate as Lady Bellona. Yet, a ray of hope glinted on the horizon.

'Curse you, Ignius! *Faster!*'

It was clever of her enemies to swap the stones of Hindsight and Foresight with replicas, for what was the crown of Strange Ground without them? A bland circlet of gold and silver which held no worth to Lady Persephone whatsoever. Juno's priests had known nothing of the deception, as surprised as Yandira to learn the real stones were missing. They died one by one, each of them clueless as to when the exchange had been made and to where the stones had been taken. But Yandira knew where they were. She saw it all now.

At first, she believed Ghador was in possession of both Foresight *and* Hindsight, but now she was certain that Eldrid's heir only had one stone. Because the other was wending its way towards the city.

Dalmyn's army had vanished on the Queen's Highway. Reports from the Coven of Bellona claimed a spell of blue light had shielded every soldier against the Serpent's Sigh before they disappeared from Yandira's magical sight. Whether Juno's Blessing had been cast from Foresight or Hindsight, Yandira did not know, but one of Dalmyn's number – perhaps Lady Kingfisher or Ghador's pompous father or some priest travelling with them – possessed a divine stone which Yandira had promised to her Oldunone. And Persephone would get it, before Her dragon tore Her disciple apart.

'It is time, Majesty,' Ignius said, flustered as he stood upright beside Yandira's sister. 'I am ready.'

'Then delay no further.'

There was a fluid simplicity to the magician's actions. He drew a small curved knife from his sleeve and ran it across Morrad's throat. The princess's eyes widened slightly, but she gave no other reaction as blood drenched her clothes and seeped over the spell she stood upon. Chalky lines ignited with red fire. The dark pool on the floor bubbled and dragons roared from an impossible depth. Yandira gasped as her insides *squeezed*. The dragons were calling for their kindred spirit to burst from her mortal body into flame and dark glory. But then Ignius pushed Morrad into the Underworld's pool and she disappeared like a stone dropped into a pond.

The relief was immediate. While lines of red fire burned out, coolness slid down Yandira's throat to douse the heat in her gut. Wild, buzzing energy slowed in her mind and the torture ended. Lady Persephone had accepted the sacrifice and paused Yandira's physical transformation.

'A fine offering,' she said, nodding her appreciation to Ignius. 'The dragon's fury is tamed.'

Obviously sharing his Empress's relief, the magician bowed.

Yandira rose from the chair, marvelling at how the shadowy armour adhered to her body like a second skin. She then glared at Lord Dragonfly.

'Are you in there, Aelfric, weeping for Morrad?' She pointed at the pool, now calm and sated. 'The blood of my blood, the richest of sacrifices – how could my Oldunone refuse my sister's flesh? But I wonder, when the dragon roars again, will Persephone accept *your* blood as payment?'

Was that a flicker of emotion Yandira spied upon Dragonfly's face? No, perhaps not, but *something* shone through the mist in his eyes, a helplessness which would only worsen when they witnessed the mysterious ways in which Bellona's old allies had evolved with their miracles and technologies. But there was a distance to travel yet before Persephone opened Her gates and brought allies to Yandira's command.

She turned to Ignius. 'Is there news from the Coven?'

'Yes, Majesty. They say that Dalmyn's army will soon be in their sights again.'

'Hmm. Divine magics are cancelling each other out. Spells and witchcraft will be of little use on the Queen's Highway now.' The magician nodded gravely. 'Send a message to the Coven, Ignius. Tell them to sharpen their knives and call down their fellow wild things. I need that stone.'

'So, Lady Maitressa spent her exile on Earth,' Seej Agda said, contemplating. 'And you say she chose an earthling to be Ghador's champion before she died?'

'I'm not sure *champion* is the right word,' said Kingfisher, 'but yes. His name is Ebbie Wren.'

They sat in the wagon, wrapped in woollen travelling cloaks, waiting to move on. Dalmyn's army had been brought to a standstill a quarter-day out from Strange Ground. Roughly a mile down a narrow stretch of the Queen's Highway that cut through a large area of woodland known as Tipper's Grove, a mighty oak with a trunk that Maxis claimed was wider than he was tall had fallen across the road. The surrounding woodland was too dense to manoeuvre around the blockage. A detachment of soldiers armed with axes had been sent to deal with it, but even this minor delay was gnawing on Kingfisher's anxiety.

'I never knew Maitressa myself,' Seej said, 'but by the way my queen speaks of her, your friend's spirit would make a fine avatar for Juno's good and light.'

'As dutiful a servant as Cursed Persephone has found in Yandira, no doubt.'

The High Priest's smile was slight, coy. 'The Oldunfolk are pitting Their wits against each other, my Lady, and we mortals are players in Their game.'

It was a relief to finally talk openly with someone who shared the secrets which had been weighing heavily on Kingfisher's soul, especially with Prince Maxis away overseeing the fallen oak's removal and unable to add his princely bluster to the discussion. He was a brave man who genuinely cared, in his own way, for the soldiers under his command, and for his daughter, but thinking rationally before speaking and acting had never been his strong point.

The wagon was positioned near the front of the army, and the dull thuds of axes sinking into wood came from up ahead. Behind them, soldiers and horses waited in a line for the road to be cleared on this miserable summer's night, gripped by the cold of a supernatural winter. The protection of Juno's Blessing had pushed the Serpent's Sigh back far enough that the foul fog was barely discernible among the dark trees. Skittish and nervous, the army knew these were dangerous times, full of uncertainty.

'Who knows?' Seej said. 'Did divine intervention compel Ghador's decision to visit her father at this time? Had she made it as far as Dalmyn, would Foresight and Hindsight now be safe behind the high walls of another queendom?'

Kingfisher often hadn't understood her role in this *game*, and the High Priest had admitted to feeling the same. But sharing their sides of events with each other had provided clarity. Yandira wasn't alone in making a pact with an Oldunone. Before her exile, Maitressa had prepared so much more than Kingfisher had ever known. If Yandira's ambition could be likened to a mirror, then Maitressa had been the rock which shattered it. The Oldunfolk had scattered the broken shards to the wind, and now it was the job of mortals to piece them back together. But whose reflection would that mirror show in the end?

Seej was looking at the twilight oval of Foresight resting on her palm. The priest said she could hear its voice.

'Is it talking now?' Kingfisher asked with a frown. 'Offering advice in these troubled times, perhaps?'

'No, its voice has been silent since casting Juno's Blessing.' Seej closed her hand around the divine relic. 'Without the crown's proper stones, Yandira cannot fulfil her promise to Cursed Persephone.' She said it with concern, not as one holding the key to Yandira's downfall. 'Yet merely keeping the stones from her is not enough. Maitressa's pact with Lady Juno was to give her daughter one last chance to live out the rest of her life in peace.'

'But to do what she should have done ten years ago if she ever rose again?' The priest nodded and Kingfisher shook her head. 'I doubt Yandira was ever able to appreciate the sacrifice her mother made to keep her safe.'

'The Underworld courses through Yandira's veins and it will take a divine weapon to strike her down. To wield such a weapon, Ghador must join to it Foresight and Hindsight both.' The look on Seej's face suggested she was struggling to find wisdom. 'In this matter, Ghador must trust to an earthling?'

'Indeed,' said Kingfisher, uncertain herself. 'I was told that Ebbie Wren is honourable to the core. Always I trusted Maitressa's judgement, but on this occasion I must confess to having doubts.'

'You and me both, my Lady. Things did not end well the last time Earth and the Realm had dealings. One need only visit the ruins of Imperium City to see evidence of that. And I find it strange that even Maitressa would not be told of Ghador's whereabouts.'

The shattered pieces of a mirror ...

'You must believe me, Mother Seej, my old friend's plans were shrouded in secrecy and I never questioned what she asked me to do. However, I wonder if Maitressa knew more about where Ghador would be hidden than she ever told. There is sense in keeping it secret from us. The less we know, the less Yandira might force from us should we be captured, thus Ghador remains safe from her attentions.'

'For the moment,' Seej stressed. 'The Oldunfolk have chosen the battlefield, my Lady, and so all our paths lead to Strange Ground. To face Yandira, the rightful heir must return to the city with an ancient weapon.' She leaned towards Kingfisher, her face incredulous. 'And I was led to believe that Lady Juno took that weapon back to Elysium after Bellona's death.'

'And I was told that it was sealed up in Minerva's tomb,' Kingfisher said. 'Nevertheless, Maitressa gave it to me around the same time she was apparently giving away the stones of her crown.' Seej snorted an astonished laugh. 'She called it a Wood Bee heirloom, but ... its blade was twilight blue and inscribed with an unknown language that could only be divine. I knew it was the sword that had struck down Bellona. Queen Minerva's sword.'

The High Priest sobered. 'But you still gave it to an earthling.'

'At Maitressa's behest, yes. She instructed me to relinquish the sword to Ebbie Wren's custody via a proxy, which I did, without question. He and his *guardian* are taking it to Ghador. I pray.'

'I share your misgivings, my Lady.'

'Oh, I do not doubt the earthling's heart, not for a moment, but I had imagined him to be a warrior of some kind. The man I met on Earth was a simple librarian, rather lonely-looking. I doubt his suitability for—'

'One moment, my Lady,' Seej said in surprise. 'You yourself travelled to the other side of the Skea?'

Kingfisher sighed. She hadn't meant to let it slip, but what was the point in keeping it secret now? 'Crossing the Janus Bridge was part of my duties, yes. And I spent a brief time in an indescribable place which I will not discuss.'

Madhouse was a better word for what little Kingfisher had seen of Earth, and she had not lingered there. She had crossed the Janus Bridge back to the Realm the instant after she gave Ebbie Wren Maitressa's satchel. Upon her return, the brooch made of Hecate's Onyx which had made the journey possible had simply vanished, and Kingfisher was glad for that; she had no desire ever again to witness the lunacy of Earth.

She shook herself free of the memory. 'Ebbie Wren does not appear to be made from the stuff of heroes, and his companion is a worry, yet we must have faith in Maitressa's reasons – *divine* reasons, as it turns out – and believe that her champions will succeed in bringing Minerva's sword to Ghador.' Because the alternative was too terrible to contemplate.

Prince Maxis was making his way back to the wagon, obviously in a foul temper. He pulled aside a soldier, who Kingfisher recognised as the scout Lina, and spoke to her while gesturing in the direction from which he had come. Lina bowed and strode away to relay whatever orders she had been given to her comrades. Muttering to himself darkly, Maxis approached the wagon.

'Is there a problem, Highness?' Kingfisher asked.

'More than one tree is blocking the road,' he rumbled. 'Three of them, evenly spaced, and I don't like it at all.'

His orders were spreading. The soldiers were readying their weapons and forming ranks as best they could on the narrow road. Many hurried past the wagon to reach the head of the convoy. The atmosphere had grown significantly tenser.

With a grim expression, Maxis addressed Mother Seej in a no-nonsense manner. 'You said Juno's Blessing is not a weapon, correct?'

Concerned by the movement of soldiers around her, the priest bobbed her head. 'Correct, Highness.'

'Then how *does* it serve us?'

'It ... It protects us from the Serpent's Sigh. It shields us from dark spells and magical sight.'

'So, Yandira Wood Bee cannot spy on our movements, but does everything lurking in this bloody fog require magic to see us? What about arrows and swords – does Juno's Blessing shield us from those?'

'No, Highness.'

'Damn it.'

Maxis looked back to where the road was blocked. Something about his stance suggested the instincts of a trained fighting man had taken over from the prince.

The hairs at the nape of Kingfisher's neck stood on end. 'What is it, Highness?'

'Healthy oaks do not fall easily,' Maxis said. 'They were cut down on purpose. I assumed our enemy sought to delay our progress, but now ...' He looked the other way then back again. 'We are halfway down a two-mile corral, the perfect spot for—'

'Highness!' a soldier cried from the convoy's head. 'There are wild things in the trees!'

And this was followed by a bestial roar and the scream of someone dying.

Brilliant sunshine beat down from a clear blue sky. A cool breeze blew in from the sea and a haze hovered over the Skea Straight, obscuring the mainland. It was a glorious summer's day in Strange Ground by the Skea, and Mrs Cory was feeling very pleased with Herself.

Foresight was travelling in the company of an army. The sword was with Ebbie Wren, though the imbecile had only just discovered its true nature – no, *imbecile* was too cruel a term. Where the earthling had at first appeared a very poor choice of champion, She was now beginning to see what Maitressa saw in him. In fact, She was on the verge of feeling rather taken with Ebbie Wren. Perhaps he could handle a grander role in the game, a special kind of mischief designed purely for him.

Nevertheless, Foresight and the sword were on course for their shared destination: the city of Strange Ground beneath the Skea. And that left just one final mystery: where was Hindsight? The answer to that should have been obvious by now to anyone with half a brain between their ears.

The trouble with divine spells designed to shield and hide mortals from other divine spells was that they could pull the wool over the eyes of divinity itself for only so long. Stealing away from Yandira the relics Juno had left in the Realm was a clever move, simple yet effective. Even so, those who the relics protected could only hide from Mrs Cory if She was not looking in their direction. And She was definitely looking at them all now, because Juno had been cheating.

The Queen of Queens had stolen a sacrifice which was intended for the Underworld. Not only that, She had used said sacrifice to speak with a mortal. No disguise, no relic – Her bare and true voice had whispered to a servant of the Serpent's Sigh – a servant gained by fair and proper means – and She had *personally* used divine magic to convert him to Her side, thus breaking the golden rule of the game in order to hinder Yandira's progress: No Oldunone was permitted to reveal Their true self to a mortal.

The sacrifice had been a young soldier who Juno thought Her adversary would deem of no consequence and therefore not notice the Queen of Queen's sneakiness. In this, She had slipped up; Juno's mistake had set a precedent which Her adversary was now free to use Herself. Delicious.

'She promised we'd always be sisters,' Ghador said, her mournful tones slicing through Mrs Cory's good mood. 'She broke that promise. She betrayed me.'

By all that was unknowable and divine, this little princess was a terrible bore!

They stood side by side up on the sea road, looking down onto the beach where holidaymakers and townspeople enjoyed summer with their towels and picnics and sun creams. The cry of gulls mixed with the chatter of voices; the discordant music of amusement arcades accompanied the thrum of traffic; and brine laced the smell of frying fish and doughnuts.

All the morning until midday, She had shown Ghador around Strange Ground by the Skea. She thought it would be fascinating to witness how one from the Realm might react to the absurdity of Earth's evolutionary differences. But far from giving Mrs Cory the reaction She was anticipating, the little princess had not been much moved by what she saw, almost as though she had been prepared in advance, and she remained contemplative and sad as she prattled on and on about the dearest friend she had loved and lost.

Now, dressed in the same simple travelling clothes she had arrived in – trousers and boots of soft leather, a woollen jersey dyed dark green, most unbefitting attire for a princess of the Realm – Ghador blended in rather blandly with the earthlings. Her entire world was on the brink of ruination yet all she could obsess about was Bek Rana, Bek Rana, Bek Rana. And it had given Mrs Cory very real concerns that She would never stop hearing that name echoing around Her mind.

'She blamed me for what happened, I know that much,' Ghador said. 'After everything we'd been through, she thought I could be so callous as to abandon her, toss her out onto the street without remorse. She didn't even give me the chance to explain.'

Mrs Cory already knew the full story of Ghador's relationship with Bek Rana, and it had never been an interesting one, not even with such a sorry ending. Perhaps it was time to move things along, if only to relieve the tedium.

The little princess's shoulders rose and fell with hearty sigh, and with reluctance in her voice, she said, 'I should return to Ebbie Wren's lodgings. I should be there to greet them when they arrive.'

If *they arrive*, Mrs Cory thought. If *they survive*.

'I'm not sure they'll be coming in from the same direction as you, dear,' She said, pointing away to the left and the dark mouth in a rocky bluff on the beach. 'See that cave down there? Local legend says it used to be a Janus Bridge.'

Ghador considered the cave with an accusatory glare and her hand slipped into her pocket where she was keeping what she thought was secret. 'You think they'll arrive from that way?'

'Couldn't hurt to keep an eye on it.'

'I fully intend to keep *two* eyes on Bek Rana, Mrs Cory. Why my grandmother would trust her again is beyond me.'

Oh, that name! 'Maybe she knew something you don't. Ten years is surely enough time for your friend to forgive and forget.'

Ghador was taken aback by the statement. '*Her* to forgive? *Her* to forget?' Her expression let the world know that no one had been more wronged than Princess Ghador. 'Let me tell you – Rana has proved herself disloyal on more than one occasion, to me and many of Strange Ground's folk. She is helping Ebbie Wren to bring a powerful relic to me, but I wouldn't be surprised if she tried to sell it instead.'

Funny you should say that, Mrs Cory thought but kept quiet as Ghador pulled her hand from her pocket and said, 'I have my doubts that Rana cares about that relic's importance.'

Here it comes. The location of Hindsight revealed!

Juno really should have been a little more creative when hiding Her relics. At times, She made things too easy for these mortals. And Mrs Cory realised ... Juno's rule-breaking had given Her license to snatch Hindsight from the little princess and deliver it straight to Castle Wood Bee. But why should She make things easier for Yandira when she insisted on disappointing her Oldunone time and time again? Besides, both stones and the sword were already destined to reach her. The finale's arena had been chosen, and thus the game was dangerously close to reaching a boringly predictable outcome. A little like thermonuclear warfare.

Ghador opened her hand to reveal what she was holding. It came as a surprise when she exposed a little pouch of purple velvet. It looked too flat to be holding a slim oval of twilight stone, blessed with the magic of a higher grace, and so it proved to be. The little princess tipped the contents of the pouch into her palm and almost proudly showed off ... *teeth*? Two of them, small, from the head of a mortal child.

'Teeth, dear?' Mrs Cory said, looking truthfully mystified. 'You're going to stop your wicked aunt with *teeth*?'

Ghador gave a sad chuckle. 'No, of course not.' She pushed the central incisors around her palm with a finger. 'I'm showing you these because they remind me of a better time. I keep them to retain my hope – hope that broken promises can be mended. I'm relying on old loyalties to bring about Yandira's final undoing, and I'm frightened that nothing of those old loyalties has survived the last ten years.'

Mrs Cory was sure that if She asked for further details, the little princess would prattle out a story about Bek Rana, so She said nothing, watching as Ghador put the teeth away and slid the pouch back into her pocket, adding, 'If Wren and Rana don't find me, I'll be without *any* of the relics I need to slay Yandira's darkness,' before sinking into brooding contemplation.

Mrs Cory had to resist the urge to laugh and clap and dance. Hindsight's whereabouts remained a mystery? It was not merely delicious, it was *miraculous*! If Ghador had not used Hindsight to cast divine protections upon her convoy and her own person, then … the Queen of Queens must have done so Herself. Personally, revealing Her true self to interfere with mortal lives. Again. Juno had smashed the golden rule to pieces. She had been cheating from the beginning. The game was now a free-for-all.

Yandira deserved to be told about Hindsight. In fact, it was high time Mrs Cory's favoured player received one last reprieve, along with a final warning. It was time to spread true mischief and give the game a less predictable outcome.

While Ghador stared into the horizon, She called to Her domain. 'Looks like a fog's blowing in,' She said, nodding out to sea.

The haze which obscured the mainland across the Skea Straight was now slate-grey and as thick as soup. A wind preceded it, bitter with winter's bite, and the instant it touched the beach, earthlings began packing up their picnics and calling their children from the water, as though a silent command was buried within the icy chill. The wind reached the sea road and took Ghador's breath away.

The fog rolled landwards, moving fast, as if with a mind of its own. A great impenetrable wall, fluid, a quirk of nature, the earthlings might well flee from it, for they could sense what the little princess could hear in the wind: the roar of dragons, rumbling like distant thunder, borne on the breath of the Underworld.

'Mrs Cory,' Ghador said gravely, 'I will walk you home where you will lock your door and stay inside.' She sounded afraid yet exhilarated. 'The Realm has come to Earth. It is time.'

Given that Lunk and Venatus had come to her house, Karin remained remarkably calm compared to Bek and Ebbie. She closed the wooden doors in the kitchen floor and cast magic upon them. An illusion spell, she said, to make the doors look like flagstones from the other side. But she added that if Yandira's servants got into the house, they'd figure out what Karin had done soon enough. 'Lunk and Venatus might be thick-headed brutes as folk, but as wolves they're shrewd and clever, and mortal magic doesn't have much effect on them. Hopefully, I've bought us enough time to escape.'

Bek prayed to Laverna: *Let* something *go in my favour, just this once. Is that really too much to ask?*

The stairs spiralled down to a tunnel beneath Oddridge's house. Under the glow of her glass ball, Karin led the way to a raft bobbing on a narrow stream of shallow seawater, which she explained ran from one side of the island to the other. Karin passed Bek a pole, then untied the mooring rope once she and Ebbie were sitting on the raft. Barely large enough to hold the three of them, the floating platform rocked precariously as Bek set off, using the wooden pole to navigate a weak current. The tunnel's rough rock walls loomed close together, slick with algae.

'Lady Maitressa left you the sigil of her House,' Karin said, once they were on their way. 'Give it to me.'

Ebbie, who had lost his earlier anger at Bek and now appeared tense, jittery, dug the amber sigil stone out of his satchel and handed it to the magician.

'Clever,' Karin said, turning it over in her hands. 'You always had a True Sight Candle. What you were looking for was someone who knew how to unlock its light. *Me.*'

'I-I don't understand,' said Ebbie.

'You will.'

Holding the stone in both hands, Karin began whispering an incantation while rubbing her thumbs over the symbol of House Wood Bee etched into it in white. Ebbie looked over his shoulder at Bek. She couldn't hold his gaze, so she looked behind, pretending to search for signs of pursuit.

Maitressa Wood Bee just couldn't keep her bloody mouth shut. She had to tell Ebbie all the things Bek didn't want him to know. Yes, the queen had adopted her. Yes, she had spent two years living in Castle Wood Bee. And *yes*, Bek and Ghador had been sisters. But that had been a long time ago and Bek owed nothing to either of them. Or so she had always thought. Because now Lunk and Venatus knew she was with Ebbie, and if they knew then so did Yandira. As for the sword – no, Bek hadn't known what she was stealing from the Kingfisher manor, would have left it well alone if she did. Ebbie was right to say they had been in this together from the beginning. Bek had been royally stitched up.

Like Ebbie, she didn't really understand what Karin was doing, but she watched, part fascinated, as the magician's spell manipulated the substance of the sigil stone. Karin had rubbed the Wood Bee symbol into a straight white line. The honey-coloured stone had become soft and pliable, almost flat like a drop-scone. Carefully, the magician folded the amber over the white line, as though wrapping wax around a wick. She shivered as she rolled it into a candle shape and whispered, 'Here we go.'

A new luminescence filled the tunnel: a deep blue glow, not glaring but enough to outshine the pale light of Karin's glass ball. It came from words carved into the wall, a strange, alien script which apparently flowed along the length of the tunnel. Bek couldn't read it, but she recognised the style even before Ebbie made a redundant statement.

'It's like the writing on the sword.'

'Oldunspeak, the language of the divines,' Karin said. 'It recognises what this sigil stone really is, and what purpose it's been given.'

Ebbie nodded distractedly, transfixed by what he was looking at.

'No one knows when or why the Oldunfolk made these carvings,' Karin continued while gently rolling the candle between her hands, 'but they protect this part of the island from dark magic. That's why Oddridge built her house on them. That's why the witch can't get to me.'

'Wait, the witch is still here?' Bek said.

'In a way.' Karin offered nothing more and resumed reciting spells while Ebbie remained mesmerised by the glowing words on the wall.

Bek bristled as she used the pole. She didn't feel comfortable around the magician and Ebbie was pissing her off. She wasn't sure if he was the one she was truly angry at, but he was irritating her more than he ever had nonetheless. All this time he had been carrying the True Sight Candle. And his bloody letter was the dog-spit icing on a huge cake of catshit.

Bek never understood why Maitressa had selected her from

among all the other orphans. She said it was because she saw fire in Bek's eyes and loyalty in her heart; but Bek had been a heartbroken and confused eleven year old, too terrified to question a queen as she was whisked off to live with the most powerful family in Strange Ground beneath the Skea.

Maitressa said her granddaughter was shy and lonely and needed a true friend, but Bek hated castle life. She hated being told what to wear, how to eat and attending school where pompous teachers were more concerned about etiquette than real wisdom like Grandma used to teach. But most of all, Bek hated Ghador, refusing to speak to her even though they shared a bedroom and sat next to each other in class.

Ghador was heir to ... *anything* a person could ever want, yet she was miserable all the time, too lofty in her privilege to lower herself into making common friends. Bek didn't see why she should take responsibility for a spoiled princess's happiness. These royals didn't know this orphan from Singer's Hope, what she had been through, what she had lost. Who was wondering about *her* needs, taking care of *her* happiness?

Backway Charlie was one of the few who knew about Bek's past, and he had once said she'd lived in a fairy tale for a while. But it hadn't felt that way. Not at first.

'Now,' Karin said, 'give me the lantern.' By this time, she had fashioned the candle into a white-tipped point and was eager to receive the lantern when Ebbie removed it from the satchel. 'Nearly there.'

In the glow of Oldunspeak, Karin opened the lantern's glass panel and began fixing the True Sight Candle onto the metal spike inside.

Bek lifted the pole from the water as a noise rattled down the tunnel. Loose stones splashing into water, or a wooden trapdoor being smashed apart?

Ebbie fretted. 'Is it them?'

Bek held up a curt hand for silence. She listened but heard nothing else. Karin had said that mortal magic had little effect on Lunk and Venatus, but did that mean Oldunspeak wouldn't stop them, either? One thing was for sure, they didn't use magic to fight. Teeth and hands were the only weapons Lunk and Venatus needed.

Ebbie was trying to see into the gloom behind the raft. 'They must be inside the house by now, right?'

Bek ignored him. Yes, he was definitely pissing her off.

Agitated, impatient, Bek dug the pole into the rocky shallows, eager to be off this island. But the tunnel, suffused with blue light, showed no sign of ending. She could only hope that it led to where Karin kept a boat and they could sneak away across the Skea well before Lunk and Venatus discovered they were gone.

The magician reached out and used two fingers to scoop glowing algae from a carving on the wall. She put her hand in the lantern. There was a bright flash, then the gentle flicker of a blue flame. 'Almost done,' she said, and more spells whispered from her mouth.

Bek still remembered the day she realised that she didn't hate Maitressa's granddaughter at all. There was this boy, the son of one noble House or another – she couldn't recall his name. He didn't like Ghador, either, and bullied her whenever he thought no one was watching. He kept telling her she was too stupid to be queen; that they would never let anyone so ugly and miserable sit on the throne. In her position, Ghador could have got him and his family into all kinds of trouble, but she bore the brunt of the bullying, never answering back, never fighting her corner, her face an expressionless mask behind which she hid her every emotion. And that was when Bek realised the princess was as confused and frightened as she was.

Ghador cried herself to sleep most nights, and nobody knew. Besides her roommate. One night, upset by the soft sound of weeping, feeling guilty because Grandma had always taught her to stick up for those who couldn't defend themselves, Bek had climbed into bed next to Ghador and held her close. In the quietest of voices, between her sobs, the princess had spoken to Bek for the first time: 'I'm sorry you lost your grandma,' and they wept together. It was the moment they became friends. Sisters. The very next day, Bek punched the bully as hard as she could and knocked out two of his front teeth.

'It's done,' Karin announced.

She closed the glass panel and passed the lantern to Ebbie. When he lifted it, light shone not as flickering blue but as a ghostly, multicoloured rainbow which cut through the luminous Oldunspeak to shine in the direction they were already heading.

'It's working?' Ebbie said. He looked back at Bek with a smile of triumph she didn't return. 'The rainbow will lead me to Ghador?' he asked Karin.

'Initially, though that's probably not its only purpose,' Karin said. 'A word of warning, Ebbie. True Sight Candles are wrapped up in all kinds of stories and legends, but they're not as easy to create as most folk believe. It takes the highest magic to make them burn, and this flame won't go out till its job is done.

'The Oldunfolk play Their games by strange rules. *Everyone* is given the chance to succeed, *everyone* is given the chance to fail. Maitressa might have supplied you with this candle, but Juno Herself has allowed you to play the game in *Her* name. *She* can see you, Ebbie. And you can wager your life She's not the only one.'

'Yandira?'

'Oh no, I mean Yandira's benefactor—'

'Shit!' said Bek.

Up ahead, the tunnel was filled with grey fog. It rolled sluggishly just beyond where the glow of Oldunspeak stopped. Although the fog didn't come towards the group, they were heading straight for it, and Bek panicked.

'The Serpent's Sigh,' she hissed, trying to stop the raft.

'Calm down.' Karin took the pole, swapping places with Bek on the raft. 'This is just where the carvings end.'

To Bek's dismay, the raft continued towards the fog rather than coming to a halt. The rainbow light shone from the lantern and speared into its thick greyness.

'If I'm right,' Karin said, 'the sword should pick up from where the Oldunspeak leaves off.'

'*If? Should?*' Bek cried.

'Well, the stones are missing, so the sword alone isn't powerful enough to slay true darkness. But if it got you through the Serpent's Sigh once, it can do it again, right?'

'Trust her, Bek,' said Ebbie. 'She hasn't been wrong so far.'

'*Shh!*' Karin had cocked her ear. 'Listen …'

A humming sound, not dissimilar to the drone of beehives, was coming from somewhere in the fog. Perturbed, Bek pulled Ebbie back on the raft, moving to the front where she drew the sword and pointed its blue blade at the Serpent's Sigh. Sure enough, just as it had on the path through the wood, the fog rolled back as they neared, shying from the divine words. It kept on backing away until parting like curtains, and the raft drifted into a large cave.

'This is where smugglers usually collect their merchandise,' Karin said, her voice raised above the hum which was now as loud as a swarm of angry bees. 'And it's where I found the witch hiding.'

She steered the raft beneath the low arch of a stone bridge

and towards the cave's entrance: a mouth big enough to swallow a rowing boat and spit it out onto the Skea. While the fog swirled and kept its distance, Karin tied the mooring rope to a metal ring fixed to the wall before leading Bek and Ebbie onto a natural walkway that sloped up out of the water and curled around the cave. At the top, they reached the bridge they had passed under moments before. It curved over to meet a wide and deep ledge, where the source of the noise raged.

'What the hell?' said Ebbie.

It appeared as though a miniature tornado, six or seven feet tall and the colour of slate, had been trapped within spiralling red bands of jagged luminescence. This close, Bek could detect a voice, low in tone and full of fury. The tornado looked to be squirming while the bands sparked and held it tight.

'This is magic beyond my comprehension,' Karin said as the group kept a safe distance at the end of the bridge. 'See, the witch did this to himself as soon as I discovered him.'

'*This* is a witch?' Bek said.

'I think he sacrificed himself, to the Underworld. The Serpent's Sigh came soon after, so I fled. This is the first time I've been able to come back.'

Bek covered her ears as the violent mass released a furious bellow which echoed around the cave.

Karin indicated the line of the True Sight Candle's light. It shone directly into whatever it was the witch had become.

'When the Janus Bridges were removed from their fixed places and stored in Hecate's Onyx, the Oldunfolk made sure the bridges would only open if They let you find the right ... let's call them *stepping-off points*.' She gestured at the swirling mass. 'I don't know when *your* stepping off point was put in this cave, but it's covered by that thing now. Because when Juno makes a move, Cursed Persephone counters, see?'

Ebbie was staring at the ring on his finger.

Bek was feeling gutted not to find a boat and a sneaky way back to Singer's Hope, but then a more daunting prospect dawned on her. 'Wait,' she said. 'We have to travel by Janus Bridge to get off the island?'

'Only if we can get rid of the witch first. Give me the sword.'

Bek didn't move until Ebbie nudged her.

'Do it,' he said, then challenged her unwilling glare. 'What, you'd rather stand here and wait for Lunk and Venatus?'

After a brief pause, and with some reluctance, Bek offered the sword to the magician hilt first.

Karin's fingers curled around it. The Oldunspeak on the blade appeared as bright, swirling lines, while the magician studied where Foresight and Hindsight were missing.

'Let's hope it's enough,' she said and started across the bridge. 'Stay within its protective circle, but don't get too close.'

Bek noticed Ebbie's expression as they approached the swirling mass: jaw clamped and lips drawn into a grim line. And it dawned on her why she was so angry with him. And it had nothing to do with the letter or the sigil stone or the situation at all. Bek envied Ebbie's ability to wade through his fear and do the right thing, to put others above himself for a land he barely understood. Ebbie Wren was a mirror, and in it Bek could see reflected the person she used to be.

'It'll be all right,' she found herself telling him.

Ebbie managed a smile, but his eyes were wide and uncertain.

As Karin neared the churning darkness, red lightning spat, and she motioned for the others to remain several paces behind her. Bek could feel magic radiating from the mass, a bitter taste and a pressure that made the hairs on her arms stand on end. It was obvious that Karin had never used a sword before. With a clumsy gait, she levelled the blue stone blade and prepared to thrust. A moment passed, in which her hand visibly shook. Bek considered offering to take her place, but then Karin gave a cry of defiance and drove the sword home.

Bellows of rage turned to wails of pain. The angry drone shattered into a million pieces, flying in all directions, and the mass ballooned like a storm cloud filled with bloody lightning. It engulfed Karin and raced along the bridge.

Ebbie turned to run. But only the Serpent's Sigh waited beyond the sword's protection, so Bek grabbed him and held him close as energised darkness, thick and acrid like smoke, billowed over them. Ebbie clung to her for dear life. Bek squeezed her eyes shut, gritting her teeth, and the harsh accusations in Maitressa's letter filled her mind. When had Bek's heart grown so hard? A change came over her then, something better than the person she had allowed herself to become.

'I won't let you fail,' she said into Ebbie's ear. 'We're in this together,' and she felt him nodding against her shoulder.

Then silence came. The pressure of magic eased. Bek opened one eye, then the other, and untangled herself from Ebbie. All sign of the witch was gone. Around the cave, the Serpent's Sigh was dissipating, clearing from the air, falling down as smoky droplets to burst on the water with lazy puffs that drifted away.

'The witch?' Ebbie said, gazing around nervously.

'Burning in the Underworld, with any luck,' said Karin. She walked back towards them, face blackened, the shoulders of her robe smoking, but unhurt. With a nod of appreciation, she handed the sword to Bek. 'Now, just imagine what that thing could do if it had its gemstones.' She winked at Ebbie. 'Let's go and find Ghador. We're *all* in this together.'

'Listen!' Bek snapped.

Voices. Someone splashing through water. Coming from the entrance to the tunnel. Then the howling of wolves.

'Your stepping-off point awaits,' Karin said, grabbing Ebbie's ring hand and pulling him to the ledge at the end of the bridge, where the True Sight Candle wanted him to go.

Bek found her legs wouldn't move. The sound of splashing came nearer.

'Come on!' Karin shouted when she saw her standing frozen. 'Grab his other hand.'

'Bek!' Ebbie pleaded, reaching for her. His voice was tremulous as though he were vibrating; the air around him and the magician rippled. 'Don't leave me now.'

Another howl echoed from the tunnel and set Bek's legs in motion. She rushed across the bridge. As soon as Ebbie's hand was in hers, the sound of a roaring sea filled her head. Some ... *force* shook her bodily. She felt Ebbie's fingernails digging into her skin, then a mighty wave of darkness swept the three of them away.

From a distance, wolves howled the name, '*Rana!*'

20

The Breath of Dragons

As a young girl, Genevieve Kingfisher had been given a strange gift by her mother: a dagger with two razor-sharp edges and a spiteful point, easily concealed in a sheath designed to be strapped to her forearm. At first, she couldn't understand why she, a noble daughter and Heir to her House, should ever need such a thing, but then her mother had explained. 'Particular individuals require a sterner deterrent from unsavoury acts than an eloquent tongue. They will think you too fearful to be anything other than compliant, and here is where you must be prepared to surprise their expectations.' And she trained her daughter to use the dagger. Trained her and trained her until the blade became a natural extension of her hand.

Twice before, Kingfisher had been given cause to draw the blade: one time to scar a mugger when he tried to steal Aelfric Dragonfly's coin-purse; the other to threaten a venal minor lord from House Sparrow who insisted on spreading lies around court about the Kingfisher heritage. But never had she drawn the blade with the intention to end lives – until today ...

When Kingfisher saw the witch coming as a black blur, covered head to foot in shadowy robes, it was second nature to dip a hand into her jacket sleeve and draw the dagger from its concealed sheath. The witch evaded Dalmyn's soldiers, sped through the defensive circle assigned to protect the noblewoman and priest, and vaulted into the wagon, curved knife glinting in his claw.

Seej Agda was no warrior; while she knelt on the wagon floor, praying for guidance from the magical stone between her hands, Kingfisher protected her by giving the witch's expectations a nasty surprise. As he raised his knife, she thrust her blade towards his eye before he could strike. Her aim had not dulled over the years. He screeched and dark blood pumped over Kingfisher's hand when she wrenched the dagger free of his socket, preparing for a second strike. But the witch clutched his face and stumbled, falling out of the wagon to the ground where soldiers silenced him for good with their swords.

Chaos reigned on the Queen's Highway. Inhuman bellows raged around Tipper's Grove, intermingled with the shouts of soldiers who fought desperately against a dark foe. The ambush had been well planned and Yandira's army had chosen their battleground wisely. Before the witches had rushed from the trees like a flock of startled crows madly flapping their wings, they sent a vanguard of wild things charging down the road.

Ogres, four of them, great big blue-grey bastards, eight or nine feet tall, hairless and naked, as broad as cliff faces, covered in muscles and thick gnarly skin as hard as stone; and they were devils to put down. While they came smashing and stamping into battle, the witches flittered like birds among them, darting in and out to peck at soldiers. Though the witches' spells were no match for Juno's Blessing, their blades were sharp and the ogres' fists like battering rams.

Soldiers screamed and died as an ogre kicked a boulder-sized foot into a group of them. Half a dozen arrows *thunked* into its chest, but they only served to enrage the beast further. While Seej prayed, begging Foresight for aid that it refused to give, Kingfisher remained braced, bloodied dagger in hand, body attuned by years of training, and she surveyed the chaos. Prince Maxis was lost in the fray somewhere up ahead, fighting alongside his men and women where the battle was thickest.

Behind the wagon, the bulk of Dalmyn's army couldn't fight through to help their comrades who were taking the brunt of the ambush. There was little room for eight hundred soldiers to manoeuvre along this narrow section of the Queen's Highway and the woodland was too dense to form flanks in the trees. Dire supernature had commanded the forest to form a high and impenetrable wall of undergrowth behind the army, choking off any chance of a retreat. The best these soldiers could achieve was waiting in line to replace fallen friends while maintaining a defensive circle around the wagon.

Kingfisher tensed as three more witches rushed from the trees nearby. None of them made it far, but this latest charge confirmed a suspicion Kingfisher had about their tactics. This close to the wagon, the witches always came in threes; two appeared to be sacrificing themselves to the soldiers, buying time for the third whose ambition was to reach the wagon itself. Yandira knew they had Foresight and she wanted it back.

A roar of pain and anger shook the ground.

In the heart of battle, amidst the corpses of soldiers, an ogre fell to its knees, peppered with arrows and criss-crossed with gashes. Maxis appeared. With a bellow, he hurled a great axe two-handed, sending it spinning through the air to smash into the ogre's face. The beast toppled like a tree and didn't move, but three more remained, each as fearless as they were savage. One was using a dead soldier as a club. It sent an archer crashing into the trees with spine-snapping force. Sickeningly, its second strike resulted in the corpse's legs tearing free and the torso sailing through the air to land in a ruined heap, scattering soldiers close to the wagon.

Witches struck and fell back, over and over, shielded by their brutes, blurs of deadly shadow and as difficult to catch. There was no telling how many there were in the trees, or what other wild things they might summon. And when they died, the witches' corpses disappeared in plumes of blackest smoke that sent a treacherous soul spiralling down into the Underworld. But still, the body count favoured the enemy. Yandira's troops were pushing the resistance back. The soldiers of Dalmyn were struggling against the tide and more than their lives was at stake.

'Mother Seej,' Kingfisher shouted. 'You must flee!'

The priest stopped praying and looked at the noblewoman as though she were mad.

'Take Foresight and run,' Kingfisher said. 'While there's still a chance. Yandira must not get that stone!'

Evidently, the enemy suspected what Kingfisher was suggesting. In unison, the three remaining ogres found a new height of ferocity. Smashing through the front line, they thundered towards the wagon, bellowing, caring nothing for the arrows spiking their bodies and the swords slashing at their thick hides. Witches ran between them, deadly and swift.

'Make your way back through the ranks and take your chances in the trees,' Kingfisher instructed, encouraging Seej to her feet by yanking her arm. 'You must deliver Foresight to Ghador.'

The priest surveyed the chaos, saw the charging ogre and cried, 'Wait!'

She pointed at the battle. Though the ogres still fought soldiers, they had halted their advance and were now covering the retreat of their mortal masters. The witches were fleeing. Everywhere, their shadowy forms bled into the forest, escaping to the depths of the Serpent's Sigh, while their brutish vanguard succumbed to arrows and blades. The ogres' ferocity waned, strength draining from them like water through a hole in a bucket, and by the time the last one died, the Coven of Bellona had disappeared entirely.

'But ... why?' Kingfisher said into the eerie hush that had descended on the battlefield. 'They had us. We were beaten.'

The same question was etched onto the faces of dumbfounded soldiers as Maxis made his way through them. His armour spattered in blood, his sword gripped tightly in his hand, he strode up to the wagon. Even he, with all his boastful pride, knew that his enemy had fled in the face of victory, as he glared first at Seej, then at Kingfisher, and demanded, 'What in my Oldunone's name is going on?'

Mr Lunk and Mr Venatus were interrogating the captain of the *Admiral's Teeth* when She appeared in the fog. They could not see Her, but She could see them, along with the ship's crewmembers standing docile on deck while their captain was held on his knees, hands tied behind his back. The Skea frothed and murmured. The Serpent's Sigh had drifted seawards from Oddridge Island to wreath all aboard with subservience to the Underworld – all except the captain, who had been spared possession.

'The last time I saw her she was rowing to the island.' By the fearful way the captain spoke, he was clearly well informed of Mr Lunk and Mr Venatus's reputation. His name was Konn and he had been sailing the Skea since his youth. 'All I know is she stole the sword from some noble and now she and her friend are on the run. She told me nothing of her plans, I swear!'

Once again, She was having to endure a tale about that bloody sneak-thief Bek Rana when Rana's travelling companion was by far the more interesting subject. Ebbie Wren was becoming more and more intriguing, especially now he had escaped the nasty surprise She had left beneath the magician's house.

However, Captain Konn was unaware of how much Mr Lunk and Mr Venatus were fearing for their own lives. While their cleverer wolf-halves accepted the truth in the captain's words, the stubborn folk in them were blinded by desperation because their master would not forgive this latest failure. All in all, She found their predicament entertaining.

Mr Venatus said, 'Last chance to tell us, Konn,' while leaving his silent companion to express the menace behind his words. 'Where did Rana and the earthling go?'

'Earthling?'

'Was it the other side of the Skea?'

The captain obviously had no idea what they were talking about. He spared a glance for his crew, a glance which longed for them to snap out of their stupor and regain loyalty to him. She considered releasing them from the Serpent's Sigh; Lunk and Venatus fighting against superior odds was truly a sight to behold. But alas, She needed these sailors alive.

'I've told you everything I know,' Konn pleaded. 'They went to Oddridge Island to get a True Sight Candle, and that's the last I saw of them.'

Because his pettiness had caused him to decide to abandon them as punishment for an unpaid debt so miserly it was hardly worth mentioning. As Konn had prepared to sail his ship back to Singer's Hope, the Serpent's Sigh had infected his crew and the *Admiral's Teeth* had sailed long enough to pick up two wolf-ish passengers before returning to the island. For that was what She wanted to happen.

Even now, the captain could not fathom this sour turn of events, while his captors were far too concerned with saving their own pelts to wonder why, when all others had succumbed to the Underworld, this one individual should remain a loyal servant of Neptune. But She could explain it. The Kiss of Juno was upon Captain Konn – there, on his thumb, a small cut made by a blade enchanted with Oldunspeak, preserving his free will.

Mr Lunk grabbed Konn by the hair and yanked his head back, while Mr Venatus said, 'If you don't start talking, he'll put out your eyes while I peel off your fingernails, one by one. And that's just for starters.'

Konn choked on words, and She interrupted proceedings before Lunk and Venatus could carry out their threat.

'Gentlemen, even your evil little souls can extract no further information from this smuggler.'

Where Captain Konn appeared startled by the voice in the fog, even a little hopeful that it might bring salvation, the wolf-ish pair acted like it wasn't so unusual, because that was how She wanted it to be. It pleased Her to allow the Serpent's Sigh to reveal Her face.

'Mrs Cory?' Mr Venatus frowned. 'Didn't we burn you to death?'

'Obviously not.'

'What are you doing here?'

'You know why I am here. And you know who I am, so let us not dally.'

Mr Venatus, along with Mr Lunk, nodded in understanding because She wanted them to accept Her presence without wast-ing time on incredulity.

'Now then,' She said, 'I cannot help but notice that your list of failures is growing, gentlemen.'

'Wren used the Janus Bridge. Again!' Mr Venatus said it as if he was complaining to an old acquaintance of how he had been cheated. 'We can't compete with that kind of magic.'

'Yes, it does seem unfair. Though I do not think your master will see it that way.'

Mr Lunk huffed and whined something which made his companion pale. 'Shit, you're right. If the Serpent's Sigh is here, then Yandira can see us. She knows they escaped.'

'No, no,' She assured him. 'Your master did not summon the Serpent's Sigh to Oddridge Island. I did.'

'Right. Of course you did. Then ... Yandira doesn't know what's happened?'

'Not as yet. But questioning this smuggler will not reveal anything that will temper her fury. By my count, this is your third failed attempt to catch your prey, yes?'

Both Mr Lunk and Mr Venatus acknowledged this harsh truth with the bleakest looks She had ever witnessed on the faces of wolf-men.

Captain Konn's eyes stared at the face in the fog, confused, afraid and uncertain as to whether or not his hopes for salvation were unfounded. His crew remained as immobile and unthinking as scarecrows.

She said, 'For what it is worth, you have My sympathies. Lady Juno should know better than to interfere with mortals so directly, and your master's expectations are impossible. Your skill and cunning are no match for divine magic, yet Yandira Wood Bee will accept no excuses.'

Mr Venatus shared a sober look with Mr Lunk. 'What do we do?'

'Oh, I have one or two suggestions to remedy your rather sticky situation.' She felt a thrill, as She always did when the chance for mischief was at hand. 'First of all, the captain of the *Admiral's Teeth* is but a distraction. Why not give him to the Skea?'

Naturally, Lunk and Venatus thought this an excellent idea. Konn struggled in vain as they lifted him by his armpits and sent him kicking and screaming over the portside. His screams lasted until he splashed into frothing waters. With his hands

298

bound, he wouldn't take long to drown, and if his crew felt in any way distressed by their captain's grisly fate, they made no sign.

'Now then,' She said as Konn rose, gave a final shout, then sank beneath the waves for good. 'Your master is a perpetual disappointment to Me, so I am willing to help you redeem yourselves before she hears of this latest failure.'

Mr Lunk growled a few words and Mr Venatus agreed with him heartily. 'How? The Janus Bridge likely took Wren and Rana to Earth. We *could* follow, but ... but not without telling Yandira what happened first. We need her permission to travel through the Underworld.'

'*Yandira's* permission?' She laughed with genuine humour. 'How adorable you are. But no, gentlemen. You work directly for Me now. You will hunt your prey in *My* name. Are you not tired of your master expecting you to achieve the impossible?'

While Mr Lunk's mood lifted visibly, Mr Venatus remained sceptical. 'We don't have to answer to Yandira any more?'

'She need not be aware of *anything* you do from here on. The True Sight Candle has been lit, gentlemen. Its light will lead us to all of Juno's secrets, not only Princess Ghador. Rules have been broken and the battlefield is no longer fixed. You may ... *slip your leashes.* Yandira will have to navigate her own way down the new path I will now set for you all.'

Lunk and Venatus gave each other what passed for them as smiles.

'What say we make Juno pay for Her misconduct, hmm? Allow Me to show you a shortcut to your prey.'

Docile sailors burst into activity, each remembering their duty on the *Admiral's Teeth* and preparing the ship for sail. She commanded the spirits of Her dragons to reveal a swathe of clear sea before the ship's prow, like an Earthly runway. At its end the Underworld opened, swirling like a whirlpool, sucking down water and fog alike. Lunk and Venatus grinned as the *Admiral's Teeth* was pulled towards it.

'A warning before you leave, gentlemen,' She said. 'Beware Minerva's sword. Even without its stones, that blade is powerful enough to cut the dirty little wolves from your souls.'

They nodded in grave understanding, and She continued, 'Do what you will to those of the Realm, but the earthling has become most intriguing to Me. He deserves ... *special* reward, and so you will curb your bloodlust until he is safely out of your way. Do not test My patience on this.'

They would do as they were told and were eager to be on their way. As the ship drifted closer to the Underworld, She faded into the Serpent's Sigh, eager to leave Herself, for the day's mischief was not yet done.

Panicked, agonised screeches blistered the air as witches rushed wildly through smoke and burning trees, directionless, with no other plan than to escape the fiery charge scorching its way through the woodlands. Tipper's Grove was ablaze.

'Where is it?' Yandira's voice came from all directions as a thunderous, disembodied roar. She had conjured spirits from the Serpent's Sigh and made them manifest into the flesh-and-blood dragons they once were, spitting fire from vengeful mouths. 'Where is my stone?'

Dalmyn's army had slipped the ambush. Kingfisher and her cohorts were once again travelling the Queen's Highway heading for Strange Ground, though Juno's Blessing was rendering them invisible to Yandira's magical sight. But the Coven of Bellona had not suffered defeat. Every witch had simply given up the fight, let their enemy go, and Yandira wanted to know why.

She selected a witch from the fleeing horde, commanded the fog to seize him, hoist him into the air, then slam him hard into the leafy ground.

'On your feet and face me!' she roared.

The witch looked up and saw a mighty dragon of old looming over him, because that was what Yandira wanted him to see – him and all the Coven members scurrying through these woodlands like foxes chased by hounds. Sacrificing her sister had cooled the lust and fire which had threatened to consume Yandira, but the dragon's rage remained within easy summons. The Serpent's Sigh recognised her as a kindred spirit and relented to her command.

Awkwardly, the witch struggled to stand as though his muscles had atrophied long ago. Stick-thin and bent within a robe of shadows, he bowed his hooded head. 'For-forgive us, Majesty.'

His voice creaked like dry rope as though he hadn't used it in years, which was likely the truth. The Coven of Bellona spent so much time in darkness, riddled with insanity and magic, it was hard to tell whether or not they retained memories of any emotion beyond the singular, blinkered desire for their Oldunone to answer their prayers and send to the Realm Her avatar who would lead them all to glory. And now that avatar was here, they had let her down.

All around, witches ran and fell, writhing as bright red dragonfire engulfed them, screaming as dagger-like talons and teeth rent their flesh and tore them in half. Merely illusion conjured in the fog, of course. In the face of Yandira's wrath, she wanted them to remember how to feel terror.

'You brought wild things to the fight, yes?' Yandira growled from the dragon's mouth, while back in her council chambers at Castle Wood Bee she glared at the witch through the

Underworld's oily waters. 'You had the element of surprise, sufficient numbers?'

'Yes, Majesty.'

'Yet you couldn't take a trinket from one simple priest?'

'We tried, Majesty, truly we did. Many gave their lives to claim your prize and we were winning the fight!' The witch trembled as his fellows burned and screamed around him. 'But ... but a voice came, spoke to us from our souls and it could not be denied. She told us to retreat.'

'*Who* told you?' the dragon bellowed.

'Forgive me, Majesty. Hers is a power greater than yours.'

And just like that, Yandira's illusions faded. Dragons and fire disappeared, and when the witches realised they weren't being shredded and roasted after all, they jumped to their feet and scurried away like startled woodland creatures. The Serpent's Sigh rushed in to obscure Yandira's vision and brought with it a crushing sense of disappointment. Then she was back in her chambers, staring into the black, sightless pool of the Underworld.

'Majesty?'

Startled, Yandira looked at Ignius Rex. Lord Dragonfly stood emotionless behind him, but the magician's face was full of concern.

Yandira lifted the crown off her head, studied its fake stones, and for the first time in many years felt the thrill of fear.

'Her Immortal Darkness is angered by my lack of progress, Ignius. She allows my enemies—'

Yandira inhaled sharply as an icy presence entered her being, and a voice spoke through the dragon squatting on her soul.

Yandira Wood Bee, you are a disappointment to Me. I give you one last chance to redeem yourself ...

21

Earthling

There was a game Bek and Ghador used to play.

Castle Wood Bee was riddled with hidden rooms and secret passageways, and these two thirteen-year-olds made it their life's mission to discover them all. The challenge was to eavesdrop on as many private conversations as possible, and they heard plenty of sensitive information in their time: who truly felt what about whom in court, what troubles were brewing with other cities – so many things two sneaky children ought not to know. Bek and Ghador didn't actually care about what they heard; they imagined themselves as spies from one of Queen Maitressa's stories, and the real trick of the game was never to get caught. And they never did ... until the day they dared each other to spy on Ghador's youngest aunt.

While the True Sight Candle's rainbow light sparkled majestically upon ankle-deep seawater, Bek emptied the contents of her stomach. The Janus Bridge had provided a turbulent and dizzying jaunt to a cold cave much smaller than the one they had left on Oddridge Island. Bek retched again but had nothing left to bring up. She coughed, spat, then felt Ebbie patting her back.

'Are you all right?' he asked.

Bek stood upright and took several deep breaths. 'I'm fine.'

His face pale, Ebbie offered her a wan smile. The rainbow flowed from the lantern in his hand and speared into daylight, filling the cave's entrance. Karin had left a minute or so before to scout the area and find out where they were, taking the sword for protection.

'Mai never stopped caring about you,' Ebbie said, suddenly, blurting out the words as though he'd been holding them in for too long. 'She cared about you a lot. I didn't realise it until now, but she told me a story about you – "The Twice-Orphaned Thief". She said you were kind, happy, but you lost everything, including your way.'

With a soft sigh, Bek sat on a damp rock to let her stomach settle. 'I should've told you about me, but ... yes, I suppose I lost my way.' She managed a small chuckle. 'The trouble with Maitressa's stories is she likes to play fast and loose with *facts*. For example, there was never a book, Ebbie.'

'Book? What book?'

'You said Maitressa told you the story of how Yandira came to be imprisoned ten years ago. There was a book of forbidden secrets, you said, hidden in the queen's library and that's what tipped her off?' Ebbie nodded. 'Well, a book didn't tell Maitressa what was going on. It was me and Ghador ...'

And Bek dredged up a nightmare which had plagued her sleep for a decade.

Those had been dangerous days in Strange Ground. Rumours were abounding that the Underworld's disciples walked the streets, blending with the commonfolk, impossible to recognise while they corrupted good hearts with spite and poison. It was a time of high paranoia in the city, a dark time when friends and neighbours learned to distrust each other. But the trouble felt so very far away for little Bek Rana and Princess Ghador, for they lived safely behind Castle Wood Bee's high walls and believed nothing bad could reach their insular life and the game they played. As it turned out, the castle was the most dangerous place to be.

The queen's private library had boasted its own hidden spaces. And it was from a hidden passageway that Bek and Ghador witnessed Yandira committing vile atrocities in a secret room.

The stench of corruption permeated the air. The foul presence of the Underworld dripped from the ceiling and ran down the walls like oily sewage. It slithered across the floor to encircle Yandira's captive. Princess Morrad appeared entranced, offering no resistance to her situation. She faced her sister with vacant eyes, while Yandira recited witchcraft in a sibilant tongue that made Bek's stomach roil with nausea.

Bek and Ghador held hands while they watched, not knowing what to do, not daring to speak lest Yandira heard and turned her attentions to them. Morrad threw her head back and opened her mouth as wide as a snake preparing to swallow a rabbit. Darkness bubbled up from her throat, frothing acidly as it ran down the sides of her face. There was something alive in that darkness, something cruel and offensive to nature. Only later did they understand that it was Morrad's diseased soul that Yandira pulled from her mouth and perched on her shoulder.

Then Bek and Ghador ran, as fast and as quietly as they could, all the way to the queen, and they told her everything.

'I'd never seen Maitressa look so lost and heartbroken,' Bek said. 'Sounds tragic now, but Ghador used to joke that Yandira was in league with the Underworld. She was always so ... well, it was just safer to stay out of her way, you know? Maitressa always treated me kindly, like one of her own. Morrad was nice enough to my face, but she was Eldrid's henchwoman and Eldrid never liked me at all. She didn't want a commoner for her daughter's sister, but her mother was queen so she had no choice but to put up with it.

'Anyway, when Eldrid found out how me and Ghador discovered what Yandira had done to Morrad, she hated me all the more. She acted like it was all *my* fault, like I was the one who wanted to kill her daughter and bring down House Wood Bee, not Yandira. Maitressa was too heartbroken to notice, but I knew right then my days in the castle were numbered.'

Ebbie's face was full of sympathy, and this time Bek was glad of his company. He didn't say anything, giving her space to talk in her own time, and she was glad for that, too.

'After Yandira was imprisoned, Maitressa went into exile. The first thing Eldrid did was kick me out. Even before she was officially named First Lady, she tried carting me off to an orphanage or workhouse. I didn't fancy that at all.' Bek shrugged. 'So I ran away, and it suited Eldrid that I never went back.'

'What about Ghador? You were close, sisters – you must have seen her again.'

Bek didn't get the chance to answer. Karin appeared in the entrance, sword in hand. 'Right then,' she said, flustered and distraught. 'The good news is we're definitely on Earth.'

Bek thought she might throw up again.

'What's the bad news?' Ebbie said.

'The Serpent's Sigh is here.'

Bek snatched the sword from the magician and rushed to the entrance to look for herself. Sure enough, thick slate fog hung above a sandy beach while a rising tide gently lapped around her boots.

'Is it Yandira's doing?' Bek said as Ebbie and Karin emerged from the cave. 'Does she know we're here?'

'Not necessarily.' Karin looked up at the sunlight struggling to shine through the fog. 'I mean, if she can send the Serpent's Sigh to Earth, then why not let Lunk and Venatus follow us?'

'Then who *did* send it?'

'Good question.'

'I know where we are.' Ebbie had stepped ahead of them, holding up the lantern. Its rainbow light speared into the Serpent's Sigh. 'This is the old smugglers' cave. We're in Strange Ground by the Skea, *my* Strange Ground.'

Bek said, 'Why would the Janus Bridge bring you home?'

'Only one way to find out,' Karin replied. 'Lead on, Ebbie.' She looked at Bek's sword. 'Probably best if you keep that thing drawn. No telling what's hiding in this fog.'

Denser than sea mist, the Serpent's Sigh rolled through the streets and alleys of Strange Ground beneath the Skea. Even if the sun blazed from its midday zenith, its rays wouldn't cut through the soupy greyness which enthralled the folk. While enchanted blacksmiths produced *chinks* and *hisses* and flashes of firelight from tireless forges, others shuffled towards Castle Wood Bee, not quite remembering why they carried sword or spear or bow. A similar state had beset the noble lords and ladies. Emerging from their grand manors, they struggled to recall when the use of weapons had become a prerequisite of courtly function. But every citizen knew in their hearts the time to fight had come. Slowly, dutifully, the folk of Strange Ground filled the city in shambling ranks, ready to protect their Blessed Empress from her enemies.

Yandira stood on the ramparts, seeing everything in the supernatural fog, *feeling* the souls gathering for war. While the citizens fortified her outer defences, every trained fighting man and woman had been ordered within the castle grounds – some six hundred soldiers and guards in all. Armed and armoured, they manned the ramparts and watch posts, guarded the gates, patrolled the inner bailey, stood sentry outside every door and in every hall the castle had to offer. Far below, commonfolk patrolled the warrens, while royal guards lay in wait in the castle crypts. Yandira felt blessed by her Oldunone's mercy.

Her Immortal Darkness had created an arena in which all the mortal players of this game were now trapped. She had sent the witches scurrying back to their burrows, the wild things to their hills, and She had revoked Yandira's sight beyond the borders of her queendom, for she had no reason to see farther now. While Juno's Champions of good and light drew ever closer, Yandira dug her trenches, and dug them deep. The centre stage in Persephone's arena was the city of Strange Ground. *Here* was where the Oldunfolk's game ended, and Yandira knew precisely where, for Her divine voice had told her so.

The dragon was restless again, its fire growing along with Yandira's anticipation. Pleased her position was well fortified, she left the ramparts, weaving between statue-like soldiers armed with bows as she hurried down the steps and across the inner bailey, making her way to the keep.

There remained only one player yet to announce herself to the game: Ghador Wood Bee. She remained the queendom's rightful heir. If the sword which had once belonged to Minerva was reunited with Foresight and Hindsight, then Ghador would have a mighty weapon and Yandira would be as vulnerable to its power as Bellona had been so long ago. In this matter, the princess had her champions, but *they* had more than Mr Lunk and Mr Venatus to worry about now.

Lady Persephone had cut off communication with Yandira's henchmen, and perhaps that meant they were doomed to fail, or dead already. It no longer mattered. After all, the sword and the stones were destined to come to this city, whether delivered by the wolf-men or not. One way or another, by divine decree, the game ended here. And soon. All Yandira needed to do was hide behind her shield and buy herself a little more time.

Reaching the throne room, Yandira swept inside to find Ignius Rex attending Aelfric Dragonfly. The First Lord to a dead House sat on Morrad's small chair beside the throne and remained vacuous as the magician used a brass needle to draw blood from his arm into a glass tube which he emptied into a vial. Yandira was pleased to see Dragonfly's blood ran quite freely.

'Here, Majesty,' Ignius said as she approached. 'Drink.'

Yandira accepted the vial as she sat on the throne. Though not unaccustomed to the taste of blood, to think this thick, salty fluid came from the vein of a man she had known her entire life gave Yandira slight pause for reflection. She drank Dragonfly's blood nevertheless, and thirstily. It cooled the fire inside, stopped the war drums pounding at her temples. With a contented sigh, she passed the empty vial back to Ignius and he set about refilling it. Yandira would need a supply of these vials to stall the dragon's hunger while she waited for her enemies to walk into her trap. Lady Persephone would have Her crown.

'Dalmyn's army is almost here, Ignius,' she said with a knowing smile. 'And my defenders are in place.'

'A masterstroke, Majesty.' The magician stoppered a vial and began filling another. 'Dalmyn won't be eager to storm the castle when they see what they are facing.'

'Yes, I am so looking forward to watching Lady Kingfisher's face when Ghador dies.' Yandira's smile turned cruel as she aimed it at Lord Dragonfly. 'And they will see each other one last time. I will make certain of that.'

'But where *is* Ghador, Majesty?' Ignius looked at her worriedly. 'Her location remains a mystery.'

'All that matters is that she is coming, and I have been told by what route she and her father will arrive. Lady Persephone spoke to me, Ignius. I heard Her true voice, deep inside my being.'

The magician's face was awed. 'Truly you are favoured, Majesty.'

And she was. Persephone's voice was made from timeless power. She was angered yet merciful, telling Her disciple this was her last reprieve, her final chance to deliver the crown of Strange Ground. And then Yandira had been shown visions of the glory that would follow when she succeeded.

'It pleases Her Immortal Darkness for me to know the place where the crown-stones will unite with Minerva's sword.' Yandira took a shuddery, excited breath. 'You see, Ignius, we were misdirected. But while my enemies believe I remain blind to their plots and secrets, I am in truth waiting for them to deliver into my hands all my Oldunone has been promised.'

'Blessed is the Underworld and all the worlds it touches,' Ignius intoned.

Rising from the throne, Yandira selected two vials from a small wooden rack beside Ignius. She lifted them and studied the slippery contents. These shots of blood would satisfy the dragon, keep her senses sharp and her nerve like iron for what was to come. But for imparting Her knowledge, Lady Persephone demanded a grander gift.

Yandira's gaze fell upon Lord Dragonfly. 'Ignius, take this old fool down to the dungeons,' she said, turning and striding for her private chambers. 'Ready him and Ghador's soldiers for the Underworld's attention. At my signal, sacrifice them all.'

It was the height of summer, yet the air had turned as cold as deep winter, making Ebbie's teeth chatter, his breath rise in smoky plumes. Following the stream of rainbow light through the fog on the beach, he held the lantern out at arm's length, feeling like the generic nightwatchman from a host of stories he had read – the one who went out alone in the dead of night to investigate mysterious noises, only to discover monsters and demons and worse. Why was the Serpent's Sigh on Earth?

Bek walked beside Ebbie, the sword drawn and pointed at the damp sand. The fog parted before them as the True Sight Candle showed them the way.

'I'll tell you what I'm wondering,' Karin said from behind them. 'Why involve Earth in all this?' The magician carried a glass ball. It was a different colour from her light sphere, giving off a green glow. Ebbie hoped this one was some kind of weapon. 'I mean ... yes, Maitressa spent her exile here and Yandira found her, but what's the point of keeping Earth involved?'

Ebbie stopped walking. For some reason, listening to Karin air the questions that were already on his mind made him think about the story of Minerva and Bellona.

'Let's keep moving,' Bek said, hurrying him along with a grave expression. 'This fog could be hiding anything.'

How far had the Serpent's Sigh spread? Beyond the town? Did it cover the Isle of Watchers, the mainland, the rest of the world? The story of Minerva and Bellona had lodged in Ebbie's brain, clinging to the foreground, refusing to go away.

They reached the sea wall and Ebbie led the way up the steps to the road. Here, there were obstacles in the fog: cars and vans, abandoned on the street, parked at odd angles. There was no sign of their drivers – or any of the townspeople, for that matter. Strange Ground by the Skea felt unnaturally subdued.

'I've never seen the like,' Karin said, transfixed by the vehicles as they weaved their way between them. 'Are they wagons or chariots of some kind?'

'Of *some kind*, yes,' Ebbie said, but offered nothing further.

How did he go about explaining the concept of combustion engines to folk of the Realm? How could he explain *any* of it? Flight, computers, space travel – how could the folk possibly understand the centuries of development that had taken place? During two thousand years of separation, Earth had become extreme, incomprehensible ...

And Ebbie realised why an ancient story wouldn't leave his thoughts.

When Bellona had used an earthling army, Earth itself wasn't much different from the Realm. But in this day and age, when Earth had spent centuries evolving weaponry and warfare? If Yandira gained control of today's armies, then ...

Ebbie paled. 'We have to stop Yandira—'

Bek gasped. 'Look at the candle.'

Inside the lantern, the multicoloured flame was sputtering, no longer streaming its light as a rainbow. It flickered on and off with a slowing strobe effect until dying down to a small, dull flame of deep blue, struggling to stay alight atop the candle.

'Why did it do that?' Ebbie said, shaking the lantern as if he could wake the candle up.

Karin gave the flame a scowl, then scanned the thick grey wall all around them. 'Someone's out there. Listen.'

Scraping, shuffling footsteps. Two figures appeared as silhouettes, moving slowly, disturbing the fog but not enough to reveal themselves.

'Lunk and Venatus?' Bek whispered, adopting a fighting stance.

'Could be,' Ebbie replied, feeling sick. 'They've been to Earth before.'

'No, I don't think it's them,' Karin said. More figures were joining the first two, one after another, surrounding the three of them. 'Ebbie, how many people live in this town of yours?'

'I-I'm not sure. Twelve thousand, something like that?'

'That's a lot of soldiers for the Serpent's Sigh to enlist.' The magician turned full circle, holding the green glowing ball like a grenade she was preparing to lob. 'And they know we're here.'

'But the sword will protect us,' Bek said hopefully. 'Like it did on your island, right?'

'From bad magic, yes, but ...' Karin looked uncertain. 'To those infected with the Serpent's Sigh, we would appear as an anomaly, a patch of ... something *good* their eyes can't see. And there's nothing to say they won't keep on following us. Or try to attack us. That's why the candle changed.'

'So we can't lead them to anything Yandira wants,' Ebbie said.

'Yandira's not controlling them. She would have had us by now, if she were—'

A clang came from the left like someone falling over a rubbish bin. The headcount was ever growing in the fog as more and more townspeople were drawn to the anomaly of Oldunspeak magic.

'Karin, what do we do?' Bek said tensely.

The magician tested the weight of the glowing ball in her hand. 'This is Hecate's Fire. I've no idea if it'll work on the Serpent's Sigh, but it shouldn't hurt us.'

'*Shouldn't?*' said Bek.

'It's a little unpredictable, but it's all I've got. I didn't exactly have time to pack for this trip. Just ... keep your sword handy and get ready to run.'

Karin raised the ball above her head and braced to throw. But she froze when a woman's voice came out of the fog.

'Stop! These are innocent earthlings and you will not harm them.'

The voice was commanding, regal. Across the road, the Serpent's Sigh parted and the woman walked towards the group. She wore a thick black parka, the hood up and concealing her face. Ebbie's first thought was to wonder if that was *his* thick black Parker, but then she came a little closer and the infected townspeople scattered before her, fleeing in all directions into swirls of slate-grey.

The woman stopped a few paces from the group. A moment passed, during which a confused sort of stand-off evolved. Ebbie felt his hand twitch. He looked down just in time to see the cream and green ring of Hecate's Onyx, the ring storing a Janus Bridge which clung to him for dear life, finally release its grip and slide from his finger. Strangely, he felt a sense of loss as it chimed on the tarmac and he watched it roll across the road to topple at the woman's feet. She picked it up, studied it, looked undecided, before finally slipping the ring onto her finger then pulling down her hood.

Ebbie's breath caught. She was in her early twenties, around Bek's age, with short black hair and eyes as green as a cat's, and her face ... She was forty or more years younger, but her face was the spitting image of Mai.

'It's you,' Bek said quietly.

The woman said nothing.

'Oh, I get it,' Karin said with a chuckle. 'You must be Ghador.' She stepped forwards, offered a hand to shake, then dropped it to her side when the woman didn't take it. 'We're having a spot of bother with the True Sight Candle. Don't suppose you know a safe place to hole up for a while, do you?'

There was no sound or sign of pursuit as the fog cleared from the group's path. At jogging pace, they headed away from the sea, deeper into town. Bek looked more troubled than ever, her lips drawn in a tight line. Ebbie felt bewildered; he couldn't work out if he had found Mai's granddaughter or if she had found him. Karin, on the other hand, was enjoying herself and full of questions for their guide.

'So, tell us,' she said excitedly, 'was it you who stole Foresight and Hindsight from the crown?'

Ghador aimed a quick, angry glance at Bek. '*I* stole nothing.'

'But you have the stones, don't you?'

'No.'

'Oh, that's going to make things tricky if you want to beat your aunt.'

'I know the whereabouts of one. The other is in a secret place.'

'Please tell me it's nowhere your aunt can get to.'

'Stop calling her my *aunt*. That murderer doesn't deserve to carry the Wood Bee name.'

'This is amazing,' Karin said, unfazed by the reprimand. 'I honestly thought the stories about Foresight and Hindsight, the crown and Minerva's sword were mostly bollocks.' She looked to Ebbie and Bek to share her excitement, but reined herself in when she caught sight of Bek's expression. 'Oh, right … Maitressa warned me it's been a while since you two saw each other. You probably have some private things to work out before you get all chummy again.'

An almost palpable tension bloomed between Bek and Ghador as they jogged along. Ebbie jumped in before either of them could say anything. 'Ghador, how long have you been here? *Why* are you here?'

'I'm here because I'm supposed to be. How and why aren't important now. The Serpent's Sigh has come to Earth and it has infected the populace of this town. It's time to go home.'

Ghador had obviously been here long enough to learn her way around Strange Ground. She cut through side roads and alleys, leading them further and further from the beach, until they were following a wide main road. Ebbie already suspected where she was taking them by the time the fog revealed a tall and dirty apartment block he knew all too well. He stopped Ghador as she approached the security doors with his key in her hand.

'We can't go in there,' he said. 'This is where I live, and Lunk and Venatus know where it is.'

'I've been living in your home for the last two days,' Ghador assured him. 'I've seen nothing of those bastards. Yandira doesn't know I'm here.'

'But obviously someone does,' Karin said, gesturing to the fog. 'Why is the Serpent's Sigh on Earth? Who sent it?'

'At this moment, I'm more concerned about getting the True Sight Candle working again.'

'Then it's not just for finding you?' Ebbie said.

'No.'

Karin *tsked*. 'I already told him that.'

'Let's talk inside,' Ghador said, turning the key in the security lock and leading them into the building.

The last time Ebbie saw his front door, Lunk and Venatus had been in the process of tearing it apart. At some point, it had been replaced with a new door; and Ebbie's secret lodger, who was more confident than him that the wolfish henchmen wouldn't make another appearance, also had the key to his flat.

Karin marvelled at the number of books crammed into cases on the lounge side of the room, while Bek sheathed the sword and eyed the kitchen appliances suspiciously. Though the flat appeared startlingly normal and pretty much how he left it, Ebbie felt that he didn't recognise his home at all.

'Got any food?' Karin asked. 'I'm famished.'

Ghador waved in the vague direction of the fridge. Ebbie

opened it. A half-eaten fish pie sat in a baking dish. He passed it to the magician, along with a spoon; she took the pie over to the coffee table, where she sat in an armchair and tucked in hungrily.

Ghador stood on the far side of the room, her back to Ebbie's bedroom door, while Bek remained close to the front door. They stared at each other across the gulf above Karin's head. Neither of them spoke, but the hostility between them was obvious and mutual, building to a head.

In an attempt to break the tension, Ebbie thumped the lantern on the table and said, 'I never believed the Oldunfolk were real, but I've seen some weird things in the last couple of days, and I keep hearing about how we're playing the Oldunfolk's game by strange rules, and I don't know what to think any more.' Ghador tore her gaze away from Bek and Ebbie pointed at the unhelpful blue flame in the lantern. 'I was told the purpose of this candle was to find *you*. Which I did, because your grandmother asked me to. But I found you almost as soon as it was lit, on Earth, living in my flat. It's like I didn't really need its help at all.' In fact, Ebbie was beginning to wonder if he himself was nothing but a spare wheel in this game. 'What's going on?'

'The candle is meant for me, always has been.' Ghador raised a hand and waggled the finger with the ring on it. 'The purpose of its light is to guide me to where the Janus Bridge will open. The Janus Bridge will then lead me to where Hindsight is hidden.'

'Which won't happen while the candle is so reluctant,' Karin said through a mouthful of food. 'And you can't use the stepping-off point in the cave. Even if Janus opened it again, it might take us back to Oddridge Island. It might take us *anywhere*.'

'There's another stepping-off point in this very room,' said Ebbie, 'but evidently it's not the right one, either.'

Karin shrugged. 'I never said it was an exact magic.'

'It was my grandmother,' Ghador said. 'She made a ... *pact* which granted her the power to set certain *stepping-off* points in this town. The one I need now is in Strange Ground somewhere, but the Janus Bridge won't open unless the True Sight Candle shows me where it is. Unless I find the bridge, I can't find Hindsight.'

'It's a conundrum, to be sure,' Karin said, tapping the lantern with the spoon. 'Let's think about this. What would Oddridge do?' She resumed shovelling food into her mouth.

Ebbie narrowed his eyes at the princess. '"*Home*", you said earlier. "*It's time to go home.*" Are you talking about *your* Strange Ground?'

'My grandmother wasn't clear on this matter, but ...' Ghador looked as though a great weight had descended on her. 'I believe Hindsight is hidden somewhere in my home city, yes.'

For the first time, Bek entered the conversation. 'Strange Ground's not a good place to be at the moment.'

Turning a slow glare on her, Ghador said, 'Nonetheless, that's where Yandira will pay for her evils. That's where she will face Minerva's sword in *my* hand.'

Bek looked down at the scabbard hanging from her waist. 'By my understanding, you'll need both of the crown-stones to do that. You're off to find one, but where's the other?'

'My father has it.'

Bek scoffed. 'Your *father*?'

'Yes, my *father*,' Ghador hissed. 'And *he* is bringing an army to Strange Ground.'

'Only if he hasn't stopped along the way to drink his fill and dip his wick.'

'Oh, you must be frightened, Bek Rana, concerned you'll be drafted for the fight. But don't worry, I only accept soldiers who don't desert their friends at the first sign of trouble.'

Bek's face reddened, and Ebbie jumped in. 'Hey, let's all keep calm. Ghador, your grandmother asked Bek to help, and she did, no matter what happened in the past.'

'And what would you know about the past, *earthling*?'

'No!' Bek stepped up beside Ebbie. 'Don't take this out on him.'

'Shut up, all of you!' Karin shouted. 'I can't hear myself think with this row, and ... what's that noise?'

With timely intervention, Ebbie's mobile phone had buzzed. It lay where he'd left it charging on the kitchen counter. He picked it up and found a message from his mother. He was vaguely aware of Karin asking what the device was but didn't reply. The message read: *It's about time you embraced your faith and got out of that town. I'm so proud of you.*

Confused, Ebbie scrolled back through a series of texts exchanged with his mother while he had been away in the Realm. She wasn't just proud, she was ecstatic, overjoyed, because, apparently, Ebbie wouldn't be able to visit her now as he had a new job in the library of a big church in Oldun City. According to the texts, he had seen the error of his ways. He had found his faith.

'What ... ?' Ebbie held the phone up. 'Have you been using this?' he asked Ghador.

She shook her head, angry eyes still on Bek. 'No, but your neighbour has.'

'My neighbour?'

'She's been kind to me since I arrived. This world is a madhouse and I might have lost my mind without her help.'

Ebbie didn't actually know his neighbours or why any of

them would pretend to be him and send lies to his mum. He read the texts again.

'So, what now?' Bek said testily.

'Well,' Karin replied, even though Bek was clearly talking to Ghador, 'while the Serpent's Sigh is out there, we're stuck in here with a True Sight Candle that doesn't want to play, but ...' She had finished eating and was peering into the lantern. 'Oddridge taught me a spell that might wake this thing up. It could *shock* the candle into working again. Maybe. It means asking for Hecate's intervention, but even if She's listening, I've no idea if She's willing to get involved in this game.'

'Worth a try,' Bek said flatly.

'Oh, do you really think so?' Ghador countered sarcastically.

Karin grumbled in annoyance. 'Look, Princess, I don't care about titles and birthrights and all that shite, but I *do* care about the Realm. You clearly need to get something off your chest – and so do you, Bek. Go and find a private space to clear the air and give me some bloody peace and quiet so I can concentrate on getting you home.'

'Excellent idea,' Ghador said frostily.

'Glad you agree.'

Mai's granddaughter opened the bedroom door and stood aside, inviting Bek to enter first. With a face like thunder, Bek strode across the room and went inside.

'Hold up,' Ebbie said before Ghador could follow. 'Which neighbour was helping you?'

'Mrs Cory from number seven.'

Ebbie blanched. 'Did you say *Mrs Cory*?'

But Ghador had entered the bedroom, slamming the door shut behind her.

Ebbie looked at the phone in his hand. 'I didn't know she lived in the building,' he said to himself. 'I thought she was dead.'

'Garlic,' said Karin.

'What?'

'I need some for the spell.' The magician had set the lantern on the table and was staring challengingly at the blue flame inside. 'Do you have any?'

'I think there's a jar of chopped garlic in the fridge.'

'What about salt?'

Ebbie nodded.

'Thyme?'

'Umm ... I've got some mixed herbs and spices at the back of a cupboard somewhere.'

'That'll have to do. Oh, and a few drops of blood.' She saw Ebbie's surprised and worried expression and rocked her head from side to side. 'All right, I can provide those myself. Just the garlic, salt and herbs, then.'

Distracted from his thoughts, Ebbie quickly gathered the items Karin requested and dropped them on the table.

'Right, this'll take a lot of concentration,' the magician said, cracking her knuckles, 'so make yourself scarce, too.'

'Sure.' Ebbie was looking at his front door. 'I need to check on something, anyway.'

22

Good Neighbour?

If any kind of blessing could be found in the Serpent's Sigh, then it was how very little it had revealed of Strange Ground by the Skea. Earth, the stuff of myth and legend, existing only in the stories told around campfires since ancient days – Bek had never wasted time thinking about earthlings, had never harboured any dreams to see their world, but here she was, frightened, out of her depth and glad a supernatural fog was limiting her experience. She couldn't quite believe it was real.

Earth's oddities were inescapable; even here, in Ebbie's bedroom, where as many books were crammed into cases as there were in the room outside, a strange black box sat on a table beside the unmade bed radiating a red light in the shape of numbers: *14:03*. What did it mean? What was its purpose? Bek stared at it until Ghador disturbed her.

'I believe *that* is for me?'

She stood on the opposite side of the bed from Bek, looking at the hilt of the divine sword poking out of its battered scabbard.

The folk had always remarked upon how Ghador looked like her grandmother, but at that moment she wore her mother's heavy, intolerant scowl. Ten years had gone by since Bek had last spoken to her. She had spent so much energy plotting her escape from Ebbie that she hadn't stopped to consider how it might feel to see Ghador again. Now, it surprised her to feel no joy or anger, only awkwardness. Because they had faded from each other's lives long ago. Bek didn't know this woman standing in front of her, and she didn't know Bek.

'Here,' Bek said, unbuckling her belt and throwing the sword on the bed. 'It's yours.'

Ghador didn't look at it, her eyes fixed on her old friend. 'I'm sorry you had to come this far.' Her voice was older, deeper, but carried the inflections of the girl Bek had known. 'If everything I've heard about Bek Rana is true, then you'll be wanting payment for your services.'

Bek didn't appreciate the tone. 'That's it? No *thanks* for risking my life to bring this thing to you? On Earth, I might add, *Your Highness.*'

'Would you have brought it to me, left to your own devices? I suspect the earthling had something to do with persuading you. *Against* your natural instincts.'

'His name is Ebbie.' If she wanted Bek to feel guilty, she'd have a long wait. 'And yes, he played a big part in bringing me around. You might not like it, but Maitressa was his friend. He genuinely cared about her, and he's done nothing but right by your family every step of the way. You should be grateful.'

Ghador wasn't moved by these words. 'Grandmother's spirit visited me.'

'She's been doing a lot of that.'

'She doesn't like the person you've become, either.'

Bek bristled. 'Perhaps *Grandmother* would be better pleased by how I decided to help *her* granddaughter in the end, despite the fact that *you* once promised me I'd never be an orphan again right before you and your family threw me out to live on the streets like a stray dog.'

'That's not fair!' Ghador's intolerant façade slipped, revealing more of the person Bek remembered. 'What about *your* promise? We'd be sisters for ever, you said. Why did you hide? Why didn't you come back?'

'What, and risk the wrath of your precious mother? What's *her* spirit thinking right now? How *pleased* is she in the afterlife?' Ghador's eyes flashed angrily and Bek backed down instantly. 'That was cruel. I'm sorry.'

'Mother didn't warn me of what she planned to do, you know. I woke up one morning and you weren't there. Gone for good, she told me. Simple as that. And she expected me to accept it.' Ghador walked around the bed to stand in front of Bek. 'But I came looking for you. I sneaked out of the castle at night and searched the streets, but I couldn't find you anywhere. I never truly forgave Mother for separating us, but in the end, after all that fruitless searching, I decided you must have learned to hate me, so *I* learned to live without you.'

'Oh, it must've been hard for you.' Bek's voice was flat and sour. 'You know, I saw you *living without me* at Eldrid's coronation. I watched your procession in all its pomp travelling through the city. You looked very comfortable with life, sitting next to the new queen, not upset at all while the folk cheered and waved. I mean, did you even notice that you'd lost your grandmother— *Ow!*'

Bek staggered back into a bookcase as Ghador delivered a quick jab to her face. At first she felt blindsided and could only stare in shock. Then Ghador pointed a finger at her and raged, 'She was *your* grandmother, too!' and a lifetime of injustice boiled up inside Bek Rana. Her hands balled into fists and her words came in a growl.

'All right, Princess, have it your way.'

*

There had never been a seventh apartment on the second floor of this building, Ebbie knew that for a fact. But here it was, a brass number seven hanging on the door to an apartment that shouldn't have been there. And was the hallway longer than it used to be? Ebbie stared at the brass number for a while before deciding to knock. The door swung inwards before his knuckles touched wood.

The rank stench of corruption assaulted his nostrils and an invisible force pulled him forwards. The door slammed shut and disappeared, leaving Ebbie to face a terrible landscape where bitter vapour steamed in the air and the sky was the colour of graveyards. This was not Earth. Nor was it the Realm.

Plant life glowed deathly green, leaves and trunks veined with dull red luminescence. A path of cracked stone, pale and ancient, stretched away from where Ebbie stood, flanked by pools of boiling oil and statues of haunted souls. At the path's end was a huge mound of black rock; atop it, a woman stood in a hooded robe. Behind her, bony spikes fanned out.

With a snap of static, the mobile phone in Ebbie's hand turned to ooze which spilled through his fingers and left not one mark on his skin. A quick and spiteful wind whipped his arms into the air and stole Mai's satchel. The tatty cloth bag, now only holding the letter, Ebbie's last link to Mai, swirled and rose like an old ghost before disappearing altogether. The woman on the rock beckoned to Ebbie. The acrid atmosphere *squeezed* against him, pushing him towards her.

Faces had been carved into the path, each holding an expression of torment. They moaned when Ebbie trod on them. As he neared the black mound, the woman pulled back her hood and looked down at him with the saddest eyes he had ever seen.

Karin! He had wanted to shout her name in surprise, but the corruption of the land had stolen his voice and he could force not one sound past his lips.

'I suppose from your perspective you last saw me very recently.' Karin thought for a moment. 'I don't know how long I've been here, Ebbie. Time doesn't have much meaning in this place.'

It was definitely Karin standing up there, but also not quite her. The magician appeared somehow intangible, almost see-through, her clothes and skin, hair and face greyer, her frame outlined by a silvery glow. *Why are you here?* Ebbie wanted to say. *What the hell is going on?* But still he couldn't utter a single word.

Karin's eyes brimmed with tears. 'I didn't make it, Ebbie. Lunk and Venatus caught up with us. Bek and Ghador got away ... I *think*. But something went wrong, *something*, and I ... I really don't know how long I've been dead.'

Dead? Ebbie wanted to go to her, but the land prohibited him from taking a single step nearer to the rock than he already was. This couldn't be real. Karin was back in his apartment, trying to fix the True Sight Candle. He had *just* left her. She couldn't be dead.

'I know what you're thinking, but you have to listen to me now,' she said – no, pleaded. 'I have no choice but to be here, to do as I'm told. *She* sent my ghost because She wants to show you a friendly face. And let's not waste time calling Her Mrs Cory – you know who She really is.'

Persephone! The name came to Ebbie with force, as if the whole of this poisonous place had risen up to shout it into his mind. The Oldunone of the Underworld – this was Her domain, and it trembled with Her presence. Ebbie felt tears on his cheeks.

'Persephone has been watching you, watching Ghador, watching all of us. But you intrigue Her, Ebbie. You fascinate

Her, and that's not a good thing.' The rocky mound shuddered and released a plume of smoke that coiled up around Karin's ghost. 'She gave me a message for you. She sends Her congratulations for coming this far, but also warns against trying to go any further. She says that now Ghador is found, it's time for you to retire from the game.'

Ebbie swallowed a hard lump in his throat. *Retire?*

Karin looked miserable, averting her gaze as though ashamed of her situation. 'For everyone's sake, you're to stay on Earth.'

Stay on Earth? Ebbie wondered if he had been drugged again. He couldn't fathom what was happening to him, what was happening to Karin, but he knew the very thought of dropping out of the game now filled him with panic.

'You'll be rewarded,' the magician said, quickly, fretfully. 'Persephone has a grand prize lined up for you.'

With another gout of smoke, the rocky mound shook and the ground before it cracked. A fissure snaked towards Ebbie. He skipped back, but it didn't reach him. Instead, it widened with a rumble, and the smoke cleared to reveal a downward view into a huge auditorium, filled with at least a thousand people. And there, on the stage, was Ebbie himself.

Karin said, 'This is the future Persephone is offering you.'

Though Ebbie couldn't hear what he was saying, he was addressing the audience with a passion and confidence he didn't know he possessed, and every person listening was enchanted by his words. On a screen behind him was written: *EARTH AND THE REALM: Two worlds, one people*, and he kept pointing at it as he commanded the stage and his audience's attention. Ebbie never knew he could look so happy. And in the front row, his parents sat watching, looking proud but sheepish, as if they had finally accepted that their son had been the wise one all along.

'Leave the game,' Karin said, 'and this will become reality. Your knowledge will make you rich, famous, revered by your peers. This is Persephone's gift to you.'

The power of the Underworld pressed in with *Her* coercion, like a venomous spider crawling across his hubris, urging him to accept this *prize* playing out in the vision. But he closed his eyes to the successful version of himself on stage and resisted Her dark insistence, despite his temptation. Perhaps Persephone thought She had locked in on the secret desires hiding in Ebbie's heart, but the truth was, when he looked into this vision of Earth, he saw a world that his heart had already walked away from. He had to get out of this place, get back to Bek and Ghador. He had to warn Karin—

The rent in the ground crashed shut with the force of Persephone's displeasure.

Up on the mound, Karin had a small smile of pride for Ebbie's defiance. 'I told Her you wouldn't be easily swayed. I said you have a deeper strength than folk give you credit for.' The smile slid from the magician's face, replaced by a look of fear. 'But She's relentless. She can't be denied. You need to think *very* carefully about what you want, Ebbie, because you haven't seen what I have ...'

To Ebbie's horror, the mound of rock opened its eyes and glared at him with black orbs lined with veins of liquid silver. Smoke came from its nostrils, and its mouth opened to reveal a giant forked tongue and teeth as long as swords. Somewhere at the back of this rank maw, a red furnace burned. Karin crouched down as the dragon unfurled itself, beat its wings and lofted her high into the air with a ground-shaking roar.

A vicious gale buffeted Ebbie, drove him to his knees before a monstrous claw closed around him like a cage and whisked him up into graveyard skies.

*

On the floor of Ebbie Wren's bedroom, the two estranged sisters sat side by side. They were now happy in each other's company when moments earlier one had been gasping for breath while the other rolled around in agony.

The fight had been an awkward scrap which hadn't lasted long. A few punches had been exchanged, a little grappling had sent books tumbling from cases, and the pair had cursed and tangled until Ghador drove her knee into Bek's stomach, while, at the same time, Bek crashed hers up into Ghador's crotch. Thus the fight ended.

Slowly, they recovered. Anger faded and tears were shared. Then, an embrace. And finally, a conversation that had been waiting to happen for ten years.

'I can't believe you kept hold of them,' Bek said, looking at the two child-sized teeth nestled in Ghador's open hand. 'What was his name again?'

'Mandor Sparrow.'

'That's the one. The look on his face when he fell on his arse and spat these out was priceless. Well worth the trouble I got into. Do you remember? I had to stand in front of court and apologise to his House. My legs were shaking so badly.'

'I thought you looked magnificent on that day. My saviour, a true sister.' Ghador returned the teeth to a little velvet pouch and put them in her pocket. Gingerly, she touched two fingers to the bruise forming under her eye. 'Why did you stay, Bek? Why didn't you leave Strange Ground?'

'I've asked myself the same question, more than once. My answers are always a little sketchy.' Bek's memory drifted through the distant past when she had first been cast onto the streets. 'I knew you were looking for me. I saw you, several times, wrapped up in a hooded cloak, pretending to be one of the commonfolk. I wanted to come to you, but I hid instead. I even reported you to the city guard a couple of times so they'd take you back home.'

'Were you really so angry with me?'

'No, I was too scared to be angry. At first. But what did you expect to happen? We'd go adventuring on the streets, explore the city like we used to explore the castle? Ghador, I had to steal so I didn't starve, run from gangs who wanted to take my food. Or worse. I had to sleep with a sharp knife in my hand, I ... I couldn't drag you into that life.'

Ghador gave a sad smile. 'You weren't quite as good at hiding from me as you think. Your name surfaced soon enough, once you started stealing more than just food. You didn't make a particularly good thief, you know.'

Bek frowned. 'No?'

'Those guards you reported me to? I paid them well to turn a blind eye if your name ever came up on an arrest warrant.'

Bek chuckled.

Ghador reached over and took her hand. 'I didn't want to live on the streets with you, Bek. I just wanted my sister back. I would've given you money, found you safe shelter, whatever you needed. We could have stayed friends, in secret.'

'No, it wouldn't have happened that way, and you know it.' Bek gave Ghador's hand a gentle squeeze. 'Your mother would have found out eventually, and what then? I don't mean that unkindly. I'm genuinely sorry she's dead, Ghador, but you know how she felt about me.'

The princess accepted the truth in Bek's words with a slow nod. 'I loved my mother, but Oldunfolk know she had her faults. Grandmother would never have let her separate us.'

Maitressa had once said she had never known two folk to share a closer bond than Bek and Ghador. Sisters in spirit if not by blood, and she was so very proud of them both. No, Maitressa would never have allowed their separation, but she left the Realm and everything changed.

'I thought I'd moved on,' Bek said. 'I honestly believed I didn't care any more. But when I found out Maitressa was dead, it broke my heart. When I heard about your mother, what Yandira had done, I knew you were in trouble, but ... everything in me denied what I was feeling. So I tried to run away. Again. I wanted to hate you, Ghador, but I don't and never did. Ebbie helped me see that.'

'Sounds like he's been a good influence on you. He certainly made an impression with Grandmother.'

'You know, he had no idea who she really was or where she came from. He called her *Mai*, if you can believe it.'

'I think I can. What was it Grandmother used to say? If you want to test the true measure of a person, let them think you're nobody, then see how they treat you.'

'Well, Ebbie definitely passes that test.'

'What about the magician?'

'Karin?'

'She seems a little ... *off.*'

Bek chuckled again. 'She's certainly not backwards in coming forwards. I think Karin has spent too much time on her own, but we can trust her, too. I mean, we wouldn't have made it here without her.'

'And what about you, Bek? What are your plans?'

'I'm here, too, aren't I?' Bek shrugged. 'Whether I planned to be or not.'

'Then here we *all* are, a ragtag army of four, facing impossible odds.' Ghador patted her estranged sister's leg. 'And now I'm a step closer to my throne than I was this morning.'

She got up and took the sword from where it lay on the

bed in its scabbard. She drew the blue blade and marvelled at its Oldunspeak decorations. 'The blade that slew Bellona,' she whispered, sheathing the divine weapon. 'And now it needs its stones to give Yandira what she deserves.'

As Bek watched Ghador buckling the sword belt, a very real concern cut through her awe at how they were playing out the stuff of ancient legends. 'Look, I don't want to start another argument, but you know as well as I do that your father is a bloody idiot. If he's got Foresight, he'll probably think he can face Yandira himself.'

'I wouldn't worry about that,' Ghador said with a smirk. 'Genevieve Kingfisher is keeping an eye on him.'

Of course. Bek had forgotten about her involvement, but if anyone had the iron will to keep Prince Maxis in line, then it was Lady Stoneface Kingfisher.

Ghador gripped the hilt of Minerva's sword and drew herself up. 'So, do I look the part?' She did, but the expression on her face matched Bek's; she looked like someone Yandira wanted to kill.

The bedroom door flew open and Karin burst in.

'It's working!' she announced, flustered. 'I fixed it. I think ...' She pursed her lips. 'I was meddling with its magic when it blazed into life, so I must have done something right.'

'The candle?' Bek jumped to her feet. 'It's active?'

'With every colour of the rainbow.' Karin grinned at Ghador. 'Just give the word, Your Highness, and we're ready to – hold on ...' The grin disappeared. She ducked out of the room, then back in. 'Where's Ebbie?'

A bad feeling crawled up inside Bek. 'I thought he was with you?'

'Said he had to check something, but he hasn't come back.'

Frantic knocking rattled the front door. The three of them

rushed out into the living area where the True Sight Candle once again shone with a multicoloured flame. Ghador opened the door and an elderly woman pushed her way in, flapping her arms in distress.

'Mrs Cory,' said Ghador. 'What's the matter?'

'A ship's docked at the harbour,' the old woman said, looking suspiciously at the rainbow light emanating from the lantern on the table. 'But it's not from this world, if you follow me.'

'A ship from the Realm?'

'Ebbie called the sailors *wolves*, told me the funniest thing to tell you – *Lunk and Venatus*. He said you'd understand.'

'Shit,' Bek hissed. 'Where's Ebbie now?'

'On the run. He's distracting the sailors to buy you time to escape. Said he'd catch up with you.' She turned to Ghador. 'I'm sorry, dear, but he was very scared, and so am I. You should do as he says.'

Ghador shared a look with Bek, then grabbed the lantern from the table.

'We're not leaving Ebbie behind,' Bek stated.

'But we can't stay here.' Ghador gripped her shoulder. 'It's *me* Yandira wants, and Ebbie Wren must know this town like the back of his hand. Let him find us along the way.' She turned to her earthling friend. 'Thank you for everything you've done, Mrs Cory. Now go home and lock the door. Don't open it again till the fog has gone.'

'All right, dear, you know what's best.'

With reluctance and certainty mixing in her gut, Bek followed Ghador as she led the way with the True Sight Candle. But Karin lagged behind, approaching the elderly woman.

'What's your name again?'

The magician didn't receive an answer as Bek grabbed her arm and dragged her out of the apartment.

*

Now weaponless, Bek took charge of the lantern, leading the way. On her right, Ghador ran with Minerva's sword drawn and pointed forwards; on her left, Karin held a glass sphere containing the green glow of magic.

How? Bek wondered. *How would Ebbie find them?* He couldn't guess where the True Sight Candle was taking them. He wasn't within the sword's protective circle. Even if the Serpent's Sigh didn't claim him, he wouldn't last long against Lunk and Venatus.

From somewhere not distant enough, a wolf barked. The group increased its speed, following a rainbow through the fog. Small snippets of the town were revealed within the tunnel they carved into the grey. Bek saw buildings, lights behind windows which she doubted were made by naked flames; and although there didn't seem to be any infected earthlings in pursuit, a new enemy had come to this place, one not so blinded by the magic of Oldunspeak, or afraid of Juno's Blessing.

It didn't take long, less than ten minutes of running, for the True Sight Candle to lead them to their destination. Unhindered, sweating and breathing hard, they came to a building upon whose door the lantern shone a multicoloured circle. On the road outside, a huge metal container was overflowing with discarded books, hundreds of them. Bek read the sign above the building's door: *St. Meyers-Bannerman Library*.

'It's locked,' Ghador said, rattling the door handle in frustration. 'We'll have to break it open.'

'No, leave it to me,' Bek said. She placed the lantern down and pulled her picks from her pocket. Crouching, she worked on the lock while Ghador stood guard.

'Somethings not adding up here,' Karin said. 'Ghador, how did you meet that earthling in Ebbie's lodgings?'

'What?'

'The old woman. Tell me.'

'She was waiting when I arrived. My grandmother asked her to help me.'

'Oh, I'd wager she didn't. Why is she protected from the Serpent's Sigh?'

'I ... I don't know.'

'That's what I thought.' Karin's voice was low, angry. Bek took a quick look away from the lock to see the magician scanning the street with her spell glowing in the glass ball. 'Oddridge used to collect all kinds of stories and accounts, some of them written on parchment as old as the hills. I read a couple of tales about this Trickster, a real bad egg who liked to cause mischief – if you can call fires and death and plagues *mischief*. Wherever She went, disaster struck, and She called Herself *Koree*.'

'What are you talking about?' Ghador said.

'You've been in some bad company, Princess. How much did you tell Mrs Cory?' The magician didn't wait for an answer, adding, 'Shite ... we've got company.'

Out on the street, figures were closing in through the fog.

'Bek, the door!'

'I'm trying!'

There was a key stuck in the lock from the other side, and Bek was struggling to poke it out.

'Karin, what are you doing?' Ghador hissed.

The magician had stepped onto the road and climbed up into the metal container. She stood upon a mountain of books, lofting her spell above her head. 'I *see* you, Trickster,' she shouted. 'You can't fool me. I was taught by the best.'

Twenty or more people emerged from the fog, stepping into the clearing made by the sword. Bek recognised the tattooed woman and the young sailor she had spoken to at the

Rudderless Swine. Captain Konn's crew, each of them infected with the Serpent's Sigh and prowling like wolves, though there was no sign of the captain, or Lunk and Venatus, among them. They closed in on Karin as if attracted to the magic shining greenly above her.

'Bek! The door!'

'It's no good!' The key was stuck fast in the lock, cocked in such a way that it wouldn't be shifted. 'It won't budge!' The pick snapped and tumbled from Bek's grasp.

With a cry, Ghador stamped her foot against the door. It shuddered but was too sturdy to be easily forced open.

'Get down,' Karin warned. She was looking back at them, speaking with an oddly serene voice. 'Don't trust anyone but yourselves now. Follow the True Sight Candle like you would your own hearts. It's the only thing in this game that won't deceive you.'

And then she hurled the spell down onto the road amidst the creeping sailors. It exploded with green fire.

The container shielded Bek and Ghador from the brunt of the blast, but still it knocked them onto their backs. The library windows shattered, showering them with broken glass, and the door was ripped from its hinges. The shock wave punched possessed sailors off their feet and sent them crashing into walls with bone-breaking force. Karin herself remained atop the mountain of books, engulfed in green flame – Hecate's Fire, she called it. She seemed to be screaming, but no sound came from her wide-open mouth as a geyser of blackest oil shot up from beneath her, lifted her into the air, doused the flames then disappeared, taking the magician with it.

Books smouldered where Karin had stood.

The Serpent's Sigh began retreating, rolling away, dragging

the corpses of sailors with it. The sun speared through the fog, warm on Bek's face but not in her gut. This was no victory.

'Come on!' Ghador urged.

Bek grabbed the lantern. Miraculously – magically? – the candle's iridescent flame still burned. She followed Ghador into the library. More books were strewn across the floor. Wooden cases had been upturned, many of them broken. The warmth of summer and a light sea breeze flowed in through the smashed window, as did sunlight – but not enough to lift the gloom.

'The Serpent's Sigh is leaving,' Ghador said, breathing hard. 'Did ... did Karin do that? Is she dead? What just happened?'

Bek didn't know, but only now was Karin's tale about the Trickster registering with her. 'Your friend in Ebbie's lodgings – She had the same name as the woman in the story. What does that mean?'

'It means *She* can see you,' said a voice from the gloom at one end of the library. Bek and Ghador wheeled around. 'It means you can't hide from Her. Or *us*.'

From among scattered books and broken cases, Mr Venatus stepped into the rainbow light. In his hand, he held a length of chain which ended at a chunky metal hook, barbed and rusted. Ghador immediately moved in front of Bek, sword levelled, poised to fight. A growl came from behind them. Mr Lunk emerged from the shadows, teeth and hands the only weapons he needed. Instead of fear, Bek felt a hard knot of fury in her gut. She dropped the lantern and grabbed the nearest thing to a weapon she could find – a sturdy hardwood pole from the frame of a bookcase – and held it like a spear aimed at Mr Lunk.

'You ready?' she asked, back to back with her sister.

In reply, Ghador leapt at Mr Venatus.

Lunk made a grab for the makeshift spear as Bek jabbed it towards his face, but he missed, taking a step back, grinning cruelly. He tried a second grab and hardwood smacked the back of his hand. That hurt him, and they circled each other. At the other end of the room, a metal hook *chinked* off a stone blade. Ghador blocked, bobbed and weaved, looking for an opening. She'd be all right, Bek told herself; she had been trained to use a sword since her youngest days. If only Bek had maintained *her* training.

Lunk made yet another grab for the pole. Bek smacked his hand away again, then sent a quick jab into his stomach. Lunk grunted and doubled, but when Bek tried delivering a head blow, she realised he was feigning as he finally caught hold of the pole, wrenched it from her grasp and threw it aside. Bek tried for a well-placed kick. Lunk punched the inside of her leg, spinning her. He caught hold of her, held her back tightly to his chest, crushing the air from her lungs.

Bek could only struggle in vain. Stinking and filthy, Mr Lunk grabbed her hair and yanked her head to one side, exposing her neck. Bek felt hot, wet breath and the closeness of sharp teeth descending on her flesh. Closer, closer, until she felt the first needle-sharp pricks stabbing at her neck.

'Ghador!'

A howl of pain answered.

Mr Lunk stopped.

Ghador had crouched to avoid a wild swing from the hook, and then she had swept Minerva's sword up to cut the hand from Venatus's wrist with a flash of pure blue light. Still clutching the chain, the appendage sailed away. Venatus was staring in disbelief at the blood pumping from his stump when Ghador drove the sword into his gut. She twisted, pulled it free and Venatus dropped to his knees with a grunt. Wasting no time, Ghador gave a defiant cry and sliced the divine blade through his neck.

Blood sprayed, Venatus fell back and his death earned a fanfare.

His body jerked violently and released its spirit. A wolf, silver and shining, standing atop the corpse. It lifted its head and howled as though worshipping the moon. Ghador prepared to defend herself, but the spirit leapt away, out of the library door and into the town.

Mr Lunk had released his grip on Bek. He moved to one of the smashed windows and whined after his friend.

Bek scurried across the floor to stand next to Ghador, and they faced him together. But Mr Lunk had no interest in the fight now. He changed before their eyes, body shrinking and snapping into a new shape, a thick pelt of silver-etched black replacing shoddy clothes. In wolf form, Lunk barked once, then vaulted through the window after Venatus's spirit. Their howls merged together and faded into the distance.

Shaken, Bek stared out at the empty street, the smouldering books in the container, and she might never have moved again if Ghador's hand hadn't gripped hers.

'The Janus Bridge is opening,' she said urgently.

She had sheathed the sword and picked up the lantern. The air wavered around them. Bek could feel the ring on Ghador's finger vibrating her hand, her arm, her body.

'Ebbie—' Bek managed before a roaring wave swept them up and carried them away.

23

Player of Games

When the dragon released Ebbie, it didn't stay with him, nor did Karin's ghost. They simply weren't there any more, and he was left alone, standing on a hill of lifeless rock, dry and crumbling. Hot air filled his lungs, acrid, tasting of soot. Before him, plains of destruction stretched as far as he could see. Heavy clouds blanketed the sky – no, not clouds, he realised, and nor was it the Serpent's Sigh. Smoke filled the sky, thick and filthy, snowing ash.

Ebbie wished the satchel still hung from his shoulder as keenly as he wished his friends were with him. Surely Mai's letter would have something to say about what he was seeing, would give him advice on what to do next, how he should feel about the huge columns of smoke rising from gigantic craters pockmarking the scorched plains, fuelling the filth in the sky. No plants grew, no trees, but a single settlement rose amidst the ash and ruin, a small village standing like the last bastion of life on an apocalyptic wasteland.

From a high place, up beyond the blanket of smoke, the roar of violent seas reached Ebbie's ears, and he knew it was the Skea, angry and restless. This apocalypse belonged to the Realm.

Screaming came from the village. Folk were fleeing in all

directions, scattering as though to escape some monstrous demon who had risen among their shanty homes. But the monster wasn't inside the settlement.

A dark shape *whooshed* by overhead, disturbing the smoke but not revealing itself. It made little sound beyond the hissing of air until an instant after it passed the hill, and then ground-shaking thunder followed it. At first, Ebbie thought he must be witnessing the dragon's return, but when the beast dropped below the smoke, he saw something made of metal and more terrifying than a hundred dragons.

What type of jetfighter it was, or what country of Earth had sent it, was impossible to tell. Trailing a slipstream of distorted air, the fighter remained visible just long enough to deliver its payload. A dozen missiles dropped from the fuselage. Almost in unison, their rear ends ignited. The fighter banked, then flew back up into the cover of smoke while its missiles powered down towards the village.

The folk were fewer than a hundred in number, old and young, some carrying babies, and none of them could outrun the wave of destruction that erupted from their homes exploding behind them. Fire raced outwards in a ring, burning and devouring each of them. Ebbie closed his eyes to the sight, covered his ears against the screams and wails. He decided he never wanted to see or hear again and resolved to stay deaf and blind for ever. But as the screams echoed away across the burning plains, a voice reawakened his senses.

'It's horrible to witness, but it can't come as a surprise.' Karin's ghost had materialised beside him on the hill. She smiled sadly, apologetically, and said, 'You've already worked out that Yandira's been promised an earthling army.'

Down below, the village was now a new crater on the wasteland, pluming smoke up into the sky.

'Karin,' Ebbie said, finding his voice returned. 'What's going on?'

'This is a vision of the future. Persephone wants you to see what will happen if you don't accept that your part in the game is over.'

'I ... what?'

'Look, Ebbie – Maitressa asked you to find Ghador and show her the way home. That's *all* you were supposed to do. And now you've done it, Persephone is offering you a life much grander than most people will ever know, as reward for overcoming the pitfalls She laid along the way. But here's the rub – all kinds of rules have already been broken, and the game is perilously close to escalating out of everybody's control, including the Oldunfolk's. If you don't take your reward and stay on Earth, it leads to *this*.'

The far distance erupted with more explosions. Blistering mushroom clouds rose one after the other to limn the horizon with fire. The ghost watched the explosions, and Ebbie couldn't decide if the anger in her eyes was for him or the destruction of her world. Perhaps both.

She said, 'Earth and the Realm were separated for a reason. Involving an earthling was a risky move, but Maitressa had no choice. Yandira struck faster than anyone anticipated. But what happens next is up to Bek and Ghador and the rest of the folk. You need to stay out of it.'

The sound of the distant explosions reached Ebbie's ears, dull but powerful concussions that sent fiery clouds blooming up towards a deathly sky.

'You have courage but you're no hero, Ebbie. Maitressa was desperate and out of time when she chose you. You were her only option.'

It stung to hear that, but in a far-off way because the

destruction before him dominated all else. '*I* am responsible for this? If I return to the Realm, Yandira gets her earthling army and wins?'

'*Wins?*' Karin chuckled bitterly. 'No, no, no. If you stay in the game, Yandira *loses.*'

An inconceivable statement as far as Ebbie was concerned, and for more than one reason. How could the scene filling his eyes be the result of Yandira's defeat when it fit perfectly the image of her victory, the aftermath, the cruelty and devastation?

'You tip the balance,' Karin said. '*This* is what Persephone has foreseen. Somehow, at some point, your presence in the Realm plays an intrinsic role in Yandira's downfall. Which means Ghador wins. She kills her aunt, claims her throne and saves the folk. And that's when the real trouble begins.'

'Ghador lets this happen to the Realm?' It made no sense to Ebbie whatsoever. 'I don't believe you.'

'Oh, I understand why you'd think that way,' Karin said. 'How could the granddaughter of the great and kind Maitressa Wood Bee allow such cruelty and hate? But how long have you spent in Ghador's company? You don't know her at all. And remember, she comes from the same stock as Yandira.' She pursed silvery lips. 'As it turns out, you're right. Ghador isn't a bad egg, but she's … *impulsive*, like her mother, like her father, as hotheaded and as prone to acting before thinking.'

The magician's ghost stepped forwards and surveyed the wasteland with her hands behind her back. 'Persephone doesn't like losing, Ebbie, and She'll allow this level of destruction if it means She can save face.

'So, when Yandira falls, She makes damn sure the victor pays the price for beating Her. See, Juno has been breaking rules, therefore Persephone is free to keep the game going as long as She likes. She makes sure Bek dies, right in front of

Ghador – and She makes the princess watch as She drags her sister's soul down into the Underworld. What happens to you from that point onwards, Persephone wouldn't tell me.'

'Bek … dies?'

'And it begins a chain of events which escalate into madness. Ghador is crushed by Bek's death, blinded by rage and the need for revenge. She vows to rid the Realm of the Underworld's influence once and for all, so, against everyone's better judgement, she takes the war to Persephone Herself. Ghador believes she can save Bek's soul. She believes Minerva's sword, with Foresight and Hindsight, can kill an Oldunone. And she's wrong.'

Karin's shoulders sagged and her head dropped. A hot wind was whipping up across the wasteland, and it carried the stench of life burned to ashes.

The magician drew herself up again and continued, 'Persephone lulls Ghador into a trap. When she opens the Underworld's gates, it's not the Great Trickster she's facing, Ebbie. It's Earth. But Persephone has been planting the seeds of spite, see? She makes it look like the Realm is invading. She's been assassinating important earthlings – politicians, religious leaders, monarchs – and committing all kinds of atrocities, then She points the finger of blame at Ghador and the Realm.' Karin opened her arms wide. 'And the earthlings retaliate with the full weight of their world behind them.'

The magician cursed and her voice quivered with the threat of tears. 'The folk don't last long, Ebbie. They have to fight tanks with cavalry, swords against guns, arrows against missiles. The Protectors of the Realm manage to raise an army of a hundred thousand soldiers, but Earth has millions – not that any of your countries need to send a single solider to win the war.'

In his mind, Ebbie saw the full horror. Bombs that could

destroy entire cities; enough firepower to rain hell from the sky; chemical weapons that made the Serpent's Sigh look like a common cold. In a war against Earth, the Realm would fall before it ever caught sight of its enemy's face. But this didn't make sense. How could this happen because of *him*?

'However ... there is another way.' Karin faced Ebbie, her ghostly face tired and defeated. 'I know it's hard to accept, but if you stay on Earth and let Yandira win, there's a very different outcome.' She pointed forwards. 'Turn around and see for yourself.'

Bek's second jaunt across the Janus Bridge was as dizzying as her first, and she had to sit down to steady her stomach and spinning head. A beam of rainbow light cut through blackness, pinpointing Ghador's location, but Bek's first thought was for Karin. Was she dead? And then there was Ebbie ... had Lunk and Venatus got to him before they found Bek and Ghador? She tried to convince herself that he had escaped, that he had just been left behind to live out the rest of his life in peace, on Earth.

A different light illuminated the darkness. One small flame, then another, and another, each flickering into life of their own accord until a dozen or more candles burned in holders sitting on a row of ornate tables. Their flames rose high and bright to bathe Bek in a warm and welcoming golden glow.

'I know this place,' Ghador said. Minerva's sword in one hand, the lantern in the other, the princess was staring around at their newly revealed environment with incredulity. 'We're in Castle Wood Bee's south tower.'

Books. Hundreds of them, thousands, neatly displayed in sturdy wooden cases rising floor to ceiling in a grand room. Ladders on runners gave access to higher shelves; a spiralling staircase led up to a balcony and a second tier of cases. To one side of the candles burning on reading tables, comfy, high-backed chairs were positioned before an open fireplace. Designed with taste and quality, this room was familiar to Bek even before Ghador said, 'This is Grandmother's private library— *Shit!*'

Ghador dropped the lantern and flapped her hand as though she had been stung. 'The ring,' she said, looking at her hand. 'It's gone.' She showed Bek that the cream and green band was no longer on her finger. 'It just … vanished.'

Then they had obviously reached their final destination. The library released memories from Bek's childhood, and also fear. The Janus Bridge's last act was to deliver them into the heart of the enemy's lair.

The princess looked confused. 'No one's been able to get into this place since Grandmother's exile.'

Which was evidenced by the decade's worth of dust and cobwebs decorating the library.

Bek said, 'Is Hindsight hidden in here?'

Ghador shook her head. 'I don't think so. Look.' The True Sight Candle's light was weak, as though unexcited by anything in the immediate vicinity.

Bek cocked her ear. 'What's that noise?'

A banging – no, a dull *chipping* sound, like a gang of miners striking away at stone with pickaxes. It seemed to be coming from above and below.

Ghador began shining the lantern's faint rainbow light around the library. 'After Grandmother left, this place became sealed off, protected by divine magic. There was no explanation for it, and my mother didn't care to find one. Nobody could get in. And I don't know if we can get out.'

The rainbow remained weak, dim, as it shone around the room, searching for the right direction. There were two main doors into the library: one above it, outside the tower, up on a high balcony; and one below, at the end of a long hall inside the keep. The True Sight Candle was uninterested in leading them to either door.

'Maybe it was sealed off for you,' Bek said, looking at Ghador nervously. She didn't like to think of divine games and plans, but if events of recent days had taught her anything, it was that some things happened for a reason. 'What if Maitressa knew you'd need a secret way back into the castle . . . ?'

Bek trailed off. The *chipping* sound had changed, lowered in tone to the unmistakable *thud* of axes biting into wood. 'I don't think the doors are protected any more.'

'Then we can get out. Right there!' Ghador was aiming the lantern into a high corner of the library. The beam had brightened into life with the change in sound, now cutting through dusty air to cast a multicoloured swirl on the books in a case up on the second tier. 'Bek, do you remember the game we used to play? The game of spies?'

No more needed to be said. As the sound of ripping wood was replaced by the clanking of armoured boots on stone steps, the sisters rushed up the spiralling stairs to the balcony and to its end where the True Sight Candle wanted them to be.

Ten years had passed since Bek last explored the castle's secret rooms and passageways, but she remembered where the library's hidden door was located. There was a book on a high shelf. As a young girl, she had needed the ladder to reach it, but she could get to it on her tiptoes now. *The Tankards of the Commonfolk*, it was called; but it wasn't a real book, and she always assumed the title was designed to bore readers away from selecting it.

Bek gave the book a firm shove. It depressed and *clicked* before snapping back into place while releasing a catch. A portion of the bookcase opened a crack. Bek yanked it wider, dislodging real books onto the balcony in her haste.

'Quickly,' Ghador said, rushing into the secret space beyond.

As Bek followed, she caught a brief flash of silver armour, swords and axes from below: royal guards clanging their way into the library.

Pulling the door closed, Bek studied the mechanisms behind *The Tankards of the Commonfolk*. Nothing too complicated and easily sabotaged. She took out her remaining two lock picks and jammed their handles into the hinges. The door wouldn't open unless they were removed, but that didn't mean it couldn't be broken down.

Stepping back, she waited for the thud of axes. Nothing. She strained her ears for any kind of sound from the other side. Again, nothing, and that troubled her. 'Why aren't they following us?' she wondered.

'Bek ...'

Ghador's voice was as strained as mooring rope. The small chamber on the other side of the library was illuminated by the lantern. A dark residue resembling dried pitch plastered one wall, the floor below it and the ceiling above. A lingering smell and presence suggested all the terrible things waiting beyond death. Bek shivered at another memory from her youth. Neither she nor Ghador needed to remind the other of where they were.

Ghador shone the lantern on the far wall where the smooth, grey stonework was interrupted by dark bricks, shiny like volcanic glass. These bricks were to be found in walls here and there around the castle, if you knew what you were looking for. They usually denoted a hidden door to a secret space; they were also specially designed to allow a person to see into a chamber, but not out. Subtle perforations in the mortar allowed sound to reach the ears of any spy hiding in the passageway on the other side of the wall. A decade ago, Bek and Ghador had been two such spies, witnessing Yandira Wood Bee's pledge of allegiance to the Underworld. The dark residue in the chamber marked where Princess Morrad had stood when she lost her soul.

'Let's keep moving,' Ghador said. Amidst the black spy-bricks she had found a secret catch. Bek followed her through a slim gap that opened up – stonework tiled onto a thick panel of wood, crafted to blend perfectly with the wall when closed – and into the passageway beyond, which offered two directions: left or right.

Deciding it was best to free Ghador of any burden other than using the sword, Bek took the lantern. The True Sight Candle blossomed and flooded the passageway when she aimed it to the right.

'Do you remember where this leads?'

Ghador shook her head. 'I stopped exploring the castle after you left.'

'Well then ...'

Bek left her words hanging and set off at a determined pace.

There was a crossroads on the Queen's Highway called Merchant's Compass. If the harbour town of Singer's Hope was a traveller's destination, they'd take the north road from this point. South led to miles of scrubland and finally the haunted ruins of Imperium City, where Minerva struck down Bellona and concluded the last game the Oldunfolk had played with mortals. But heading dead west for no more than half a mile would lead a traveller to Strange Ground beneath the Skea.

The city should have been visible from the crossroads, but the Serpent's Sigh had put paid to that. The fog was as quiet as a grave and just as cold. Kingfisher wondered what manner of horror lurked within its slate-grey mass, what *fate* watched her with hungry eyes. She stood next to Maxis at the head of the army. On the prince's other side, Seej Agda stared at Foresight in her hand, running a finger up and down the smooth, blue stone as though encouraging a pet to speak by stroking it.

Seven hundred soldiers had formed ranks at Merchant's Compass. Wagons had been unloaded of spears and arrows, but no tents had been erected, no campfires lit; the army was prepared for battle, and the battle was almost upon them. Wagons had been moved to the rear. A small cavalry flanked foot soldiers, and they were ready for the command that would send them marching on Strange Ground.

Kingfisher had been thinking about Aelfric Dragonfly. She doubted Yandira would deign to let him live. *Has Juno ever smiled kindly upon any of us?* she wondered.

The Queen of Queens' divine blessing protected them all from Yandira's dark sorceries, but Dalmyn had lost around a hundred men and women to the Coven of Bellona and their ogres. There seemed to be no explanation for why the witches had retreated, but if the ambush had achieved any purpose at all, then it was to remind Yandira's enemies of how they remained susceptible to sharp metal and claws. The bodies of the fallen had been left on the Queen's Highway.

Maxis stamped his feet against the cold and grumbled something about how he hated waiting. Earlier, he had demanded, 'What now?' of his High Priest.

Seej had shown little emotion when replying, 'Foresight must be taken into the city.'

'And there Ghador will meet us?'

'With Minerva's sword and Hindsight, Oldunfolk willing.'

No one wanted to air their questions of doubt. What if Ghador hadn't made it this far? What if Dalmyn had arrived too late? What if Yandira had got to Ghador before she could complete the divine weapon that might save the Realm from a terrible Empire? What if all Dalmyn's army had achieved was to bring Yandira the final piece of her victory?

Not knowing the state of play inside Strange Ground was as hard to take as the waiting. It was tempting to rush the city gates, strike hard and fast, for the sake of everything that was good and light; but of all people, it had been Maxis who showed restraint, shrugging off his usual bravado and sending his scout Lina to discover what they were facing.

Lina had yet to return, and Kingfisher feared what she would find. Without doubt, Yandira would have all of Strange Ground's trained fighters – royal guards, soldiers, city guards – defending her position, but the commonfolk? The Serpent's Sigh blanketed the city.

Kingfisher's heart thudded as the fog parted and Lina emerged, on foot and running hard, bow in one hand, a long knife in the other. Many of the soldiers stirred anxiously at the sight of her, no doubt wondering, as Kingfisher was, if foes were hot on her heels. But when Lina called, 'Peace, Highness,' Maxis ordered his troops to stand fast and stepped forwards.

'What did you see?' he demanded as Lina approached.

'It's worse than we feared,' she said, sweating and out of breath. 'The enemy is everywhere.' Blood speckled her face and more dripped from a wound on her arm and coated the blade of her knife. The quiver on her back was empty of arrows. 'Outside the city ... inside ... *everywhere*. Yandira's army outnumbers us, Highness.'

'So it is fashioned from more than trained fighting folk,' Kingfisher said.

'Witches and wild things, then?' Maxis asked Lina. 'How many are we facing?'

'Thousands, Highness, but ...' The scout dropped her bow and knife, then held a hand to a stitch at her side, bending double to properly catch her breath. Kingfisher took a waterskin from a nearby soldier and handed it to the scout. She drank deeply and gratefully as Seej came forwards to check the wound on her arm.

'It is nothing, Mother Seej.' Lina gently pushed away the priest's attentions. 'A shallow cut from an arrow.' She addressed her prince. 'Highness, the enemy does not fear Juno's Blessing. At first, they were nought but shadows in the fog, none of them hindering my passage. But when I came too close to the city, they attacked, rushing into my circle of divine protection in an endless swarm. I had to flee, fight my way out. They retreated once I was far enough away, but I had to kill many to get back here. And I am ashamed of it.'

'Nonsense,' Maxis said. 'You are a soldier at war, doing as she must. I'll hear nothing of *shame*.'

'You don't understand, Highness.' Lina turned troubled eyes to Kingfisher. 'I also thought to meet witches and wild things, but these were no beasts of the Underworld I faced. They carry weapons but wear no armour. Nobles and commonfolk alike ... Yandira's army is Strange Ground's citizens.'

'Citizens?' Seej said. '*All* of them?'

Lina looked helpless. 'I saw nothing to tell me otherwise.'

A charged silence fell upon the four, broken by Kingfisher saying, 'She wanted you to see them,' in a cold, hard voice. She began pacing, clenching and unclenching fists. 'Ten thousand live in Strange Ground. Even if our army was twice that number, could any of us easily cut down children, the elderly and anyone in between who can carry a weapon? Yandira has surrounded herself with a shield of innocent folk, and they are not the true enemy.'

Maxis swore, and Seej Agda said, 'Yandira knows she can outwait us.'

'But why wait at all?' Maxis shouted, venting his frustration. 'If I were in Yandira's position with such superior numbers, I'd attack and take what I wanted.'

'She doesn't need to, not yet.' Kingfisher gritted her teeth. 'While Yandira keeps us at bay, she can focus her attention on the city, prepare for Ghador's arrival. Damn it. Without Foresight, Ghador will fail.'

'But the same goes for Yandira,' Maxis said, showing fear for the first time on this quest. 'She needs it as much as my daughter.'

'That won't be a problem for her,' Seej replied. 'We're stuck in the mud. We can't attack, we can't flee and Yandira knows exactly where Foresight will be waiting once Ghador is dead.'

Evidently, Maxis felt the cold bite of those words as keenly as Kingfisher. 'No!' he blustered. 'There must be another way to get that damn stone to my daughter.'

'Please, Highness,' Lina said. 'We might have one friend among the enemy.' She was facing the direction of Strange Ground, head cocked as though listening, studying the Serpent's Sigh. 'There was a moment while fleeing when Yandira's servants surrounded me, and I believed I was done for. I might not be standing before you now if not for someone in the fog who distracted them, helped me escape.' She pointed ahead. 'And whoever it was has followed me here.'

Indeed, a tall and burly man came into view, stamping towards the army wearing a leather apron and carrying a cudgel. He did not look to be infected with the Serpent's Sigh, or in particularly good humour.

'Halt!' Maxis shouted.

'I'll give you bloody *halt*,' the man shouted back. 'I'm looking for Lady Kingfisher.'

'Peace,' Kingfisher called, stepping up alongside Lina. She

recognised this man. He was the landlord of a drinking establishment in the city. Jester's Tavern. His name was Charlie, but those in the know called him Backway. '*I* am Lady Kingfisher.'

'Good.' His face bruised, Charlie nodded at Lina, looked unimpressed by the army behind her, then settled his gaze on the noblewoman. 'I'll show you how to get into the city.'

With the apocalypse raging behind him, Ebbie's eyes were filled with a utopia somehow existing peacefully on the other side of the hill.

The sea in the sky was as clear as crystal. Ships sailed upon it, but not just those of the Realm: Earthly cruise ships and ocean liners meandered across the calm and gentle Skea. The sun shone down through serene waters, brightly, warmly, to glint and dance upon glass skyscrapers rising tall in a sprawling city like the peaks of a crown. Lush forests and fields of crops surrounded the city, dissected by a snaking network of roads upon which cars travelled. But these vehicles were not restricted to the ground. Many of them flocked in groups like migrating birds.

One car soared by close to Ebbie. Its wheels were folded into its undercarriage, but no wings held it aloft. Though air rippled around the car's rear end, it emitted no exhaust fumes, and the only sound was a melodic humming as it veered away towards the glass skyscrapers and joined the flock.

Electric? Ebbie wondered. *Magic?* How far into the future was this vision? The air tasted so clean, sweet to breathe. Everything looked so ... *healthy*, like he gazed upon a fantasist's rendition of a perfect world.

'So,' said Karin, stepping up alongside Ebbie. 'You stay on Earth and Yandira wins. Ghador dies in the process, but Bek survives. In fact, she goes on to lead the rebellion that helps put Yandira down for good.'

The magician's ghost stood in front of him, a perfect world behind her. 'When Yandira completes the crown of Strange Ground and delivers it to the Underworld, Persephone honours Her promise. She opens Her gates and gives Her disciple the earthling army she craves. And that's when Yandira realises she never understood what she was asking for.

'When the earthlings come, they see the situation for what it is. They size up Yandira straight away and sympathise with Bek's rebellion. Earth doesn't bring all the horrors of warfare at their disposal, Ebbie. They capture Yandira and hand her over. They respect the Realm and let the folk deal with her by their own laws. Yandira is executed, naturally, but after that everything changes. The earthlings come in peace. They offer the hand of friendship and the folk take it.'

From somewhere in the city of sparkling glass, bells began ringing, chiming out a melody of celebration.

'Earth and the Realm,' Karin said. 'Two worlds, one people. Science and magic. The miracles of technology meet the mysteries of supernature, and they reap some very positive results. Our peoples build a bright and wonderful future, *together*.'

Ebbie struggled to take in all that was assaulting his senses. It was too much, too blinding, to let him think straight. But in that moment, the image of Mai popped into his mind. She was looking at him with the face she pulled whenever she wanted him to stop accepting, to consider alternatives and use his own sense of reason.

'I don't get it,' he said. 'Everything will be bright and brilliant *if* I stay on Earth, *if* I leave the game. You're telling me this future is entirely dependent on me making that one, simple decision?'

'Oh no, you'll do much more than that.' Karin smiled as the bells rang out. 'See, the Priests of Juno are impressed by Bek,

355

her passion to save the Realm, her leadership skills. I mean, she goes all out to stop Yandira, and thousands of folk line up behind her. Bek wasn't born of noble blood, but she was adopted by a Royal Family. The priests decide to crown her Queen of Strange Ground. She changes her name to *Wood Bee* and becomes the Realm's first ambassador to Earth. And who do you think she wants as her principal advisor?

'Ebbie, if you accept the reward Persephone is offering now, then later you'll already be in a position to become the go-to mediator between Earth and the Realm. Your insights and knowledge prove invaluable during the early days of negotiations. You and Queen Bek Wood Bee begin a chain of events that lead to *this*.' Karin swept her arm across the sprawling city in all its futuristic glory. 'You're looking at Strange Ground beneath the Skea, Ebbie, where the Janus Bridge is always open. Travel between Earth and the Realm becomes free for all, and there's a bridge in every city, permanently connecting both sides of the Skea. But here in Strange Ground is where it all begins, because of you and Bek. They even erect a statue in your honour.'

'What?'

'It's down there right now. Do you want to see it?'

'No!' Because it was utterly inconceivable. 'This is mad, Karin. You're saying I've been given the power to decide whether a world lives or dies.'

'No, I'm saying you're the first link in a chain of events which has one of two outcomes.'

'It doesn't make sense.'

'Look, the escalation has already begun, Ebbie. Juno and Persephone only care about beating each other. They don't give a toss about what happens to Their players, but Juno *cannot* win.' The magician was pleading. 'You have the chance to make the *right* decision. Focus on that, because how can any mortal really make sense of *anything* the Oldunfolk do?'

No, that was the age-old argument endorsed by high and mighty shepherds who had been using fear of divinity to keep their flocks of sheep in line for time immemorial. And Ebbie had stopped buying into it when he was eight years of age.

Rumbling came from behind him. He turned around to see a firestorm had whipped up on the wasteland. Burning a dull orange, it rolled across the Realm as a blistering smog of fiery debris.

'I'm just the messenger,' Karin said, 'but I'm glad for that. It gives me the chance to beg you to leave the game like you're supposed to. Don't let my world burn.' The ghost gripped Ebbie's shoulders from behind with surprisingly strong and corporeal fingers. 'Surely *this* is the better way?' She turned him around, so he was once again struck by the healthy, clean vision of utopia. 'I'm dead, and that won't change whatever you decide. But if you ask for it, Persephone will let me show you the way back to Earth.'

'And ...' Ebbie inhaled deeply. The air was so pure; the sky so blue beyond the crystal waters. 'And if I ask you to show me the way to the Realm?'

Karin sighed. 'Listen to me, Ebbie. What you're looking at is the better way. Sacrifices *will* be made, there'll be a *lot* of hardship at first, but Persephone and Yandira winning *is* the lesser evil. Could you live with yourself if you chose the *other* way?'

A wave of fiery wind buffeted Ebbie's back as though pushing him towards Strange Ground's better future.

His thoughts were all over the place; but cutting through the confusion in his mind, Mai was still looking at him, sternly now. And she was making him recall advice she had given Ebbie weeks ago, concerning his unwillingness to face life beyond the closure of the St. Meyers-Bannerman Library.

She had said, 'Whenever the future looks bleak, full of details I do not like, I become frozen with confusion. At such times, I like to close my eyes to the world and drift into my past. I retrace my steps, in my head. I study the chain of events which have brought me to the present. Every detail, as best as I can recall, and I face my conduct with honesty, the good along with the bad, and then consider what changes I might make to unburden future turmoil before it arrives.

'You'd be surprised, Ebbie Wren, at how efficiently a clear mind can swim through a bleak outlook to break the surface with a fresh alternative in hand. In times of confusion, hindsight is foresight's greatest teacher, and we should never accept—'

'Ebbie!' Karin's voice shattered the memory. 'The Realm needs you to do the right thing.'

'I-I need to think.'

'You need to *choose*. Hundreds of thousands of lives are depending on you.'

'No, just ... give me a minute.' Ebbie sat down on the crumbling hill, crossed his legs and clasped his hands before him. 'Please, let me think.' And he closed his eyes to the future worlds on either side of him, retracing the past experiences which had brought him to this moment.

24

Old Haunts

Bek and Ghador made their way along the narrow passageways secreted between the walls of Castle Wood Bee. Tense and silent, not giggly and excited as they had been as children, for the game they now played was far deadlier than pretending to be spies; and one way or another, the game ended here.

The passageway spiralled around the south tower, heading down all the while before levelling out to a straight run which cut into the keep. The way dog-legged to the left, but the lantern didn't steer them into making the turn. Instead it led them to the wall, where a ladder descended into a darkened shaft in the floor.

Nothing stirred Bek's recollection as she looked down at a circle of yellow firelight marking the shaft's end. 'I don't remember using this way before, do you?'

Ghador didn't reply and started her descent.

Still holding the lantern and climbing with one hand, Bek followed and discovered the ladder ran down through the hollowed back of a tall statue, then out into the oily torchlight of the place where the Wood Bee bloodline had been laid to rest since the beginning of its rule: the castle crypts.

The statue from which they emerged belonged to one of Ghador's ancestors or another. Bek frowned at its stony face.

'Why aren't the guards chasing us?' she wondered aloud. Undoubtedly, they were under Yandira's power, infected by the Serpent's Sigh, so why had they stopped in the library? 'Maybe Yandira doesn't realise you're here.'

When Ghador didn't reply, Bek whirled around. The princess was approaching an open chamber in the crypts. Bek hurried after her with the lantern, recognising the chamber as the Chapel of Elysium. Inside, an intricate stone carving of Lady Juno gazed at a central table of stone. Upon the table, a dead queen had been laid.

Bek kept her distance, shining the lantern away, while Ghador, as still as any statue, stood over her mother. Surrounding Queen Eldrid, candles had burned their wicks down to nothing. Ghador brushed what looked to be ash from her mother's pale face, and Bek could guess what she was thinking. Yandira would rather leave her sister here to rot than show her any kind of respect.

When Ghador turned, Bek expected to see anger or tears; but as the princess stepped towards her, there was little expression on her face at all, though she was gripping the sword so tightly her knuckles had turned white. Bek thought hard for something to say, but a sound caught her attention. A small noise, dry like sun-baked sand blown across a beach. And then Bek saw it. A patch of something dark moving across Eldrid's body.

Ghador caught the sound herself and cocked her ear, keeping her eyes on Bek with a questioning frown. Bek gave her sister a specific look which she hoped she would remember as one of many within a lexicon of coded expressions invented by two children years ago. *We're in true danger*, the look said, *and there's no hiding from it*. Ghador signalled that she understood, and Bek mouthed the word *Shade*. Subtly, but not turning, Ghador adjusted her stance.

The cancer grown from Morrad's soul slithered as a smoky mass from Eldrid's corpse to the table. It ballooned and deflated, ballooned and deflated as though breathing hard, and finally the merciless assassin opened its eyes.

Bek kept hers on Ghador's. *Get ready to act*, her look said, and the princess prepared to strike with the sword.

Yandira's servant was formed from magic, but stories claimed its physical attack was as corporeal as a barbed arrow to the heart. The Shade condensed into a diamond shape, black and hard like spider chitin, and quivered as though bunching muscles, preparing to spring.

'Now!' Bek shouted.

Ghador spun, sweeping the sword downwards just as the Shade vaulted from the table. The stone blade met the creature's rise, and Oldunspeak poisoned it with a venom administered with a snap of blue sparking through rainbow light that smacked the Shade to the floor. It hissed and thrashed, squealing like a rat in boiling water. Ghador tried to deliver a killing thrust, but the Shade jumped away and fled into the crypt's murk.

'Come on!' Her voice panicked, Ghador prepared to give chase. 'We have to kill it!'

'Wait!' Bek grabbed her sister's arm. 'Listen ...'

The clang of armoured boots on stone echoed around the crypts, sounding as though many feet were running from all directions, closing in.

'Guards,' Bek said.

'Hide,' said Ghador.

'No.' Bek tugged her arm and encouraged her to follow the direction of the lantern's beam. Because the True Sight Candle was the only thing that wouldn't deceive them now.

*

'These tunnels turned me over a tidy profit down the years,' Backway Charlie grumbled. 'Never thought I'd need them myself, though.'

He led the way through the warrens beneath Strange Ground, his torch flame casting dancing shadows on the walls. Rather than acting terrified of the situation and of what they were heading towards, Charlie sounded put out, like all he wanted was for a bad day to get better and his life to return to normal.

'Are you sure about this?' he asked no one in particular. 'Where we're heading is not a good place to be at the moment.'

All eyes turned to Seej Agda. The priest was holding Foresight between her hands, listening to an ethereal voice only she could hear. 'Yes,' she said in a quiet voice. 'Ghador will meet us at the castle.'

Charlie puffed his cheeks and continued on.

To the uninitiated, the warrens formed a miles-long network of confusing twists and turns, but Charlie navigated with ease and without breaking stride. In fact, he had probably memorised the layout before he learned to walk. Kingfisher remembered his mother. In her younger days, she had often used the warrens to meet up in secret with Maitressa and Aelfric. Together, they would sneak into Jester's Tavern, where the landlady – Charlie's mother – knew who they were but turned a blind eye as they got drunk on honey beer. Happier days. But now, through all his grumbling, Backway Charlie had provided a way forward, a plan of action, such as it was.

Dalmyn's army had remained a short distance from Strange Ground's gates. While the hundreds of soldiers gave Yandira an enemy to focus on, a few agents had sneaked away to a secret entrance into the warrens. There was Charlie, of course, and Maxis had selected Lina as a companion, who now guarded the small group's rear with her bow. Seej Agda walked alongside her prince, and no one had dared refuse Kingfisher's participation. The army stood ready for the signal to march into the city. What that signal might be, no one could say for sure. The group couldn't even be certain exactly where it was in Castle Wood Bee that Foresight wanted them to meet Ghador.

Charlie's memory of what happened to him was vague. He had been infected with the Serpent's Sigh, he said, but a cleansing light and voice had freed him. The voice had told him he was a *reserve strategy* in some 'stupid bloody game' he didn't claim to understand and didn't want to play. After that, he had somehow simply known that Kingfisher would arrive, and that she would need smuggling into the castle grounds.

'I'll tell you who I'd like a bloody word with,' Charlie said. 'Bek Rana. She's got some explaining to do.'

'Rana?' Prince Maxis replied with surprise. 'I remember her. A snot-nosed vagabond who Maitressa hauled in off the streets to be friends with my daughter—'

'Hey!' Charlie's change of tack was swift and defensive as he rounded on Maxis. 'She might be a pain in my arse, but she knows when to do the right thing, even when it's for the folk who treated her like dirt. You should pray that Bek's helping your daughter right now because she'll need her.'

'Should I?' Now it was the prince's turn to be offended and he drew himself up, though he remained a head shorter than the burly landlord. 'If you think for one moment—'

'Gentlemen, please!' Kingfisher interrupted with a whiplash tone. 'Perhaps we might remember where we are and lower our voices. Whatever we might think of Bek Rana, Ghador is counting on her *and* us.'

The stark reminder had the desired effect, not least of all because they were not alone down in the warrens.

Earlier, Charlie had told them, 'There's a lot of folk down

here, still infected like I was. Whatever that light did to me, it frightened them away. At first. But they're not scared to come near me any more, so keep a look out.'

The Serpent's Sigh was present in the warrens, always receding from the group. There were a couple of moments when Lina called for silence, listening to darkness beyond the torchlight, watching for what the fog might be hiding. But whatever the scout's keen hearing had detected proved to be nothing, and thus far Yandira's assassins had not revealed themselves or shown any sign they knew the group was down here.

After a dizzying number of twists and turns, Charlie led them to where the tunnel sloped upwards, claiming that this marked the beginning of Castle Wood Bee's grounds. The landlord was reluctant to move closer, stopping to stare down at the bloodied corpse of a young soldier.

'This is who brought the light,' he said with a shudder. 'This is who brought the voice. And he was already dead when he came to me.'

'The dead spoke to you?' Maxis said dubiously.

'Something did, *through* him.'

'Are you sure you haven't been at your own stock?'

'I'm not a bloody idiot, *Highness*. He moved like a marionette. His eyes glowed, and he ... spoke without speaking. I don't understand it, but I know what I saw, and when this boy found me, he was already dead.'

While Seej Agda knelt beside the corpse and whispered prayers, Kingfisher wondered if Juno was using innocent folk as Yandira was, as Cursed Persephone would. She tore her gaze from the young man's lifeless face and looked at the ascending path. 'Whereabouts in the castle does this lead?'

'The dungeons,' Charlie said. 'But there's a snag—'

'Highness ...' Lina had moved away from the group, facing

the way they had come. She reached over her shoulder, drew an arrow and nocked it. 'Someone's approaching.'

It was more than just some*one* approaching. The scraps and clicks of many shuffling feet headed towards them. Charlie stepped up alongside Lina, but his torch illuminated no threat. The landlord lobbed the torch underarm down the tunnel. The yellow flame spat and flared upon hitting the ground, shining on a wall of fog; but then, folk marched in shambling fashion into firelight. They packed the tunnel wall-to-wall, stretching back who knew how far in the fog. Clearly under the Serpent Sigh's influence, they carried knives and fire pokers; Kingfisher saw a shovel, a rake – anything that could be used as a weapon.

The front line halted the slow march as if to consider the burning torch on the ground. Smoky eyes found the small group of interlopers. Makeshift weapons pointed at them, and in unison the horde released a deep, baritone moan. It filled the warrens with the ghosts of tortured souls.

'Time to leave,' Maxis said, sword in hand.

'You don't understand,' Charlie said as he and Lina backed away. 'The way into the castle is blocked—'

The horde shed its laborious gait and charged with the ferocity of wild things.

The end was coming. Aelfric Dragonfly could feel it, just as he could feel the last of his true self dwindling, breaking, crumbling like dirt ready to be blown away on a desolate wind. His voice, which had once commanded respect and reason in court, was a now a jaded whisper inside his head, and it was saying, *Today, madness claims sovereignty over the Realm.*

In the stifling dungeons, Ignius Rex had opened the Underworld. He had chalked his spells onto the flagstones in a wide circle, murmuring all the while in a foul language until the spell collapsed, imploded, into an agitated pool of fetid oil, just like the one in Yandira's private chamber. But Ignius hadn't stopped at that point. Even now, he continued crafting symbols and alien words as though creating a mosaic in which the swirling, hungry oil was the bitter central jewel. Dragonfly stood close to the pool. He could smell its acrid fumes, taste the corruption, and he knew he would be the first to see Cursed Persephone's domain.

At my signal, sacrifice them all, Yandira had said. She had gained so much from only one sacrifice. What kind of power would she reap from fifty?

The members of Ghador's entourage were oddly subdued as they watched Ignius – except Lieutenant Davil, who stared at Dragonfly with a pleading gaze. She and her soldiers would have fought, and fought to the death, to save this queendom if they could only be freed. But what could Dragonfly do, trapped in his own cell as he was? The nobleman was as stripped of weapons and caged behind iron bars as these brave soldiers. None of them could do anything but await their fates.

And yet ...

Dragonfly could see what apparently Davil could not. As Ignius Rex chalked his spells, a shadowy creature had materialised behind him. The Shade. No one else seemed to notice its arrival. At first, Dragonfly thought Yandira had sent her servant with orders for Ignius to commence the sacrifices, but the Shade was clearly in distress. Silently, it flopped about like a landed fish, jumping this way and that, as though struggling in its death throes. No, it wasn't dying; it was changing.

The Shade grew, its throes calming. Its shape expanded and moulded into that of a fully-grown woman, lying curled on her side, weak as a newborn foal. Still, not one soldier reacted; still, Ignius did not notice. So intent was the magician on his work, he failed to see the Shade rise behind him in the grey and silvery image of the very soul which had created it.

The ghost of Princess Morrad smiled at Dragonfly, and a spark of flame rekindled his own dwindling spirit. She drifted towards him, her eyes bright and clear of affliction, almost the woman she had been before her sister's terrible deeds. Dragonfly wanted to embrace her, but he couldn't move; instead, Morrad gathered him into an embrace of her own when she reached him, an embrace that sank beneath his skin, entered his soul, and it felt ... it felt like cool blue water, clean and pure. Juno's magic flowed from her.

Morrad spoke to her mother's dear old friend, but with emotions, not words. There was regret, heartbreak and then hope. Ghador had returned, she told him; she was here, Minerva's sword was here, Foresight and Hindsight were close. Together, Dragonfly and Morrad could help pave the way to Yandira's end. Was he willing?

Yes, he answered, with all his heart, wanting nothing more from this life.

Morrad burrowed into Dragonfly's soul and shared Juno's Kiss. The Serpent's Sigh hissed in its blue water and Dragonfly was as free as Morrad's ghost. He was weak, broken, and he staggered on unsteady legs at first; but then he gasped a breath as Morrad injected the strength into his muscles to approach Ignius Rex.

On his hands and knees, the magician finally sensed something was amiss. He looked up to see Dragonfly looming over him. Confusion quickly turned to shock and he jumped to his feet.

'No!' Ignius cried as Dragonfly grappled him.

The prisoners stirred and shouted encouragement. The magician was strong, but a fight was not Dragonfly's aim. With

Morrad fuelling his actions, his heartbeat racing, he leaned into his adversary, catching him wrong-footed. Seeing they were stumbling towards the Underworld's filthy maw, Ignius Rex struggled desperately, screaming, but Dragonfly wouldn't release his grip, not even when they toppled and splashed into the oily pool and were sucked down into its impossible depths.

Dragonfly clung on and looked up, seeing the Underworld's mouth close and swallow him into absolute darkness.

Divine favour saved them down in the warrens.

With an untold number of possessed folk chasing them, the insurgents of Dalmyn closed in on where the tunnel to the castle dungeons had been blocked. A latticework of thick metal bars, floor to ceiling, wall to wall, each stabbed deep into hard rock, with a heavy central gate. Charlie shouted a warning as they approached it: this gate was secured by more locks than a queen's vault and warded by age-old spells.

The feet of Yandira's troops hammered up the slope behind them, but they made no other sound, not a single shout or curse to smother the ragged, fearful breaths taken by those who fled from them. Kingfisher drew her dagger from the sheath in her sleeve. The gate might well trap them in front of an insurmountable foe, but she wouldn't go down without a fight. Perhaps her companions shared her defiant spirit. In the end, it didn't matter.

Foresight had begun glowing in Seej's hand and she lit the way with it. When the priest and the stone closed in on the blockage, the sharp clunks of mechanisms and the hum of magic filled the tunnel. Juno's Blessing, the power of Oldunspeak, released locks and wards and the gate swung open. When the five of them rushed through, the gate crashed shut behind them and reset its precautions.

Bodies crashed into the barrier. One after another, hitting metal like arrows smashing upon a castle wall. Faces squeezed through the gaps between bars, veins popping, eyes bulging as more and more piled in.

So enthralled were these folk by the Serpent's Sigh, so obsessed with Yandira's orders, they didn't think to stop. None of them understood that a hundred rampaging ogres could not break down this barrier before them. Prey was in their sights, and that was all the motive they understood. It was impossible to tell how far back the stream of folk went, but they formed a great weight, pressing forwards without thought for those at the front. The crush was lethal. Bones broke with snaps and crunches.

'Foresight!' Kingfisher cried. 'Use it, Mother Seej! Save them!'

'I'm trying!' Voice full of despair, the priest held the stone close to her lips. 'Please,' she begged it. 'They will die …'

Already, the front line of folk were losing consciousness. Expressions fell lax, eyes rolled to whites and noses bled. The horde held them in place, pushing forwards, allowing no room in which they might slide to the ground.

'The stone won't listen to me,' Seej said. 'It just tells me to move on.'

The priest turned away, tears in her eyes. But Kingfisher couldn't stop watching the faces of the possessed. The front line was dying now. Eyes glassy with a lack of life, death rattles escaped bloodied lips. But still the horde pressed forwards without voice.

Charlie stood alongside Kingfisher. 'When Yandira Wood Bee is in my sights,' he said with a flat tone, 'I'll strangle her myself.'

He tried to steer Kingfisher away, but she shrugged him off and kept watching. What difference would ridding the Realm of Yandira make ultimately, when the Oldunfolk could be so perversely ambivalent about who to save and who to damn in this sickening game of Theirs?

In the end it was Maxis who took charge, stealing her attention from the relentless crush of bodies and speaking with courage and reason despite the angry, distraught tremble in his voice. 'Come, my Lady. If we continue on to meet my daughter, perhaps this senseless charge will end and lives will be saved.'

The prince then ordered Lina to scout the way ahead, while he, Kingfisher, Seej and Charlie followed at a distance, each of them pale and perturbed as the stomach-churning and disquietingly subdued sound of innocent folk dying fell into the background.

It didn't take long for the tunnel to level out, and the walls changed from hard-packed dirt to stonework. There were no dangers ahead, only a wall where Lina waited for them.

'Dead end,' the scout said, face pained.

'Not so.' Kingfisher moved to the front of the group and peered at the wall in the light of Foresight. There were dark, shiny bricks in the stonework, and she knew what they signified. Stepping closer, she cupped her hands around her eyes and looked through one of the glass bricks.

'What can you see?' asked Maxis.

'The dungeons.' Though the view was a little smoky through the tinted glass, Kingfisher could see clearly the mutilated corpse strapped to a torture rack opposite. Her stomach turned to witness more senseless death, but the corpse itself encouraged an incongruous flush of victory. Captain Gavith. And to his right the cells were full to bursting with folk, many of whom she recognised.

'Ghador's personal guard,' she announced, stepping back. 'There's a secret door in this wall. Help me find the catch.'

It was Charlie who located it: a low brick that depressed with a click, releasing a catch in a narrow section of the wall which had to be wrenched open.

A shout came from the cells as soon as Kingfisher entered the dungeons. 'My Lady, here!'

'Lieutenant Davil!'

Kingfisher tried to get to her, but Maxis blocked her way, brandishing his sword and saying, 'Careful of a trap, Genevieve. These folk have been in Yandira's care.'

'Peace, Highness,' Davil said. 'Yandira murdered Captain Gavith for information. Her sorceries do not work on us. We have free will, we are angry and we are ready to fight.'

'Juno's Blessing,' Seej said, listening to Foresight. 'It is upon them.'

'So, do we let them out?' Charlie said, returning from where two jailers lay crumpled beside the rack with a bunch of keys in his hand.

Maxis took the keys and began opening cells while Lina moved to guard the stairs leading out of the dungeons with her bow.

Bruised and battered, but strong and willing, the convoy mainly comprised soldiers, forty of them at least, with a smattering of servants and diplomats whom Kingfisher vaguely knew. There was a stench of rot and corrosion in the dungeon. Strange and disturbing symbols had been drawn on the floor in chalk.

Davil came forwards and Kingfisher took her hands.

'My Lady, you're a sight for sore eyes,' the lieutenant said. 'A few moments ago, we were all destined for the Underworld.'

'Have you seen her?' Kingfisher said. 'Have you seen Ghador?'

Davil shook her head. 'Not since she disappeared on the Queen's Highway. My Lady, there's something you should know. Lord Dragonfly was here—'

'Form ranks,' Maxis commanded, energised to be around trained fighters again, even if they weren't his to command. 'We are my daughter's army and we will bring down Yandira Wood Bee.' He frowned at the state of the newly freed soldiers, concerned that most were dressed in their undergarments. 'Lieutenant, perhaps your troops should visit the armoury?'

'And then to the Temple of Juno,' Seej Agda said. The priest was holding Foresight close to her chest, eyes closed, listening to its divine voice. 'That's where Ghador will meet us.'

25

The Sins of the Mother

Something terrible was happening. The feeling came suddenly, crawling over Yandira's skin with icy claws as she sat in the protected shell of her private council chamber. On the floor, the dark pool of the Underworld stirred with weak, lacklustre swirls and somehow appeared sickly. Inside Yandira, the dragon's agitation increased steadily. She popped the cork from a vial and swallowed its contents. The blood dampened the threat of uncontrollable rage but did not soothe a troubled mind.

Was she experiencing ... *doubt*?

The trap had been set and everything was moulded to Yandira's advantage. Though her vision could not see Dalmyn's army, she could sense it as a magical anomaly hiding within the Serpent's Sigh; and, as planned, the bulk of Dalmyn's soldiers remained immobile outside the city gates while Yandira feigned ignorance of the few assassins who had sneaked into Strange Ground. She had been tracking their not-so-clandestine progress through the warrens, just as she had been watching a second anomaly which had appeared down in the crypts – the shield of Juno's Blessing, just as Lady Persephone had predicted.

From behind her fortifications, with the insights of Her Immortal Darkness guiding her, all Yandira had to do was wait for her enemies to spring the trap that would deliver both crown-stones into her possession and render Minerva's sword useless. So why this doubt? Why this sudden, unshakable feeling that something was terribly wrong?

Yandira flinched as the pool gave a sudden belch. The sickly oil burst to expel a blast of rancid gas, along with an item of a more material nature. A bag ... a satchel, made from dark cloth, flapped into the air and landed in Yandira's lap. Her instinct made her swipe it to the floor and stand over it defensively. But the satchel merely lay limp by her feet and offered nothing more sinister than its apparent emptiness.

Narrowing her eyes, Yandira picked it up and looked inside, confused to find a letter, perturbed to see it was addressed to her.

Yandira, my youngest and only surviving daughter,

I once asked what you hoped to achieve. What ultimate goal were you working towards? You refused to tell me at the time, and I have been wondering why ever since. But now, after a decade of contemplation, I believe your silence was more than telling. You did not answer my question because you didn't know how to, and still don't.

If you think the sole purpose of this game is to help you become the new Empress of the Realm, then you have never understood the nature of the Oldunfolk – yours, mine or any other who has ever heard our prayers. Whether or not one more mortal sits upon yet another throne is of little consequence to either of our Oldunones. We are but fleeting moments, sparks of intrigue who occasionally relieve divine ennui.

My greatest failure as a mother was my inability to make you understand that to rule by subjugation is to not rule at all. It is choiceless, empty. It is tyranny. The power for which you have bargained with your soul is mighty, but have you considered the tyrants who control it? You sold your soul for self-glorification. You murdered your sisters for delusions of grandeur. Will the earthlings be so eager to play this game by your rules?

I may have given up my throne years ago, but I remain a Protector of the Realm and still care greatly for my world. I can only hope, pray, that your choices and actions will come back to bite you, Yandira Wood Bee, without leading to the ruination of us all.

In heartbreak and regret,
Your mother.

Yandira sat down and let the letter slip from her hands. It drifted into the Underworld's pool. Oily waters blackened the paper and sucked it down into its dark depths: Fury came in many forms. Yandira's was a storm in the bowels of an ancient volcano and would have buried the land in magma and burning ash if not ... if not for this cold doubt crawling on her skin.

The letter had come from the Underworld. Why would Her Immortal Darkness permit this?

Yandira looked into the Serpent's Sigh. She sensed the anomalies inside the castle, saw her soldiers moving into position; but when she looked for the Shade, it could not be found. She searched again, calling for its presence, but it wouldn't respond. All Yandira could detect was a stark absence. The Shade wasn't missing or hiding ... it didn't exist any more.

Yandira surged to her feet. *Ignius!* Her command was a lightning bolt cracking through the Serpent's Sigh. She couldn't understand why her Oldunone was punishing her at this time, but she knew how to regain Her favour. *Do it now!* she commanded. *Sacrifice them all!*

But the magician did not respond. As with the Shade, Yandira felt only the absence of existence. Ignius Rex was dead—

The dragon roared in Yandira's chest. She drank another vial of blood, but it wasn't enough, not any more, and the beast's hunger was beyond compare. The pool of the Underworld paled and swirled and closed like a ghost abandoning its haunting place. The dragon roared again, rattling Yandira's ribcage like a prisoner shaking the bars of a cell. The empty vial slipped from her hand and smashed on the floor.

'My Lady, no!' Panting, gasping, Yandira stumbled and staggered towards the door. 'I beg Your Immortal Darkness, please, a … a little more time. I can give … I can give You …' But the agony was too great to talk further.

Yandira fell through the doorway to the throne room. She crawled to her throne, didn't have the strength to pull herself up into it and rolled down the steps to the base of the dais. Inside her, the dragon was clawing its way to freedom and blood frothed from her mouth. The royal guards in the room didn't come to help, couldn't do anything even if Yandira had retained the presence of mind to command them. Subjugated and docile, they watched as their would-be Empress succumbed to the spirit of a monster.

But it didn't bring death.

When the dragon took over, a new and alien strength flooded Yandira. Something old and impossibly volatile. The roar in her chest worked its way up her throat and bellowed from her mouth with such volume it shook the very foundations of Castle Wood Bee. Yandira hitched and jerked up onto her hands and knees. A second roar cracked pillars as two appendages burst from Yandira's back. Lengths of black and bloodied bone at first, they quickly unfurled like a ship's sails into long and leathery wings.

With a single beat, Yandira lofted herself into the air. Her next roar produced a stream of red, molten fire. She vomited death. Tapestries incinerated, stonework melted, royal guards cooked inside their armour. The grand throne room doors disappeared in a swarm of angry cinders. Yandira beat her wings and sped through the opening.

This was no punishment; this was a gift, and all would burn in her fire.

Bek couldn't shake the feeling that the Shade was somehow on her, crawling over her skin, searching for tender flesh to pierce. Perhaps even now it was watching their desperate flight through the crypts; perhaps the wound Minerva's sword had given it was fatal, and it had crawled into a dark corner to die. Either way, the Shade didn't show, but Yandira had sent her servants after the rightful heir.

It was impossible to tell from which direction the enemies came but the din they made suggested many of them, and they were closing in. When the True Sight Candle led Bek and Ghador to an old tomb, at least thirty royal guards converged on their position, each armed with pikes and swords and axes, cocooned in silver armour.

Bek's heart banged against her ribcage as they formed a semicircle that pressed the sisters back towards the tomb. All that stood between them was a blue-bladed sword which did not seem half as powerful now it faced so many.

Bek turned. The True Sight Candle shone an iridescent swirl upon the tomb's ancient entrance, and she realised it was the oldest tomb in the crypts, the final resting place of Queen Minerva Wood Bee. This tomb hadn't been opened since the day Minerva died, *couldn't* be opened. High magic had sealed it shut long, long ago, so how did the candle expect them to enter?

Perhaps it was the proximity of Minerva's sword that the seals recognised. When the guards pressed the sisters close enough, Ghador flinched as Oldunspeak flared in the blade. There was a rumble and grind of stone on stone. Releasing a cloud of dust and an age-old breath, the tomb opened. Its stone door slid back and then descended into the floor, revealing a space which legend said hadn't been seen for two thousand years.

And from it came the radiance of Juno's Blessing.

The guards halted their progress. Bek's eyes were dazzled, but she could see, somewhere at the light's centre, the source was a small oval of deep twilight. Hindsight ...

Ghador recognised it as well, encouraging Bek to follow her into the tomb. A wall of wispy, watery translucence had risen between the sisters and Yandira's soldiers. The guards pressed forward again, and as each one touched the rippling barrier, they were repelled with enough force to send them crashing and tumbling across the crypt's stone floor.

If, as legend said, the tomb held the golden sarcophagus rendered in the likeness of Minerva Wood Bee, surrounded by a priceless horde of treasure, Bek saw nothing of it in the blue light. Not even the radiance of the True Sight Candle penetrated the glare. She could make out Ghador, however, reaching for Hindsight with a trembling hand. Had Maitressa opened this tomb ten years ago? Had the stone always been here, right under Yandira's nose?

The answers were unimportant. Ghador had Hindsight, her father was bringing Foresight and soon Yandira Wood Bee would know the true meaning of fear.

But that wasn't what happened.

As soon as Ghador's hand closed around the stone, it disappeared and its light died in an oily blackness that wrapped around the sisters, snatching them away into a void of corrosion.

Kingfisher thought she would feel safer to be surrounded by soldiers again. If anything, she felt more vulnerable than ever. Davil had told her that Lord Dragonfly was in the dungeons moments before she arrived. Every prisoner had been prepared for sacrificing to Cursed Persephone, but Dragonfly had somehow broken the spell of the Serpent's Sigh, and his last act was to wrestle with the foul magician Ignius Rex and send them both tumbling into the Underworld, thus saving every other soul held captive.

Dear Aelfric, Kingfisher thought. *Had I arrived sooner, would you be standing with me now?*

She had to harden her emotions; she could acknowledge the heartache later. This army was heading for the inner bailey and the Temple of Juno; and though each member was loyal to Ghador's cause, they were ragtag, ill-prepared for what dangers lurked in Castle Wood Bee.

The armoury had been practically stripped of anything useful – no armour whatsoever left, two or three swords with chipped blades, a few broken spears and enough hammers and pokers to arm less than a third of Ghador's soldiers. Their situation was improved a short time later, but only by grim remedy when the first wave of Yandira's troops met them in the banquet hall.

A score of soldiers waited at the opposite end of the hall, each armed with a new, shining blade, but wearing the clothes of castle servants. Innocent folk, subjugated by the Serpent's Sigh. Ghador's army hesitated at first; but when the servants rushed at them with the same mindless ferocity as those in the warrens, Maxis and Davil had no choice but to order the charge met.

There was no training in their fighting skills. As disorganised as children, the servants swung their weapons with reckless abandon, without regard to any defence. They lived to serve Yandira Wood Bee and understood only that they had to fight her foes for as long as they drew breath. But they were no competition for trained soldiers. As these subjugates were struck down, Kingfisher turned away and met Lina's gaze. There was an arrow in the scout's hand but she hadn't nocked it, and she bowed her head to the sound of metal meeting skin and bone.

In the heavy silence that followed, Davil ordered her soldiers to collect weapons from the fallen.

'Servants,' Maxis spat, then cursed the ground Yandira Wood Bee stood upon. 'Where are her royal guards? Where are her soldiers?'

No one answered. Was it cruel luck that had sent so unworthy a foe to impede the progress of trained fighters? Kingfisher could think of a more pertinent question: where was Yandira herself?

Seej Agda said prayers for the dead and Ghador's army moved on. With most of their number now armed, the soldiers made cautious progress through Castle Wood Bee. At their centre, they shielded the few servants and diplomats of Ghador's entourage. Maxis and Davil led the fighters, Mother Seej behind them. Foresight was in the High Priest's tight grasp, its whispers encouraging them to reach the Temple of Juno, where it was hoped the princess was already waiting. If not, they'd have to barricade themselves inside the temple long enough for Ghador to arrive with Hindsight already shining from Minerva's sword. They hoped.

'That bloody stone,' Charlie said, eyeing Seej. He walked beside Kingfisher, brandishing his cudgel menacingly, while she held her dagger. 'If it protects us, why wouldn't it protect those poor souls back there? They didn't *choose* to serve the Underworld.'

'I've been asking myself the same question,' Kingfisher said darkly. 'I can't find an answer.'

Charlie grumbled an expletive. 'This is a sorry day for the Oldunfolk.'

There was no arguing with that.

Curiously, their passage met with no further resistance, and Kingfisher began to wonder if they had surprised the servants in the banquet hall, stumbling by chance into a fight rather than walking into a planned ambush. Perhaps they had sneaked in without Yandira's detection. There was no sign of the Serpent's Sigh inside the castle, not until they neared the doors to the inner bailey. The corrupting fog hazed the end of a long, wide corridor and the edges of the grand reception hall beyond, always keeping a distance from the blessed soldiers, and they made it outside surrounded by a clear bubble inside a world of thick slate-grey.

The temple stood two hundred paces at least from the keep, and as they headed straight for it, Kingfisher allowed herself to believe they would reach it unimpeded. But when the temple appeared in the fog, so did the first walking corpses.

Priests, robes charred, skin blackened and red – undoubtedly dead, but shuffling around in a mindless cluster, forming a barricade before the ruined temple doors in a number that might have comprised every priest in Strange Ground. Even as Ghador's soldiers slowed, a shout went up from the back: royal guards were streaming from the keep behind them. From the left and right, soldiers of the city guard stepped from the fog with trained precision to flank their enemy.

The Serpent's Sigh receded to reveal the full size of the trap. Archers lined the ramparts above and behind the temple, standing shoulder to shoulder, aiming arrows at the insurgents. Davil made an attempt to rally her troops, but the quiver in her voice negated any orders she could give. The ranks of royal and city guards wore armour, were better armed and outnumbered Ghador's army three to one at least. And who knew how many more thousands Yandira could summon from the fog at any moment? This was their last stand.

Yet the enemy did not press its advantage. Instead of attacking, Yandira's troops waited, content for now to contain the insurgents in the inner bailey.

'Come on, you bastards.' Maxis bared his teeth. 'What are you waiting for?'

The answer came from above.

The beating of huge wings swirled what was left of the Serpent's Sigh as a black shadow soared through the grey. A bellow of rage and power blistered the air, and Ghador's army cowered as a monster released a blood-red stream from its mouth.

Burning with the fury of the Underworld, fire cascaded into the inner baily almost liquidly, like a cloudburst of molten metal. Ghador's army pushed against the barricade of bodies. Yandira's soldiers didn't try to stop them. Kingfisher raised her hands, expecting death. She felt the heat, saw the anger and flames swirling around the inner bailey, and ... the fire did not touch her. Nor any other person protected by Juno's Blessing. But the enemy troops were incinerated where they stood. In a crazed attack, driven by a lust to destroy, to kill anything living, the servants of the Serpent's Sigh died without a sound.

'Dragonfire!' Seej cried from somewhere in the confusion. 'It cannot harm us!'

'To the temple!' Davil ordered.

'Move, damn you!' Maxis shouted. 'Everybody – *run!*'

A dragon? Kingfisher thought with panic as, from out of the chaos, the soldiers fled into the temple, slipping and staggering over burning priests along the way. Davil was the last to enter the main prayer hall and immediately started barking orders. 'Pews, barrels, beds! Anything we can use for a barricade!'

The order was barely out of her mouth when a fresh gout of dragonfire shattered the stonework around the doorway and sent her tumbling across the floor.

'Stand forward!' Maxis shouted, helping Davil to her feet. 'Form ranks!'

Without thinking, Kingfisher joined the front line, surprised to find Charlie beside her.

'Be a good time for Ghador and Bek to show up,' he said, face stony.

'Yes, wouldn't that be a sight ...?'

Kingfisher trailed off. Out of the fire, stepping through the ruined doorway, Yandira Wood Bee walked into the temple, wearing the crown of Strange Ground.

Maitressa's youngest child was barely recognisable. Leathery wings fanned from her back like ebony blades. Her face was a bestial grotesquery, dark eyes lined with veins of silver. Black scales covered her skin like armour, and her fingers were as long and sharp as knives. The power of the Underworld was upon her, and Kingfisher somehow knew that not one weapon in this prayer hall could put her down. Though Lina tried, releasing an arrow that Yandira swatted from the air with casual ease.

The beast began speaking in an incomprehensible language, a sibilant rumble, nauseating to hear. Her forked tongue flicked between pointed teeth, spitting and spraying smoky saliva that burst into red flame wherever it spattered the floor. Yandira's knife-fingers clacked together, itching to rip every person present to shreds.

It was Seej Agda who confronted the beast first. Kingfisher hadn't noticed, but the High Priest wasn't among the main group. She had waited outside in the raging inferno. She entered the temple now, Foresight held aloft, glowing with an intense blue which made the beast snarl and wheel around to face her.

The look on Seej's face was empty, lost. Was she seeking revenge for the dead priests and folk outside? Or was Foresight whispering to her the method of Yandira's demise? What if it was saying that Ghador was dead—

'In the name of Juno's good and light.' Tears streaked Seej's cheeks and hatred blazed from her eyes. 'I stand in your way!'

Instead of attacking with the stone, Seej closed her eyes and lifted her face to its divine radiance. Yandira's response was almost too swift for mortal eyes to detect. She sprang forwards and rammed a handful of finger-knives into Seej's stomach. Impaled and lofted above the beast's head, Seej struggled weakly as Yandira faced the insignificant army of Ghador, blood pouring over her scales. Lina loosed another arrow. It shattered in the air before it could thud into the dragon's heart. Yandira spoke once more in that hideous tongue which could only be of the Underworld, then she threw the priest at her foes.

Without thinking, Kingfisher rushed to where Seej landed nearby. Blood pumped from her wounds and there was no stopping it. Seej gasped for breath, her eyes rolling back. Kingfisher cradled her head, vaguely aware that orders were being given for the soldiers to spread out. But even if their weapons could have any effect, it was too late.

Yandira raised a glowing hand to her forehead. There was the sound of cracking glass and broken shards fell to the floor. When she moved her hand, the real Foresight shone from the crown. Yandira roared her victory with a geyser of dragonfire that set light to rafters high above.

The soldiers backed away from her.

But something else was happening, something the beast had not seen. While Yandira roared, her talons splayed, Foresight shining from her forehead, a darkness bloomed into existence behind her. A great swirling disc of oily liquid, giving off an overpowering stench of corruption. When Yandira finally noticed it, her rumbling voice became panicked. She beat her wings, springing into the air, and spat fire at the darkness.

The disc swallowed everything she vomited. Yandira's wings folded as she was trapped by a powerful force that slammed her down onto the stone floor and dragged the beast towards its hungry blackness. Yandira roared again, but oily water filled her mouth and doused her flames. The anomaly swallowed the beast whole, Foresight and all, then diminished to the size of a gold coin before blinking out of existence.

In the stunned, shaken silence that followed, Kingfisher realised that Seej Agda had died in her arms.

'What happened?' Maxis demanded. He stood over Kingfisher but appeared to be addressing the deceased priest. 'Ghador was supposed to meet us here. Where is she?' There was panic in his eyes. *Where's my daughter!*

With his eyes closed to the apocalypse on one side of him and the utopia on the other, Ebbie drifted through his recent past. He was remembering the last conversation he had shared with Mai, in her little nook on the high street between the launderette and the newsagent's – she with a hot chocolate, he with a cappuccino – on the morning before she died.

They had been discussing *faith*, and Mai had been interested to know when it was that Ebbie had turned his back on divinity. He told her about his childhood and how his parents forced him to go to church every Sunday. Those weekly trips made him feel uncomfortable, right from the first he could remember, but he never said anything, never complained, because he felt there was something wrong with him for not feeling the same way as his parents. They always seemed happiest in church, nodding along to sermons, agreeing with every word, never questioning, never doubting. Why couldn't he experience this happiness? And then one Sunday the simple answer struck Ebbie like a bolt from the blue: he did not believe.

Faith, as he felt it to be true, was not something that could be taught for the sake of *compliance*. What he witnessed in church was his parents bending to a strict interpretation of a story, which held no tolerance for doubters and offered damnation to those who strayed from the path. This was earthlings controlling earthlings; and to make his parents believe, down to the core, that they led a good life because it was founded on divine edicts without providing a single shred of evidence, was a great and terrible trick.

'My parents weren't happy when I sat them down and explained that I didn't believe,' Ebbie had told Mai, 'and they've been trying to convert me ever since. But I suppose that was the moment I fell in love with the Realm. The stories of the Oldunfolk made more sense to me. If divinity existed in any form, then They acted like an honest representation of it, cruel and kind and everything in between. They celebrated Their own power.'

'Oh, I agree wholeheartedly,' Mai said. 'The Oldunfolk revel in who They are, unashamed of Their true nature, while bathing in the folk's glorious worship. When They are content, They are wondrous. When They are angry, They are terrible. But when They are bored – *that* is when They become truly deadly. And for some Oldunfolk, playing great and terrible tricks on mortals is the grandest pastime of all.'

In the nook on the high street, Mai sipped her chocolate,

savoured the taste and gave an odd, crooked smile. And suddenly it was as though she were speaking in the present, not from a memory.

'I'll tell you something to remember, Ebbie. If deceit is required, Great Tricksters, whether they be mortal or divine, follow the same game plan. First, they gain your confidence to better cloud your judgement and sense of reasoning. Then they make you believe life will be unbearable unless you buy whatever they are selling. Finally, they walk away, having achieved their goals without you ever realising you've bought into a pack of lies.'

And there, on the hill, Ebbie broke through his quagmire of confusion and saw that his future was not founded upon two alternatives.

'This is all utter catshit.'

He opened his eyes to find Karin's ghost standing over him. Her lips were set in a grim line. A sudden thought of Bek came into Ebbie's mind and he couldn't stop a burst of laugher. That Bek might lead a rebellion wasn't implausible, but the image of her sitting on a throne, wearing a crown ... Queen Bek – even she would find that funny.

Karin was frowning at him, clearly offended, and Ebbie's laughter stopped.

'I'll tell you what I believe,' he said, getting to his feet and brushing dust from his hands. 'The future holds infinite possibilities. Every decision, every action, creates a multitude of differences. You can't whittle it down to predictions so precise.'

Karin shook her head. 'You're wrong about that, Ebbie. Trust me, the Oldunfolk *know*.'

'So, I should roll over and accept there're only two options for the future, two extremes? The very worst –' he motioned to the fire and destruction on one side of the hill, then to the peace and serenity '– and the very best. You want me to believe this is proof that there's nothing in between because *you* say so?'

The magician stared at him, staying silent.

Ebbie continued. 'If I was supposed to stay on Earth after finding Ghador, Mai would've told me. If my job was done, I'd have been removed from the game, simple as that, not given the choice over who wins and loses. To suggest otherwise is absurd.'

Karin's face creased with anger and her voice growled like a monster's. 'I would not be so sure about that if I were you.'

Ebbie shied from her anger but somehow bolstered his courage to press on. 'Every story I've ever read about You, every conversation I've ever had that mentions Your name, the same word is used – *Trickster*. Can't get away from it, whenever You come up. So I use it now. *Trickster*. You're not fooling me any more.'

'Astounding. All you had to do was choose.' Karin's anger was lost in a smirk and Her voice adopted an impossibly old and dangerous tone. 'Still, you must be frightened.'

'Like I've never been before, but not for my life. Not here, not yet.'

'Oh?'

'You have to remember who I am – an earthling who doesn't experience *anything* through Oldunfolk-fearing eyes. Moves and countermoves – that's how the game is played. Where's Karin?'

'Do you know, I am really not sure. The last I saw of the magician and your other friends, Mr Lunk and Mr Venatus were breathing down their necks.' The ghost split down the centre and parted like gates opening. 'I lost track of them after that. Or did I?'

The true image hiding inside the ghost stepped out onto the scorched and crumbling hill and stood to Her full height.

Cursed Persephone, Oldunone of the Underworld, towered over Ebbie, eight feet tall at least. She stared down at him with ebon eyes. Her obsidian hair was styled into a topknot, as slick and dark as Her leather armour – which might have been Her skin. Her ears were pointed and Her face familiar. Ebbie wondered how he had ever missed it, but She radiated a corroded immortality, dangerous and powerful, something far beyond the guise of a funeral director called Mrs Cory. She smelled like every bad thing that could ever happen.

'*Trickster*,' She mused. 'I am usually quite fond of that moniker, but when I hear it from your faithless lips?' She opened and closed massive hands while the silvery remnants of the ghost dissipated. 'It is more than tempting to crush your head until your skull shatters.'

'You won't kill me – not personally – because there are *rules*.' Ebbie tried to sound confident, but his heart was racing and he couldn't meet the Oldunone's lightless, knowing gaze. 'If you kill me now, Juno will have licence to remove one of Your players, maybe Yandira herself, and where would that leave You?'

'On the losing side, *you* might presume.'

She clapped Her hands with a concussion that might have raised mushroom clouds on the burning plains of the dying Realm. Instantly, like a stage curtain dropping, the lies of two extreme futures disappeared, replaced by a poisonous landscape beneath graveyard skies. Stinking of corruption, the Underworld bloomed into dread existence all around.

'So,' Persephone said. 'Here you are, little Ebbie Wren, custodian of stories. You have caught an Oldunone in a barefaced lie, and your insights are keen. Not exactly trying to spare My blushes, are you?'

Her voice was laced with thunder. *I won't die here*, Ebbie told himself. *She won't kill me. She can't.*

She continued, 'Juno and I have already broken the rules. That the game stands on the cusp of wild escalation is all too real.'

'You don't care about that,' Ebbie said meekly. 'You only care about winning.'

Persephone laughed. 'If Maitressa Wood Bee has convinced you that Lady Juno's priorities are any different from Mine, then I am not the only trickster in your life.'

'Maybe not, but You *are* the greater evil.'

'Don't believe every story you've read.' Persephone stepped closer to him, and he didn't have permission to move away. 'Shall I tell you why you are a clever choice of player? You can claim to have no faith, but only because Earth spoiled you first. For generations your kind have struggled beneath the shadow of tyrants who might destroy your existence with the push of a button or a single command. You are not fazed by higher power because you have been saturated in the concept since birth. You understand the mechanics of *divine rules* better than the folk ever could because earthlings have made divinity *mortal*.'

Emboldened by his conviction that She could not kill him without compromising Her position, Ebbie forced himself to meet Her dark, dark eyes. 'I'm no *link* that begins a chain of events that decides the fate of worlds. I have a role in this game because a good friend asked for my help and I said *yes*.'

Persephone considered him, not quite in admiration, but close to it. 'I should have chosen an earthling champion myself. Perhaps I will, next time. As for your role, well ...' She rocked Her head from side to side. 'It certainly started out as simply as you describe, but I am afraid it amused Me to *up* your status within My strategies. And now I find I have painted Myself into a corner somewhat.'

It was strange to hear an Oldunone laugh in mockery of

Herself. The Underworld laughed with Her, bending to its master's mood with a dangerous self-deprecation that would soon seek vengeance.

'Why did you bring me here?' Ebbie said.

'That I might convince Maitressa's champion to embrace his cowardice and greed, thus turning his back on the hero she believed him to be, was simply too delicious an opportunity to pass up. All you had to do was choose Earth over the Realm and let Yandira win, but instead ... you chose to call My bluff.'

Again, the self-mocking laugh. 'Juno gambled on you being the bait on a hook that I could not resist swallowing. And She was right. I honestly did not bank on you seeing through the grandeur of My trickery. Bravo. However, I really am a sore loser and see no other way to save face than by offering you a pact.'

Ebbie felt cold, remembering the visions of Karin and all she had shown him. 'A pact?'

'Would you like to hear My terms?'

A hard knot formed in Ebbie's gut as Persephone held out Her fists, side by side, as though She was about to perform a sleight-of-hand trick. 'Here is Earth,' She said, moving Her left fist forward. 'And here is the Realm.' Her right fist replaced the left. 'I will deliver Maitressa's champion to whichever place he chooses.'

Ebbie swallowed. 'You'll let me leave? Unharmed?'

'And in return, you will ensure that I do not lose the game.'

'What?'

'Fail me, and I will make the nightmare of apocalypse a reality. Now, *choose*.'

In his mind, Ebbie saw the terrible visions of the Realm burning to cinders. *It's a trick*, he told himself. *A lie, a lie, a lie!* And this time, the Underworld was laughing at him because

Persephone, Immortal Darkness, was relentless and couldn't be denied.

'I am waiting,' She said.

'You already know my decision,' Ebbie said through clenched teeth. 'I won't abandon my friends.'

'Then this belongs to you.' Persephone opened Her right fist. An oval stone of twilight blue sat on her palm, twinkling with majestic light. 'Take it.'

She didn't give Ebbie the option of holding back. He reached out and plucked the stone from Her shovel-sized hand. Its light danced and sparkled, and a voice whispered in his mind, pure and cleansing, and told this earthling its name.

He became short of breath. 'This is … This is—'

'Our pact is sealed, Ebbie Wren.'

He saw nothing of Persephone's dragon returning apart from a giant shadow descending with speed and a pressure that crushed him to his knees. Ebbie clasped Hindsight tightly in his hands as darkness scooped him up and carried him away.

26

Ruin

It felt different from the Janus Bridge. There was no dizzying jaunt, no speed, no motion sickness. Instead, some divine brand of spite had enveloped Bek, sucked her out of Castle Wood Bee with a slow drag through viscous corrosion to throw her up onto damp wild grass in the chilly outdoors. Fighting for breath, she got to her hands and knees, coughing dark mucus from her lungs.

Beside her, Ghador suffered similar distress. When the coughing eased, they both rolled onto their backs, gulping air. Somehow, the princess still held Minerva's sword. Bek sat up and saw the lantern nearby. It stood upright, but its rainbow light was fading. Less and less it shone, until the flame shrank to a flicker of blue that was finally extinguished. Bek crawled to the lantern, opened its glass panel, releasing a puff of smoke, and saw the candle had exhausted itself.

This was the end of the line. But where were they?

The Serpent's Sigh's relentless fog was nowhere to be seen. Overhead, dawn blushed the murky and unsettled Skea. A fine rain fell almost sadly upon ruins. All around, as far as Bek could see, ancient stones, broken and weatherworn, poked up through a sea of wild grass and brush like the bones of history.

'I had it,' Ghador said. She was on her feet, staring at the sword. 'Hindsight was mine. I felt it in my hand. Where did it go?'

Bek joined Ghador in taking stock of their environment. A landscape of ruins beneath miserable weather with a charge in the air that made it feel dangerous. 'What is this place?'

As if in reply, a growl rumbled from a short distance away. A huge, muscular figure came out of the rain-misted air, prowling between old pillars sticking from the ground at odd angles. A wild thing, a great beast.

The part of Bek's brain not panicking over the sight of this monster would've guessed it was a wolf, if wolves grew to the size of horses, with no hair covering their tough, leathered skin, and had two heads – one of flesh and blood, the other a silvery phantom. Their faces resembled wolf and folk melted together.

Absurdly, Bek's reaction was to wonder, 'Is that thing Lunk and Venatus?'

Ghador cursed. 'What happened to them?'

The beast was stalking towards their position, both its noses sniffing the air.

'Don't just stand there looking at it!' a voice hissed from behind Bek and Ghador.

They wheeled around in unison. Where the remnants of a floor gleamed whitely between patches of grass, from within three walls still standing of an ancient house, topped with a portion of roof, a woman in a russet robe beckoned the sisters to her position with angry, urgent gestures.

'Karin,' Bek blurted.

'*Hide*, you bloody idiots!'

Rushing to the magician, Bek and Ghador entered the ruined house and ducked down behind a cracked and crumbling wall. Karin remained standing, peering through a hole in the stonework, watching the beast outside.

'So, if it's not after me or you, what's it doing?' she said, as though continuing a conversation she'd been having with herself. 'Sorry, I meant what are *they* doing.'

'Lunk and Venatus?' said Bek.

'Oldunfolk only know how they ended up as this abomination, but I've been watching it for a while and it doesn't seem interested in doing anything but prowling around and sniffing the air. It must be able to smell us, so why won't it attack? Why is it here?' The magician looked down at the sisters sharply and with a heavy frown. 'Why are *you* here?'

'I was about to ask you the same thing,' Bek said. 'What happened to you, Karin? We thought you were dead.'

'So did I – at least for a while. You wouldn't believe the things I saw before I was dumped here.'

'Where is *here*?'

'The ruins of Imperium City.' Karin pursed her lips in thought 'Is that ironic? Poetic?'

Imperium City? Where Minerva defeated Bellona? This *game* was supposed to end at Castle Wood Bee. Ghador's father was bringing Foresight. Hindsight had been ... *right there*! But now they had been thrown to where people said ghosts and bad magic had reigned since the last time the Oldunfolk fought?

'This is madness,' Ghador said. 'Karin, how did you get here?'

'Same way as you, I suppose.' The magician made an angry noise as she resumed watching the beast outside. 'Her Divine Arse-Face of the Underworld – She didn't like me rumbling Her tricks, so She booted me out of the game. Surprised She let me live, to be honest.'

Ghador expressed shock. 'Cursed Persephone brought you here?'

'And you, I should imagine. Anyway, Princess, I thought you were calling Her Mrs Cory?'

'What?'

'She must have got to Ebbie, too.'

Bek tensed. 'Have you seen him?'

'No, not since Earth. But it doesn't matter now.' Karin peered hard through the hole in the wall. 'Something's gone badly wrong in the game, and if you ask me, Lunk and Venatus are waiting for someone who isn't *us*.' The magician's shoulders tensed as a deep, baritone bubbling sound came from outside. 'And that *someone* has just arrived. Shite ...'

Bek and Ghador were quickly up and looking for themselves. The Lunk and Venatus creature was braced, hackles raised as it faced a swirling black disc which had appeared above it. From the disc, a figure burst into the air, borne on jagged wings of leather, more terrifying than the giant wolf-folk hybrid.

'Dragon,' Karin whispered. 'Look at its head ...'

The monster wore the crown of Strange Ground, no mistaking it. The gemstone set into its front gleamed with Juno's Light.

'Foresight,' Ghador said, sharing a meaningful look with Bek. This creature was Yandira, had to be, but transformed into an abomination; and if she possessed Foresight, what had become of Ghador's father and Dalmyn's army?

With the ferocity of a monster three times her size, Yandira roared a jet of red fire at the sky that dazzled in the rain, turning droplets into falling rubies. The Lunk and Venatus hybrid growled and barked at her and she turned her attention to it, floating down to the ground but keeping her wings spread like scythes. The two beasts circled each other, and Bek realised this was no happy reunion between master and servants.

'How is *anyone* supposed to defeat *that*?' Ghador said, voice leaden.

'Maybe Lunk and Venatus will do it for you,' Bek replied,

but she doubted it. And without its stones, Minerva's mighty sword was not powerful enough to slay the creature Yandira had become.

'I can't see the back of the crown,' Ghador said. 'Maybe she doesn't have Hindsight.'

'No, we're too late,' Karin said, shaking her head. 'Yandira's got the upper hand in the game. Persephone's opening the Underworld's gates. Look ...'

The black disc from which Yandira had appeared was expanding, growing and growing, becoming a vast backdrop to the circling monsters. The darkness cleared to reveal a crystal-sharp view into a world that could only be Earth.

Karin said, 'Before She left me in these ruins, Persephone wanted me to see one or two things. She's bringing Yandira an earthling army, and you can't even begin to understand how powerful it is ...'

Bek could see thousands of earthling soldiers carrying strange weapons, marching between bizarre technologies of warcraft. But the view was obscured as the two monsters finally stopped sizing each other up and engaged in battle.

With an ear-splitting bark, the wolf-folk hybrid pounced at Yandira. She rushed to meet it and their bodies clashed with an impact that shook the ground. Talons slashed, teeth bit and they fell, thrashing and tearing in the rain, lost among brush and wild grass, until the dragon roared and red fire erupted at a blistering speed, like a volcano spewing lava, towards the ruined house where a thief, a princess and a magician could not hide from its violence.

Hindsight was talking to Ebbie, but with garbled nonsense that phased in and out of his mind like a badly tuned radio. He couldn't quite remember leaving the Underworld, but

Persephone was leading him through Earth on his way back to the Realm. No one could see him, no one could help him, and Hindsight was only adding to the chaos.

At breakneck speed, Ebbie was flying over a military procession. Thousands of soldiers marched along a main road in a city ... *somewhere* on Earth. Fully kitted out, rifles resting on one shoulder, their polished boots rose and fell in well-trained unison to a fanfare of waving flags and cheers from innumerable patriotic spectators. Interspersed among the marching legions, huge missiles and cannons trundled along on carriers and mobile launchers; tank divisions powered forth on their tracks, the barrels of their guns aimed forwards. High above, jet fighters performed aerial displays.

Trapped between the air and ground forces, unable to slow or halt his flight, Ebbie found it impossible to identify what country the army belonged to, but he'd seen this kind of thing before on newsfeeds. This was a display of power, a flexing of muscles, and the procession was miles long. It was real, not one of Persephone's *visions*. Ebbie knew this because the Oldunone of the Underworld wanted him to know the truth before he returned to the Realm. She wanted him to *see*.

Hindsight's voice phased in and phased out.

With wind stealing his breath, Ebbie flew towards the procession's head, hurtling over a tank division. Up ahead, Persephone had unlocked the Underworld's gates, ripping reality wide open and creating a huge hole between the two worlds, a portal leading to where the sea was in the sky, easily large enough to swallow a fully mobilised army ready for war. Ebbie thought he saw Bek in a landscape of ancient ruins, Ghador and Karin with her, all of them alive and well but obviously in a dire situation as red fire ballooned around them to obscure his view.

The army might have been celebrating itself, unhurried as it flexed its muscles to intimidate neighbouring countries, but not one of these soldiers had any idea that divinity had bigger plans for them. Ebbie knew – because Persephone *wanted* him to know – that Yandira already had Foresight, just as She wanted him to know that should She lose the game, She would march this army straight into the Realm and make all those visions of annihilation come true.

Ebbie held the final piece of Yandira's victory, but how could he simply hand Hindsight over to her? How could he betray his friends? How could he bring about Ghador's death, the person he had promised Mai he would help, the very reason he had gone to the Realm in the first place? He had seen the bigger picture, the escalation, the consequences, but what was the right choice? What was the *trick*?

With no control over his flight, Ebbie hurtled clear of the military procession and sped towards the Realm. Ghosts swirled around Persephone's gate, spinning like silver Catherine wheels, eager to shepherd him into red flames and death. Wind snatched away Ebbie's shout as he felt the blistering heat coming closer and closer. Hindsight chattered nonsense in his head, and the ghosts gathered him up. Chaotic and silver, they launched him through the gate and into the furnace.

Yandira's dragonfire flooded into the ruins of the house, shattering stone and burning foliage to cinders, but it could not break the shield of Juno's Blessing.

Bek felt its heat, sensed its desire to incinerate her, but it was as though clean air kept the flames at bay, cool as a lakeside in springtime. But she lost sight of Ghador and Karin almost immediately. As the dragonfire burned and destroyed, Bek called their names, yet her voice was tiny, inconsequential against Yandira's roars, and she could see nothing of them in the blistering red storm.

Stumbling, staggering, Bek knew there was no safe harbour from the beast's heat and passion. Yandira's fire seemed endless, as though she were a conduit through which all the Underworld's fury was channelled, and perhaps it would cover the ruins of Imperium City in their entirety. When the dragon roared next, it was in victory, and the Lunk and Venatus hybrid's howl of pain died in its furore.

The fire parted to form a clear arena in the red, and a shadowy beast strode towards Bek, barbed wings open, Foresight gleaming from her crown. Yandira spoke in a hostile language, incoherent but conveying a long-held hatred of the Wood Bee orphan. She pointed one of ten razor-sharp talons at Bek, showing her the weapon that would end her life. Closer, she came; closer and closer, relishing the moment.

'Ghador!' Bek shouted.

But her sister didn't answer her plea. Someone else saved Bek Rana from the dragon's hate.

A blur of motion came from the fire, trailing a streak of blue in the red like the tail of a shooting star. A man crashed into Yandira like he had been shot from a catapult, throwing the beast aside before he came tumbling to a halt a few paces before Bek. Slowly, he got to his feet, standing on scorched ground between Bek and the beast.

'Ebbie!'

He didn't reply and faced the dragon as she once again emerged from the fire. Ebbie's fist glowed with the same light that shone from the crown of Strange Ground. Yandira saw it and her roar was full of longing. Hindsight, Bek realised, but … was he about to give it to her?

'Ebbie, no!'

Yandira lunged for the stone, but as she did so, Ebbie turned and lobbed it to Bek. She caught it. An instant later, Ebbie cried out and his face creased in agony as Yandira's talons burst from his chest. In horror, Bek watched him die.

Yandira lifted Ebbie's limp body and cast him into her dragonfire. Bek scurried backwards, struggling to get to her feet and escape with the divine stone glowing in her hand. Yandira came for her, rumbling in that dark, sibilant tongue. Bek held Hindsight out in her fist, praying it would frighten the dragon away. Then she yelped as someone laid a strong hand on her shoulder.

Yandira halted as Ghador pulled Bek to her feet, took what she was holding and stepped protectively in front of her sister.

Hindsight released a musical chime when Minerva's sword snatched it from Ghador's hand. For the first time in two thousand years, it *chinked* into its oval frame, and all along the sword's blade Oldunspeak came alive with white light and icy vapour.

Yandira snarled and spat.

Ghador shouted a war-cry and attacked.

They moved with supernatural speed, radiating otherworldly strength. The dragon's talons slashed down and Minerva's sword rose to meet them. They should have clashed like a battering ram striking a castle door, but a line of blue energy prevented contact. It flashed like lightning, bellowed with the voice of a hundred thunderstorms and released a force that repelled the combatants. Ghador was thrown onto her back, Yandira was sent spinning into the air and Bek stumbled in the after-shock.

Ghador was quickly on her feet, sword at the ready. Yandira flapped her wings madly to level her spin, then she soared down from the sky for a second attack. They met. Lightning blazed and repelled them both as ferociously as before. But this time, the energy released a reverberating din like the tolling of a gigantic bell that chased away the dragonfire completely, revealing the blackened ruins of Imperium City and the cool rain falling from the Skea.

Bek looked for Ebbie. She could see where the Lunk and Venatus creature lay, severed head of flesh and blood lying close to the corpse, phantom head vanished, but of her friend there was no sign.

Yandira crashed to the ground in a heap. She stood up on unsteady legs, one of her wings unfurled, the other broken and hanging useless. Behind her, through the gates of the Under-world, the earthling army marched ever closer to the Realm with a promise of the greater storm to come; but Foresight wasn't shining so brightly from Yandira's crown now.

When Ghador faced her aunt for the third time, it was with an eerie calm that sent prickles up and down Bek's spine. There was nothing defensive in Ghador's stance, nothing threaten-ing. Absurdly, madly, she sheathed Minerva's sword and stood proud, unfazed as the dragon snarled and ranted at her.

'No!' Bek shouted. 'What are you doing?'

'Leave her be,' Karin said, appearing alongside Bek. The magician's face was pale and serious. 'This is between Ghador and Yandira now. Nothing we can do.'

'Ebbie was here,' Bek said, feeling small and lost. 'He brought Hindsight.'

Karin nodded as though this news made perfect sense. 'Then maybe I should've said this fight is no longer between Juno and Persephone.'

Ghador looked away from Yandira to give Bek a slow nod. A gesture of reassurance or farewell?

'Don't you see?' said Karin. 'They have a stone each. They're cancelling each other out.' The magician bowed to Ghador. 'The game's up, Bek.'

Yandira charged with a roar and a fresh gout of flame. A shield of ethereal light shone around Ghador. Fire and talons splashed and sparked upon it, but Foresight wouldn't destroy Hindsight, and the princess faced the onslaught regally. Slashing and roaring in a frenzied, desperate attack, Yandira couldn't break through the shield, but she struck and struck until the dragonfire died in her throat and her talons shattered.

Her serpentine voice panicked, she staggered back, nursing crippled claws. Ghador stepped towards her, calmly, without threat, and Yandira continued to retreat towards the Underworld's gates and the marching army. Her bestial face was somehow as frightened as a child's in the dark.

Bek held her breath, wondering whose killing stroke would end this game. But the killing blow, when it came, was neither Ghador's nor Yandira's to make, and Karin whispered, 'When darkness comes, lightness must follow, but never to shine upon a clear and easy road ...'

The Underworld's gates darkened, hiding the view of Earth's army behind a vast wall of rippling, bubbling oil. Yandira had time to turn and stare at it before the whole thing crashed down on her. Like a black tidal wave, it swallowed the beast, then Ghador, and flooded the ruins as it came for Bek and Karin.

Unstoppable, somehow sentient, Bek knew it wanted to drag her soul into a place where mercy had never thrived.

But it didn't.

The wave froze before it touched Bek and then receded. With a sound like a vicious gale over violent seas, it twisted up into a waterspout, leaving Ghador cowering with her arms over her head inside her divine shield. But it claimed Yandira, along with the corpse of her merged former servants and swept them up into a huge sphere of oil it formed in the air. Yandira managed one final, weakened roar before she disappeared, and the sphere shrank – shrank and shrank – until it imploded with the deep toll of a bell.

Persephone had closed her gates. The earthling army had no way through, but the look Ghador gave Bek across the ruins was not one of victory.

'Yandira still has Foresight,' she called.

'Princess, get your arse over here,' Karin said. 'This isn't finished yet.'

Where the Underworld had first opened, a mass of swirling silver was rising from the ground. Drawing the divine sword, Ghador backed away until she stood alongside Bek and Karin, and they faced the phenomenon together.

'What is this?' she said.

'Ghosts,' replied Karin.

The cluster of swirling silver separated to reveal individual spirits, and as each spiralled into the images of the living folk they had once been, Bek, Ghador and Karin saw they had nothing left to fear.

Lord Aelfric Dragonfly and Princess Morrad smiled at the three living women. Queen Eldrid stood with them, wearing the crown of Strange Ground, complete with the shining stone of Foresight, and her expression was an eyebrow arched in disapproval for her daughter's choice in friends. And lastly, wearing the biggest smile of all, was Lady Maitressa Wood Bee.

Maitressa's ghost drifted forwards. She nodded thanks to Karin before coming to Bek and Ghador. Her eyes brimmed with silvery tears and pride as she breathed two words: 'My granddaughters,' and then drifted back to where Morrad, Dragonfly and Eldrid waited.

Ghador looked as surprised as Bek felt to see Minerva's

THE WOOD BEE QUEEN

sword now with Maitressa and no longer in her granddaughter's hand. Hindsight's light glowed warmly from it. In silence, the ghosts bowed to the sisters and magician before fading, taking the sword and stones with them into the afterlife. But they left behind a gift.

'Ebbie!' Bek shouted.

She rushed to where he had appeared, lying on his back in the damp grass, arms crossed over his chest. Bek knelt by his side and took his hand. He bore no wounds, but he didn't move, didn't open his eyes, and his skin was ice cold.

'Let me see him,' Karin said, nudging Bek aside. She felt for his heartbeat, put her ear to his mouth.

'Is he alive?' asked Ghador.

'He's certainly breathing.' Karin tapped Ebbie's cheek, saying his name. His eyes fluttered, then closed again. The magician grinned. 'Lazy bastard's asleep.'

Bek discovered she had nothing left – no emotion to express, no strength to hold her upright – and she collapsed to the ground, lying back on the grass.

Ghador lay down beside her and said, 'Let's go home.'

Bek felt for her sister's hand and squeezed it. Together they let the rain fall on their faces.

27

Bloodline

Lady Kingfisher was watching the sunrise from the ramparts of Castle Wood Bee. A blushing pink dawn filtered through the gently rolling swells of the Skea, and gulls had begun their morning cries. It would be a glorious summer's day in Strange Ground beneath the Skea, but the folk had a lot of work to do before their city was healed.

The threat of a dark Empire had vanished with Yandira Wood Bee. No one could say for sure why she had been snatched away from the Temple of Juno, but four days had passed since the dragon disappeared and she had not returned. The Serpent's Sigh disappeared along with her, and the citizens of Strange Ground were now picking up the pieces of their lives.

A cool breeze carried the tang of brine, and Kingfisher breathed in deeply. She hadn't been sleeping much of late, but watching the sunrise helped to ease a troubled mind.

Prince Maxis and his soldiers had been a great help to her in the aftermath, maintaining order and supervising the grim task of collecting the dead. In the city, inside the castle and from its grounds ... so many corpses had been found, so many friends and loved ones. Even now, bodies were still being discovered down in the warrens. There were too many to bury. Huge funeral pyres had been built outside the city.

Now that the gulls would fly again, messages had been sent to Dalmyn with news. In response, Queen White Gold sent aid, which had arrived two days ago. More soldiers, along with many priests who were the real blessing; it was reckoned that every one of Strange Ground's own priests had been called to their temple when Queen Eldrid died. Yandira had murdered them all. Dalmyn's priests had worked wonders among the citizens, offering faith and comfort to the thousands who had survived the infection of the Serpent's Sigh.

Kingfisher had spoken to a few of the survivors herself. They all had a similar story to tell. They said they remembered not wanting to serve Yandira, but also how she bent them to her will and made them *feel* like serving her was a great vocation. They remembered wanting to kill in her name. The senseless desire, the sheer *need* to wield a weapon and destroy life – the memory of it lingered long after the Serpent's Sigh faded. One woman had told Kingfisher that it felt like waking from a nightmare only to discover you had murdered a loved one in your sleep. The guilt, the shame, bit deep and perhaps it would never leave those who had been infected.

Strange Ground would be well again in time, Kingfisher had faith in that, but she suspected that plenty more sleepless nights lay ahead of her. And on this dawning of the fifth day since Yandira vanished, she found her heart heavier than it had ever been. Later that day, she was due to meet with Prince Maxis and the High Priest who had succeeded poor Seej Agda. The meeting's purpose was to discuss the Wood Bee Throne's future.

Princess Ghador was still missing. What had become of her was unknown. The folk were beginning to ask questions, grow restless – where was their queen? Who would lead them through this tragic time? The answer was not easy to stomach. Kingfisher liked to believe that wherever Yandira had disappeared to, Ghador had a hand in sealing her fate, but she didn't want to admit that in ridding the Realm of her unhinged aunt, Ghador had likely perished herself. Maxis was ready to face the likelihood, however, as was his High Priest, hence the meeting later that day.

Kingfisher wished dear Aelfric were with her. She could have used his wisdom and counsel in all of this. Maitressa had been an only child. All her daughters were dead, and there were no cousins or other relatives – at least, none who were worthy of the throne. Ghador was the last of the Wood Bee bloodline—

Kingfisher flinched as a gull landed on the wall before her. It screeched and cocked its head, pecking at the leg where a message had been tied. With a frown, Kingfisher untied the message and read. *My Lady, come to Jester's Tavern right away. Come alone.*

With a cry, the gull flew from the wall and Kingfisher watched it soar away. She read the message again, then strode from the ramparts.

Strange Ground was quiet at this early hour, just a few guards patrolling the streets, some of whom nodded respectfully at House Kingfisher's First Lady as she marched to Jester's Tavern. When she arrived, the door was locked, so she rapped her knuckles upon it.

Charlie's face appeared at the window, glaring at her suspiciously. 'You alone?' he said through the glass.

Irritated, Kingfisher gestured around her. 'Do you see anyone with me?'

Charlie opened the door and locked it again once the noblewoman had stepped inside.

'What's the meaning of this, Charlie?'

He held a finger to his lips and beckoned her to follow him. The tavern was dark inside. Only two candles had been lit, illuminating a woman – a magician by the looks of her – who was tending a man lying on his back upon a table. The woman was trying to spoon-feed the man broth but was having no easy time of it as he was clearly hurt and only semi-conscious.

Kingfisher recognised him and turned a shocked expression to Charlie. 'This is Ebbie Wren.'

Charlie spread his hands helplessly. 'They sneaked up through the warrens a couple of hours ago, asking for you. Scared the life out of me when they appeared in my cellar.'

'But how ... ?' Kingfisher swung to the magician. 'How did you find him?'

'Ah, well, there's a bit of a story there, my Lady.'

'Has he spoken? Did he mention Princess Ghador?' Kingfisher's heart thudded. 'Tell me, damn you! Is she alive?'

'Don't fear, Genevieve,' said a voice from behind. Kingfisher whirled around. 'Yandira didn't win the game.'

From the darkness at the back of the tavern, Princess Ghador stepped into the candlelight with a smile on her face. Behind her came Bek Rana. They both looked as though they had been dragged through the Underworld backwards.

Kingfisher wanted to rub her eyes to ensure this vision was real. Her joy and relief welled up with the prickle of tears, but she maintained courtly composure by drawing herself up regally, arching an eyebrow and saying, 'Well, you two certainly took your sweet bloody time.'

28

A Royal Librarian

On the day of Princess Ghador's coronation, Ebbie Wren was making slow progress through the library in the south tower of Castle Wood Bee. Leaning heavily on a walking cane, he took careful steps towards a reading table, short of breath, trying to preserve what little energy he had. Weak as he was, the smell of paper and leather bindings, reeking of stories and knowledge, invigorated him. To be surrounded by books again was the grandest reward he could have been given.

He had died, his friends told him – killed and dragged to the Underworld. He knew it was true, though he retained little memory of death, only a vague awareness that Persephone had been there, close by, watching. He recalled nothing of the ghosts She allowed to bring him back to the mortal world. But he remembered rising through cold darkness to find himself lying in the back of a wagon being driven by Ghador, while Bek and Karin sat over him as he dipped in and out of consciousness.

Reaching the table, Ebbie groaned as he lowered himself into a chair. He had a lot to come to terms with, but he wouldn't have wished to be anywhere else.

He took a moment to admire the hundreds, thousands of titles collected by his dear old friend Mai. Books and books and books, all in his care. He had been wondering if the library should move to a different location in the city, to a place where the folk could borrow these books at their leisure. They deserved to be read. But there was a lot of work to do before that could happen. Mai had never catalogued her collection, and it would take Ebbie weeks, months, to do it for her – a job he was looking forward to. Plus, Ghador wanted the collection checked over by a magician, for lurking among the many titles in the library might be dangerous books that had once belonged to Yandira.

Karin would have been the one to conduct a search for any dark and dangerous tomes, but Karin was no longer in the city. Ghador had asked her to be the new royal magician, but she wasn't interested in the position, nor any other kind of reward. She had been fixed to one place for long enough, she said. She didn't want to stay in Strange Ground, didn't intend to return to Oddridge Island, either. All Karin wanted was the freedom to travel across the Realm and, in her own words, *see what's out there*. It had been an odd sort of farewell. Ebbie, Bek and Ghador didn't want her to leave and were sad to see her go, but it also felt like saying goodbye to someone they'd hardly got to know, despite the experiences they had shared.

Ebbie looked up as a loud click disturbed the silence. On the balcony of the library's second tier, a bookcase swung open and Bek hurried through. She leaned over the rail and whispered down to Ebbie.

'Have you seen her?'

'Who?'

'Kingfisher.'

'No.'

'Good.' Bek closed the secret door and descended the spiralling steps, grumbling, 'I'm happy for Ghador. I mean, I *want* her to be queen, but I don't see why I have to be standing beside her when they put the crown on her head.'

'Because you're her sister,' Ebbie said. 'She's proud of you.'

'Is she?' Striding across the library floor, Bek gestured to her attire. 'Then why is Kingfisher making me dress up like a bloody peacock on *her* orders?'

She wore breeches and a matching jacket of dark blue velvet, embroidered with gold thread. Her cream shirt had more ruffles down its front than the 1980s on Earth. White stockings covered her legs from the knees down, dirty at the feet because she was running around with no shoes on. Bek's hair had been plastered to her head by whatever passed for gel in the Realm, and she wore a tiara set with stones more colourful than a True Sight Candle. As for her face ... it looked as though Bek had fled halfway through having make-up applied.

'You look ...' Ebbie rocked his head from side to side. 'Nice?'

'Shut up.' Bek dropped into a chair on the opposite side of the table. 'Do you realise how big this thing is? How many people are going to see me looking like an idiot?'

Two weeks had passed since they had arrived back at the city, and Ghador's coronation was to be a grand affair. With so much damage still being repaired at Castle Wood Bee and the Temple of Juno, the priests had decided to crown the princess at the public square in Golder's Fairway. Thousands of citizens would come to join the celebrations, but Strange Ground was also teeming with royals and members of noble Houses from all over the Realm. They all wanted to see Maitressa Wood Bee's granddaughter sitting on the throne. She and her sister would be facing a crowd of monumental size.

'Yeah,' said Ebbie. 'You're going to look like an idiot today.'

'Thank you for that.'

'Hey, it's the least I can do for the new royal advisor.'

Bek muttered darkly, 'I might go back to robbing houses.'

Ebbie chuckled. 'You'll be fine. I only wish I could be there to see you in all your glory.'

Bek managed a small smile. 'Me, too.'

It had been decided that Ebbie should keep a low profile for the time being, especially with so many delegates from other cities in Strange Ground. He was not from the Realm, and until he learned to blend in as a native, no one could risk the folk discovering he was an earthling.

'Come on,' he said. 'Let's find Ghador before Lady Kingfisher catches you hiding here.'

Ebbie tried to rise, but his strength failed him and he crashed back into the chair, wincing at a pain in his back.

Bek came to his side and laid a hand on his shoulder. 'Are you all right?'

'I'm ... I'm fine.' Ebbie patted her hand. 'Just a weak moment.'

They came and went with frequency. Persephone had left an icy splinter of death in Ebbie's soul, like a little reminder, and it would take him some time to thaw back into life. Fragile, but growing a little stronger every day, he felt like an old man slowly aging backwards.

The last couple of weeks had been a strange time for them all. Bek visited Ebbie regularly, sometimes two or three times a day. He enjoyed her company, was grateful for her friendship, and he never let on that he knew she visited so often because she was feeling insecure. Bek was struggling to adapt to castle life, and in Ebbie's company she didn't feel so lost. She and Ghador were firm sisters again, every bit as close as Mai said they had been, but the soon-to-be queen had her work cut out for her in the aftermath of Yandira's brief but savage regime, and it was hard for them to spend quality time together. Although Ghador found time for her sister now.

The secret door in the bookcase clicked open again and

Ghador appeared over the balcony, aiming an accusing finger at Bek.

'You!' she said as though discovering a great conspiracy against her. 'You're not getting out of this.'

Bek put her half-made-up face into her hands and groaned.

The princess hurried down the stairs, having first gathered up the hem of a flowing dress of the same velvet and gold thread design as Bek's clothes. She stormed towards the reading table, trying to loosen the high neck, looking as uncomfortable in her attire as her sister.

'What are you doing in here?' she demanded.

'Hiding from Kingfisher, what do you think? Why did you tell her to chaperone me?'

'Because I know what you're like, and I'm not doing this by myself.'

'Do you realise how hard it is to escape that woman?'

'Yes, of course I bloody do.'

Bek's frown was full of suspicion and she clenched her teeth. '*That's* why you told her to keep an eye on me – so *you* could get away from her.'

Ghador grinned. 'Honestly, I feel like I'm hiding from a pack of wolves.'

Bek snorted a chortle. 'Do you think she'll howl when she picks up our scent?'

Ghador doubled into a belly laugh and Bek collapsed with her. Seeing them like this was infectious, and Ebbie couldn't help laughing along with them. The mirth ended abruptly, however, when Lady Genevieve Kingfisher cleared her throat.

She appeared at the top of the stairs leading up from the library entrance. She approached straight-backed, dressed regally for a coronation, her face expressionless yet somehow admonishing. Bek and Ghador huddled together, giving Ebbie a glimpse of the children they had been. Children who got into a lot of trouble together.

Kingfisher inhaled and exhaled heavily, then addressed Ghador. 'Highness, your grandmother and your father are rather impatient for your company. Apparently, you have kept them waiting quite long enough.'

Ghador's shoulders slumped. Bek nudged her sister, but her smirk died as Kingfisher's stern attention fell on her.

'And for you, Miss Rana, I have a message from Charlie. He says if he has to attend this *stupid bloody thing* then you do, too. So get your *arse* down to Golder's Fairway. I added that last part myself, for both your ears.'

'All right, Genevieve,' said Ghador. 'You've made your point.'

'I'm glad to hear it, Highness.'

Ghador took Bek's arm and began steering her towards the library's lower exit. 'We'll see you later, Ebbie.'

'If I haven't died of embarrassment first,' Bek added.

Ebbie wished the sisters luck and Kingfisher waited for them to leave before saying, 'Maybe I should *howl* after them, yes?' Ebbie smiled and the noblewoman relaxed her stern exterior.

'As children, those two could put years on any guardian,' she said, looking around the library. 'It is good to see them together again. If only Maitressa were here to see it, too.'

Kingfisher looked as though she had aged since the first time Ebbie met her, back in a different life on a different world, as if a great weight refused to lift from her shoulders.

'So,' she said wearily, 'Ghador will wear a new crown. I like to believe that Juno is keeping Foresight and Hindsight, along with that damn sword, in Elysium, and we will never need to see their like in the Realm again. But who knows?' She approached the table. 'My faith in the Oldunfolk has been tested to breaking point, but at the same time my faith in we *mortals* has risen.'

She reached the table and Ebbie noticed the envelope in her hands.

'Here's a confession, Ebbie. For the longest time, I had grave doubts about you. I'm far too proud to admit I was wrong, so let me say this instead … Maitressa always was a fine judge of character. And *this* –' she placed the envelope on the table '– is for you.'

Without further word, Lady Kingfisher left the library, heading for the coronation of a new queen.

Ebbie stared at the envelope for a while before breaking the wax seal stamped with the crest of House Wood Bee and pulling free the letter inside.

My dearest friend, Ebbie Wren,

Pardon me if I'm wrong, but aren't you the gentleman who pitted his wits against an Oldunone and lived to tell the tale? Didn't you sacrifice yourself to fire and death for the sake of your friends and the greater good? Well then, it seems you were a hero all along. Not bad for a librarian.

I sorely doubt you are capable of feeling proud of your actions, so allow me to express my pride, for you and all you have done for us. The Realm owes you a debt it can never repay. Because of you, my daughter is gone, though it is hard to believe that we won the game. Perhaps to say that Cursed Persephone did not lose is a truer claim. And in this, you have paid a personal price.

It is safer to separate our worlds. The Janus Bridges have vanished once more, and perhaps this time they will never be found again. The folk must remain ignorant of the deeds of an earthling hero, while Earth is the home to which you cannot return. Your parents will never know what became of you. Strange Ground by the Skea will never realise it has lost its greatest son. But I believe, with all my heart, that your world's loss is my world's gain. The Realm will suit you well as an adopted home, I think.

Thank you, Ebbie Wren, keeper of lifetimes. My gratitude is boundless, and be certain that somewhere in the afterlife I will be raising a hot chocolate in your honour, just as you will be taking great care of my library.

Be well. Be happy.

Your friend,

Mai

Ebbie read the letter a second time before slipping it into his jacket's inside pocket. With a smile both contented and sad, he looked around at the countless stories in this grand old library, and he whispered to himself.

'They say that in the Realm, the sea is in the sky ...'